Sara Moliner is the pseudonym for the writing duo Rosa Ribas and Sabine Hofmann. Rosa Ribas was born in 1963 in Barcelona, and since 1991 has lived in Frankfurt, where she teaches at the university. She is the author of six previous novels. Sabine Hofmann was born in 1964 and is a former lecturer in philology at Frankfurt University. *The Whispering City* is their first novel together. Highly acclaimed in Spain, it has been translated into several languages.

'*The Whispering City* is not simply a magnificent thriller: it is a vivid and forensic dissection of an era cloaked in a tyranny of silence' Marc Pastor, internationally bestselling author of *Barcelona Shadows*

'One of the most original, dynamic, convincing and addictive crime novels around today' *El Mundo*

ENGLISH PEN

FREEDOM
TO **WRITE**
FREEDOM
TO **READ**

This book has been selected to receive financial assistance from English PEN's Writers in Translation programme supported by Bloomberg and Arts Council England. English PEN exists to promote literature and its understanding, uphold writers' freedoms around the world, campaign against the persecution and imprisonment of writers for stating their views, and promote the friendly co-operation of writers and free exchange of ideas.

Each year, a dedicated committee of professionals selects books that are translated into English from a wide variety of foreign languages. We award grants to UK publishers to help translate, promote, market and champion these titles. Our aim is to celebrate books of outstanding literary quality, which have a clear link to the PEN charter and promote free speech and intercultural understanding.

In 2011, Writers in Translation's outstanding work and contribution to diversity in the UK literary scene was recognised by Arts Council England. English PEN was awarded a threefold increase in funding to develop its support for world writing in translation.

www.englishpen.org

THE WHISPERING CITY

Sara Moliner

Translated from Spanish
by Mara Faye Lethem

ABACUS

ABACUS

First published in Spain with the title *Don de lenguas* in 2013 by Ediciones Siruela SA
First published in Great Britain in 2015 by Abacus
This paperback edition published in 2016 by Abacus

Published by special arrangement with The Ella Sher Literary Agency

1 3 5 7 9 10 8 6 4 2

Copyright © Rosa Ribas and Sabine Hofmann 2013
Translation copyright © Mara Faye Lethem 2015

This book has been selected to receive financial assistance from
English PEN's 'PEN Translates!' programme, supported by Arts Council England.
English PEN exists to promote literature and our understanding of it, to uphold writers'
freedoms around the world, to campaign against the persecution and imprisonment
of writers for stating their views, and to promote the friendly co-operation
of writers and the free exchange of ideas. www.englishpen.org

The moral right of the authors has been asserted.

A CIP catalogue record for this book
is available from the British Library.

ISBN 978-0-349-13995-1

Typeset in Bembo by M Rules
Printed and bound in Great Britain by
Clays Ltd, St Ives plc

Papers used by Abacus are from well-managed forests
and other responsible sources.

MIX
Paper from
responsible sources
FSC® C104740

Abacus
An imprint of
Little, Brown Book Group
Carmelite House
50 Victoria Embankment
London EC4Y 0DZ

An Hachette UK Company
www.hachette.co.uk

www.littlebrown.co.uk

To you, Celia, forever in my memory

There she lay. Mariona. Pale, blonde, voluptuous, and . . . dead.

Abel Mendoza paced from one side of the massive desk to the other like a caged ferret, raising small clouds of dust as he shuffled piles of papers that hadn't been touched in months. He turned towards shelves filled with medical reference works. His hands seemed to have taken on a life of their own and moved wildly, pulling out books and picking up others that had fallen to the floor, closing open drawers and opening closed ones.

Finally he found what he was looking for. Just at that moment, with the back of his left hand, he inadvertently knocked a plastic skull to the floor. Half of it was covered in muscles and had an eye; the other half was bare bones. Skulls wear a permanent smile, even when they've fallen to the floor. The impact sent an eyeball flying, bouncing like a ping-pong ball towards the recumbent body.

He picked up the skull and, despite his nervousness, or perhaps because of it, couldn't resist returning its smile. Then the rolling plastic eye hit the heel of the dead woman's single shoe. The hollow thud it made sent him over the edge into real panic.

Abel Mendoza fled the room, running out through the door he had opened just minutes earlier with a picklock.

1

'Mariona Sobrerroca's been murdered.'

As always, Goyanes sounded neutral, professional. Joaquín Grau switched the heavy black receiver into his other hand so that he could rub his right temple. The headache he'd had since getting out of bed that morning flared up when the Commissioner gave him the news. Yet the voice at the other end of the line kept talking, oblivious to the effect it was having.

'Her maid found the body this morning, when she came back from a weekend with relatives in Manresa. The house was turned upside down; must have been a break-in.'

His headache intensified still further. Grau reached out for the glass of water his secretary had left for him on the table, grabbed a little packet of powdered painkiller, stuck it between his teeth and ripped it open. He poured its contents into the water and stirred it silently with a teaspoon. He drank it down in a single gulp before interrupting the Commissioner.

'Who's assigned to the case?'

'I gave it to Burguillos.'

'No. I'm not so sure about him.'

A snort was heard at the other end of the line. Grau ignored it. 'I want Castro on this case,' he ordered.

'Castro?'

'Yes, Castro. He's the best you have.'

Goyanes could only nod.

'OK,' he conceded, but he sounded displeased.

The public prosecutor responded irritably. 'And I expect results soon. The Eucharistic Congress is going to be held here in a month, and I want the city clean. Is that clear?'

'Crystal clear.'

After hanging up, Grau analysed the conversation. He had made the right choice. Castro was one of the most capable inspectors in the Criminal Investigation Brigade, if not the most capable. And he knew him to be absolutely loyal. He wasn't as convinced about Goyanes, despite the fact that the CIB's Commissioner had, once again, just shown him the necessary degree of deference. For some time now, Grau hadn't been sure he could trust Goyanes and his closest men, including Inspector Burguillos.

For the moment, his position in the public prosecutor's office was secure. For the moment. But he was aware that he had many enemies, and their number was growing. He knew too that they were clever, and capable of hiding in the shadows until the opportune moment arrived. He had to stay sharp. Goyanes had followed orders, but Grau had noticed that he was even more distant than usual. Or was it just his imagination? He had to stay focused, on guard, as always. The lion who takes the first swipe is usually victorious.

Relentless, that was how he liked to think of himself. Just like during the war, when he had been a military judge known for his ability to pass death sentences without wavering. That was why, after the war, when the Regime appointed trusted people for the new Justice Administration, they'd named him public prosecutor of Barcelona. The work they'd begun during the war wasn't over, there was still a lot to do. And he was still relentless.

He leaned back in his seat and looked at the pile of letters on his desk. He had never allowed his secretary to open them, just as he hadn't invited any familiarity between them. He always made sure to check out his staff thoroughly, but his secretary didn't know a single thing about her boss that wasn't strictly necessary. Not his secretary, not anyone. He would never understand some people's need to tell others their personal stories, to open flanks of attack to the enemy gratuitously.

His gaze remained fixed on the unopened envelopes. It still made him feel slightly uneasy to see the day's correspondence on his desk. For several weeks after the commuters' strike last spring, he had opened the post with some trepidation. The popular public transportation boycott over the increase in fares and the ensuing general strike had caused many heads to roll. The first to go was Barcelona's prefect, followed immediately by the mayor. Two Falange officers ended up in jail because they didn't show sufficient enthusiasm for sending their units to fill the tramcars and break the strike. Other old-guard Falangists had also lost their posts. No one could be sure of holding onto their position.

He grabbed one of the letters at random, an envelope of fine paper that he tore with a sharp thrust of his steel-handled letter opener. It was an invitation to an official reception. Of course he would go, if only to avoid giving them the opportunity to whisper and plot behind his back. Yes, he was on his guard.

And now the Sobrerroca murder. Mariona Sobrerroca, dead. He had known her; he'd had social dealings with both her and her husband, the late Jerónimo Garmendia. Life takes so many twists and turns! Their magnificent mansion on Tibidabo had emptied over the course of just two years. In that brief stretch of time, the Grim Reaper had caught up with them both. 'I'm becoming morose,' he thought. 'And that's no good; that and this headache are a bad combination.' There was only one solution for both things, and that was to keep a cool head. Mariona Sobrerroca's death was just work – it was a case, a police investigation. One that involved sniffing around among the Barcelona bourgeoisie. On the one hand, that could be complicated. Who knew what they were going to turn up? Every investigation, no matter where, aired dirty laundry. It was like digging for wells: go deep enough and you always find shit. And those people didn't want you looking into their sewers any more than anyone else did. The differ-ence was that they were well connected, so he had to treat them with kid gloves. They were quick to complain, and they knew exactly whom to address their complaints to. Later, he'd have to hope that the results of the investigation were satisfactory. Perhaps, as on other occasions, he'd have to hide some things. And he wasn't sure whether this case would distinguish him in the public eye.

And then again maybe it would.

He picked up the phone and dialled Goyanes's number.

He got straight to the point. 'I want this case to get priority treatment in the press.'

'Why?'

'Because it's important to show the world that this country pursues its criminals and punishes them efficiently.'

He didn't care whether Goyanes believed those words, lifted from official speeches, or not. Grau knew they were incontestable.

'What does "priority" mean?' the Commissioner wanted to know.

'That we're going to give one newspaper the exclusive: *La Vanguardia*.'

'*La Vanguardia*? Why them? Remember what they did with the information in the Broto case . . .'

'That's exactly why. This time, as the only official source, they won't be able to start speculating.'

That conversation was even briefer than the first one.

Afterwards, he tipped his head back and closed his eyes, in the hope of mitigating the pain, which was now making itself felt as a throbbing in his ears.

On the other hand, he told himself, returning to the train of thought he'd interrupted in order to call the Commissioner, it was very likely that these enquiries would yield some interesting information, which he'd make sure to file away for future use. Maybe he'd even get some material that could help him solve a few of his own little problems.

He began to notice his headache easing slightly.

2

At nine that morning, as she contemplated her half-empty cup of coffee with sleepy eyes, Ana Martí heard the telephone in the stairway. It was kept in a nook beneath the first set of stairs, inside a box with a shutter door that closed with a lock. Only Teresina Sauret, the doorkeeper and the Serrahimas, the building's owners, who lived on the main floor, had the key. When the telephone rang, the doorkeeper picked it up and told whomever it was for that they had a call. If she felt like it; sometimes she wasn't in the mood. Tips or Christmas bonuses, either the expectation of receiving them or the generosity of their presentation, spurred her on to climb the stairs.

That day, it was the possibility of claiming the two months of back rent Ana owed that made her legs swifter, and soon after the shrill ringing had got her out of her flat, the doorkeeper had already reached the third floor – which was really the fourth, when you counted the unnumbered main floor – and was banging on the door.

'Señorita Martí, telephone.'

Ana opened the door. Teresina Sauret, planted in the middle of the doorway, blocked her exit. Cold, damp air came in through the spaces not filled by her plump body, which was squeezed into a plush robe. Ana grabbed her coat, in case the call was long, and the keys to lock up against the doorkeeper's prying eyes. Teresina must have thought she was looking for the money, and she moved aside. Ana slipped through the gap to exit her flat and closed the door, leaving Teresina's face a few centimetres from the wood, at the height of the bronze peep-hole, round like a porthole. The peepholes on the other three doors shone in the light of the bare bulb that hung from the landing ceiling. There were no lamps in the hallways of the floors for let, only in the entryway and the main floor, for the Serrahimas' visitors. The owners seemed completely uncon-cerned by this fact, or what the tenants might think about it.

The doorkeeper muttered something; it was unlikely to have been anything nice or pleasant, but Teresina Sauret took the precaution of not saying it too loudly. That way, Ana, the layabout, would get the message just from her tone, yet anyone overhearing it would fail to understand.

Meanwhile, Ana ran down the stairs, reached the nook and picked up the heavy Bakelite receiver Teresina had left resting on the box.

'Hello?'

'Aneta?'

It was Mateo Sanvisens, editor-in-chief at *La Vanguardia*.

'Do you know Mariona Sobrerroca?'

How could she not? She had been writing for the society pages for almost two years; there was no way she could have escaped knowing who she was. The widow of a posh doctor and heiress to an old Catalan lineage, she was part of the fixed cast at all the city's important parties.

'Of course,' she replied.

Moving away from the door to Ana's flat, Teresina Sauret had begun her descent, slackening her pace to be able to catch part of the phone conversation. Her feet drew closer with exasperating slowness.

'Well, now you don't know her, you *knew* her.'

'What does that mean?'

'She's dead.'

'And you need the obituary for tomorrow ...' she started to say.

The lines of text were already writing themselves in her head: 'Illustrious Mariona Sobrerroca i Salvat is no longer with us. Garmendia's widow, generous benefactor of ...' Sanvisens's next remark snatched the mental typewriter right out of her head.

'Aneta, dear, are you daft, or has watching too much opera made you feeble-minded? You think I would call you for an obituary?'

She had been ghostwriting for the newspaper long enough to know when she should leave Sanvisens's questions unanswered. She took advantage of the silence to nod goodbye to the doorkeeper, who had finally reached the last stair. Teresina Sauret went into her flat. The sound of her slippers against the floor stopped, as was to be expected, just behind the door.

'She's been murdered.'

She must have startled the doorkeeper with the exclamation that slipped out when she heard those words, because there was a bang against the door. *I hope she hit her head good and hard*, thought Ana.

'I'd like you to follow up on the matter. Will you do it?'

She had a lot of questions. Why me? Why isn't Carlos Belda doing it? What are the police saying? What do you want me to do? Why me? She had so many questions that she simply said, 'Yes.'

Mateo Sanvisens asked her to come into the office immediately.

She hung up, then raced up to her flat with long strides, put on some shoes, grabbed her bag and headed down the stairs. Teresina Sauret was closing the little door to the telephone.

'Such manners! What's the rush?' Ana heard as she went running out onto the street and headed towards the Ronda.

She passed, without a glance, the graffiti of José Antonio's face over block letters that read 'HERE WITH US!' Stencilling the founder of the fascist Falange party – the martyr, as many called him – was considered less an act of vandalism than one of patriotism. Which was why no one had dared to complain about it. They were too afraid of drawing attention to themselves. Since there were no trams heading towards the Plaza de la Universidad, she chose to walk rather than wait. She walked so briskly to Pelayo Street that soon her legs didn't feel the cold. At the newspaper office she waited for Sanvisens to answer her questions. Maybe he'd even tell her why he'd called her instead of Carlos Belda, who always handled the crime news.

'Carlos is off sick. He'll be out for at least a week, if not two,' Sanvisens said after greeting her and looking at his watch, as if he had timed her progress since the call.

Out of courtesy, she asked, 'What does he have?'

'The clap. They treated it with penicillin and he had a reaction.'

'Maybe the penicillin was bad.'

It wouldn't have been surprising. There had been more than one case of adulterated medication that had left a trail of the dead and chronically ill. Adulterating penicillin was a crime punishable by death. So was tampering with bread or milk. But it was still done.

'Maybe,' said the editor-in-chief.

Mateo Sanvisens wasn't particularly fond of small talk. He was a man of few words; curt, some said, like his gaunt build, the sinewy body of a veteran mountain climber, with hands covered in ridges as if they'd been carved with a chisel. In his youth he had scaled several high peaks in the Alps and he knew the Pyrenees, where he was from, better than the smugglers did. In his office he had pictures of some of the highest peaks in the world, including Everest.

'The tallest mountain, though not necessarily the most difficult. That's something you often find out when you're already on your way up. I'll get there soon,' he would say frequently.

Beside it was the marked page of *La Vanguardia* that had announced, two years earlier, in 1950, that the French expedition had reached the summit of Annapurna.

As soon as Ana had settled in front of his desk, Sanvisens immediately started in on the details of the case.

'Mariona Sobrerroca's maid found her dead at her home yesterday.'

10

'How was she killed?'

'She was beaten and then strangled.'

'With what?'

She was embarrassed by the thin little voice that asked the question, but a growing excitement had seized her throat.

'By hand.' Sanvisens mimed strangulation.

The how, where and part of the when had been resolved in few words.

'Is this news really going to be covered?' she asked.

News of murders wasn't well received by the censors. In a country where peace and order supposedly reigned, local crimes weren't supposed to bring that image into question. There were clear orders on the matter, but also, as with everything, exceptions. It seemed this case was going to be one of the latter.

'It can't be swept under the carpet. Mariona Sobrerroca is too well known, and her family, particularly her brother, is very well connected, both here and in Madrid; so the authorities have decided it is better to report on the investigation and use it to demonstrate the effectiveness of the forces of order.'

The last few words sounded as if they were in quotation marks. Ana caught the sarcasm.

'What if it turns out she was killed by someone close to her, a top society person?'

A series of photos of Mariona Sobrerroca in the society pages paraded through Ana's mind, as if she were turning the pages of an album: in evening wear at the Liceo Opera House beside the wives of the city's high-ranking politicians; delivering armfuls of Christmas presents to the children of the Welfare Service, along with several leaders of the Women's Section of the Falange; at a debutante ball; with a group of ladies at a fundraiser for the Red Cross; at dances, concerts, High Mass ...

'Well, it would serve as an example of how we are all equal under the law.' The sarcastic tone was still there. 'But I don't think so. It seems to have been a break-in. Whatever it was, we are going to report on it. In an exclusive.'

He paused as his eyes searched for something on his desk.

'The case is in the hands of a specialist, Inspector Isidro Castro of the Criminal Investigation Brigade.'

Isidro Castro. She didn't know him personally, but it wouldn't be the first time she'd written about him, although it would be the first time she did so under her own name. Castro had solved some important cases in recent years.

She remembered one in particular: the disappearance and murder of a nurse at the San Pablo Hospital, because she had written the copy that had appeared under Carlos Belda's byline.

Castro had hunted one killer after another. The first was ratted out by an accomplice, who in turn accused a third man. Not a terribly long chain of betrayals, but even if it had had ten links in it, Castro would have managed to connect them all. The police used brutally effective methods, and Inspector Castro, over the years he'd been working in Barcelona, had earned a reputation as the best. Soon she would meet him. What would he look like? What would the person behind 'the magnificent investigative work carried out by the Criminal Investigation Brigade' – as she had written in the article – be like? It was impossible to report on crimes in Spain without using those kinds of formulas. Crimes were to be solved, and order – the country's natural state – restored. She had done a good job. You had to do things right, even if someone else was going to get the credit for them. Perhaps Sanvisens appreciated her work, even though he had never said it, and this opportunity was her reward.

The editor-in-chief had given up his attempt to find whatever it was with just a glance and was now rummaging through the mess of documents, newspapers and notebooks that covered his desk. Ana knew that he was searching for something for her.

She owed a lot to Sanvisens and his friendship with her father, despite the political differences that had irrevocably distanced them. He hadn't spoken to her father since he had been released from jail and dismissed from his post, and Sanvisens never even uttered his former colleague's name. In fact, he grew angry if Ana even mentioned him. As for Ana, she struggled to banish the suspicion that her job at the newspaper was some sort of compensation because Sanvisens had the position that should have been her father's. When he offered Ana her first article, she'd asked her father for 'permission' to accept it. He gave it to her tacitly, with the phrase, 'We are a family of journalists.' The name Mateo Sanvisens was still taboo.

And now, finally, she was getting to do some serious journalism, writing about a murder case. Her surprise, and the question 'why me?', must have been written all over her face, because Sanvisens, as he pulled a small piece of paper out of a pile of letters, looked at her and said, 'Isn't this what you've always wanted? Well, here's your chance. Make the most of it.'

At the theatre or the opera, every understudy dreams of the lead losing his voice. That's their moment, having mastered their role while watching in the wings: to step onto the stage and dazzle the audience.

And she had got a lot of answers, but she still had one final question. 'Will it be my own byline . . .?'

Sanvisens seemed to have been expecting it.

'Yes. What you write will appear under your byline.'

He read her the note he held in his hand.

'Now get moving. You have to be at police headquarters at eleven. Don't forget your ID. Olga is doing an accreditation for you.'

Suddenly Ana realised exactly where she had to go.

'On Vía Layetana?'

'Yes, that's what I said. Is there a problem?'

'No, no. I just wanted to make sure.'

There was no way she was going to admit to him that she, like so many others, was frightened by the mere mention of that building. Sanvisens looked at her somewhat suspiciously. Ana averted her eyes to avoid giving him any cause to doubt her suitability for the job. She had to step into the spotlight and shine, even if the setting was one of the most threatening in the entire city. This was her chance. '*Ritorna vincitor*,' ran the aria from *Aida* that struck up in her head.

'Eleven o'clock, Vía Layetana,' she repeated, as if making a mental note.

'Inspector Isidro Castro will be expecting you,' added Sanvisens.

She tried to thank him, but Sanvisens wouldn't hear of it.

'Do me a favour, Aneta: when you leave, find the errand boy and tell him to go to the pharmacy and get me some of those little sachets of magnesium.'

Bringing a hand to his stomach by way of explanation, Sanvisens then abruptly turned round and started banging away at his typewriter. So she didn't get a chance to ask him if Isidro Castro knew that the person covering the story was a woman.

A woman who, after giving the errand boy the message, was so euphoric that she didn't realise she was speaking aloud: 'This time, the dead woman does have a name.' Unlike the macabre joke Carlos Belda had played on her when she first started working at the paper.

She remembered the rat. A dead rat lying swollen on the steps, its pink tail hanging almost all the way down to the stair below. No one had bothered to move it aside: not the police, not the undertakers, nor any of the curious bystanders who came to take a look. Someone would eventually end up stepping on it.

The dead woman she supposedly had to write about was on the first floor of an abandoned building on Arco del Teatro, a street that led into the lower Paralelo and the filthiest part of the Barrio Chino, Barcelona's red light district. Some children had discovered the body wrapped in an old blanket.

She didn't get to see it, but she didn't need to. She had seen the space where the woman had tried to take shelter from the cold, a wooden box, part of what had once been a wardrobe. It was as if she'd been buried alive.

'Was she elderly?' Ana had asked one of the officers she'd met in the building.

'About forty, but she'd packed a lot of living into those years.'

The case turned out to be a dirty trick. Belda knew this type of news wasn't usually published, that a piece about one of the corpses the police removed each week from abandoned buildings and the shelters where the hundreds of indigents swarming the city took refuge for the night wouldn't pass the censors. It had all been for nothing. The stench of piss and putrefaction on the street, in the building, in the flat. The impoverished faces of some, the bloated features of others, the dogs that ran terrified along the pavements, fleeing grubby, feral children.

The mere fact that Belda had been the one who'd offered her the chance to go to the scene had put her on her guard. Her humiliation over having fallen so naively into his trap hurt more than her frustration when she realised she wasn't going to be able to write a word about it.

Belda was waiting for her in the offices of *La Vanguardia* like a boy on All Fools' Day who can barely stifle his laughter when he sees the paper figure stuck to his victim's back. No one on the staff had opposed her joining the newspaper as vehemently. That was more than a year ago, but he still hadn't accepted her.

To get to her desk, Ana had to pass Belda's. That day, when she returned to the office, he waited until she was close enough, looked up, took the cigarette from between his lips and, with feigned disappointment, said, 'Oh, so you missed the stiff? Well, maybe you can write a feature on the latest fashions the whores in the Barrio Chino are wearing.'

He let out a laugh and looked around him, seeking the applause of his colleagues, who were following the scene more or less willingly.

He raised a few chuckles, which turned into cackles when they heard Ana's retort.

'I'm sure you're much better informed on their underwear.'

She turned on her heel and left him first with his mouth agape and then spewing a torrent of insults that only stopped when Mateo Sanvisens came within earshot.

So her first case had been a death with no body, the only record of it some court archives filed away along with those of the other nameless souls found dead that week.

But this time, the corpse waiting for her was a dead woman with a name — a very prominent name.

3

'Look, I got Ruiz to buy that silver piece from me. You should be glad to be rid of it, it was only gathering dust.'

Encarni put the shopping basket down on the table. She was pleased. Ruiz, the pawn shop guy, had paid her well for the centrepiece, and she had been able to buy plenty of groceries. The basket was overflowing. She was sure the missus would say she could take something to her mother.

'Good,' answered her employer, but Encarni could tell she hadn't been paying attention. She was sitting at the kitchen table with a cup of coffee in front of her, and her hand held a holder with the nub of a cigarette in it. The coffee and cigarette must have been her breakfast, and it was already noon.

She started to pull things out of the basket, making as much noise as possible: she crushed the newsprint so that it would crunch, she clinked together two bottles before placing them heavily on the ground. She liked things to make noise: the tinkling of the silverware when she put it in the drawer, the creaking of the drawers of the many cupboards when she opened them, the lids banging onto the pots.

The noise was practical, too, when Encarni wanted to attract Señora Beatriz's attention.

She turned towards Encarni, pulling her gaze from the distance and focusing it on her. 'How much did Ruiz pay you for it?'

'He gave me ninety pesetas.'

'Good.' Then she smiled. 'That's a lot.'

Encarni grinned with satisfaction. She was proud of her

17

negotiating skills, but she thought it more elegant to accept the compliment without comment, to downplay it, so she changed the subject. 'Do you know what? Up in Tibidabo, they found a dead woman.'

Was Señora Beatriz still listening to her? There was no way of knowing. If she was thinking about the dusty papers and the yellow cards she had in the desk, there was no point telling her anything. It would be like talking to a wall or a hatstand. But she lifted her head; it seemed she wanted to know more. Encarni continued, 'A rich widow. Horrible thing. The chicken guy told me that it was real butchery. Everything covered in blood. How awful!'

She turned to put the half-pound of butter she'd bought into the fridge. Before putting it away, she took it out of its paper, sniffed it to make sure it wasn't rancid and placed the stick on a porcelain butter dish.

'The maid found her. Poor thing. She had a day off, came back and there was the widow. Stiff as a board. Thank goodness I'm not in her shoes.'

'Yes, what luck! Especially for me.'

Señora Beatriz sounded amused. She was still wearing her dressing gown. Her blonde hair was wrapped in a turban, a damp lock escaping on one side. Another night that she had stayed up into the wee hours with her books.

Encarni smiled.

'Forgive me, Professor, ma'am. But imagine, Fermín the fishmonger said the poor girl almost died of a heart attack.' Encarni paused for dramatic effect. 'But the worst thing is the eye ...'

The missus leaned forward and shook some ash from her sleeve. Encarni sighed. She was going to make another hole in her dressing gown. She didn't seem to care much, though it must have cost a bob or two. She had to have bought it before the war; you couldn't find those designs these days. If she wanted to, the missus could be very elegant, but no; in the end she just put on whatever she pulled out of her huge wardrobes. There was even a cassock in one of them.

'It was my Uncle Lázaro's,' Señora Beatriz had told her when she'd asked about it.

'And what's it doing here?'

'I don't even remember.'

'The priest in my town would have sold his soul for a cassock of such quality.'

'Encarni!' Señora Beatriz pretended to be scandalised. 'Well, if you'd like, we'll send it to him.'

'That's expensive. Forget about it.'

She'd responded evasively, instead of telling her that she still remembered with shame how the priest of her town – El Padul, in Granada – had called her a 'bitch in heat', pointing at her during a sermon in church, because he had seen her kissing her boyfriend the previous afternoon. If it weren't a cassock and made of such good fabric, she would have used it to make dust rags. Encarni knew about clothes. She and her sister used to study the display windows on the Paseo de Gracia on Sunday afternoons.

'They ripped out one of her eyes and it was rolling around on the floor.'

Encarni bent and picked up an orange that had fallen and rolled along the kitchen tiles. She placed it in the fruit bowl.

'Her eye was rolling on the floor?'

'That's what she told me in the greengrocer's and while she did, nothing to it, she slipped me an overripe apple.'

She produced the apple and put it on the table in front of the missus. It seemed that the apple was about to begin rolling too, but Encarni stopped it with her hand and placed it firmly beside the coffee cup.

'Look, all four of them are perfect,' she said. '"Let me see," I said to the produce lady, "because last time there was one that was overripe." "Please, for the love of God," she told me, "don't be like that. It's just that this murder's got me all *a-frit*."' Encarni imitated the fruit seller's accent and way of speaking. 'What nonsense! She only tells her stories so her customers are distracted and she can sell them rotten apples and disgusting oranges.'

19

'Can you say that again?'

'What?'

'The *disgusting* part.'

'Ay, ma'am! Don't start again with my zeds,' lamented Encarni, but with little conviction.

She hadn't forgotten that her zeds were what had got her the job in the first place.

She had been working at Señora Beatriz's house for almost two years, ever since one afternoon when she'd sat down, exhausted, on one of the circular benches along the Paseo de Gracia. She had been going from house to house looking for work since the early morning. She was so tired that she didn't notice the woman sitting to her left until she pulled out a box of matches from her handbag and lit a cigarette fitted into a long black holder. A woman smoking in the street. But she wasn't a whore: she was elegant, even if her clothing was a bit dated; Encarni had guessed she was over forty, but forty in rich women's years, which take less of a toll than a poor woman's forty. She had a book on her lap. After lighting the cigarette, she held the holder with her free hand and continued reading. A woman smoking and reading; Encarni couldn't contain her curiosity.

'Is it good?'

The woman turned towards her in surprise.

'Pardon?'

'No, nothing, just wondering if the book you're reading is good.'

'Very. It's Dauzat's *Introduction to French Dialects*.'

'Gosh ... Well, it sounds good,' she said, intimidated by the obscurity of the title.

She was expecting the woman to turn back to her reading, but she didn't, instead asking, 'You're from Andalusia, aren't you?'

'Yes, ma'am.'

'From Granada, if I'm not mistaken.'

'Yes. From a town that ...'

'I knew it had to be Granada! From the capital or its surrounding areas, right?'

'Near the capital, from a town, El Padul, that ... How did you know?'

'From your s's. Or, I should say, from the s's you don't pronounce, from your lisp.'

The woman then told her that her way of pronouncing the letter 's' was peculiar to Granada. She spoke with such enthusiasm that it occurred to Encarni that the woman wasn't exactly normal, but she still responded gamely to her next question.

'Have you been in Barcelona long?'

'Only a couple of years. I live in *Monchuí.*' That was her pronunciation of Montjüic.

She didn't want to tell her that she lived in a shanty town, but that thought reminded her of why she was there: to get out of that slum once and for all.

'Listen, you wouldn't happen to need a girl to help around the house?'

The woman looked her up and down. Encarni permitted the scrutiny, but lifted her chin proudly. She was clean, and although her clothes were mended, they were at least well mended.

'The truth is, I could do with someone because I have a lot of work, but I can't pay much.'

'Room, board and what you can spare. I'll settle for that.'

'When can you start?'

'Tomorrow morning.'

The address the woman gave her was in a good part of the city, on the Rambla de Cataluña. Encarni was pleased to find out that there was no man of the house, but sad there were no children.

The next day she turned up at the home of Señora Beatriz Noguer and learned that she was a professor who wasn't teaching, for some political reason, but she wrote books. Books about how people around the world pronounced different words.

Yes, she owed a lot to her zeds, which was why she picked up one of the apples, held it aloft and said to the missus, '*Dizguzting orangez.*'

Her 's' sounds always came out like zeds, and vice versa. The missus laughed.

Encarni unwrapped the chicken. It was a bit lean, but she had haggled a good price. And she had made sure they gave her all the leavings.

'The man in the chicken shop says they were Masons. They need eyes for their rituals. They dry them on a low flame, like prunes or mushrooms. Then they cut them into slices. They prefer blue eyes, says the chicken man.'

'Then we're safe,' responded the missus.

'Yup. Unless the Masons change their mind and all of a sudden start collecting brown eyes.'

It seemed the Masons were to blame for everything. They probably didn't even exist. Just like the bogeyman, who supposedly snatched away naughty children. If they did exist and needed eyes, then they wouldn't leave them rolling around on the floor. The chicken man was talking rubbish.

She looked around. All the shopping had been put away, everything was in its place. The missus was distracted again, lost in contemplation of the smoke rising from her cigarette. Encarni wondered whether it was the right moment to talk to her about the refrigerator. She seemed to be in a good mood.

Señora Beatriz's voice pulled her from her thoughts.

'Encarni, was there any post for me?'

No, there were no letters in the postbox. Yes, the postman had been and had left a thick envelope for Ramírez, on the second floor. No, nothing had come for her.

The missus got up. She seemed displeased. Goodbye, good mood. She had been waiting for some letter for several days. Encarni sighed and started to peel the potatoes.

4

Beatriz watched the street from the window of her study. A dense layer of darkening cloud had covered the entire city. It was starting to rain, and along the Rambla de Cataluña people had opened their umbrellas and quickened their step.

Her letter hadn't come that day either. She gently pushed her armchair and swivelled inside it. The titles of the books on the shelves were barely visible. On the other hand, the gaps were perfectly discernible. Dark rectangles between the leather-bound volumes. Every time her eyes landed on one of the gaps she felt a stab of bad conscience, but it couldn't be helped. There was no other choice. The old editions were worth more than the silver cutlery. Which would be the next to go? she wondered fleetingly. One of the emblem books? One of the Virgils? Probably *The Consolation of Philosophy* by Boethius; the edition on her shelf was printed in Lyon in 1515. It had been read, like all the books in her library, but it was in perfect condition. Perhaps it wouldn't be necessary. When the letter arrived with the message she was waiting for ... her ticket out.

In Spain, she couldn't work at any university, couldn't even teach sixth-formers. In order to be able to work she needed a certificate that guaranteed her adhesion to the Regime. And they would never give her that. When she had come back from Argentina she'd tried to get a post at the University of Barcelona. They had soon made it clear that there was no place for her in a university that was 'free of subversive elements'.

'I'm sorry, Doctor. There is no place here for people who wish to undermine the principles of the Movement,' one of the professors told her sarcastically, a man whose face she thought she remembered from her student days in Madrid.

She had never considered herself a subversive element; she had never even been particularly interested in politics. But some articles that she had written at the start of the Civil War defending the legitimacy of the Republic had meant she'd had to go into exile and, on her return, she found she was ostracised from academia.

Returning from Buenos Aires in 1948, she went to live with her mother in the enormous family flat on the Rambla de Cataluña. Her father had died many years before. She settled into her old room. Her mother was already very ill by then. Beatriz read her French novels and her mother, who listened with her eyes closed, corrected her pronunciation every once in a while.

'Young lady, I think you should take another trip to France.'

Later, the intervals where her mother was awake grew shorter; her comments about her pronunciation grew few and far between. Finally Beatriz stopped reading and would sing softly to her, the same songs her mother had lulled her to sleep with more than thirty years earlier. She died the same day the national football team won against England, against 'Perfidious Albion', as the president of the Spanish Football Federation said on the radio. When she went into her mother's room to tell her about it and give her a little laugh, she found her dead in her bed.

Now she lives alone in the flat with Encarni. But not for much longer, if the letter she's waiting for says what she's hoping it will. And what if it doesn't? Then she'll have to continue hibernating.

5

'Goddamn it to hell. This is the last thing I need.'

Inspector Isidro Castro, of the Criminal Investigation Brigade, had had a bad night. Daniel, his youngest child, had been coughing incessantly.

The coughing had woken him at dawn. Every time he heard it, it stirred an old fear in him, a fear rooted in something he avoided mentioning despite knowing full well what it was. He got out of bed to see how the boy was doing.

As he put on his flannel slippers, he heard a violent coughing fit from the children's room. It gave him a stab of panic. Only the sight of Araceli, his wife, who continued sleeping peacefully, calmed him down a little. 'If it were serious, if the lad was in danger, her mother's instinct would wake her,' he told himself.

He left the room without turning on any lamps. He had enough light from the street lamp, light that entered through slits in a blind that didn't close properly.

He went into the children's room. Cristóbal, the eldest, was sleeping face down, tangled in the blankets. He had inherited his own restless way of sleeping. Very carefully, so as not to wake him, Castro managed to undo the knot formed by his lanky legs, sheets, blankets and bedspread. 'What a growth spurt this boy's had.' He covered him up. It was bad enough having one child ill.

As if wanting to remind him, Daniel coughed again. He went over to him. On the night table, between the two boys' beds, lay the comics they'd read before falling asleep. He touched the small lamp. It was cold. He didn't let them read for more than half an hour, but they would wait for their parents to fall asleep and then continue. Once, he discovered that they had covered up the slit under the door with clothing so that the line of light in the hallway wouldn't give them away. He scolded them, of course; but inside he was proud that they had turned out clever. But even if they'd been stupid, the important thing was that they were there. Alive. Breathing.

And coughing. Daniel had been coughing for several days.

'A cold,' the doctor had said.

It was normal with the chilly, damp weather.

'Chicken soup.'

And, to Daniel's delight, two days off school.

Daniel. Dani. Daniel.

Had it been a mistake to give him the same name as his son who'd died?

His first Daniel had died in 1937, at eight years old. A superstitious fear made him believe that this one, the second Daniel, would only be safe once he had passed that age. He was still six months away. Six months of anguish, of trembling every time he coughed or got a bump. His wife wouldn't understand his fears, which was why he hadn't told her about them. She didn't know, and Isidro hoped she never would, what it was like to lose a child. He also knew what losing your wife felt like.

'They died in the war.'

If anyone asked, that was all the explanation he gave.

He had lost his first wife in Galicia. After the war he went to Barcelona, where he had married Araceli, a woman from Navarra who worked as a salesgirl in the El Siglo department store, in 1941. She was twenty-four years old; he was pushing forty. Araceli had fallen pregnant; when they married, she was already three months along. It was a boy, named Cristóbal after her father, although when she was seven months pregnant a woman from the neighbourhood had predicted, based on the shape of her belly, that it would be a girl.

26

'If so, we'll name her Régula,' said Isidro when he heard the news.

That was the name of his first wife.

'No,' Araceli had protested. 'Not that! How can we give her a dead woman's name?'

It was the first and last time Isidro raised a hand to her. Seeing his threat, she protected her bulging belly with her left hand and used her right to grab his looming wrist.

'I'm not one of the thieves and murderers you deal with at the police station. I'm your wife.'

She didn't have to say it twice. He never again mentioned the name of his first wife, and she didn't seem to remember that the lost boy, who gave his name to their second son, was also called Daniel.

That 29 April, Isidro's sleep-deprived ill humour was exacerbated by the prospect of having to investigate the new case with someone looking over his shoulder, a journalist. Isidro had been at the police headquarters on Vía Layetana since seven and had already had an interrogation, two dressing-downs of subordinates, a wrangle with a typewriter and now, to top it all off, the conversation with Goyanes.

'And from *La Vanguardia*, no less?'

Isidro didn't understand it. The newspaper's treatment of the investigation into the murder of the high-class prostitute Carmen Broto in 1949 had raised hackles in police circles. Articles in *La Vanguardia* had questioned the police version, giving rise to all sorts of speculation about the important people who might have an interest in seeing that woman dead. The rumours about illustrious men among Broto's 'friends' hadn't bothered them as much as the insinuation, albeit very discreet, that the police investigation wasn't being carried out as zealously as it should be. Gil Llamas, head of the CIB, went into a fit of rage that was still vivid in Isidro's mind, one of those that could give you a stroke.

'But weren't we at loggerheads with *La Vanguardia*?' he replied, although he didn't usually ask questions, and especially

27

not since Goyanes had become his superior. He knew that he wasn't exactly among his favourites.

The Commissioner looked at him in surprise, and, despite the fact that he wasn't in the habit of explaining himself, answered him.

'The order comes from higher up. Grau, the public prosecutor.'

Another hothead, thought Isidro. The difference being that the fits his boss Gil had were flashes in the pan, intense but fleeting explosions, while Grau cultivated a stubborn rage that continued to corrode after detonation. It was dangerous for his enemies. The Commissioner wasn't a declared enemy, but everyone knew they hated each other. Goyanes tried to hide it, with little success, struggling to keep a neutral tone as he said, 'And he's already spoken with the Civil Governor, it appears, since Acedo Colunga has shown a lot of interest in the case.'

He certainly didn't need to provide any more arguments. Which was why Goyanes's shock turned to disbelief when Isidro insisted on his objections.

'I still don't understand why the press . . . '

'This is going to be a model investigation, Castro. Get that into your thick head.' Goyanes shook a piece of paper in the air. Isidro understood that it was the note from the governor.

When Felipe Acedo Colunga took an interest in something, the matter became absolutely top priority; everyone knew about his 'little notes'. If they reached a newspaper, publishing them was mandatory; if they arrived at a police station, they had to be obeyed.

'Mariona Sobrerroca was a very important person in Barcelona's society circles.'

His dislike for the Catalan capital city echoed in his pronunciation of its name. Both men were from elsewhere: Goyanes was from León; Isidro, Galicia. Their police careers were quite different. Isidro had always been a part of the CIB and was unfamiliar with and uninterested in other aspects of the force; Goyanes came from the Social Investigation Brigade,

28

the Regime's political force. Some said they had transferred him to the Criminal Investigation Brigade so that they could better control its movements. Although their careers followed divergent paths, they shared a distrustful view of the world. But Goyanes suspected everyone of being a communist, a Mason or hostile to the Regime, observed Isidro. His own distrust was simpler, clearer: crime was nothing more than a confirmation of the criminal nature of humans.

Goyanes kept talking. 'Sobrerroca comes from a good Catalan family, they're pro-monarchy but covertly, and we are going to put all our effort into clearing up her death and shutting up all those throughout Europe who conspire against the Caudillo in order to put that Bourbon whoremonger Don Juan at the helm of this country.'

So the case had political connotations and, as if that weren't enough, he'd have to contend with society people. 'Fucking brilliant,' he thought but didn't say out loud; to his boss he replied, 'I don't understand all that stuff.'

'And you don't need to. As always, what matters is that you do a good job and that this journalist, this Señorita Ana María Martí Noguer, reports it as she should.'

'Señorita? It's a woman?'

Isidro could tell that Goyanes didn't like the idea at all either. Still, he nipped his new objection in the bud. Not even in this unpleasant situation could he expect any understanding from his superior.

'Yes, a woman. And you are going to make sure she writes what she has to write. Is that clear?'

'Yes.'

'By the way, how's it going?'

'Just getting started.'

'Which means . . . '

'Notifying relatives, talking to the maid, waiting for the forensic report, talking to the neighbours . . . '

'And?'

'Not much, for the moment. But it looks like a break-in. A neighbour in the house across the street thought she saw a man running out of Sobrerroca's townhouse, and the door looks as though it might have been picked open; the garden gate must have been unlocked.'

'Yes. And?' Goyanes made an impatient gesture.

'The neighbour gave us a description of the man she saw, but it wasn't very helpful. That's all we have for the time being.'

'All right. Well, give it to the journalist nice and tidy, and don't forget to say that we're going to find the murderer soon. With a bit of luck, he reads the paper, and he gets nervous.'

'Maybe.'

Isidro waited until he was outside Goyanes's office to mutter, 'Fucking brilliant.'

He repeated it again as he went down the stairs and passed two of his colleagues, noticing their breath. The one who walked past him on his right wrapped him in a cloud of poorly digested raw onion; the one on the other side left a trail of alcohol, the first splash in his morning coffee. Who knows how many more would follow it. Thinking that he didn't have to work with Burguillos the drunkard gave him a spark of joy. It lasted for six, maybe seven steps. Until he remembered that a Señorita Ana María Martí Noguer from *La Vanguardia* would be waiting for him downstairs.

'Fucking brilliant.'

That last time he said it out loud. Over the next few days he would repeat it many more times, but to himself, because you didn't say 'fucking brilliant' in front of a woman.

The woman waiting for him was about twenty-five, maybe less. She was sitting on a bench in the hallway in front of his office. She kept her back very straight to avoid touching the wall, where many resting heads had left dark, greasy circles. Her hands were in her lap, her black jacket covering them like a muff. She wore a long skirt, dark stockings and flat shoes that couldn't hide the fact that, when she rose to greet him, she was a couple of centimetres taller than him. 'One sixty-nine,' estimated Isidro, unwilling to concede all three of the centimetres that separated him from being a metre seventy. He didn't like tall women – women taller than him. Nor did he like women who stood up to greet him and shook his hand firmly like a man. This one was pretty, besides. She looked at him expectantly, with enormous light brown eyes the same colour as her pulled-back hair; her plump lips slightly open as she smiled timidly, lifting her pronounced cheekbones and slightly square chin.

'A magnificent skull.'

That was what morbid César Sevilla would say to Isidro several hours later. He was the officer who had accompanied her to Castro's office door. Sevilla bragged about his 'x-ray' eyes and he never missed an opportunity to make a comment about someone's bone structure.

'Long femurs, short humeri,' he said about Commissioner Goyanes.

'Asymmetrical clavicles,' he might comment about a new arrest.

'Holy Mother of God! That was some slap ... you dislocated his inferior maxillary!' he said about another after an interrogation.

The first thing he admired about Ana Martí was her skull.

'So, Señorita Martí, you're covering Señora Mariona Sobrerroca's death for the newspaper.'

He invited her into his office.

6

This was Inspector Isidro Castro of the CIB? The man who extended his hand to her wore a poorly cut suit. It wasn't a terrible fit, but it seemed too big and made him appear rectangular and stumpy. Legs too short, head too small, further reduced by his black, firmly pomaded hair, torso too big ... but all her first impressions were erased as soon as he extended his hand and greeted her without smiling, 'So, Señorita Martí, you're covering Señora Mariona Sobrerroca's death for the newspaper.'

She had rarely heard a male voice as smooth, and as unsettling. It sounded restrained, with a deep tone, yet not low; a baritone in which half of the air expelled from his lungs didn't vibrate his vocal cords, instead passing like a sigh along with the other sonorous half.

The word 'newspaper' had emerged from his mouth loaded with disdain. She wasn't welcome. Had Carlos Belda been?

'My colleague, Señor Belda, is ill and that's why ... '

Castro made a face that drew two wrinkles between his brows. It seemed that Carlos wasn't received there with a warm round of applause either.

'Do you have experience in violent cases, señorita?'

His tone left no room for doubt: *Don't lie to me, or ...* Or what? *Or our first conversation is over, and the whole case with it.*

'No,' Ana replied.

'Are you at all familiar with police work?'

'Yes. From the newspaper.'

If Castro didn't ask her what her experience consisted of, she wouldn't have to tell him that all she had done was write and correct countless crime articles for colleagues at the paper. She particularly didn't want to have to tell him that she worked for the society pages at *La Vanguardia* and several women's magazines, writing about debutante balls, receptions and weddings. If it hadn't been her first day working with the inspector, she would have already known that merely thinking it and hoping he wouldn't ask her awakened in him the hunting instinct of a natural-born interrogator. But that was their first conversation, and she was still unaware of Castro's ability to hit on precisely what others didn't want to reveal. As a result, he asked her, 'What does your job entail?'

And she, of course, told him the truth, adding at the end, 'But I also have knowledge of criminology and police work . . .'

'You do? And where did you learn it? Did you take a correspondence course from the CCC Academy?'

Her pride wounded, she couldn't keep from replying, 'Reading. Did you know what Chandler said, for example? He said that the easiest murder case in the world is the one somebody tried to get cute with; the one that really bothers police is the murder somebody thought of only two minutes before he pulled it off.'

'Very nice. Excuse me.'

Castro stood, opened the door and shouted into the hallway, 'Sevilla! Can you come here for a second?'

Almost instantly the officer appeared, grumbling. He was about Ana's age, thin, with pale white skin from his forehead to his nose and the rest of his face darkened by the shadow of an incipient beard that emerged just hours after he shaved.

'What is it?'

'If I tell you that the easiest murder to solve is one where somebody tries to be too cute, and that what really bothers us is the murder that somebody thought up two minutes before doing it, what would you think?'

'What would I think? Well, that's stupid.'

'You see? Señorita, don't read so many foreign writers. We're in Spain.'

Ana couldn't help but admire the inspector's memory, seeing how he repeated her words almost like a tape recorder. Castro laughed half-heartedly, then waved the young officer away. Sevilla disappeared without another word. He seemed accustomed to jumping when his boss ordered him to.

Once Sevilla was gone, Castro recovered his seriousness. He perfunctorily pulled some papers out of a file and, before even glancing at them, started to give her information about the case.

'The victim was discovered dead this morning by her maid, Carmen Alonso, at her home on Tibidabo Avenue. The body was found in the office of her late husband, who had a private medical practice in the house. The maid was returning from Manresa, where, according to her statement, she had spent Sunday with relatives. The information was confirmed, although I haven't personally verified it.'

She didn't understand what he meant by that last bit. Ana had pulled a notepad out of her bag and was taking notes on what Inspector Castro said, though avoiding the policeman's abuse of the passive voice; like her father, she was a sworn enemy of the passive, that 'barbaric Anglicism'.

'The body of the victim was lying in a supine position with the head turned somewhat to the right. Like this.'

A photo was placed between her eyes and her notepad. It showed Mariona Sobrerroca on the floor, wrapped in what could be a nightgown or a sheer dress. It wasn't the first time she'd been shown an image of a murder victim, but it was the first time she'd seen one of someone she had met. Her habit of always focusing on people's hands and feet was a big help. She saw that one foot wore a high-heeled shoe. So the garment wrapped around the right leg had to be a dress.

'And the other shoe?'

'We found it on the other side of the desk.'

'So there was a struggle?'

'Señorita Martí, don't get ahead of yourself. I'll give you the information.'

'Of course.'

The tone with which she said those words didn't entirely match their deferential content. Castro noticed because he gave her a severe look before continuing.

'The messy room and the loss of one shoe reveal that the victim fought with her aggressor or aggressors. We are conjecturing that she surprised someone who had entered her house to burgle it.'

Ana's hand holding her pencil came to a stop. She wanted to ask if they knew how many people it could have been, but she didn't dare, at least not so soon. Castro, although he had perhaps guessed her unspoken question, didn't reply to it. Instead he answered one she hadn't yet formulated.

'The white ball is an eyeball.'

He had put the photo so close to her that she hadn't realised it was an eye until he'd said it.

'It belonged to a skull that decorated, shall we say, the office of the victim's husband, Dr Jerónimo Garmendia, who died more than two years ago, in January 1950.'

She already knew that. Dr Garmendia had been the preferred doctor of a certain class of Barcelonian. He had died in a car accident on the Garraf coast. Ana remembered it well. His car had skidded on a curve and plunged into a rocky cove. She wasn't yet writing for *La Vanguardia* then. She had only recently started publishing brief, uncredited articles and writing photo captions for women's magazines.

'According to the forensic assessment, her death was caused by manual strangulation, but first the victim was persistently beaten on both the face and body.'

Another photo.

Mariona Sobrerroca's plump, cherubic face showed several haematomas, her lower lip was swollen and darkened by blood and her right earlobe was split. Ana pointed to it with her pencil and looked at the inspector. This time he was willing to respond.

'Probably the victim's earring got caught on something in the struggle and tore her ear.'

Ana tempted fate with another question: 'Did they find the lost earring?'

Castro looked at her condescendingly. He responded as he showed her another image, 'Yes, with a piece of the ear.'

Another photo. She glanced away, but only for a second. She forced herself to look at the small strip of flesh with irregular edges that hung from the golden clasp of a bunch of small white and black pearls.

She started to take notes again. Castro stopped her in her tracks.

'Don't bother with so many notes, señorita, we'll give you everything in writing.'

He hadn't sunk her with that comment, but he'd left her clinging to the lifeboat.

'To avoid unwanted errors and speculation,' added Castro. 'What you need to do is to pretty it all up.'

'Then what you want is for me to take the official communiqué, fix a couple of commas, smooth out a few passives and decorate it with adjectives?'

'The improvements in style are up to you.'

That would be like taking dictation. She'd be better off writing her articles for the society pages.

'No,' she heard herself say before thinking of the consequences.

'No, what?'

'No, I'm not going to do that. You can find yourself a copy editor. I'm a journalist.'

They were both silent, regarding each other carefully. Ana was already saying goodbye to the case, to *La Vanguardia* and to a career in journalism that was over before it had even begun. Why couldn't she have accepted the conditions the policeman had given her and then work out how to get round them? But it was 'her' first article. Or it would have been, since her eagerness to finally write something of her own had brought on this absurd refusal and now, if Sanvisens didn't fire her for being an idiot, he would leave her for ever stuck in the glittering dungeon of society parties. But, at that moment, it was Sanvisens himself who came to her aid.

'My boss told me that it is very important our readers see the efficiency with which you work to solve this case.'

Castro observed her with a neutral expression. Instinctively, she resorted to adjectives. 'In a delicate case such as this one, it is crucial to highlight the extensive police work, the noble spirit with which a diligent and efficient investigation is carried out, to find the perpetrators of such a horrendous crime.'

'Of course. And?'

'And my articles could be of great help to you. Which is why I dare to suggest that you allow me to follow your work closely and present it in my newspaper. Based, of course, on the information you provide me with.'

She noticed a slight lift at the left corner of Castro's mouth. It seemed that her efforts to keep the job had at least amused him. She saw the 'yes' timidly rising to the policeman's lips while a 'no' kept it tightly shut. The 'yes' bounced against his teeth and fell back, but took a running start . . . It tried twice more and both times the inspector stifled a smile.

Then the door opened and Officer Sevilla came in.

'What is it?' asked Castro, and Ana saw the 'yes' squashed in the inspector's annoyed expression.

'Carmen Alonso is already here.'

'Mariona Sobrerroca's maid,' said Ana.

Castro looked at her and she felt compelled to add, in an attempt to impress him, 'I have a very good memory for names, and you mentioned her a moment ago.'

She hadn't given up completely, and she was trying to earn points, even fractions of points, to nudge him in her favour.

Sevilla stood in the doorway awaiting orders from his boss.

'Bring her here.'

Ana understood that her arguments hadn't convinced him. She accepted defeat, closed her notebook and got up to leave the office. But Castro stopped her.

'What? Don't you want to see the extensive police work and

noble spirit with which we carry out a diligent and efficient investigation? Well, now's your chance.'

She didn't miss Castro's satisfaction when he saw the astonishment he had caused by repeating her words almost verbatim. They were like two cocksure gunslingers in a western. That the policeman in turn wanted to impress her with another display of his memory could be a good sign. It also meant she had to be careful with what she said.

Castro addressed his subordinate. 'Sevilla, put the lady from *La Vanguardia* in a chair there, in the corner, so she can see well.'

The officer obeyed the order. He placed a chair behind Castro's desk. From there, Ana would be able to see the woman's face. She settled in her place with a gesture from the inspector.

'Don't worry,' Sevilla told her in a joking tone, 'the blood splatters won't reach you there.'

'Sevilla!' reprimanded Castro.

'But she's a witness, isn't she?' said Ana timidly.

'That remains to be seen,' Castro replied.

The officer went out to look for the woman.

Again Ana felt the anxiety that had seized her when she'd approached the police headquarters. The building was covered in a slick of fear that emanated from its innards, from the basements that were the setting for torture and death. As with so much else, it was something that was known and not talked about. The fear that impregnated the headquarters' walls was nourished by stories told in hushed voices, by unexplained absences whose causes were nonetheless clear, by the cruel echoes of denunciations. Fear penetrated the building's walls and spread into those surrounding it, infecting them. It had reached her as far off as Condal Street, and had gradually tightened around her, crushing her a little more with each step. She had almost forgotten it as she spoke with Castro, but now it was back again, the fear.

She saw the same fear in the face of the woman who was now entering Inspector Castro's office.

*

Carmen Alonso took a few shaky steps and sat down in front of the inspector in a chair indicated to her by Officer Sevilla. She was wearing her Sunday best to make her statement at the station; she was about Ana's age, but infinitely more tired and afraid.

Castro didn't even greet her or say a word as she sat down. As if he didn't see her, he picked up a piece of paper and started to write briskly. The other three remained in silence, their attention on the sound of the pencil that scraped against the paper as if trying to tear it. Footsteps were heard through the closed door, some muffled voices and the halting tap-tap of a typewriter.

Carmen Alonso kept her gaze down. Ana hadn't been able to see her eyes.

The inspector finished writing, folded the paper and held it out to Sevilla, who was standing behind the maid. The woman shivered at the officer's arm passing close to her shoulder as he took the paper. She looked around and saw Ana for the first time. Her gaze asked the question 'Who are you?', but Castro's voice giving instructions to Sevilla attracted all of her attention.

'While I take care of this, go to the Ramblas and bring me what I wrote down here.'

Ana wondered if this exchange was already part of the interrogation. Carmen Alonso had to be aware of Sevilla's body just a few centimetres from the back of her chair; she had to feel walled in between the two policemen, who seemed to regard her as just another piece of furniture. The woman remained immobile as Castro looked over her head at his subordinate.

'Don't be long.'

Sevilla left.

'OK,' said Castro, and he addressed Carmen Alonso for the first time. 'Let's proceed.'

He picked up another piece of paper where there were some handwritten lines and he began, 'Your name is Carmen Alonso Ercilla, born on 8 January 1927, in Valencia de Alcántara, Cáceres. Father, Rafael Alonso García; mother, Belén Ercilla Montero?'

'Yes, sir.'

'How long have you been working for Señora Sobrerroca?'

'Two years, since she was widowed.'

'Did you live in her home?'

'When I first started I did, because Señora Mariona was afraid to be in that big house alone, but for the last six months I've been sleeping at my sister's, in Hostafranchs.'

She had clearly been living in Barcelona for some time; she already referred to a house with a garden as a *torre*, thought Ana.

'That night, too?'

'No. I was coming from the house of some relatives in Manresa.'

'What time did you get to Señora Sobrerroca's home?'

'At seven, like always.'

'And she was no longer afraid?'

'No, she didn't seem to be.'

Castro spoke as if he were having a friendly conversation with Carmen Alonso, who seemed less intimidated.

'Tell me what you did on Sunday, and what you saw when you entered Señora Sobrerroca's house.'

She recounted the same things that Castro had told Ana. The inspector pretended to be checking her statement against the paper he held with both hands. From her corner, Ana could see the page – there was only the maid's personal information on it.

Her story ended with her calling the police after finding her employer's corpse.

'Very good, very good, Señora Alonso. You studied that perfectly.'

'I beg your pardon?'

'You understood me. You repeated word for word what you said to the officer who took your statement.'

Carmen looked at him with wide eyes.

'I don't understand.'

'You are reciting, ma'am. You are smarter than you look, and you know that the best way not to contradict yourself is to repeat exactly the same story from beginning to end.'

But you also do that when you are telling the truth, thought Ana, though she kept quiet. Perhaps it was just Castro's strategy for verifying her statement.

'How do you want me to tell it to you?'

'Try the truth.'

'That's what I did.'

'Well, tell it to me again.'

'How?'

'However you want, but without lies.'

The woman began her story again, this time hesitating; the effort not to repeat literally what she had said, to search for synonyms, add details, was clearly causing her difficulties. She was concentrating hard, with the lost gaze of someone who is recalling images to mind.

Castro didn't let her finish, interrupting her with another question. 'Did Señora Sobrerroca keep valuable objects in her husband's office?'

As if coming out of a trance, Carmen replied, 'Not that I know of.'

With a wave of his hand, the inspector indicated for her to go on.

'Dr Garmendia's office was like a museum. No one was allowed to move anything. When I cleaned, she would come in afterwards and make sure that everything was where it should be.'

'How do you know that Señora Sobrerroca wasn't keeping anything of value in there?'

'I don't know. But what would there be of value in a doctor's office?'

'Don't make conjectures, that's not your place.'

'Yes, sir.'

'Did she have valuable jewellery? Money?'

'She had jewellery, in her dressing room. And that isn't conjecture.'

The slap came so quickly that Ana almost leapt out of her chair with fright.

Castro, who had stood to deliver the blow, sat down again,

put his hands on the desk and said, in the same monotone he had maintained throughout the entire conversation, 'You're trying my patience. How about you start telling me something I can believe?'

'What?' asked Carmen, tearful and scared. 'What do you want?'

Her left cheek was red.

'For example, you could show me your hands.'

The woman obeyed. She lifted her hands and showed them with the palms facing up, parallel to the desk. She was trembling. Castro sat up to look at them, indicating to the woman that she should show him the backs. She did. With a quick movement, the inspector seized the woman's hands with his left. Reflexively she tried to free them, but she was prevented by the right arm of the policeman rising up to hit her again.

'Too small to strangle Señora Sobrerroca. What's your accomplice's name?'

Ana didn't know what was more menacing: Castro's hand, which seemed impatient to fall on the woman, his sudden familiarity or his impassive expression.

'What's your accomplice's name?' he repeated.

And, although the question 'What accomplice?' was logical, it earned the woman another slap; a brusque, precise slap on the same cheek as the first, as if Castro were fitting his hand to the pre-drawn contour.

Carmen Alonso would have fallen from her chair if the inspector hadn't been holding her by the hands. She hid her face between her outstretched arms. She was crying; her tears stained the thin blue cardboard folder that was on the policeman's desk, right beneath her face.

'Why are you hitting me?'

'Listen, you don't know how much it irritates me to be taken for a fool. We weren't born yesterday, you know.'

Nothing in the inspector's expression showed rage, or even anger. Castro spoke and slapped with the coldness of an automaton.

Ana was trembling. Why didn't she get up and tell Castro to stop? Out of fear. Two fears, if she was honest, and one of them made her feel ashamed. Being scared to confront a man capable of such sudden violence and who, moreover, had the protection of his authority, was at least understandable. But that she didn't dare to do it out of fear of losing her job was degrading, it sullied her.

And even then she remained glued to her seat, as Castro let the maid go, sat back with his hands on the desk and told her, 'If you, as you confessed, knew that Señora Sobrerroca had valuable jewels and was alone in the house, how do I know you didn't give in to the temptation of stealing them?'

Carmen lifted her head. Tears dripped from her chin. She dried them with the back of her hand, took a breath and, with a trembling but resolute voice, answered, 'I haven't confessed anything, I only said something.'

She raised her arms to protect herself from the slap she was expecting. Both she and Ana had their eyes fixed on Castro's hands, but they didn't move.

With the determined fatalism of a martyr in the Roman circus, the woman continued speaking: 'I'm no fool. The missus treated me well and paid me much better than those of her class usually do. Sometimes she gave me clothing, and she even used to take me with her to the theatre and the cinema. Why would I do anything bad to her?'

Carmen Alonso, despite her fear, was arguing from logic and common sense. Castro was interrogating her from inquisitorial omnipotence. Ana wondered if any victims of the Inquisition had appealed to common sense and saved themselves from persecution that way. She didn't know, but it seemed that here, somehow, it was working.

The maid lowered her arms. 'Hit me, if you want,' her expression said.

But Castro was interested in something else now.

'You say that she used to take you to shows and that you used to sleep at the house. What changed? Did you do something wrong?'

'No. It had nothing to do with me. I think that she was no longer afraid of being in the house alone.'

'Oh, no?'

'That's what she said.'

Castro stared at her; his silence forced the maid to continue talking.

'I didn't do anything wrong. The missus was very pleased with me.' She lowered her eyes and added, more to herself than for the other two people in the room, 'And I with her. What am I going to do now?'

Castro didn't bother to answer. After a few seconds he turned in his seat and told her, 'You can leave. But you should know that we will be watching you.'

'Can I start looking for a new job?'

'No one is stopping you.'

What would stop her is that she had been Mariona Sobrerroca's maid, whose murder hadn't yet been solved. Who was going to want her in their house?

Carmen Alonso got up and left. First she nodded towards Ana. Perhaps it was a farewell. She couldn't hold her gaze.

Castro remained staring at the closed door. Behind his back, Ana didn't dare to move or speak. As if suddenly remembering her presence, the inspector turned and told her, 'Well, you heard what the witness said.'

Her 'yes' came out in a croak. Her throat was dry.

'So, prepare your article, a test run.'

'Here?'

'You aren't suggesting taking our reports home to peruse over tea and biscuits?'

'No, no.'

She was sure they didn't treat Carlos Belda like this, but she was already learning what she was allowed to think and what she should keep quiet.

The door opened and Sevilla poked his head in.

'Back already? Did you run my errand?'

'Yes. Should I bring them to you?'

'Later.'

Castro signalled to Ana with a movement of his head. She understood that whatever Sevilla had gone to get wasn't meant for her eyes.

'Another thing,' said the officer. 'We have a rag-and-bone man that the dead woman's neighbour saw passing by the house.'

'Where is he?'

'Waiting outside the door.'

'Bring him to an interrogation room. I'll be there shortly.'

He rose and, before Ana's questioning gaze, handed her a sheaf of case papers.

'I have things to do. Write your article. You can use my desk.'

He was already leaving the room when he added, 'Don't even think about sitting in my chair.'

He closed the door.

It hadn't even occurred to her, but, like Bluebeard's wife, the warning was an incentive to go around the desk and sit in the inspector's chair. She didn't feel anything special about his seat. 'Why should I feel something special?' she thought to herself. It was a wooden chair with green padded leather arms worn from use. From sweat? As she thought this she involuntarily lifted her arms and rested them on the desk. Her eyes landed on a page from the newspaper *Arriba* that peeped out from beneath some papers and bore a list of names. She recognised what it was before she had a chance to read it: the names of those put to death the day before. She looked away before any of them could stick in her memory.

She heard footsteps on the other side of the door. She leapt from the chair and took her place again. She buried the list of the executed beneath the blue folder that still bore the damp stains of Carmen Alonso's tears.

She started to write. By hand.

When Castro returned, she would have to give him her handwritten text, as if it were her homework. That would never do. She got to her feet and left the inspector's office. She remembered that when he had called to his subordinate, he had shouted towards the right, and she moved in that direction along the hallway. She reached a room that smelled of sweat and aftershave lotion; among the ten or twelve policemen distributed over several desks, she made out Officer Sevilla with a cigarette between his lips. Sevilla saw her too and leapt up. The others stopped what they were doing and turned towards her. Only one, who was furiously hunting and pecking on his typewriter, remained completely unaware of her presence, absorbed as he was in his own tumult.

'Need something?' Sevilla asked, without taking the cigarette out of his mouth.

'A typewriter,' she said, pointing to his preoccupied colleague.

Sevilla looked in the opposite direction. Along one of the nicotine-stained walls he spotted a typewriter on a little table with wheels.

'I'll bring it to you.'

She returned to Castro's office followed by the squeak of little wheels. Sevilla heaved the typewriter onto his boss's desk. He didn't leave, standing in the doorway as if he needed to keep a zealous eye on what she was going to do with the equipment. Ana turned her back to him, stuck paper in the carriage and started writing. An admiring little whistle behind her back indicated that the policeman was impressed by her speed.

Once again, the hours she'd invested in learning to type were paying off. She had taught herself with a little dog-eared book that her father had bought at the second-hand book market in the San Antonio district. Her mother had complained many times about the noise of the typewriter as she was practising her A-S-D-F-G-F, her Ñ-L-K-J-H-J and then the more advanced speed exercises. But she let her keep at it; Ana was ten years old and it was a game. They still lived in the enormous flat on Paseo de San Juan, and her mother could avoid the percussive clatter of the keys by going to the other end of the apartment. A few months after, a real clatter would come, that of the Italian air force bombardment in March

1938. Ana, wedged beside her mother against the wall of the Triunfo-Norte metro station, would try to trick her fear by doing exercises on a book cover as if it were an invisible keyboard.

Now she was writing the article for Castro to read and approve. When he returned, she was only a few lines away from finishing. She didn't let Sevilla's chatter distract her.

'You should see how she types. She must have steel metacarpals!'

She wrote the last two sentences and turned.

'Done.'

She pulled the sheet of quarto from the typewriter's carriage and handed it to him. Castro sat at his desk and began reading the text. Sevilla hadn't moved from the doorway. She knew that it was only her imagination, but she could feel when the policeman's eyes were fixed on the inspector and then turned on her, at the nape of her neck. Both of them were waiting for Castro to finish reading, and she imagined that the officer was maliciously anticipating the opposite response to what she was hoping for.

'Fine,' the inspector said at last. 'This can be published. You just have to take out this part here.'

Castro pointed to the sentence that described the position of the dead woman's body.

'Take out the part about the dress. This isn't for the society pages.'

She accepted the deletion with the private satisfaction of knowing that he was forcing her to erase a petty detail because he hadn't found anything he could reproach her for.

'What are you still doing here, Sevilla?'

'Waiting to take the typewriter back.'

'Well, go on, take it.'

Sevilla put the typewriter on the little trolley and dragged it out of the room. Castro looked at Ana and said, 'Don't even think about changing a single line of the text you showed me. Even though you forgot to make me a carbon copy, I will notice any differences.'

She was sure about that.

Ten minutes later, she left the headquarters with a smile on her face, which was such an unusual sight that two women walking down the Vía Layetana stared at her in surprise.

7

Pablo Noguer liked his new office. He liked it even though the furniture had been scavenged from other parts of the firm and the various styles didn't match. But it was his, and it was on Bruch Street at the corner of Consejo de Ciento, far enough from his father's law practice, which was further north in the Ensanche district on Londres Street. Also, he had a huge picture window that opened on to the block's large central courtyard. You could look out and let your gaze wander over the changing choreography of blinds and curtains.

The office was a bit remote from the firm's reception area. His clients, or more accurately the clients Calvet, the second in command, assigned him were less important and less well off than those of the other attorneys, and he received them in the firm's conference room. And he had many cases where he was acting as a public defender. 'To break you in,' Jaime Pla, the head partner of the firm, had said. 'There is no better school for a good lawyer than daily contact with the dregs of society. Take good note of everything you see, Noguer. Get an unvarnished look at what humans are capable of.'

So Pablo learned from all sorts of conmen, pickpockets, pimps, prostitutes and murderers. If that was the idea, Pla was a good teacher.

He hung his coat in an old art deco tallboy that no one had wanted. It was time to go and see Maribel.

He found her, as always, sitting at her desk in the anteroom to Pla's office. When she saw him, she gestured for him to come over. In her white blouse and navy jacket, she looked just like any secretary in a well-established firm: tidy and competent. She was pretty and pleasant too. Pablo smiled at her and she smiled back. He presumed that Maribel had taken a certain liking to him because she was much more friendly and gracious with him than with the other lawyers in the firm. But that morning, there wasn't time for the usual small talk.

'Pla wanted to talk to you as soon as you got in. I'll let him know you're here.'

Pablo was surprised. What did Pla want? He normally worked with Calvet.

Maribel hung up and looked at him. 'You can go on in.'

She stood and opened the door for him as she did for the head partner's clients. She waited until he had taken a couple of steps inside and closed the door discreetly behind him.

Pla pointed to a chair in front of his desk and continued writing with his solid, robust body leaning over the table like a novice schoolboy, an impression that Pablo knew very well was deceptive. No one was less clumsy and innocent than Jaime Pla. For a while, the room was silent except for the scratch of pen on paper, the dull blows of the blotting paper he applied with vigorous movements and the rustle of the signed documents as he put them away in their folder. Finally his leather desk pad was clear. Pla lifted his head and stared at Pablo as he twirled the fountain pen between his fingers.

'I'm pleased you came quickly, Noguer!'

He held up a hand to keep Pablo from replying.

'It's an unpleasant matter. Extremely unpleasant. And serious.'

Pablo took the precaution of saying nothing. He looked at Pla squarely, trying to maintain a neutral expression.

'The day before yesterday you were in an ...' Pla paused briefly, 'establishment.'

Pablo nodded.

Two days before, he had gone out with some of his young colleagues from the firm. Calvet had invited them. Pablo had understood it as some sort of initiation rite: going out for drinks together, going to a brothel and the next day toasting the occasion with Alka-Seltzer dissolved in water.

'There, there were some . . . ' Pla hesitated again, 'some excesses. Various excesses.'

That was also true. He would have preferred to forget about them, and he felt embarrassed by some of the images that came into his head.

Pla's gaze became kindly. Pablo was familiar with the strategies his boss used in the courtroom. This expression worked to reassure reluctant witnesses so that he could then deliver a well-timed blow and destroy their credibility entirely. He prepared himself.

'All of us, when we are young, have to let off steam. Well, later too, because a man is a man and has his needs. But' – the kindness vanished – 'there are limits.'

Pla opened the main drawer of his desk and pulled out an envelope.

'Someone filed a complaint with the police. It seems that on the night in question you consumed illegal drugs, namely cocaine. It seems you also sold the drug.'

This was only partly true. That night there was plenty of everything: food, alcohol, women. Cocaine too. But he hadn't brought it. He didn't know where it had come from or who started spreading it around. No one sold cocaine there, only consumed it and, from what he could remember, the other three young colleagues, Miranda, Ripoll and Gómez, did too. Perhaps Pla knew as much, perhaps not. Pablo reacted as he had learned to. 'Never admit to anything. It's always better to counter-attack,' his father would hammer into him.

'That's slander. Who filed the complaint against me?'

Pla stared at him. 'It was anonymous.'

Before Pablo could reply, he continued, 'Well, the complaint, due to fortunate circumstances that I don't want to go into now, came from Vía Layetana straight into my hands. Luckily. So, give thanks to the goddess of Fortune or,' Pla smiled, 'light a candle to Saint Martin, the patron saint of drinkers, who must have been looking out for you.'

Stay objective, don't show any emotion, control your body language.
Pablo struggled to do so and hoped he was more or less managing it.

'Don Jaime, of course I am most grateful, and I appreciate your attempt to protect me, but could you tell me what it says in the accusation?'

Pablo extended a hand, but Pla didn't give him the piece of paper. He unfolded it and smoothed it out.

'I'm going to read it to you.'

Pla ran his hand over his thin moustache, fitted some reading glasses onto his nose and looked at Pablo once more before directing his gaze to the piece of paper in his hand.

'It's almost impossible to read this scribble. The handwriting is a disaster.'

He started to read. '*Your Excellency . . .*'

He glanced up.

'It seems that our friend doesn't have a good grip on the whole title business.'

He continued reading. '*As a good citizen of new Spain I have to denounce something. The consumption of prohibitive drugs –* I guess he meant prohibited *– is rising, and they even sell them in bars. Were will we end up if solisotors do these things and skorn morality? Yesterday I was in a bar and was witness to thus. Neer eleven at night a group of posch young men, among them one named Pablo Noguer who I wanted to denounce to the proscecutor for the crime below. They all wanted champain and women. They were partying for a wile with plenty whore, as you can imagine. Round one I saw the aforesaid Pablo Noguer sell cocaine to several people. It wasnt the first time, I saw him several times sell in La Paloma Blanca, on Tapia Street, and La Gallega, on the Rambla Santa Mónica, both rough place where the poch little lord go looking for cheep women.*'

Pla looked at him.

'That last part isn't particularly important because it doesn't give any precise information. But in the first accusation, there is a place, date and time. I still haven't spoken with your colleagues. Given your name and your family's name, Noguer, I chose to talk to you first. Which is why I am asking you: is what he says true?'

Pablo swallowed hard. If he denied having taken cocaine and any of the other three admitted it, he could lose his credibility with Pla. He had no choice but to lower his eyes and say, 'Only one of the points is true, Don Jaime; I think I tried the cocaine. I admit it was foolish, but ... '

Pablo trusted that Pla would see it as a minor infraction. The fact was, cocaine could be bought in the pharmacy on prescription. Although it had to be registered. But not everyone had a doctor who would prescribe it. Which was why the black market flourished. Those who did business in it ran the risk of a long sentence. The repercussions that an accusation such as this one could have on a career in the law were obvious.

' ... But I assure you that I was not the one who passed it round, much less sold it.'

Pla nodded gravely. Did he believe him? Pablo continued his counter-attack, trying to deflect attention away from himself. 'Besides, the declaration doesn't hold much weight. An anonymous eyewitness who surely wouldn't be willing to testify under oath.'

'You already know, Noguer, that anonymous accusations are taken very seriously in this country.'

He knew it well. An anonymous denunciation was enough to get you called into the police station. It was enough to make you the victim of interrogations that some people came back from with broken arms or legs. When they came back. But that couldn't happen to him, could it? If it did, perhaps his father could pull strings. He would have to write pleas, pay large sums of money or perhaps call in a favour to stop the process. His shame turned to mortification as he thought of what his father would say, the disdain in his voice when he spoke to him, his mother's aggrieved face.

Yes, he would get him out of the jam, but there'd be no end to his reproaches. And his father wouldn't be able to stop everyone in Barcelona from finding out about it, and his career would be ruined.

Then Pla asked him, 'Do you have any idea who could have written this letter?'

'No. I haven't the slightest idea. Maybe someone from the brothel? One of the girls? One of the pimps?'

'One of the girls? Did you treat them . . . did you treat them badly?'

Pablo blushed.

'No. For the love of God! It was just the regular,' he cleared his throat, 'the services we agreed upon and the corresponding remuneration.'

Pla started to twirl the fountain pen around again. It was a German model, a Pelikan with green and black stripes that blended together as the lawyer spun it fast.

'But the man or woman who accused you knew your name,' he said finally.

'That's not hard. We were all calling each other by our names.'

He remembered that when Calvet had ordered the champagne, he had egged him on: 'Come on, Noguer, let's see what you're really made of. In court you act like an altar boy.' Pablo held the bottle between his legs. They all shouted when the foam started to emerge in a spout and chanted his name when Calvet held the bottle to his mouth for him to drink. He didn't want to remember anything from that point on. That night wasn't one of the proudest moments of his life.

Pla's voice took on a strict tone. 'I can't say that I'm pleased about this matter. I expect model behaviour from my lawyers. I expect that, in every situation, they know where the permitted and tolerated limits are. On the other hand, I value your work highly and I would like to continue to employ you. I am going to have to reflect on how to proceed in this case.'

He got up from his chair. The conversation was over.

Pablo managed to mumble a few words of gratitude and exited the office.

He passed by Maribel's desk. She called to him, 'The minutes from the Molina case. You have to draw up the buying contract.'

He turned and took the papers she held out to him.

'Forgive me, Maribel. I was distracted.'

Maribel smiled at him.

He returned the smile mechanically and went to his office with the minutes under his arm.

8

Once a week Ana offered her services as a scrivener in one of the stalls near the Bouquería market. Seated inside one of the wooden booths, she wrote and read letters for people who were illiterate or who wanted to ensure a standard of writing. Letters to family members, to friends, to institutions; to give news, communicate births and deaths, marriages, First Communions; having got work, having lost it, asking for money or demanding the payment of debts. And love letters.

One of her regular customers was Carmiña Orozco, a young woman from Galicia who worked as a chambermaid at the Hotel Majestic, a luxury hotel on the Paseo de Gracia. Carmiña wasn't illiterate: she knew how to read, albeit slowly, and how to write, but she preferred the letters she sent her boyfriend, Hernán, in prison, to be 'in nice handwriting'.

Hernán still had three of the seven years he'd been sentenced to for stealing a Singer sewing machine from a warehouse, time that Carmiña had used to put together a trousseau by means of petty theft from the hotel.

That day she wanted to let her boyfriend know that they already had a complete set of bed linen, with two sheets and pillowcases.

'Carmiña, you know that's a crime, and that you could end up in jail like your boyfriend, don't you?'

Ana told her the same thing each time, but mostly to feel that she had fulfilled her moral obligation. This time, after having seen the treatment Castro had meted out to Mariona Sobrerroca's maid, she feared for what would happen to Carmiña if they caught her. As she pulled out a sheet of paper to begin the letter, she imagined Castro slapping the young woman.

'Yes, ma'am. But you aren't going to grass on me, are you?'

'Of course not! What you tell me remains a professional secret,' lied Ana, 'like what clients tell priests or solicitors.'

'Clients? Priests?'

'You know what I mean.'

Carmiña nodded. Ana picked up her pen.

'How should we put it this time?'

'Put that the head of housekeeping gave me a bed set because she is very happy with my work.'

In Carmiña's letters, her thefts were disguised as gifts from her boss when they were textiles, or from the cafeteria supervisor when they were dishes, or from the owner of the hotel when they were other things, such as an ashtray, a pitcher and other decorative ornaments she'd managed to take without, for the moment, arousing suspicion.

'And that I'm going to have them embroidered with our initials.'

This was how she had erased the monograms that had once proclaimed the towels, bathrobe and sheets to be the property of the Hotel Majestic.

'The sheets and the pillowcases are embroidered too?'

'Of course. It's the Majestic.'

'Well, you can leave the H for Hernán.'

'No. It wouldn't look right. They're machine-embroidered, and you can tell the difference.'

Carmiña had her dignity. Or perhaps she was aware of the irony that Hernán was in prison for trying to steal sewing machines.

'You're right.'

Ana wrote.

Dear Hernán,
   I hope that these lines find you in good health.

Ana had tried several times to convince Carmiña that such formalities weren't necessary in a letter to her boyfriend, but she insisted on them so it would be clear that it was a serious letter, a proper letter.

Sra Gómez, the head of housekeeping, praised me again for my good work. She says I'm an example of diligence, tidiness and care, that when we marry I will be a perfect housewife, as befits a Spanish woman. That is why she gave me a full bed set. It is linen, and I'm going to take it to the embroiderer so she will put our initials on it.

She read it over and crossed out the part about the 'Spanish woman'.

She didn't want to go too far. The letter had to get through the prison censors, but it was enough, in her opinion, that the news she was transmitting was inane, and at the end she put the obligatory repetitions of 'long live the Caudillo'.

She read it to Carmiña.

'Do you want me to add anything else?'

'Put something nice. Something sweet and nice. Don't make me say it, it really embarrasses me.'

Since she couldn't think of any verse she could camouflage into prose, she put a piece of a bolero by Antonio Machín, with a few changes:

I don't care what state we live in, or how, or where. All I care is that it is by your side.

She showed it to Carmiña, who read it slowly, excited when she reached the end. She approved it. Ana wrote a clean version on the paper Carmiña had brought with her.

Carmiña left, after paying her for her work, with the handwritten letter – you don't type love letters – folded carefully and placed inside an envelope. Ana watched her go, thinking that when she sealed the envelope perhaps she would shed a couple of tears onto the paper that was already scented with a few drops of perfume she'd stolen from a hotel guest. Hernán didn't realise it, but he had sniffed some of the world's most expensive perfumes.

The stalls to Ana's right and left were also occupied. From the one to her right she could hear the voice of Oleguer Pons, a retired man who spent his days in the National Library of Catalonia reading history books and who earned a few coins writing letters.

Oleguer Pons was lucky to have been born a lefty (although in school he hadn't been allowed to write that way) because a stay in the police headquarters on the Vía Layetana had rendered his right hand useless. To make him confess to the whereabouts of his son, an underground militant in the Communist Party, the police had hung him from a pipe by his wrists with handcuffs for two days. He held out, as did one of his wrists. The right wrist was contorted and twisted inward for ever.

But Oleguer Pons – called by the Castilian version of his name, Olegario, during the two weeks they'd held him in the Social Investigation Brigade prison cell – remembered when he was released that his hands had been tied on another occasion. In school, the teacher had tied his left hand to the back of the chair with string to keep him from writing with it. Which is why, when the bruises disappeared from his left wrist, he needed only a week of practice to develop lovely handwriting with that hand. Since he couldn't go back to work, now that he was crippled and had a police record, he survived by writing postcards and invitations for a printing house and helping people with their letters near the Library of Catalonia.

Oleguer was reading a letter to someone. It seemed as though it was something difficult, because the woman interrupted him frequently to ask, 'What do you mean by that?'

'How do you expect me to know, woman?'

Ana resisted the temptation to look over. As much as she

had been exaggerating when she'd explained the secrecy of her profession to Carmiña, she did believe that her work was subject to an ethic that demanded discretion. Besides, she was going to find out anyway, since old Oleguer didn't share her reservations and enjoyed talking about his work. He was also more in need of conversation than she was, and clung to the few chances he had, even when it was telling her about the letters he had read or written that day. He didn't talk about his deformed hand. They had discussed it once, and that was enough.

She thought that if they had a lull at the same time, she would tell Pons about her article, but she decided not to tell him that she had been at Vía Layetana and worked with the police inspector. Perhaps it would be better to stick to their customers and their stories, as always. Now that she thought about it, most of the conversations they had were about other people's lives. But this time she felt like talking about herself, about her article, about Sanvisens congratulating her on it, about getting up early to go to a kiosk and buy a copy, turning the pages with nervous fingers and finding it there, her article.

She pulled a book out of her bag, an edition of *Nada* by Carmen Laforet that she had bought second-hand at the Cervantes Bookshop. She had read about five pages, when, out of the corner of her eye, she noticed a familiar figure approaching her stall; it was the unmistakable silhouette of another of her regulars, Pepe 'The Spider', a slight man in his thirties, barely five feet tall spread out over thin legs, a narrow torso and a pair of skinny arms in which all the muscles seemed to have been replaced by tendons. With them he could climb up any wall that had even the slightest texture. Pepe the Spider was a cat burglar. And illiterate.

For more than a year now, The Spider had come once a week for Ana to write a letter to the girlfriend he had back in his village in the province of Seville and to read him her response to the previous letter. He always turned up, except for those three weeks when he had had to disappear because he was a suspect in a break-in at a house in San Gervasio. That was four months ago.

'Every time there's some break-in that involves climbing, they nick me, even though I had nothing to do with it. And once I'm there, they shave my head. You don't know how much it hurts to have them take all this off.' The Spider pointed to his hair, rough as a brush.

'Why do they do it?'

'Because they can,' The Spider lamented as he explained to Ana the reason for his absence.

When he could allow himself to be seen on the streets again, he brought three letters from his girlfriend for Ana to read. He had them sent to an ironmonger's on the street where he lived. It was a precaution in case they ever sent him down for a long stretch, so that his girlfriend's letters wouldn't end up in just anybody's hands. The shop assistant there was an old friend of his from his village.

The Spider's girlfriend, Azucena, knew how to read, but she too had someone write her letters for her. Ana didn't dare ask her client, but she assumed it was a woman.

'Is there a school in your village?'

'Of course. I didn't go, but there is one.'

'And is the teacher there a man or a woman?'

'A woman. Why?'

'Just curious.'

Perhaps the teacher was the author of the letters that The Spider received. In any case, they were definitely written by a woman. Not only because of the style, with fragments such as, 'Today I pick up my pen to write to you' and 'I am at a loss for words to show the depth of my appreciation for the effort I know you are making so that we can marry soon', but for one sound reason: a woman wouldn't dictate her love letters to a man, no matter how prosaic they were and how filled with cliché. That was also her experience as a writer and reader of letters. For love letters, both men and women preferred that the scrivener be a woman.

She read The Spider his letter. The man could barely hold

back his tears when Azucena sent him greetings from his family. Then he explained to Ana what she should write to his girlfriend.

'Tell her that I will soon be able to bring her here.'

When he'd finished, he said, 'Can you give me this one on credit, Señorita Ana? I'll pay for it next week, I swear.'

'Yes, all right.'

The Spider left happily with his letter in an envelope and, thought Ana, with a scheme for some burglary in his head, if he was thinking of bringing his girlfriend to Barcelona.

'One of these days a gust of wind will come and blow that one right away,' said a voice from the booth to the right.

Oleguer Pons had also finished with his inquisitive client and was watching The Spider as he disappeared around a corner. Then, as Ana had expected, he told her about the contents of his client's letter. She listened to it with the impatience of someone who knows that the story she has to tell, when it is her turn to speak, is going to be infinitely more interesting. And it was. Old Oleguer was the perfect listener: attentive, curious and enthusiastic. Ana went on in depth and then held out the copy of *La Vanguardia* that she had brought with her to show to her parents. Oleguer Pons read the text and told her, 'The family tradition continues. Has your father or your grandfather seen it?'

No. Not yet. She was planning on going to their house later, for lunch. And taking them a copy of the newspaper. She was eager to see her family's reaction to her first success.

All the same, she helped two more people with some official papers. Afterwards, she said goodbye to Oleguer Pons, closed the stall and headed to her parents' house.

9

'The taxi's here.'

Calvet appeared in the doorway of Pablo's office and started laughing when he saw his disconcerted expression.

'We're going to have lunch with Pla. I reserved a table at Siete Puertas. Weren't we going to talk about your problem? Don't tell me you forgot! I can't believe that.'

No, of course he hadn't forgotten. Since he'd been told about the lunch, the hours had both stretched on interminably and passed in a flash; now it seemed that the meeting with his bosses was catching him unprepared. Calvet went off, leaving the door open.

Pablo put on his jacket and went after him.

'Calvet and Señor Pla have already gone downstairs,' Maribel told him.

They hadn't waited for him. Bad sign.

'Bon appétit!' said Maribel in farewell.

Siete Puertas was an expensive restaurant near the port. Was that a good sign? If they took him to eat there, surely they weren't going to fire him. Or was that perhaps the last meal of a condemned man?

Pla and Calvet sat in the back seat of the taxi and closed the door, making it clear that he should sit beside the driver. Another bad sign. During the ride Calvet talked constantly. Pablo saw out of the corner of his eye how the lawyer accentuated each of his words with gestures that he drew in the air like Chinese calligraphy. Sometimes he talked about the traffic. 'There are more and more cars in this city! Soon you won't be able to cross the road.'

Or he commented on the building work being carried out for the Eucharistic Congress: 'Did you know they are finally knocking down the rookeries on the Diagonal?'

Pla's worrying silence was broken only when Calvet talked about the new Civil Governor, but it was nothing more than an approving grunt. 'A hardliner, just what this city needs,' added Calvet, not allowing himself to be disheartened by his boss's reserve.

Pablo didn't think that what the city needed was more of a hard line, but he was very careful not to state his opinion.

'Noguer, I guess you must have noticed the change since they put one of the hardliners at the head of the CIB. Goyanes, the one who used to be in Social. A tough nut to crack.'

And he was. Since Commissioner Goyanes had been in the CIB, not only had the number of arrests for common crimes gone up, but the penalties handed down by the public prosecutor's office were much harsher. Rumour had it that they had put one of the political officers into the CIB to keep an eye on the investigators so they wouldn't 'go easy'. Goyanes had the support of the Civil Government. The Commissioner, Governor Acedo Colunga, and his right-hand man, Sánchez-Herranz, were outsiders and, judging by their declarations, seemed convinced that they were in a city whose inhabitants were, to a man, potential criminals who had to be kept at bay.

Soon they arrived at the restaurant. Calvet took charge of ordering; he also chose the wine. Then Pla intervened. 'Don't even think about bringing us an Alvariño, for the love of God. We'll have a Blanc D'Anjou,' he said to the waiter.

He shot a furious look at Calvet, who shrugged and went on talking about something or other.

Shortly afterwards, the waiter brought a serving dish laden with seafood: cockles, clams, oysters, shrimp, crayfish, even two lobsters were piled up on a mountain of ice. Such merchandise was usually only obtained on the black market. At the summit of the seafood mountain an enormous spider crab lifted its pincers towards Pablo and glared at him with its dead, malevolent-looking eyes. Pla helped himself to the largest lobster and opened it with a surgeon's precision. He turned towards Calvet. In all that time he hadn't deigned to exchange a single word with Pablo.

'Have you heard about Mariona Sobrerroca?'

Calvet nodded as he deposited a crayfish head on his plate of shells with a vexed expression. Then he turned to Pablo, 'Did you know her, Noguer?'

'Slightly. My father had some business dealings with her husband. I saw her a few times at social events.'

He remembered a night, six years or so ago, during an intermission at the Liceo Opera. He had finished secondary school and his father had insisted he accompany him to, as he put it, learn how to move about in society. In that encounter, Mariona had looked him in the eyes and told him something about one of the singers, he didn't recall what, while her husband spoke with his father. He offered to bring her another glass of champagne and he felt worldly and gentlemanly because she accepted it with a childish smile. Still very naive, he interpreted what happened next as a series of coincidences. First, her clutch bag fell and he had to bend down to pick it up for her; as he did so, she gave him a little pat on the shoulder that forced him to look up in such a way that for a few seconds he looked like an enamoured young man at the feet of his beloved, an image that she must not have minded. In another moment the fur stole that covered her back slipped and he helped to replace it on her rounded white shoulders; she thanked him with a flirtatious smile. When the bell rang announcing the second act, Mariona tripped on a stair and had to grab onto Pablo's arm to keep from falling.

To his left, Pla lopped off a shrimp's head as he asked him, 'Did your father represent Garmendia?'

Pablo nodded.

'But I don't know in which matters.'

His father had defended him when a patient denounced him for medical negligence, but it didn't get to court.

If Pla's question was designed to test his discretion, he had passed. If it was testing his loyalty, he had failed.

Pla lifted a glass, swirled it around and looked expectantly at Pablo.

'From what they say, Garmendia had very particular methods.'

Pablo didn't know much about that subject. He shrugged as he decided on the last king prawn over the shrimp.

Then Calvet intervened. 'What a looker Mariona Sobrerroca was!'

'Lush. A bit over the hill, but that has its charms, too,' commented Pla.

'A real stunner.' Calvet wiped his lips with a napkin.

Pablo didn't say anything, and not only because a waiter was there, taking away the plates before bringing the second course. All three had ordered meat. As they polished off a Catalana chicken and leg of lamb with rosemary, Pla and Calvet continued discussing Mariona Sobrerroca's murder. Pablo ate his veal in silence. He didn't find the subject very interesting, and he wondered why the other two were taking so long to get to what they were supposed to be discussing.

To his right, Calvet's voice demanded his attention: 'Noguer, Noguer.'

'Yes?'

'That veal must be heavenly, because your head is in the clouds,' he joked. 'I was saying that the article in *La Vanguardia* about Sobrerroca was written by a woman.'

Pablo thought Calvet was expecting him to show surprise.

'A woman?' he said, although he didn't really care.

But that wasn't what Calvet wanted to talk about either.

'Ana María Martí Noguer. When I read it this morning I said to myself, "Look, like our Noguer." Is she a relative?'

Pla observed the exchange with indifference.

'No. I don't know of any Ana María Martí in the family.'

'Of course, of course. It's not such an uncommon last name. Could she be the daughter of the Martí who also worked at *La Vanguardia*?'

Now he was talking to Pla instead of him.

Pablo didn't pay any special attention to the stories they were telling him about the journalist, and a couple of other people whose names were familiar but which didn't spark his interest.

When the coffee arrived, Calvet leaned back in his seat.

'What are we going to do with you, Noguer?'

Pablo lifted his cup to his mouth too quickly and burned his lips. Luckily Calvet started to speak again. 'Well, I don't see it as such a serious problem. We were just having a little fun.'

'You were having fun? I don't think I share your definition of fun. It's not simply that Noguer admitted to taking drugs, it's that they saw him selling them.'

Calvet extended his arms as if to an auditorium crowd whose applause he wanted to win.

'It's not a capital crime. Your doctor can prescribe cocaine.'

Pla set his cup down on the saucer and the teaspoon gave a slight tinkle of complaint.

'I don't want drug addicts in the firm, or neurasthenics who require to be prescribed cocaine.'

Calvet nodded pensively, his forehead filling with wrinkles. For a moment he looked like a wise Buddha deep in contemplation. But it lasted just a moment, since he soon began to gesticulate and speak again.

'That's true, my friend, totally true. But surely our good Noguer isn't a drug addict or a neurasthenic.' He opened his arms again, this time to show that the world was how it was and that you had to take things with a pinch of salt. 'We were young once, too, for God's sake, and we've made plenty of slips.'

Calvet put a hand on Pablo's shoulder.

'Our Noguer is young.'

Pablo looked towards Pla, who drummed his fingers on the tablecloth.

'All right, we'll give our young friend the licence of youth. There's still the drug trafficking. That isn't a youthful peccadillo, is it? If I remember rightly, it's punishable with a jail sentence.' He said the last part with clear sarcasm.

'We don't know whether he did that or not. I was there, and I didn't see it. Of course, I wasn't watching him all night. Here we have his word against the accuser's. In fact, in my view it's slander.'

The drumming stopped. Calvet continued: 'And if I had to choose sides, I'd believe a colleague with whom I got along well over some anonymous letter.'

Pla looked pointedly at Pablo.

'Perhaps Noguer could do something to quash these rumours. Have you looked into it at all?'

He shook his head. He hadn't done anything. Why should he? Digging into the matter would only make it worse. Before he could say so, Calvet spoke again.

'You did the right thing, Noguer.' Then he addressed Pla. 'Intervening in the situation would just give us more headaches.'

Calvet put a hand on Pla's forearm and looked at him.

'Jaime, leave it be. The problem is solved. The accusation is no longer in police hands, and our anonymous author isn't going to take any action against us.'

He gestured to the waiter, who brought them three glasses of cognac.

Pla nodded his head slowly.

'Fine, you are responsible for Noguer. Let's leave it at that.'

Calvet stuck his nose into the glass with gusto.

'French. Imported. Ten years old.'

Pla tilted his head in satisfaction. They lifted their glasses. Pablo raised his, too. He was doubly thankful to Calvet, who had saved him from an ignominious dismissal and had exonerated his guilt. Or had he? The cognac left a bittersweet taste in his mouth; they hadn't done him justice by believing him, they were merely condescending to let him off the hook.

10

'It's dark in here!' said Ana as she entered her parents' dining room. It was two in the afternoon, but already the curtains were drawn at many of the windows and kept out the light of the one cloudless day that week. The room was dark, it was true. It was also true that the phrase was more of a ritual than a complaint. Ana knew that her mother wouldn't agree to open the curtains.

'What do the neighbours care what we eat?'

They didn't, of course, but ever since the day a neighbour across the street had waved to Patricia Noguer from the balcony, the curtains remained drawn at mealtimes and as soon as nightfall forced them to turn on the lights. Her mother wasn't used to such proximity. Before – the time prior to the war was simply called 'before'; it was neither necessary nor desirable to spell out before what – they lived in a flat of palatial dimensions on the Paseo de San Juan, where the houses opposite were merely a landscape, but after – 'after' what needed no explanation either – following her father's fall from grace, the family had had to move to a much smaller flat in a more modest neighbourhood.

'Modest' wasn't Ana's word, it was the one her mother used to whitewash the dirty streets, the perennial odour of damp and urine in some of the doorways, the laundry hung on the balconies that dripped slow, heavy drops onto the pavements and the skeletal little plants that tried in vain to rise towards a sun that never touched those blackened walls. 'Modest' was a word as soft as the bobbin lace doilies that Patricia Noguer used to hide the worn arm of the chair Father sat in each evening, on the side where the radio was.

'Poverty is narrowness,' her mother would say. 'Narrow streets, narrow staircases, narrow rooms.'

Narrow rooms, even more so because she had insisted on bringing part of the furniture they'd had on the Paseo de San Juan to the new flat on Joaquín Costa Street. While the pieces were enormous and disproportionate to the dwelling, they kept alive her faith in returning to her rightful place, to streets with generous pavements, to grand entranceways which horse-drawn carriages had passed through not long before, to large picture windows that opened far, far away from the houses opposite.

Now, in order to reach the little balcony that opened on to the street, she had to pass between the rectangular table and a bulky china cabinet that displayed a porcelain service that appeared complete. It was actually missing a cup from the coffee service, but Patricia Noguer had replaced it with a similar one, though one of ordinary china, like a person might disguise a missing tooth.

'Where is Grandfather?' asked Ana.

'In his room, but he's already up.'

'That's good. Will he eat with us?'

'He will.'

It was something. No one ever knew how long Grandfather would stay at the table, but they all counted the mouthfuls he managed to cut, chew and swallow before he noticed his dead grandson's chair, shot a confused glance at the rest of the family and asked, 'When is Ángel coming?'

It hadn't helped that they'd taken away all the photos of Ángel and stopped mentioning him in front of Grandfather. He still noticed his absence from the house, despite the fact that his grandson hadn't ever lived in that flat.

But today Ana would ignore her brother's ghost, and she wouldn't count her grandfather's mouthfuls. She wouldn't complain about her mother either, even though she not only condemned them to eating without natural light but also deprived them of much of the electric kind. She had brought from the other house an enormous chandelier with candle-shaped bulbs, four of which were lit. The other eight had been unscrewed. Sometimes Ana would climb up on one of the chairs, covered in cloth to protect the upholstering, and screw in two more bulbs.

'Come on, Mamá. Just while we eat.'

'Certainly, and how are we to pay the electricity bill? With what your father makes at the grocer's ...'

But no, not this day. She wouldn't screw in any more bulbs or try to open the curtains a few more centimetres.

Not this day. Because this was the day the first crime article with her byline had been published. Ana María Martí Noguer. Her name on a text of almost four hundred words, the left-hand column on page eleven. The headline: 'Police investigate brutal murder in Tibidabo'. Sanvisens hadn't wanted to reveal the victim's name in the headline. Then, 'Initial enquiries by the Criminal Investigation Brigade' and the text under her name.

Several times that morning she had passed in front of the display window that *La Vanguardia* had on Pelayo Street. The pages of the day's newspaper were exposed to the view of all onlookers, who read it for free, leaning forward with their hands clasped behind their backs. She had watched them, but the effort of pretending she wasn't had made it impossible for her to determine how many were reading her text.

She had left it on her father's old desk.

He too was waiting to return someday to what he had been 'before', even if it wasn't at a large national newspaper like *La Vanguardia*. It would be enough for her father to be able to set foot in even a small paper's editorial office and listen to the music of the typewriters. The sounds her father now heard were the bell on the grocer's door, the keys and crank of the enormous cash register that reigned over the counter in front of which, she recalled, the sacks of beans and chickpeas gave off a rancid, dusty odour that impregnated the place. It had been a while since Ana had passed by there; her father didn't want her to see him in the store, stuffed into a dark grey smock with the name of the grocery embroidered on the breast pocket.

More reading than writing was done these days at her father's desk. When he came home at midday he went into his office for half an hour before lunch and he read 'so I don't get soft in the head' after a morning spent loading bundles in the warehouse or serving customers.

But he still kept his old typewriter, a majestic Underwood. Ana was surprised to see it without its protective cover on a small low table beside the desk. That was another of the pieces of furniture that the family had refused to abandon and, along with a bookshelf and her father's chair, almost completely filled the small interior room he called his office, which in the other flats in the building must have been a utility room. She left the copy of *La Vanguardia*, open to the page with her article, on the leather blotter, another of the surviving castaways from the family's economic shipwreck. The two silver inkwells, on the other hand, had been pawned several years earlier while her father was still in jail.

Her father arrived punctually. He was surprised to see her. Ana ate with them every Sunday, but she hadn't come for lunch on weekdays since she had moved into the flat that had been her grandfather's, on Riera Alta Street.

'I left something on your desk,' was Ana's reply to her father's inquisitive look. 'Something good,' she added, so as not to alarm him.

Like so many others, he had learned that often news wasn't cheery.

Before going into his office, Andreu Martí opened the door to Grandfather's room and greeted him as he did every day; sometimes he got a response and other times, only the silence that announced that he wouldn't be leaving his room that day.

'Father, I'm home. I brought you two new "Coyotes".'

Grandfather, like her father and brother after him, had been a journalist, but now he read nothing but comic books and adventure stories. On Sundays her father sometimes managed to coax him out of the house to go to the second-hand market in the San Antonio district to buy copies of *TBO*, the *Coyote*, the *Masked Warrior* or books by Salgari, Verne or the *Just William* collection. He never bought *War Deeds*, because it made him anxious.

Ana heard her grandfather's voice, although she couldn't make out the words; her father responded and her grandfather's voice replied. Then came the sound of the door closing and her father's footsteps heading to the next room.

Meanwhile, she helped her mother set the table.

'So you're sticking to your guns,' her mother said without looking at her.

Ana took advantage of the fact that she was fetching the napkins from a drawer of the bureau to pretend she hadn't heard.

'Should I take out the plain ones?'

'Yes, the plain ones. What did Gabriel say about you publishing a crime piece?'

'Nothing yet. I still haven't told him; I'll talk to him on Sunday.'

She distributed the napkins without looking up, as if doing so demanded all her attention.

'What? You did it without his permission?'

'I don't need his permission to do my job,' she replied, her gaze still lowered.

Her mother snorted, and she couldn't help echoing her with a huff. Separated by the table, they both stopped in their movements. Patricia Noguer opened her mouth to begin her next reproach, but the rage that began to show in her daughter's eyes made her change not her opinion, but at least her strategy, and with a plaintive voice she added, 'I can't wait for him to finish his studies, come back from abroad and marry you, so you'll abandon these silly dreams!'

She could have been cruel and reminded her mother that

73

Gabriel, after his stay abroad, still had two years, two long years, before he finished medical school, and that there was no promising that they could marry after that either. Perhaps she could have added that she wasn't sure she wanted to, that frankly she didn't miss him much. Or she could have thrown the last napkin onto the table and left, as she'd done on other occasions. She didn't. Not today. Not with her article sitting on her father's desk.

But she could have, and her mother knew as much, so she held her tongue, swallowing the rest of her laments and reproaches and simply pointing to the napkin Ana still held in her hand like an indecisive boxing coach who's not sure if he should throw in the towel or let the fight continue.

'Fold it well, this isn't a charity soup kitchen,' her mother said.

For her, the soup kitchen was the antechamber to hell, like all those places you don't arrive at but rather fall into. The only way to avoid them, despite the family's precarious situation, was to keep up appearances with exacting discipline. They never ate in the kitchen, always in the dining room, and while there were fewer silver settings, they still had to be properly placed.

When she had entered the house she'd seen a basket with clothes for the children of the welfare service. In reality the basket contained only two or three items of clothing – the rest was stuffed with newspaper – but her mother wanted to go out onto the street with an overflowing basket, like before, when she and all the friends she no longer saw prided themselves on taking several bags of clothes for the 'poor'. The poor are always those who don't have what you do, even if it's only three old jackets.

No, it wasn't the soup kitchen. Ana folded the napkin carefully. Her mother changed the subject and began to tell her that a relative, on her side, the Noguer side, had died. She nodded without paying the slightest attention as her mother told her when and where the funeral would be. She was really more interested in making sure that the silver settings were placed at the proper distance. Spoon, which meant there'd be soup. Knife and fork.

'What's for the second course?'

'Stewed meat.'

Stewed meat for a weekday lunch? Where had she got that from?

It seemed the day was filled with successes, large and small. Her mother had bought meat, her grandfather was coming out of his room to eat and she had published her article. She heard the sound of a door opening. It wasn't the exasperatingly slow creak of her grandfather's; it was her father turning a handle before giving a vigorous pull. But his steps headed to the bedroom, not the dining room. Father had to change for lunch: another of the appearances kept up in that house.

In her parents' bedroom, behind the door of the large wardrobe, hid the shrine that her mother had erected to her dead son. The firstborn son, *l'hereu*, dead at twenty-seven, executed by firing squad in prison in 1943. There her mother prayed for forgiveness for her Red son, for her daughter-in-law exiled in France with a grandson they wouldn't get to see grow up. As her father changed for lunch, he saw the photos of Ángel.

Soon she heard the bedroom door again.

The fact that her father hadn't immediately come to congratulate her after reading the article had already somewhat diminished her expectations. That he still went by Grandfather's room to ask him not to be late reduced them a bit further, although not enough to avoid her disappointment when her expectant look was met with nothing more than a curt, 'Good, maybe a little formulaic. Have they paid you yet?'

'No.'

'How are you doing for money, Aneta? Do you need anything? Are you up to date with your rent?'

Her father was taking advantage of her mother being in the kitchen. She avoided his questions, pretending she heard noises in the hallway.

'I think Grandfather's coming.'

Her father approached her and whispered, 'Don't mention your article during the meal. It's better if Grandfather doesn't read it or even know about it.'

11

Abel Mendoza, on the other hand, read it several times.

After fleeing Mariona's house that Sunday, he had travelled across the entire city to take refuge, once again, in Mercedes's bed.

He got to Hospital Street, in the Barrio Chino, at eight in the evening and was surprised to find the door to the house locked. He knocked but there was no movement inside. Then he saw the police notice warning that the establishment would remain closed for two weeks by order of the judge. Why did he have to find the doors locked that day?

He knocked one more time, out of pure obstinacy.

A bang and the creaking of hinges made him look up. Mercedes's head peeped out of a first-floor window, framed by a cloud of tousled black curls.

'Can't you read, you dolt? You must be really horny . . . Oh! Hello, Abel! Wait, I'm coming down.'

She hurried him inside, afraid that the watchman might see them and tell the police that he saw a client entering in defiance of the temporary shutdown order.

Mercedes, despite her youth – twenty-four according to her papers, two fewer according to her mother – was already the madam's right-hand woman, which gave her the privilege of being a kind of gatekeeper and having her own room. A room that customers didn't have access to; only the men whom she allowed in. One of them was Abel.

Mercedes – never call her Merche and never, ever

Merceditas – had let him take refuge in her bed on many of his stays in Barcelona. Abel's visits were a luxury for Mercedes, whose regular clients didn't usually provide her with memorable moments: 'It's well known that the poor are not big on attention to detail in lovemaking.'

It was a phrase she had learned from the madam.

With the place shut down, the owner had gone to spend a few days at her family's house in Vic, and had left Mercedes in charge of the empty building.

Mercedes was very grateful to the owner, who had picked her up on the street before the family she was working for delivered her to the Foundation for the Protection of Women so that she could be locked up in a refuge for 'fallen' women. They were willing to make a large donation to rid themselves of the 'lost woman' who had got knocked up by the boss. No impropriety from a client could compare to what she'd heard you could expect from the wardens in the internment centres. Mercedes was grateful, and loyal.

As they went up to her room, she told him why they'd been closed down.

'Thank goodness the inspection didn't happen on the owner's niece's first day on the job.'

'Underage?'

Mercedes nodded.

'Twelve.'

'Twelve? Just a girl!'

'It was with a big boss from Social.'

'But twelve years old . . . '

'If they want girls, we give them girls. There are some people you can't say no to.'

'But . . . '

'Look, we all win. Her parents, who need the money; the client, who needs a hairless pussy and us, because the last thing we need are problems.'

'But what about the girls?'

'They have to put up with it, just like we all do! Their turn will come.'

She opened the door and they went in.

Mercedes's room was kept almost as white as a convent cell. White sheets, white curtains, white pillows, white upholstery on the armchairs. On a dresser rested a photo of her parents, who still lived in a town in the Extremadura region. There was also some sort of little altar with a plastic statue of the Virgin Mary filled with holy water and topped with a screw-on crown against which leaned a photo of her son, Alvarito, whom her parents were raising.

'A couple of girls ended up in jail because they challenged the policemen who came to close the place down. We got shut down for two weeks, and a fine.'

'Why?'

'Formalities. We don't register customers the way we're supposed to.'

'That was the reason?'

'Partly, but the truth is that one of the inspectors has a thing for the new girl, the one from Majorca, and he wants too many freebies.'

'Two weeks isn't so bad.'

'You think we eat air? Or love?'

'You must have something stashed away ...'

'If I did I wouldn't tell you about it.'

'I don't want money, just a bed and a roof over my head.'

'Well, you should have said so. I can give you a bed and a roof, but only at night. We can't have a man around during the day; they might think we aren't meeting the terms of the ban.'

'That's fine.'

It was fine for both of them. They had met on one of Abel's visits to the brothel, and Mercedes had offered him a bed any time he was in Barcelona on one of his business matters, whatever they might be; she didn't seem too curious. She didn't seem too curious about anything Abel did outside of her room, for that matter. A fortune teller had predicted that the man of her life would arrive by ship, so he wasn't the one, but, while she was waiting, she had to have a good guy in her bed every once in a while, and practise having a boyfriend who would take her out for a bite to eat or a drink.

As for Abel, he was happy not to have to spend the night in a boarding house. That way, the time he spent in Barcelona didn't appear in any registers.

'Abelín, you must be the son of nobility,' Mercedes said on Tuesday morning, stretching ostentatiously. And she added, in a version of the madam's phrase, 'What art! What attention to detail!'

Then, as she had done on Monday, she put him out on the street. Abel had another day of wandering the city before him. He was still dazed, directionless, overwhelmed by everything that had happened, first at home, then in Barcelona, at Mariona's house.

Since Mercedes had given him a little money in the end, he went into a barber's shop and paid extra for a nice lotion after his shave.

'But nothing that makes me smell like a queer.'

It threatened rain. He went into a tavern, El Cocodrilo on San Ramón Street. He had been in once before, with Mercedes.

It was a day when he had got quite a bit of money from Mariona, and he was feeling generous.

'Come on, let's go and have a vermouth. Where do you want me to take you?'

He had expected Mercedes to say, 'Take me to the Rigat in Plaza Cataluña, or one of the outdoor tables in Calvo Sotelo Square,' but her universe ended at the border surrounding the Barrio Chino.

'Let's go to El Cocodrilo.'

So that was where they went to drink their vermouth, surrounded by stevedores, prostitutes and local families. They were unified by their Sunday clothes and dignified by their clean shoes. Abel looked at them that day somewhat nostalgically, as if they were the remnants of a world he would soon abandon.

Just as he had known from the beginning that at some point he would abandon Mercedes. He looked at her with the gaze of the protagonists of the many romantic novels he had read, for professional reasons. He looked at her the way he had learned to: 'tenderly, tilting his head a little, parting his lips ever so slightly, letting his eyelids droop with a hint of languor'.

Not even a woman like Mercedes, a professional used to hard dealings with men since she was practically a girl, could resist that gaze that made women feel unique, somewhere between girlfriend and princess. She blushed furiously and, although when she'd had a few she could take on any sailor who showed up at the brothel spoiling for a fight, she took a couple of dainty sips from her glass of vermouth.

Lucky he hadn't said his last goodbye to her the previous time, thought Abel as he slipped once more into a seat at one of the tavern's tables. Otherwise where in the city would he go? This time he didn't drink vermouth; all he had in his pockets was the money Mercedes had given him, as he had spent his own on the train ticket and the suit he was later planning to use to start his new life. He had left it hanging in the wardrobe of Mercedes's white room. She had lent him a jacket that had been left by a customer after a raid. It was a bit small if he buttoned it up, but since he was forced to walk hunched over by the rain that had begun to fall while he was in the barber's, he guessed it wasn't as noticeable.

He asked for bread and cheese and a small glass of wine. An early regular had left a copy of *La Vanguardia* on one of the chairs. He picked it up and began to read absent-mindedly until he reached page eleven. There it was. The news of Mariona's death. The text said that the police were on the trail of a man who had been seen hastening away from the dead woman's home.

They were looking for him. Who could have seen him?

He took the page out of the newspaper and folded it carefully so the owner wouldn't see, but the man was busy polishing glasses and arguing with an unseen woman's voice that was coming from the kitchen. Abel stuck the article in his pocket, paid and left.

12

'Tieta Beatriz! Hello!'

His Aunt Beatriz jumped. She had almost passed him on Pelayo Street without noticing him.

'Pablo! What brings you here?'

His aunt pointed with one finger to her left cheek, so that he would kiss her, something she'd always done.

'I was doing a few things for the firm, and now I want to have a coffee. Why don't you join me?'

'It's just that ... '

It was always the same with Aunt Beatriz. On the one hand, it was obvious that she was very pleased to see him; on the other, she kept her distance. Perhaps she was thinking of some of those authors she was so fond of. 'Beatriz is married to her books,' his father would sometimes say.

Pablo imagined it bothered his father that his sister had never married because if she had, she might have added some good connections to the family.

'Instead, she went off to South America. Who knows what she was doing over there?'

His Aunt Beatriz had lived for several years in Buenos Aires. She had come back a year before Pablo finished his secondary school studies and had taken care of his grandmother until her death. Pablo had got on well with her straight away, and he often visited her at the old family flat on the Rambla de Cataluña. During that last year of school she had organised and corrected several of his pretty disastrous essays, which had enabled him to get a decent grade in Language Arts. As she revised and read his texts, she let out occasional grunts of displeasure and quoted, through gritted teeth, Latin aphorisms on application and discipline, but then she had sorted out the essays for him. He always left her gifts of black market cigarettes and coffee on the sideboard in the parlour.

This chance encounter was a stroke of luck: he needed to talk to someone about what had happened with Calvet and Pla, and who better than her? He couldn't shake the uneasy feeling that had taken hold of him after the lunch at Siete Puertas. He couldn't go to his father with the matter, but his Aunt Beatriz was a good listener and often hit the nail on the head. And he was increasingly convinced that, in this story, there had to be some nail that needed hitting.

He waited for her to light a cigarette and take two slow drags on the holder and then, with barely any preamble, he gave her the lie of the land. Their privacy was assured by the surrounding din of customers' voices, the shouting of the waiters, the banging of cups and glasses and the constant roar of the coffee machine; but all the same he drew close to her when he spoke. He explained it all quickly, without pausing for questions or interruptions, as if he had kept the story bottled up and now couldn't contain himself. Beatriz looked at him, and every once in a while brought her cigarette holder to her lips. She was a good listener. Or was she? Because at that moment her gaze shifted towards the large window, towards the street; really, noted Pablo, towards nothing in particular, just into the distance. Then he fell silent.

'What are you thinking about, Tieta Beatriz?'

'About Cardinal de Retz.'

'Oh,' he said, unable to hide his disappointment.

'Don't pretend you don't know who he is. Jean-François Paul de Retz. He lived in the period of Richelieu and Mazarin. He died in 1679.'

Why was she bringing up a French cardinal now?

'Are you writing about him?'

'I'm not one of those dispassionate idiots who only reads an author when they're writing some article about him.' His aunt paused and changed her tone.

'No, sweetie. It's just that your story reminded me of him. There is an interesting passage in his memoirs where the Cardinal de Retz tells how he won over a young courtier, a nobleman from a minor house. First he scared him by accusing him of a crime he hadn't committed. Then he summoned him to clarify the matter. On that occasion a third person intervened, one of the Cardinal's trusted men, whose role was supposedly to defend the young man. This "defender" refuted all of the Cardinal's accusations, but without proving the young man's innocence entirely, merely questioning his guilt. The young man, of course, became indebted to the Cardinal and, above all, to his trusted man, which in the end was the same thing.'

Beatriz gestured to the waiter and ordered another dry sherry.

'What happened to the young man?' asked Pablo.

'They cut his head off with an axe. The guillotine was invented later.'

Pablo waited for the explanation.

'They sent him on an espionage mission for the Cardinal, and he was discovered. Retz boasts in his memoirs of managing to plant in the young man's spirit a mix of fear, indebtedness and gratitude. He bragged about being able to do what he wanted with him.'

Here she paused again and looked at him. Pensive, Pablo took a napkin and wiped off a few drops of sherry that had spilled on the table.

'You mean that it was all a set-up?'

Beatriz stuck another cigarette into the holder.

'Maybe.'

Pablo lit it for her. Then he said, 'The anonymous letter is still at the firm. Pla could take it out of the safe whenever he wanted to, and spread it around.'

Beatriz released a mouthful of smoke. Pablo understood that she was waiting for him to keep talking. Talking and thinking.

'I'll have to get that letter.'

'I think so.'

It would be difficult.

'How can I do it?'

Beatriz laughed. 'You'll think of something.'

13

Isidro Castro kept a complete register of the names of people they were looking for, those they'd already had in custody and those they had released. Isidro was methodical, a quality many members of the CIB boasted about, and which Goyanes said he truly appreciated in him. Methodical, systematic, and rigorous were adjectives that the Commissioner used in his assessment of his subordinate's work.

On the list were the names of the city's notorious criminals, and some of its most illustrious families. The two columns were separated only by a fine red line drawn by hand with the help of a ruler. Some of the names were already crossed out. They had good alibis, or were the result of fake leads. The article in *La Vanguardia* had led to a few reports being filed: a woman from the Barrio Chino who accused her lover of the crime, since she hadn't seen him for a while. The woman's spite quickly turned to regret and insults directed at God knows whom when they told her that the man's absence was due to the fact that he'd spent the last two weeks in jail. The doorman of a block of flats neighbouring Mariona Sobrerroca's also turned up, but all he really told them was what had appeared in the article.

'The guy's just a show-off,' declared Sevilla.

Two more people came in, anxious to 'cooperate', but after talking to them the policemen didn't understand what their story was nor why they were telling it.

'Slim pickings,' said Isidro. 'There are some people who aren't even good at informing.'

He had also talked with some of the names from the right-hand column of his list, the list of 'good' people. He hadn't got much, except the uncomfortable feeling that he smelled bad, judging by the looks on their faces when they let him in.

If the murderer had read the article, he hadn't felt the need to turn himself in. It's not that he'd thought Goyanes's expectations would be met, but he felt somewhat frustrated and he took it out on the author of the article. He couldn't shake the impression that Ana Martí had muddled him with her arguments and that he had allowed himself be softened up by her eagerness and – he had to admit it – by her appearance. What was it that Gil, the head of the CIB, always told them? 'Be careful with women in investigations. No one should let themselves be swayed by personal charm.' He immediately put the rest of Gil's speech out of his mind because he'd warned that 'women use other methods to achieve their goals', and that was unfair to the journalist. But she was a woman and, while she struck him as very honest, the couple of times he found himself repeating Sevilla's words – 'magnificent skull' – as he thought of her made him uneasy. Really, the fact that he was thinking of her at all bothered him. As soon as she arrived he would tell her that, since they had to continue working together, he would prefer, as he had initially suggested, to give her the official texts so she could rework them. And if she didn't like it, that was her problem.

Now he had something more important to do.

'Sevilla, bring Boira up to me,' he ordered his subordinate.

Ten minutes later, the man walked into his office.

Lorenzo Boira was the most veteran of Barcelona's confidence men. He was sixty years old and, despite having been arrested an infinite number of times as a suspect, he could boast that he remained in the clear: he'd never been prosecuted. The same prodigious imagination that allowed him to concoct elaborate scams with absolute precision, and the same power of conviction he had used for years to deceive his prey, also came in handy for distorting the prosecutors' accusations, the victims' testimonies and even the judge's intentions.

But Boira had a weak point: his family. As in any other family business, he had taught his sons all the tricks of his trade. The three of them had been well schooled, but the eldest, Alfonso, hadn't inherited his father's composure and they had caught him after a knife fight with his accomplice in a tavern on Blay Street. That had been on 24 December 1950. Alfonso Boira had been given ten years; he had been saved from capital punishment because Isidro made him confess quickly and they found the other guy in his hideout in Hospitalet. They arrived before he died from his wounds, though it was a close call.

Boira senior tried everything to shorten his son's sentence, but it was no use. When the old conman threw in the towel, Inspector Isidro Castro – who was the one who'd arrested his son and persuaded him to confess – turned up at his house and offered him, in his words, a deal. 'Information. In exchange, better treatment for your son in prison.'

They had sent him to the notorious Modelo prison.

Lorenzo Boira didn't think it over for long before accepting. Part of the deal was to give him a certain degree of immunity.

'Thank you, Inspector. I have a large family to support. Now I have to take care of my daughter-in-law and the two grandchildren Alfonso gave me.'

Deep down, Isidro disdained the victims of Boira's scams, who were as hurt by their own greed as they were by the scammers. Besides, it was important that Boira remained active and respected in the city's underworld. There wasn't much he could inform on if he stayed at home.

He'd had him arrested on Tuesday, left him to marinate for a night in the cells and now, when Sevilla brought him to his office, he was going to go over the list of usual suspects with him.

'Come on in, Boira, come on in.'

Sevilla closed the door and left.

Despite his night in the cells, Lorenzo Boira maintained his decorous appearance, which was one of the secrets of his success. His sixty years gave him a gravity that was very useful in his profession.

'How can I help you, Inspector?'

'Mariona Sobrerroca, what have you heard?'

'There's not much being said, even though there's a lot of talk.'

The case was gossip all over the city. Boira adjusted the cuffs of his shirt, which was somewhat the worse for wear after a night on a straw mattress, but still looked as if it had been ironed. Isidro saw the gleam in the conman's eyes; clearly he was already calculating what he could request for his son. I won't haggle too much this time, thought the inspector.

'Let's see then, what are they saying?'

Isidro opened his notebook and picked up a pencil.

'They say that what they did to the woman was horrific, that they took out her eyes.'

Isidro didn't correct the increasingly morbid version that was being spread by gossipmongers; he wasn't there to give information, rather to get it.

'They mention she had a lot of money, jewels, furs ... And that since she lived alone she was an easy target.'

'Is there a specific name being mentioned for the killer?'

'There are a few names.'

He gave them. They were all burglars. Isidro knew most of them, but there were also a couple of new names, Roc Vives and Diego Gascón.

'Do you know if they're violent?'

'Don't know. Only that it seems they steal for politics: for the party in exile and for the resistance.'

'Then I'm not surprised they were so rough on the woman. Cowardly Reds, they're bastards.'

'I'm not one to judge, sir.'

Boira's son still had eight years left in jail, but in the next visit from his wife and kids he was going to get several parcels containing food, tobacco and Western novels, his favourites. An hour and a half later, Boira was on the street and several people on the list would soon find out they'd be spending that night and the next few in a cell. Isidro asked the guys from the Social Brigade for information about the two men Boira had mentioned. One was soon eliminated. Gascón had been killed by the Civil Guard a week earlier in Lérida, at a country house where he was taking shelter with several of his men before crossing the French border.

They said that there were rumours that Vives was in Barcelona gathering funds for the Communist Party. He was suspected of being behind the break-in at a jeweller's shop on Rambla de Cataluña ten days earlier. But Vives seemed more interested in big jobs. In Mariona Sobrerroca's house they had found jewellery the thief had left behind, probably because she had surprised him, but it wasn't worth enough for Vives to go to that house in particular. In any case, he would follow up on the lead.

14

At first there is only a bare wall. Time and creeping ivy, now long gone, have broken away the plaster in several places. The holes in the middle are from bullets. There is also one way up high, perhaps from someone who didn't want to kill any more.

Ángel appears to the right, as if coming on stage, shyly, insecurely. He looks at the uneven floor, afraid of falling. He is alone and his hands are behind his back. A voice gives him instructions: 'Further to the left', 'Closer to the wall', 'Not so close'.

He complies because of the photographers. 'That's it,' says the voice. Ángel stops, separates his legs slightly and lifts his head. He looks ahead, not at the firing squad but at someone behind the men gripping their weapons. He looks at her. Then he parts his lips to say something, but the shots come before his voice does. Then, he closes his eyes and remains standing as the blood starts to emerge from the wounds on his chest. His white shirt becomes completely soaked, but Ángel doesn't fall. He never falls.

Ana woke up, once again, just at the moment when his lips started moving.

She gave a start in bed. She was covered in a thin layer of sweat that made her tremble with cold when she pulled aside the sheets. It had grown cooler overnight. She sat up in bed without putting her feet on the floor. The floor tiles were always freezing in that flat, and she found her slippers by tapping around quickly with her feet. The old felt slippers that had belonged to her brother were cold too. She headed to the bathroom with hesitant steps and turned on the water heater. The pressure left much to be desired; a straight trickle fell from the shower, sending out a few streams of cold water at regular intervals. Her body responded by moving to one part of the shower tray, which was cold too because the hot water hadn't touched it.

She dried herself off, wrapped herself in a robe and went into the kitchen. She turned on the radio while she made coffee. It was real coffee – she wasn't willing to give that up, she'd rather have terrible coffee with reused grounds than drink a mug of roasted ground chicory or carob beans. Her father had given her a small new packet from the grocer's when she left, soon after lunch. 'A reward for the article,' she thought.

As the coffee percolated she let her gaze wander along the walls of the inner courtyard her kitchen windows overlooked. The news theme tune sounded on the radio.

'Barcelona, opulent Spanish and Mediterranean city kissed by the Latin sea, refuge for foreigners, seat of courtesy, as Cervantes wrote, opens its arms to Catholics from the world over and to all men in a vast prayer for inner peace and peace from war, the peace from God of which the angels sang beside the cradle in Bethlehem, and which transubstantiated Christ's majesty. After fourteen years of disruption, the glorious work of the International Eucharistic Congresses will resume in this city thanks to the Pope's fondness for Catholic Spain. Our country is an oasis of peace in our tormented world, and here Christians will gather for the thirty-fifth International Eucharistic Congress.'

The announcer's leaden voice gave way to sacred music. She turned off the radio before the music made her even more gloomy.

The Eucharistic Congress. This meant that at the end of the month the city was going to fill with priests, nuns and the devout from all over the world. There would be holy music on the radio and more police in the street. Masses, sacred images,

Mother in an overexcited state, insisting, since Ángel's death, on saving the whole family herself with her prayers and penitence. And Father sunk further into resignation with each passing day. Or maybe not. Why had he uncovered his old typewriter?

15

'Goyanes is hopping mad,' a colleague warned him when he saw him heading to the Commissioner's office. Isidro thanked him with a nod of the head. Like sailors out on the high seas, knowing that a storm was brewing didn't mean he would avoid it, but it did help him to confront it with the hope of emerging not too battered.

'Come in, Castro.'

He had called him by his last name. The storm was going to be a tempest, unleashed by a small piece of paper on his superior's desk. His arms framed it like grey fabric parentheses. Isidro recognised the official letterhead. He pointed to the paper.

'Acedo?'

'Even worse: Grau.'

Notes from Acedo, the Civil Governor, were indisputable orders. Those of his enforcer, Public Prosecutor Joaquín Grau, were no less binding. But they also carried with them the fear inspired by his furious fits of rage. If, for some reason, Grau formed the impression that his orders, his will, were not being followed, he wouldn't hesitate to assert his position and turn up unannounced at the office of the civil servant in question to threaten him, no matter who was listening. And everyone knew that he followed through on his threats.

'What a leader the Legion lost!' Sevilla had once said after one of Grau's tirades.

It's true, thought Isidro. There was something of a swagger

in Grau's tone, as if there was a military man inside him, beating on his chest as he fought to get out of those dark suits he wore, perfectly cut by one of Barcelona's best tailors. Grau was feared by his enemies and surely by his friends as well.

So the note on Goyanes's desk was from Grau. Bad news.

'What does he say?'

'Well, it's a short note, but it says a lot about you.'

'About me?'

'Don't get too excited, it's not a birthday card, although he was the one who insisted I give you the case.'

He could imagine whom Goyanes would rather have entrusted it to, Burguillos, whose words were slurred from drink. He wasn't a bad cop, but Isidro couldn't stand arselickers. While the Commissioner informed him of Grau's complaints, he counted the lines on the note with lowered eyes and wondered how Grau had put everything his boss was recriminating him for into so few words.

'Not only did the men you sent to the Tennis Club turn up scruffily dressed, they acted like real louts, both when announcing the news of Señora Sobrerroca's death and when making their enquiries. Some members complained directly to Grau, who is also a club member. He also mentions you directly. The Señores Parés complained of your bad manners not to Grau, but to the Civil Governor, who then conveyed to Grau his interest in having this case resolved not only as quickly as possible, but also with courtesy and respect. Acedo strictly demands that it be wrapped up before the Eucharistic Congress.'

'And when is that?'

'What world are you living in? Don't you listen to the radio? Don't you go to the cinema? Don't you read the newspapers?'

'Only the sports pages.'

And, as of two days ago, the society pages, too. And the women's magazines he'd had Sevilla buy for him.

Goyanes told him the dates as if he were doing him a big favour: 'It'll be from 27 May to 1 June. But you will tie this case up before then.'

Ten minutes later, he left the office. Less than four weeks. The jails would fill up with suspects and informants. If he didn't have anything by then, he could always pull some unlucky rake from up his sleeve, but tampering with the outcome always left him unsatisfied. That meant he'd failed.

Sevilla met him in the hallway. He was going to say something, but Isidro spoke first.

'How do they expect me to solve this case if all they do is give me deadlines and conditions?'

'Isidro . . .'

'We still have to talk to several of Sobrerroca's little lady friends, but we have to treat them like delicate crystal figurines; Goyanes, Acedo and Grau have got us fixed in their sights, ready to leap on my jugular as soon as any of her pals have their feathers ruffled.'

'Isidro . . .'

'And all for a routine job, because Goyanes knows full well that none of these people is a suspect, and no matter how much he says we can't leave any loose ends, that we might turn something up, I don't know who he thinks he's fooling. Mostly we're talking to them so they can see that the police are bending over backwards to solve this case. I mean, this is just . . .'

He was about to say 'fucking brilliant'.

'Isidro . . .'

'What the hell do you want, Sevilla?'

'The girl from the newspaper is here again. I sent her to your office.'

'The society news lady. Just what I need to complete my collection.'

'What collection?'

He didn't answer. He had hit on a possible solution to the problem he was having with 'those people'.

Which was why he never got round to saying 'fucking brilliant', as Sevilla was expecting him to. Although he was trying not to show it, he was glad to have the journalist there, and not just because of her magnificent skull.

16

Castro stepped into his office. Ana noticed that he was enveloped in a surly black cloud. As at their previous meeting, he didn't greet her. Unless you considered accusatorially grumbling 'You are very punctual' a greeting.

'It's important in my profession.'

'Of course, I almost forgot that you call yourself a journalist.'

She had prepared herself before coming, by putting together a short speech with arguments about her suitability to shadow his investigation. She decided to postpone it for a little while.

The inspector sat down and shot her a sullen look.

'What brings you here?'

'I came for the next article, as agreed.'

'We agreed, did we?'

'Yes.'

She didn't allow herself to be intimidated by the pause that followed; she avoided filling the space, out of fear of silence, with unnecessary words that were dangerous around someone like Castro.

He stared at her blankly. Suddenly he started rummaging around on his desk. He found what he was looking for – several copies of ¡HOLA! magazine with little pieces of paper sticking out of them. He opened one at a marked page and, still holding onto it, placed it before her eyes.

'Here,' he said, and pointed to an article.

It was a piece about a reception at the Tennis Club. The photo showed Mariona Sobrerroca dressed in a tennis outfit, among other members of the exclusive club. That would be Mariona Sobrerroca's final appearance in the society pages. Perhaps the penultimate, Ana corrected herself: there was still the funeral. The rest would be material for the crime pages, her material.

The article praised the elegance and sportsmanship of the participants in a charity tournament whose donations would go to a hospice. Those that weren't counts or marquises were their spouses, and they posed willingly for the photograph that would immortalise them.

The society news page reported on two debutante parties, a baptism and a charity ball. Castro's bony finger pointed to the photo illustrating the last of these.

'Do you recognise her?'

Even though her head was covered by the inspector's not very clean fingernail, she knew who he was talking about. It was Conchita Comamala Abad, the wife of Narciso Rocafort, owner of the Hilaturas del Segre textile mill.

'I wrote that article. It says so right there, you see?'

As she pointed to her byline, she realised that Castro had already seen it. What was he playing at?

'I suppose she was pleased with it.'

'I suppose so,' she said before he could read her the string of adjectives that decorated her text. Without them, there were only a couple of lines without much content. It was the moment to give him the persuasive speech she'd developed and practised in her head on the way over.

'I wanted to tell you that—'

'It's good that she was pleased, because I have to go and see her today and you are coming with me.'

Castro didn't allow for many questions, but he knew how to pre-empt answers.

'I'm sure that Señora Comamala and a couple of other women we have to talk to will be more willing to give us information on the late Mariona Sobrerroca if you are the one asking the questions, since they already know you. And you are a woman.'

He didn't end the sentence with a 'Don't you think?' or 'What's your opinion?' Not even a 'Right?' that would have given her a chance to object (which, of course, she wasn't planning on doing) or at least to give an opinion, which she kept to herself.

According to what Castro had said, at this point they were treating it as a break-in.

Did they suspect that someone like Conchita Comamala could have something to do with the case? Hard to imagine, if it were a break-in. The other two people Castro wanted to visit that day were just as hard to fit into the policeman's investigation. Neither the industrialist Anselmo Doménech and his wife, nor Isabel Mira, one of the city's music patrons, seemed likely candidates for roughing up Mariona Sobrerroca and tearing off part of her earlobe.

As if, once again, he had read her mind, Castro explained what he was trying to find out: Mariona Sobrerroca's habits, both mentionable and unmentionable; who was in her circle of friends; who counted themselves among her enemies; her financial situation.

'That's the content. You can give it whatever shape is fashionable among those people.'

Hearing his disdain, which began with the first 'th' of the demonstrative, ran through the 'o' and closed with the 'se' in a sneer of displeasure, she understood that he needed a mediator. She reproached herself for not having had the courage to take the initiative a little earlier. Then Castro would have owed her a favour and not the other way round. The inspector put an end to her train of thought, 'Get used to the idea that it'll be just like your receptions and premieres, except dirty and ugly.'

They went out to the car.

Ana climbed into the vehicle apprehensively. It wasn't a patrol car, but it was a police car and it was impregnated with human odours, mostly tobacco and sweat. Her imagination put on its sadistic little clown hat and played a dirty trick on her as she closed the door and the window handle touching her arm made her aware of the car's narrowness; then she thought of how many people had made their last trip sitting on that back seat, on their way to prison. She was unable to reign in her impulse to look back at them.

'Are you comfortable?'

At the sound of Castro's voice she turned and faced forward again, but she couldn't shake off the feeling of claustrophobia.

'May I roll down the window a little?'

'Of course.'

She tried to turn the handle, but it wouldn't budge.

'Wait,' said Castro. 'There's a trick.'

The policeman extended an arm. She pressed herself back into her seat with all her strength but she couldn't avoid some slight contact and, above all, breathing in his scent of aftershave lotion and tobacco.

Castro didn't notice her unease.

'Is this all right?' he asked, opening it a few centimetres.

'Yes. That's fine.'

They set off, heading into town. In less than fifteen minutes they reached a stately building on Provenza Street.

Conchita Comamala lived in a grand first-floor apartment whose palatial dimensions were indicated by the number of steps it took the maid to cross the front hall to put away her jacket and Castro's mackintosh in a cupboard hidden behind a dark wood door.

They had arrived punctually, but Conchita Comamala, in a little show of power, kept them waiting for fifteen minutes. Castro suffered through the wait. Ana, seated on an art nouveau sofa to the left of the inspector, noted how his tension grew with each minute of a delay that he too knew was intentional. Castro wore a darker suit than when they'd first met, but with exactly the same cut, as if he had inherited the suits from the same person, who was clearly taller and wider than him. The inspector tried to adjust it to a body it hadn't been tailored for. A slight pull on the right leg, a shift of the lapel, a movement of the collar, another tug of his left hand, each of the gestures demonstrated his growing impatience. Despite being a good friend of Prosecutor Grau, the lady of the house was still toying with the authorities.

Which was why Ana sighed with relief when the double doors finally opened and Conchita Comamala appeared, stiff and haughty. She remained for a few seconds with her hands gripping the doors, and then she placed them on her waist. In that defiant pose she approached them with the small steps permitted by her knee-length black pencil skirt. Conchita Comamala had always known how to turn even the most prudish piece of clothing into something provocative.

The policeman's unexpected female companion threw her off guard, causing her to utter an 'Oh!' which she clumsily linked to a greeting, 'Oh! Aneta Martí. What a surprise! I haven't seen you since *Turandot*.'

Conchita Comamala's familiar tone was masterful. Anyone would have realised that they hadn't watched the opera together, and it was clear which of the two women had been sitting in a box and which in the gods. But the only one listening was Castro, and he couldn't have cared less. He stood up when she came in, but he punished her lateness by refusing to take a single step towards her. She had to approach him to hold out her hand.

The greetings over, she invited them to sit down in the drawing room. As if she had been waiting outside the door, listening for the creak of sofa and armchair, at that precise moment a maid in uniform and cap entered the room.

'Coffee or tea?' asked Conchita Comamala.

Castro, impatient, was about to refuse, but Ana spoke first. 'Coffee, please.'

'I'll have the same,' he said, as if he were in a coffee bar.

The maid left.

'This is about poor Mariona, isn't it?'

'It is. You saw her the day prior to the murder, didn't you?' asked Castro.

'Yes.'

Conchita Comamala responded to the policeman, but then glanced at Ana.

'Did you know her well?'

'She was a good friend.'

Her eyes turned back to Ana.

You didn't have to be particularly well versed in the language of the upper echelons of society to know that this meant she was an acquaintance. A close acquaintance.

'How long had you known each other?' Castro went on.

'We were at school together with the Theresian nuns, although she was a little older than me.'

She shot a knowing look at Ana. Castro's silence was her sign to intervene.

'The night before her death, ma'am, you were with Mariona Sobrerroca at the premiere of *Tannhäuser* at the Liceo.'

'Please, Aneta, no need to be formal with me. Just speak to me as you normally would. And yes, we saw each other there.'

'I heard that Victoria de los Ángeles was fabulous.'

'Well, fabulous would be overstating it. She was good, but she's had better nights. That's what I said to Ramiro Sagunto and his wife Alicia during the intermission. And we ran into Doris Dorée, who'd been feeling rather poorly.'

'And Mariona?'

'Mariona was a little strange, to be frank.'

'In what way?'

'In that she thought everything was fine, better than fine, everything was marvellous. And she was wearing make-up! And those clothes!'

'What was she wearing?'

Conchita Comamala lowered her voice and brought her face close to Ana's. 'As if she were twenty years younger.'

She knew that tone. She was speaking with the same haughtiness and scorn that women who consider themselves decent use when referring to whores or the floozies their husbands used to let off steam.

Isidro Castro's voice inserted itself between the two women's heads and they drew apart.

'The person who killed her was looking for something at

her home. Do you know if Señora Sobrerroca kept valuables in her flat? Money? Jewels?'

Didn't he realise that Comamala had just begun to confide in her? Ana told herself that Castro was used to getting information the hard way, with his fists. She looked at her hands to avoid fantasising about seeing him leap up and slap Conchita Comamala like he had Mariona's maid in his office. She responded sharply, 'How would I know? I suppose she had a safe at home. Or she kept them at the bank. Why are you asking me such nonsense?'

She crossed her arms when she'd finished her sentence. Ana intervened before all conversation was closed off to them.

'I remember her having some very pretty pieces,' she said in an evocative tone.

'Pfft,' was Conchita Comamala's first reaction.

'The tiara like Greta Garbo's in *Mata-Hari* . . .' she tossed out as bait.

'Ah! Yes! Divine! I'm sure she kept that at the bank, and had someone collect it when she wanted to wear it. I have to admit that it was the only piece of hers I envied. That doesn't make me a suspect, does it?' she said in a frivolous tone.

She had Comamala on side again, but Ana heard the inspector beside her take in a breath to say something. Before he could she tapped his foot with hers and turned towards him with an angelic smile, 'Of course not, isn't that right? Aren't you drinking your coffee, Inspector?'

To her surprise, the inspector obeyed her, picking up the cup that the maid had left on a little low table beside the sofa and taking a couple of sips. Meanwhile, Ana kept talking to the woman. 'Do you remember what she wore to the Liceo that night?'

'I do, diamond earrings that her husband had given her for their silver wedding anniversary. Someone told me, though I don't remember who, that she had had to pawn them when Jerónimo died. He was surely a great doctor, but it seems he was a real disaster when it came to finances, and he left Mariona in quite a fix.'

She didn't know Mariona's financial situation, but she knew she'd had a brother who, as is traditional in Catalonia, had inherited most of the family wealth. Still, Mariona should have received a good income.

'Did he speculate?' she asked.

'I don't really know, but I heard talk of his getting burned over something in Germany. Besides, he was a gambler.'

Half an hour later, when it became clear that the conversation had run its course, they bid Conchita Comamala farewell.

Castro waited, starting the car and drawing away from the house before thanking her.

'For what?'

'For making conversation with that old windbag so she'd tell us things. What a waste of time!'

'You think so?'

'What did we find out? That the woman had bad taste in clothes and jewellery, even though it was expensive.'

'But it's interesting to know that she had showy pieces. Perhaps one of them was what the thief was looking for.'

'We didn't have to suffer the woman's gossiping to find that out.'

'Then why did we have to talk to her? She's not a burglary suspect, is she?'

'Being that you're so well read, you should know that a police investigation isn't a one-way street, it's a network of paths. We have to try them all before deciding that they don't take us where we want to go.'

'Can I use that image for my article? It's very evocative.'

'No.'

'Why not?'

'Because I was pulling your leg.'

Ana looked at him in surprise; Castro sounded genuinely amused, as he did when he added, 'Don't you dare quote me saying evocative things or any other queer stuff.'

'Fine,' she answered, offended.

'Don't be like that. Now, seriously. Look, we do it because we have to do it. Because even though they pull a disgusted face when they see us, if we didn't make these visits they'd complain that we weren't doing our job. It's that simple. And it's still a waste of time.'

'Well, I thought it was interesting.'

'What could have seemed interesting to you in that string of gossip?'

'Just that, the gossip. Remember what Mariona's maid said?'

Castro shot her a quizzical look. Ana continued.

'That she hadn't been sleeping at her employer's house for some time.'

'Yeah. So?'

'And Conchita Comamala said that she was euphoric, rejuvenated. Do you know what that could mean?'

The inspector stared straight ahead as he drove. He didn't answer, merely shrugged. His lips curved down in a scornful grimace.

'That maybe Mariona had a new love.'

'Señorita Martí! A new love! How twee!'

With those words, he turned the steering wheel abruptly and parked. They got out without saying another word.

The Doménechs lived in another grand first-floor flat beside the Hotel Majestic. As they passed the hotel, Ana looked at the facade. Perhaps Carmiña was behind one of those windows, making beds with one eye on a towel set, or slipping into her uniform pocket a used bar of soap that had been brought from Paris and left behind in Barcelona.

They reached the entrance. Once the policeman had flashed his ID, the doorman hastened to open the main door for them and only Castro's curtness got him to stop insisting they take the lift.

'We aren't handicapped,' said the inspector, starting up the stairs.

Ana gave a look of silent apology to the doorman, who was: he wore a prosthetic leg.

She went up behind Castro.

'Let me speak first,' she told the inspector when they reached the door to the flat.

106

A uniformed maid opened the door and took them to a small room where Claudia Pons, the lady of the house, was already waiting for them. The wife of textile industrialist Anselmo Doménech was about forty years old and, unlike Conchita Comamala, she received them immediately in a parlour where she waited, wrapped in a grey knitted jacket. She seemed as timid as Joan Fontaine in *Rebecca*, the film that gave cardigans their name in Spanish: 'rebecas'.

'My husband isn't here. He's at work.'

'Surely you can be of help to us,' said Ana, sitting on the opposite sofa. Castro followed suit. Claudia Pons gazed at her questioningly.

'We met at Mariló Fígol's coming-out,' Ana explained to her. 'I wrote it up for *¡HOLA!*' Claudia Pons seemed to relax a bit. Ana hoped that Castro had noticed.

'Poor Mariona!' she said suddenly. 'Who could have imagined it, that day?'

'She was also at the coming-out,' Ana explained to Castro before he had a chance to ask.

Then she addressed Claudia Pons. 'Terrible. Just as it seemed she was starting to get over the loss of her husband.'

'Yes, poor thing. She'd stopped mourning a few months ago, although I must say black suited her, with that pale, porcelain skin, which she still had despite her age.'

Ana avoided looking at Castro, to keep him from interrupting.

'The last time I saw her it seemed that she was doing very well; she was quite rejuvenated,' said Ana, making Conchita Comamala's words her own.

'Indeed. Even Anselmo, my husband, said so. He's at work.'

The last part was said in a tone reminiscent of children justifying a missed day of school.

'That makes her death even sadder. Do you know of any reason that might explain this "rejuvenation"?'

'Reasons, reasons ... We're always looking for reasons and motives. Why isn't it enough to know that we are alive, healthy, have a roof over our heads and our daily bread?'

'Do you know or not?' interrupted Castro.

He scared her with his impatient bark. Before she retreated like a snail into its shell, Ana intervened like a protective shield.

'Forgive Inspector Castro's somewhat brusque tone, but resolving this matter is the police's top priority, and all information is of the utmost importance.'

Claudia Pons looked at them, unable to decide which one she should address. She opted for Ana.

'I didn't want to seem like a gossipmonger, but I would say that poor Mariona had a beau. I think she wanted to hide it, because at her age, and being a widow ... well, you understand. But she was invited to my middle girl's First Communion celebration, and she said she wouldn't be coming alone.'

'When is it to be held?'

'Next Sunday. Anselmo would have liked her to do it at the end of the month, during the Congress. He is very into symbols and these things, but I don't want it to be during a mass event, where you can't see her, and since the priest at San Justo church is a friend of the family's, a cousin of ... '

Ana chose to interrupt her. Castro wouldn't be able to stand too many digressions. 'And Mariona didn't say who she was planning to attend it with?'

'No. I was dying of curiosity, because I hadn't seen her in the company of a man since Jerónimo's death. She only survived him by two short years,' said Claudia Pons after a sigh. 'I hope the same doesn't happen to me.'

Seeing the surprised expression on the faces of both visitors seated in front of her on the sofa, she added, 'My husband is more than twenty years older than me. It wouldn't be fair, would it?'

After an hour of conversation, they left Claudia Pons grateful for the three hundred square metres of roof over her head and much more than daily bread for her supper.

When they reached the bottom of the stairs, the doorman limped into the lift, closed the outer grille, shut the glazed inner doors and pressed a button. He ascended, very upright, and ignored their farewell waves.

108

'You offended him,' Ana said to Castro.

The inspector shrugged. They left the building. Then she decided that now was the moment to analyse the conversation they'd had in the flat.

'You see?' she said triumphantly. 'I'm not the only one who thinks Mariona must have been in a romantic relationship.'

'You were very pushy about it. Why did you insist so?'

'Well, because I think she had a date with him the night she was killed.'

'Where'd you get that idea from?'

'From the dress she was wearing.'

'Maybe she was returning from somewhere when she surprised the thief in her house.'

'The thief? If the culprit is a thief, he's a very shoddy one.'

They had reached the car. Castro stared at her with the key already inside the lock on the driver's side door.

'Why?'

'Because for one thing, he didn't take Mariona's earrings. Maybe they fought because she didn't want to give them up, and that was how he ripped her earlobe. But then, after all that, he left it behind.'

Castro didn't respond. He opened the door, climbed into the car and unlocked the other door so she could get in. He indicated she should sit down with a couple of pats on the seat.

He started the car and pulled away.

'And now?' she asked.

'One more. The last one.'

In the station Castro had mentioned Isabel Mira.

'Where does she live?'

'Paseo de San Juan.'

The mention of the street where she used to live was like a punch to the stomach.

'Is something wrong?'

'No. Nothing.'

Castro drove slowly. She lowered the window, this time without difficulty. She appreciated the fresh air on her face as she contemplated the streets bustling with people. Where were they going? Why were they walking so quickly? There was no place to go; the entire city was the same, a uniform grey mass. Even the sea was grey.

'Why didn't he take the earring?' insisted Ana.

'He must have had a scare. He wasn't expecting her to be at home. She surprised him, they fought and he killed her without meaning to.'

'But once she was dead, why not take such easy booty?'

'I told you, he got scared. A fight like that makes a lot of noise.'

'But you won't deny that what Conchita Comamala insinuated and Claudia Pons conjectured reinforces the idea of a relationship? And if so, why didn't anyone appear after her death?'

'He must be ashamed. The rumours . . . '

'And you don't want to know who it might be?'

'Why? He'll show up if he wants to.'

Why was the inspector closing off that theory so categorically? Why was he insisting that it had to be a break-in? Convenience? A thief was less difficult than a possible lover who, given his silence, was perhaps a member of society who could cause problems for them.

Castro's voice to her left gave her a start.

'I deduce from your silence that you're wondering why I'm not following up on the lover hypothesis.'

'But how can you—'

The policeman cut off her show of astonishment.

'Look, I'm not following it up because for the moment nothing points in that direction. Over the years I've seen enough to recognise a break-in and the traces left by a crime of passion, even when the killer tries to make it look like a break-in. You can tell by the way the drawers are gone through and how the contents are scattered, in the knocked-over furniture . . . Let me try to explain it to you, in case you haven't read about it in some American book. When they fake a break-in, they knock down chairs. Why would a thief do that?

To make noise? Somebody was looking for something in Sobrerroca's home.'

They reached Isabel Mira's house. Around sixty years old, she received them dressed with the simplicity seen only in people who know that their lineage exempts them from social convention.

Castro barely opened his mouth during the conversation with the patron of the arts. Ana wondered if it was because he understood that it was better that she spoke, or because he was already bored and didn't want to have anything to do with whatever might be said. Either way, the image they formed of Mariona was very similar: she didn't have great friends or, therefore, any real enemies, only a few people who didn't like her much. To Ana's disappointment, Isabel Mira didn't mention, or even hint at, the existence of a new man in Mariona's life.

They headed back to police headquarters. On the way, Castro began to list the things that she could put in her article.

'We are on the trail of a thief. We will soon find him, thanks to the collaboration of citizens who have given us valuable information.'

'Is that true?'

'That they've given us information is. Put that after speaking with several people close to the victim, they have all emphasised what a great loss her death is, and . . .'

'You don't have to dictate it to me. You're going to read it anyway.'

Ana couldn't get the mention of that unknown boyfriend out of her head. Waiting at traffic lights, Castro turned to her and said, 'Not a word about the story of the supposed lover.'

She looked at him in surprise.

'How do you do it?'

'How do I do what?'

'Know what other people are thinking . . . and choosing not to tell you.'

Castro focused his gaze back on the traffic.

111

'I'm from Galicia,' was all he said before turning right on to Balmes Street. 'So not a word. Understood?'

'OK.'

For the rest of the journey Ana stared out of the window.

Soon they reached headquarters. On a table in the inspector's office she saw several cardboard boxes and files piled up. Castro noticed her curious gaze.

'Yes, they are documents on the case.'

Ana was barely able to keep herself from stepping towards them.

'The dead woman's personal papers.'

'Can I ...? It would help me to build up a picture of Mariona Sobrerroca.'

She didn't want to tell him that she had learned from the American press that there was a particularly attractive component for readers, something they called 'human interest'. His reaction to her quoting Raymond Chandler had already shown her that he wouldn't appreciate it.

'I would only mention things that would help readers get to know the victim a little better ... '

The inspector looked at her with an amused expression, although he tried to show annoyance. 'You're as insistent as Chinese water torture! But I don't want you to think that I'm ungrateful. You helped me a lot this afternoon. If you want, have a look at the things in that box. Sevilla's already been through them. But if you find the solution to the case, don't hesitate to let me know.'

He laughed half-heartedly at his own joke and, before leaving the office, said, 'I'll tell Sevilla to bring in the typewriter so you can write the article.'

While she was waiting for the officer to arrive, she started to look at the material. Mariona Sobrerroca's life passed before her eyes in no particular order: photos of winter holidays, a furrier's receipt, postcards from friends, invitations, letters, brochures, magazines, press cuttings. She had made a small album of her appearances in the society pages. Ana found many of her own articles there. Mariona also saved all the invitations she had received: a collection of large cards that were a chronicle of Barcelonian social life over the last few years. There was also another packet with postcards; Ana could have used them to make a guide to her favourite places, from San Sebastián to the Swiss Alps. In an album of sorts, she had saved the condolence cards she'd received after her husband's death. A professional letter writer such as herself couldn't help noticing how formulaic almost all of them were. She set aside the few where she thought she could make out a hint of real grief.

All of a sudden some handwritten letters caught her eye. She read them. They were love letters. So it was true that Mariona had – what was it Claudia Pons had said? – a beau. She had been right. She smiled triumphantly. She had to tell Castro, show him that bundle of letters. Then suddenly she realised that the inspector already knew, since they had examined the material. So she hadn't discovered anything; at least, nothing that the police didn't know and hadn't already deemed irrelevant. It seemed Castro was quite convinced about his break-in theory.

A voice behind her made her jump.

'Here's the typewriter. What are you doing, looking at those things?'

'Inspector Castro gave me permission.'

'What a chore! I had to read all that crap, pardon me. It's all just precious nonsense. Well, maybe you'll like it.'

'Goodness, thanks. Can I copy some of the documents?'

'What did the boss say?'

'That I can look at all I want.'

'But he didn't say anything about writing, did he? I'd better ask.'

He returned shortly.

'He says that you can copy what you want, but to remember that you can't publish a single line about any of it without his permission.'

That said, he stood in the doorway.

'It's hard for me to concentrate with someone watching.'

'Suit yourself.'

He left.

Ana put paper into the carriage and started to copy some of the documents: the letters from the boyfriend; the less stereotypical of the condolence letters; also a few of the bills demanding payment from a furrier, a dressmaker. She didn't have a very clear idea of what she wanted to do with them, just the vague impression that Mariona Sobrerroca's papers could help her understand the dead woman's life better. María Eugenia de las Mercedes Sobrerroca i Salvat, according to a birth certificate she also copied.

She copied it all word for word. She typed very quickly, but still had trouble stifling the occasional giggle at the obvious affectation of some passages of the love letters signed by a person calling himself 'Octavian'. When she had finished, she put the copies in her bag so Castro wouldn't see them and regret his generosity.

Then she began to write her article.

When Castro returned, she was still writing.

'I've almost finished.'

Castro didn't have a chance to answer; the office door opened after a few knocks. A policeman entered followed by a whiff of alcohol and tobacco.

'What do you want, Burguillos?'

'Commissioner Goyanes wants to see you, Castro.'

Ana turned; the man's lisp had caught her attention. He must have been around forty; his thinning hair made it hard to be more specific. He wore a narrow pencil moustache that failed to hide the disproportionate thickness of his upper lip compared to his lower one.

'Again?'

Just then Ana pulled the paper out of the typewriter carriage. She handed it to Castro, but he waved it away, saying, 'I trust you. Don't let me down.'

Castro left without closing the door. Burguillos stayed in the office as she gathered her things. He had approached the small table that held the information on the Sobrerroca case and was openly browsing the papers in front of Ana, who didn't dare say anything to a policeman. She stepped out of the office and closed the door behind her. Sevilla was at the end of the hallway talking to another policeman. He broke off his conversation and approached her.

'Is that it? Can I take the typewriter?'

'Yes.'

He went into the office without saying goodbye to her.

She hadn't taken even a single step further before she heard angry voices from inside.

'What are you doing here, Burguillos?'

'Well, if it isn't Sevilla . . . '

'Come on, get out. If the inspector finds you've been snooping around in his things, he's going to haul you over the coals.'

'Fuck's sake! I was just having a quick look.'

'Get out. I hope you haven't messed all this up.'

Ana slipped away so that they wouldn't catch her snooping as well. She pressed the bag with her article and the copied documents close to her side and walked swiftly out of the headquarters.

17

It held up. Beatriz went over all the steps one more time. When she was at that point in her work, she always imagined it as a rope ladder. She had to control each rung. Would it break with the next step? She climbed it again in her mind. Every once in a while she looked down at the books on her desk. The argumentation was solid; Beatriz tensed the ropes, thinking of possible counter-arguments and jotting down those that seemed particularly cogent. But she could refute those, too. No, there was nothing more to say; her thesis was well constructed. And the best part was that she would give a conference about it in Tours, then she'd write her article and publish it in a prestigious French journal specialising in the subject. It wasn't just going to sit in a drawer. She would write it up and people would read it.

Satisfied, she leaned back in her chair.

Then Encarni came through the door.

'Can I make you a coffee, Professor?'

Why not?

'Sure. I'll be there in a moment.'

She emerged from her office. When she sat down at the kitchen table, her eye was drawn to a tin of powdered milk that Encarni had put there.

'Why have you bought that?'

'Because of the refrigerator, ma'am.'

Encarni looked at her as if she were from a distant planet

and generously put three heaped spoonfuls of powdered milk into the cup of hot water.

The refrigerator was made of wood, painted white and had to be filled regularly with blocks of ice. Encarni hated it with all her soul. She opened the drawer that held the ice with noisy tugs and shoved it back into the old contraption with the same aversion and no less noise. Every time she turned the spigot to let out the thawed water, she spoke to it like a nurse bringing a bedpan to an annoying patient.

'Come on, now we're going to do a little wee-wee, we're very old and not good for much, just for pissing in the chamber pot. Come on, let's see you do it.' The spigot creaked when she turned it and the water started to come out. 'Good job. Look at you go.'

'Are you going to buy powdered milk and tinned goods so that we can throw out the refrigerator?'

Encarni sighed.

'The milk company is raffling off a prize. We have to fill out this form and tear off the label from a tin of milk and send them in together.' Encarni searched with her finger on the paper on the table, 'To Nestlé in Barcelona. With a bit of luck, you can win a refrigerator.'

She looked at Beatriz triumphantly.

'A modern, electric refrigerator.'

She showed her a photo of a refrigerator that she had torn out of a magazine. A large box with rounded edges and a smooth bright surface. You couldn't see any joints or seams, only a slightly convex metal sheet of light blue. An American Cadillac for the kitchen.

'But, Encarni! You don't have a chance of winning that refrigerator. How many people do you think are going to take part in the raffle? Half of Spain, I bet.'

'And someone's going to win it. Why not me?'

'Yes, why not?' sighed Beatriz.

There was no point; nothing was going to make Encarni change her mind.

'Look, we have to put the answers here.'

'We have to? It's up to you to respond, not me.'

'But maybe you could take a look and tell me if they're right. It's the least you could do for a new fridge! Because I would leave it here.'

'Gee, thanks.'

'Where my mother lives, in Monchuí, there's no electricity. She would get on fine with the old one.'

Encarni's family lived in a shanty town on Montjuïc.

'Come on then, let's have a look at those answers.'

Encarni held out the form for her. Beatriz read aloud.

'What do most consumers use La Lechera condensed milk for? A. To make coffee a sweet, creamy delight. B. To prepare a delicious rice pudding.'

'I put A.'

'That's what I'd put, too.'

'But those are the easy questions. Look at this one.'

She pointed to question seven with one finger.

'In what year did Enrique Nestlé invent the powdered milk that saved so many infants' lives? A. 1867. B. 1810. C. 1905.'

She looked up.

'I'd say that—'

Encarni didn't let her finish.

'We have to put 1810, Professor.'

Beatriz thought. When were soup cubes invented in Germany? Surely the milk was made in a similar way; in the end it was the same thing, extracting the water in order to conserve it. It must have been at some point in the mid-nineteenth century. She was irritated with herself because she used to know and her memory was failing her.

'It's clear, ma'am, that the earlier it was, the more lives they can say it has saved.'

'Bring me the encyclopedia. The N volume. Let's check when Mr Nestlé invented powdered milk.'

While Encarni was in the library, the doorbell rang.

'I'll get it, Encarni.'

Beatriz saw through the peephole that it was Manolo, the doorman's son. She opened the door and the boy handed her a letter. She took it. Her mother had always kept a small bowl of coins on the pedestal table in the entryway. Now Encarni filled it up so that she would always have some to hand. She took out a few coins and put them into Manolo's hand. He mumbled 'Thank you' with a surprised expression. She must have given him too much. The boy quickly hid the coins in his fist and turned and disappeared down the stairs even faster.

Beatriz closed the door. Just then the hand that held the envelope started to shake.

For a second she considered waiting until evening to open the letter, so that she could enjoy the feeling of being the one to decide when the big moment arrived. But as she was thinking this, she found she'd already entered her study and was gripping her father's letter opener. The blade made its way along the bright white paper with the Oxford University seal. *Dominus illuminatio mea*. The Lord is my light.

She pulled the letter out of the envelope. She lowered the reading glasses she wore on her head; a few blonde and grey locks were tangled around the arms.

'Esteemed Doctor . . . '

It was a no. They hadn't given her the visiting professor job. Jackson, who she'd known since the days of Don Ramón in Madrid, had told her it wasn't going to be easy.

There went her opportunity. Her ticket to another world. Her personal escape. She would have to stay here. The sky closed over her. This year, maybe the next one as well. There wouldn't be many more such chances. She contemplated the frieze that ran around the room's entire ceiling, a key pattern that repeated over and over. Always the same. Like the years that awaited her. In that city, in that narrowness; an endless succession of grey days.

Then she jammed the letter into a pile of papers.

18

Two envelopes, one white, the other with black edges. A
funeral notice. Ana grabbed them and closed the postbox.
Then a metallic click warned her that perhaps it would be
better to leave the building again. She recognised it straight
away: the sound that preceded the opening of Teresina Sauret's
door.

The old woman was familiar with the sound each of the
postboxes made on opening, Ana was convinced of that. It
wasn't possible that she always had something to do at the very
moment Ana was collecting her post. The doorkeeper could
see which neighbours were going up and down the staircase,
but in order to know who was arriving, Señora Sauret had to
wait for the person to approach the stairs.

Teresina Sauret's door was to the right, hidden in a recess at
the foot of the staircase. From her peephole she completely
controlled the first flight and landing, but the row of twelve
postboxes was out of her line of sight. In the world of door-
keepers, some have more good fortune than others. Teresina
Sauret hadn't been lucky in her guard post.

Like musical instruments, which develop an unmistakably
unique character over years of use, each of the postboxes had
a sound of its own, the sum of the dents, creaking hinges and
the rustiness of the lock. As for the doorkeeper, she had an
incredibly sensitive ear, trained by hours of attentive listening
behind the door, and thanks to which she also knew the footsteps of each tenant.

But that day it would do her no good, because Ana too had an excellent ear and immediately recognised the stealthy but not imperceptible sound of the door being opened with cunning slowness. Like field mice who are alerted not by the flapping wings of the owl who hunts them, but the slight creak of the branch when the bird leaves the tree. She put the two envelopes in her bag and in a couple of strides was back out in the street. Teresina Sauret's voice reached her, muffled by the door to the building, which had closed behind Ana's back.

'Señorita Martí! Señorita Martí! Remember that . . . '

She knew full well what she had to remember; actually it had been on her mind all week. She also knew that Señora Sauret was lying in wait for her. It wasn't the first and, given the situation, it wouldn't be the last occasion when the doorkeeper would chase after her for the rent, but that evening she reached home too tired and hungry to face the disapproval in Teresina's little weasel eyes.

It pained her to remember that the flat had belonged to her family. Hers and the one next to it, because her paternal grandparents had lived in twice the space before the war. Then, when things changed, the Serrahimas bought the flats and divided them into two. They rented out half of her grandfather's old home and, as long as someone in the family lived there, and paid the rent, they could carry on living there. When her grandfather had begun to have problems managing on his own, Ana had moved there to take care of him. She was pleased to do it because it got her out of the house. Then two years ago her parents had decided that it was best that Grandfather live with them. But she stayed in the flat. Her parents had been reluctant to accept that, but conceded because it would allow them to hold onto the property. Since she had lived there with her grandfather, there wasn't, as far as she knew, talk about a woman her age living alone. She gave the tongues no reason to wag. She never had visitors at home and had never even let Gabriel come up. Not that it was necessary; the hypocritical city offered plenty of options to slip past the gaze of its moral guardians.

She left Riera Alta and turned on to the Ronda de San Antonio. When she passed by the café Els Tres Tombs, she saw a free table and went in.

'What can I get you, sweetheart?'

'A café au lait, please.'

'Any pastries?'

She had to say no to the waiter, although the sugar glaze on the heart-shaped puff pastries attractively laid out on the bar seemed to shine in the lamplight just for her. And the cigarette smoke couldn't cover up the scent of the pile of madeleines beside them. But she only had enough money in her purse for the coffee.

She put the two envelopes on the table. She didn't know which one to open first.

The waiter approached with the cup of coffee and the jug of hot milk. His short white jacket was small on him; it must belong to another waiter, who would put it on at the end of this shift. The waiter's hands looked disproportionately large. He began to pour the milk. Ana saw that he was about to lift the jug before the cup was full.

'A bit more, please. I don't like my coffee too strong.'

The waiter grumbled, but she pretended not to hear. A finger of milk, even when watered down, is a lot. Defiant, the waiter filled her cup to the brim without spilling a single drop.

Once he had headed off, she considered her dilemma again: whether to open the funeral notice or the other envelope first. She remembered what Carlos Belda had once asked her, 'Tell me, what is the page that women look for first in the newspaper?'

Of course, she'd replied that it was the society pages, the section that for the time being was keeping food on her table and paying her rent, though not always on time.

'You're wrong, dollface,' Belda had declared somewhat pedantically. 'It's the obituaries.'

It was true.

So she opened the black-bordered envelope first.

The deceased was a woman named Blanca Noguer

Figuerola. Who was Blanca Noguer Figuerola? She recalled that her mother had told her recently about a relative dying. She hadn't paid much attention, and didn't remember how closely they were related, but she had received the funeral notice, which meant that other members of the family did remember. She would have to go to the funeral, even if only not to disappoint her mother again.

She looked at the birthdate. She guessed Carlos Belda also knew that the first thing women do when they read an obituary is calculate the deceased person's age and mentally pronounce one of the two de rigueur phrases, depending on the results of the calculation: 'Poor thing, so young', or 'Well, she had a long life'. In this case, the latter was the appropriate one and, reviewing the deceased woman's list of relatives, Ana came to the conclusion that she must be one of her mother's cousins. The burial was the next day in the Montjuïc cemetery. Yes, she would have to go.

She felt the irksome sensation at the nape of her neck that she was being watched. She turned. It was the waiter, who was openly following her movements. She understood that he was waiting to see how she managed to drink her coffee without spilling half the cup. In such situations she was always grateful she had grown up with a brother. Eschewing the manners befitting a lady, she leaned over the table, brought her mouth to the full cup and took a good slurp. Then she turned to the waiter, ostentatiously wiped her lips with the back of her hand and smiled at him. He immediately looked away.

Which was why he missed her surprised expression when she opened the white envelope. It was from her father. A brief little note that read: 'So you can give yourself a treat', along with several twenty-five-peseta notes. How had he managed to save up so much money? He hadn't mentioned it the day before when she had eaten with them.

'I am going to give myself two treats, Papa.' She would go back home and walk through the door unhurriedly; she would reach the foot of the stairs without her heart pounding and she would start walking up at a leisurely pace. And when Teresina

Sauret's door opened and she started to say, 'Señorita Martí, remember that you have to pay the ren—'

She would answer her offhandedly, 'Of course.'

Then she would open her bag and hand the money to the doorkeeper. And in the same careless tone she would add, 'May I please have a receipt?'

But first, the other treat.

'May I have a *palmera*, please?' she asked, pointing to the heart-shaped pastries. 'One of the darker ones. And another café au lait.'

Then she pulled out the documents she had copied in Castro's office. The letters that Mariona had received from her boyfriend had particularly awakened Ana's curiosity. There were fourteen of them.

The boyfriend was called Octavian. She repeated the name several times under her breath, searching her memory for someone with that name in the circles closest to the victim, but she couldn't remember anyone, which was strange considering the Catalan bourgeoisie's fondness for patrician names. Reading the letters, she realised that she shouldn't actually be looking for an Octavian. Even though the letters were rather cryptic, and without Mariona's replies it was impossible to understand some of the allusions, soon she could tell that Octavian was a pseudonym, behind which hid a man who called Mariona 'my Marschallin'. They were adopting roles from the opera *Der Rosenkavalier*! That surely meant that Mariona's lover was significantly younger than her. She understood now why they had wanted to keep their relationship secret, and she felt sad imagining the fiftysomething widow with a new spring in her step while her friends looked on disparagingly.

Was that how Castro and his people had seen it, as well? Given the indifference with which they had let her copy the material, clearly not. It occurred to her that there wasn't only gratitude behind Castro's generosity in letting her see all that material. Perhaps he was hoping that she would happen on something that the police hadn't been able to find. But most likely, she admitted with a stab to her pride, it was just a way to keep her busy, as if she were a child who had to be distracted so she wouldn't be too much of a bother.

She took a sip of coffee and kept reading. But nothing in those lines revealed to her who Octavian was, although she knew he had to be hidden in there somewhere.

The next day she took a taxi to the cemetery, but first she walked to Paralelo so it would cost less. She was splurging, but in moderation, she told herself.

She carried the funeral invitation in her bag. She had inherited it from one of her cousins, one of the rich ones, who gave her their old clothes so that she could attend the society parties she wrote about with some respectability. She inherited them in good condition, an advantage of having cousins who followed fashion. She had three coats, and hadn't worn any of them yet. She also had several handbags, but this was her 'journalist' bag. She had managed to cover its few scuffs with shoe polish, and luckily no one besides her looked inside it, because the lining was coming apart.

'The Montjuïc cemetery, please.'

Along the way she realised that she hadn't brought her veil. Her mother was going to be furious.

She pulled out her notepad and, even though it made her a bit sick to read in the car, took a look at her notes on the Sobrerroca case. She had the letters with her. She wanted to read them one more time before the funeral; she was sure that at some point she would manage to get some information out of them.

Sitting in the taxi on the way to the cemetery, she felt excitement at finally being involved in her first real case.

After getting out of the car she entered the city of the dead and, for the first time, the sight of the rows of funereal niches that completely covered the hillside didn't weigh on her heart.

19

'Imagine, they had to open the poor woman up three times.'

'For the love of God! Couldn't they just have emptied her out the first time?'

The first of the two women in black nodded; the feather in the small veiled hat she wore bobbed in time. A third woman brought her hands together over her handbag and added, 'Those the Lord calls to his bosom . . .'

One of the three women was married to one of Beatriz's many cousins; the other two she had never seen before. She quickly turned her back on the small group. She didn't want to be drawn into any conversation, especially not one like that. As she turned, the funeral invitation rustled in her jacket pocket.

The doorman's son had brought it to her the previous night. That time it had been Encarni who had opened the door and tipped him.

'Cheeky little Manolito told me that you're more generous, ma'am,' she'd said as she delivered the black-bordered envelope.

Encarni held it with two fingers, somewhat apprehensive, and sighed in relief when she put it down on the table. But then she had stood over Beatriz, waiting for her to open it.

'Family?' she had asked after Beatriz had taken out the funeral notice.

'An aunt.'

'My condolences. Should I prepare funeral clothes?'

She nodded, and Encarni left the room.

From the study she heard the muffled sounds of the young woman's laborious search through the wardrobes for the appropriate attire.

A funeral notice. More bad news. First she had thought about stuffing it in a pile of papers as she had done with the letter from Oxford, but then she'd decided to leave it out so that she wouldn't forget the exact time and place of the burial.

She joined the funeral procession that was slowly beginning to move. She heard the crunch of footsteps on the gravel path, the swish of mourning dresses and the occasional discreet murmur. The retinue wound its way up Montjuïc mountain along a path flanked by cypress trees. About a hundred people followed the coffin that swayed on the shoulders of the bearers as they took one of the many curves. The May sun fell on the oak wood that shone as brightly as the silver-plated, solid iron fittings. Blanca must have chosen it herself. It had been a long time since Beatriz had last seen her aunt, but unless she had changed a lot in her final years, the coffin perfectly reflected her discreet elegance.

The cemetery, with its profusion of angel sculptures, irritated her. On a tomb to the right of the path one angel lay drooping over the headstone. It seemed overcome by immense grief, its long hair covering its face and its bare arms lifted in a final gesture of entreaty. Beatriz turned away. But soon her eyes came across another angel with fallen wings and its gaze lifted up to heaven. Frankly, I prefer the dogs of hell in the medieval representations of purgatory, thought Beatriz. Doomed souls fighting against emaciated demons; sinning bodies devoured by snakes; nameless winged monsters – that is how grief and pain should look. Grief when her mother died. Grief when Jakob disappeared from her life. Furious beasts, not gloomy angels with languid robes dragging their wings along the ground.

Beatriz called herself to order. If she kept carrying on like this, she'd turn into a bitter old lady hauling around her permanent inventory of losses. Her mother, Jakob, lost friends, missed opportunities. A bitter, old, resentful woman. In a word, unbearable. Not even she would be able to put up with herself. She knew of only one antidote. Getting on with work, and not thinking about things too much.

She decided to listen to the conversations going on in whispers around her.

'Poor woman, in the end she was a shadow of her former self.'

'And so alone, in that enormous house. And no relative to take care of her.'

Beatriz went over to her brother Salvador, whose wife had begged off with a migraine. On the other side of Salvador was their cousin Bernardo.

Bernardo was trying to extract information from Salvador about the division of their aunt's assets. He was particularly interested in some properties on the Costa Brava.

'I'll tell you one thing, in a couple of years half of Europe will be coming to sunbathe on our beaches. They'll come in hordes; they'll rent rooms en masse to be able to tan their pale skins.'

Felipe, the husband of another cousin, turned round to join the conversation.

'And don't forget the Americans. They're going to need land for their military bases.'

Salvador sketched a smile.

'Not only that. They will need food, alcohol and women,' added Bernardo.

Felipe chuckled silently and whispered over his shoulder, 'You want to invest in a brothel in the Barrio Chino? And in English classes for the girls?'

'I don't think they'll need to talk much.'

Both men laughed quietly.

Bernardo wouldn't let the matter drop. He pulled on Salvador's sleeve and murmured, 'So you don't know who's going to inherit Blanca's properties?'

Salvador shrugged and whispered, 'No idea. Maybe Joan.'

'Not Joan, I already asked him.'

Salvador nodded pensively.

'Well, I can't think of anyone else. Maybe the Brotherhood of the Holy Cross.'

Beatriz smiled. Blanca had never been a religious person. Going to church had been a social duty for her that she had fulfilled when it seemed necessary. At family parties she had taken her revenge for those dutiful church visits by making fun of the intellectual poverty of the sermons. In her youth, Blanca had read Freud avidly and made good use of her reading when expounding her observations and hypotheses about the hidden passions of the local clergy. The representatives of God on earth were a band of neurotics and criminals, according to Blanca. Which was why Beatriz thought it highly unlikely that she had left anything to a religious brotherhood. Bernardo sounded offended: 'But Aunt Blanca couldn't stand priests!'

Beatriz assumed that her brother knew full well who the happy heir was. He was probably already pondering how he himself could close some advantageous deal with him.

By the looks of it, Bernardo had come to the burial to do business, and he was not going to be deterred. Since Salvador wasn't giving him any information about Blanca's estate, he moved on to the other recently deceased woman of note.

'Weren't you in charge of Sobrerroca's affairs?'

He didn't wait for a reply, just continued with his offensive: 'Who's getting the house on Tibidabo? That's worth a fortune. Must be going to her brother. But what's he going to do with it, when he lives in Madrid? With that location, it's a gold mine.'

Salvador reacted to these questions with the same show of ignorance as before; Bernardo slowed his pace and was left behind, a cyclist returning to the peloton after an attempt to take the lead. Maybe he was searching for a new source of information towards the rear of the funeral procession.

Just behind them walked an older woman whom Beatriz only vaguely remembered. A cousin of Blanca's. She had been reproaching her daughter in a low voice for some time: 'Where have you come from? You're late again! Why aren't you wearing a veil?' The young woman seemed to take the scolding calmly, but then she launched into her counter-offensive: 'Mama, we are at a funeral. Be quiet, people are starting to stare.'

It was true that Beatriz had turned to glance at the mother and daughter. She had greeted them with a friendly nod. The young woman was in her twenties, very pretty, with a slightly square chin and a lively gaze. When her mother tried to start on again with her reproaches, Beatriz listened to what she said.

'Please, Mama, let's accompany Aunt Blanca with dignity on her final walk.'

That somewhat pitiful tone was effective and the conversation behind Beatriz ceased.

A minute later, Pablo appeared by her side. It seemed he had been making his way from the rear of the procession towards the front.

'Good morning, Aunt Beatriz. Good morning, Papa.'

Pablo kissed her first and then his father.

'It's nice to see you again after so long, Tieta, even though it's at a funeral.'

Beatriz understood. His father shouldn't find out about the problems he was having.

So she asked him, 'How are things going?'

'Well, I'm learning a lot at the new firm.'

He sounded perfect: the obedient son and promising lawyer. The boy was a chameleon. Beatriz saw that her brother was eyeing his son suspiciously.

'Something new every day,' said Pablo without batting an eyelid.

That was another sign for her; she understood that there was new information. Then Salvador intervened, 'Glad to hear it. What are you working on at the moment?'

'A very interesting case. Listen, Papa.'

Beatriz smiled. Even as a child his father had forced Pablo to give spontaneous speeches on every possible subject. Pulling a case from up his sleeve was the easiest of exercises for him.

But then he was interrupted from behind by one of Blanca's

cousins, the woman who had been scolding her daughter earlier.

'Silence, please. We are going to accompany Blanca with dignity on her final journey.'

They walked the rest of the way in silence. Blanca belonged to the wealthy branch of the family. They had a mausoleum halfway up Montjuïc, in front of which the bearers placed her coffin. When her turn came, Beatriz set her crown of flowers on top of it. She stood in front of the coffin for a moment and murmured her words of farewell. As she moved to one side to make room for other mourners, Pablo whispered to her.

'Come, Tieta, I have the letter.'

Beatriz nodded.

20

Pablo led Beatriz to one of the benches that stood in front of an ostentatious mausoleum and they sat down. He drew the letter and a cigarette case from his suit coat pocket.

'How did you get it?'

He was very proud of how he'd made off with the letter, so he indulged in a small prologue.

'Partly thanks to Maribel, Pla's secretary. She's the perfect secretary, who always tries to remove all obstacles from her boss's path. If possible, even before Pla has realised they're there. Maribel even keeps Pla's family's birthdays in her diary so he won't forget them. She got them out of his wife and wrote them down so that she can remind him in time. She told me that once.'

And though his aunt hadn't asked him, he added, 'Because let's just say that Maribel is very, very fond of me ... ' He smiled as he recalled the scene.

He and Maribel were alone in the anteroom to Pla's office, which smelled faintly of her perfume. He had complimented her, and in the conversation that followed ...

'And?'

His Aunt Beatriz didn't leave him time for daydreaming, interrogating him with her gaze. Pablo continued.

'This morning I went to the firm very early and I copied out the dates in Maribel's diary. Later, when she had arrived, I told her that I had to go into Pla's office to gather some papers that I needed for the early appointment in court. I searched a little,' he sketched a smile, 'and then the phone rang. Maribel's mother calls her every morning. She lives in Santander. Maribel calls her back, and that way they can talk at the firm's expense until Pla arrives. That was how I had time to try the safe combination using all of his family's birthdays. I opened it with his eldest daughter's. And here you have the letter.'

He saw that Beatriz was rummaging through her handbag. First she pulled out a book and put it on the bench. Pablo turned it over so he could read the title. Something about French dialects.

'Leave the book alone. I don't want the notes to fall out.'

There were little pieces of paper in his aunt's fairly illegible hand sticking out from between the book's pages. So many that the cover was already buckled and some pages had large gaps between them. Pablo withdrew his hand. Beatriz was still searching. The book was followed by a packet of cigarettes, an elegant powder compact, a small perfume vaporiser, a bit of chewed pencil and a silver-plated case. Finally she also found her glasses.

After reading the letter, she put it down on her knees and turned to Pablo.

'I think you should find another firm.'

He looked at her, confused.

'This letter wasn't written by the person they've led you to believe wrote it.' She paused briefly. Pablo waited in silence. Surely she would follow her thesis with an explanation. 'The way a person speaks, the way he writes, the way he expresses himself, all of these give us pieces of information about that person. We can hear where he comes from; we can often also hear what his social class is. Your Spanish, Pablo, is the Spanish typical of Barcelona, as it is spoken in the wealthy neighbourhoods. Your vowels are nasal . . .'

'But Tieta—'

Beatriz interrupted him, answering his objection before he had a chance to formulate it.

'In written texts you can't hear any voice, but there are obvious signs.' His aunt peered at him over her glasses. 'The

133

way someone formulates their thoughts, what words they choose, how they connect sentences and what expressions they prefer. All this reveals a lot about the person. It's like a fingerprint. Look here, where he writes: 'a group of posch young men came in'. Is there anything about this that raises a red flag for you?'

Beatriz scrutinised him expectantly. It was his turn. At least he had to try.

'It sounds a bit odd. I wouldn't write it like that.'

'Exactly. Would you call yourself a "posh young man"?'

'You're asking whether I would choose that expression?'

Beatriz nodded.

'Of course not. Marisa, our old cook, would say I'm a "posh young man". That was actually how she spoke about my parents. She worked for "posh people". The servants speak that way. And other people who don't include themselves among the "posh".'

It seemed he had given the correct response. Beatriz continued, 'Very good. And look: "Were – sic – will we end up". It sounds more like spoken speech. On the other hand, he writes "the aforesaid Pablo Noguer". It's another, completely different style, the type of expression found in police reports or juridical texts.'

'Perhaps he thought that he should express himself like that when writing to the police.'

Beatriz gave him an approving glance.

'A good observation. And it would be correct, too, if not for the fact that the text as a whole contradicts it. Look at the spelling.'

Pablo read the letter again and commented, 'A catastrophe.'

'Well, not really.'

Pablo stared at her uncertainly.

'Look here. He often leaves off the s's; he writes that he is going to denounce you to the "proscecutor" instead of the "prosecutor". He writes the way he speaks. That one is a plausible error, but look here: "rough place" instead of "rough places", "plenty whore" instead of "plenty of whores".'

'Where is the problem? That's how they pronounce it as well.'

'Yes, but when you learn to write, one of the first things you learn is that plurals are written with an s.'

Beatriz gave him another owlish glare over the top of her glasses. He decided it was better to say nothing, and just waited. So that was what he did, and she continued: 'It's a very simple rule that is taught very early. And the author of this letter learned to write.'

She points to the text.

'There are a lot of errors, including some very typical ones. But notice that most of the punctuation is in the right place, and he wrote a word like "brothel" correctly, even though it is much less common than "whores" or "places". That indicates that the author learned to write, and if he has,' Beatriz paused and pointed with the pencil, 'if he has, there is no reason to leave off all the s's at the ends of the plurals, even though he does when speaking. The person who wrote this letter wrote it the way authors write their Andalusian characters to identify them as such by their vernacular.'

'So who wrote the letter? I'm sure it wasn't a novelist.'

'I can't give you the name. Definitely a well-educated person. Perhaps someone with some juridical knowledge.'

Beatriz was pensive for a moment as she chewed on the pencil.

'Well, for the moment that is all I can tell you. And that you should look for a new firm.'

She rose. Pablo followed suit.

Then they both noticed the scrolls of smoke coming from the other side of the mausoleum. Out of curiosity, she went around the stone construction. On the other side there was another bench. Beatriz could only see the back of a young woman who had also been in the funeral party. She trotted quickly away and disappeared around a corner. She had left her cigarette on the edge of the stone bench. Beatriz put it out against the naked foot of a grieving angel.

21

As was to be expected, her father hadn't attended the funeral. Her father didn't set foot in cemeteries, much less in churches. Perhaps if he had been able to bury Ángel ... but her older brother lay in some mass grave in Aragón; they had refused to hand over his body. Her paternal grandmother rested in the cemetery of Pals, too far away for someone like her father, whose blacklisted state forced him to work long hours to survive. Where had he got the money he had sent her? The stew she'd had on Tuesday at her parents' house was made with good meat. Her mother knew how to haggle, but that only went so far. That cow wasn't some old cow sacrificed because the cost of feeding it outweighed the profits it brought in. Now that her disappointment at how little fuss he'd made over her article was partly forgotten, she could remember how the stewed meat, which she in turn hadn't praised sufficiently, had been tender and juicy.

She watched her mother talking to a group of women, all in black, all with veils. Relatives, surely. Her mother had four siblings and Ana couldn't even say how many cousins, uncles and other relatives. Some of the women wore very expensive clothes; even in mourning the differences were clear. Her mother's clothes had been good. Years ago. Observing the crowd of mourners, she came to the realisation that, in her mother's family, beauty was unequally distributed between the genders: the women were far better-looking than the men. So that it didn't sound like she was praising her own appearance, she formulated the theory for herself by saying that the men were uglier.

'Hideous,' she said, appraising two of her male cousins from a distance.

'Homely,' she corrected herself, recalling with a pang her brother's 'monkfish mouth', as he himself used to say to make her laugh.

She wanted desperately to leave the cemetery, but she couldn't go without saying goodbye to her mother and she preferred not to approach the group in order to avoid introductions and comments. At least other groups were heading towards the exit, but the one her mother was in seemed to have their shoes nailed to the ground.

The cigarette she had sneaked off to smoke in secret after the ceremony hadn't sat well with her. Even though she didn't know the dead woman, or at least didn't remember her, she had needed it to shake off the sadness inherent to funerals.

Just then, the young man she had heard speaking behind the mausoleum walked past. They gave each other the once-over. She noticed he wore fine black leather gloves. She guessed they must be about the same age and, because she found him quite handsome, she came to the conclusion that he wasn't a member of the family. Or perhaps he was the exception to the rule that she had formulated, and the only attractive male Noguer.

Patricia Noguer finally broke away from the circle of women.

'Do you know what I could do right now?' her mother asked her as they walked towards the exit.

'What?'

'Eat a nice dish of whipped cream with walnuts. How about you?'

Ana accepted, despite the signals her body was sending her. They took a taxi to the city centre and then walked to the Dulcinea Café on Petritxol Street, a side street in the Gothic Quarter so narrow that the sun never reached it.

As they opened the café door they were enveloped in an aroma of coffee and warm milk.

'Order whatever you'd like, darling.'

'Really? Have you and Papa won the lottery?' she said, instead of asking directly where the money for the veal and the treats had come from.

'How could we, when we don't even play? I sold some things,' her mother replied evasively. 'What are you going to order, Aneta?'

They both ordered the same thing: a dish of whipped cream with walnuts and a café au lait. Funerals always made them hungry. Their stomachs' initial protests were silenced by scoops of whipped cream and caramel sauce. Perhaps because it was a strange time of the day for that dessert, the waitress had been especially generous with the caramel, and the drizzled lines that criss-crossed the mountains of whipped cream were thick and rose a few millimetres off the white surface. As they ate, her mother told her all about the people they'd seen at the burial.

Then Ana's thoughts returned to the strange conversation she had accidentally overheard while she was smoking behind the mausoleum. She wouldn't have paid much attention, but she had been drawn in by their tone: both conspiratorial and intimate. The woman was the one who had turned to glare at them during the funeral procession, thanks to which Ana had been able to call a halt to her mother's spiralling reproaches. She had noticed her again during the burial because she was wearing a jacket that, in another era, must have been very expensive. She estimated she was about forty years old. The conversation about papers and letters had awoken her curiosity.

'Mama, who was the woman beside Aunt Adela at the burial?'

'Which one? There were a lot of people.'

'The one who wore a black jacket with batwing sleeves and embroidered lapels with a black rose brooch.'

'Goodness, you really know your clothes.'

Ana couldn't help but smile, both because it amused her to find that the vast knowledge of the subject she'd accumulated on the job wasn't entirely useless, and because of the glimmer of good mood she had managed to extract from her mother. She added a couple of details, imitating the style of her articles.

'With discreet yet elegant black buckled shoes and honey-blonde hair pulled back into a chignon slightly streaked with grey and accentuated by a delicate tortoiseshell clasp.'

'You're a funny one! She wasn't wearing a veil either, was she?'

Please don't let her get started on that subject again.

'No.'

'I know who you mean. Beatriz.'

'Is she a relative?'

'Yes, of course. Beatriz Noguer is the eldest daughter of my cousin Josep. Why do you ask?'

'No reason. She just caught my eye.'

'Yes, they are striking; she is the intellectual of the family.'

The word was generally pejorative when applied to a woman. She even recalled it being used as an insult when she had shown a fondness for reading in school. It wasn't positive coming from her mother, either; even so, she kept digging. 'Intellectual?'

'Beatriz writes articles.'

'She's a journalist?'

'No, something to do with literature. She is the younger sister of Salvador, the lawyer.'

Her mother assumed Ana knew who she was talking about. Seeing Ana's questioning expression, she added, 'The lawyer who helped us so much with Papa's thing, to get the sentence reduced.'

Salvador Noguer: now she remembered who he was. It was hard for her to believe that he was the brother of the woman with the blonde bun. In that branch of the Noguer family there was also that marked difference in the appearance of men and women that she had noticed at the burial.

All of a sudden, Beatriz Noguer's name began to ring a bell in her head, accompanied by the title *Spanish Dialects*. A title from the bibliography of one of her classes in philosophy and language. She recalled having asked her mother at the time if they were related. She was overcome by a strong feeling of déjà vu, remembering that during that first conversation she'd had with her mother about Beatriz Noguer she had also thought she'd like to meet her.

'And do you know where she works?'

'Works? At home. She lived abroad for a while after the war, but she returned a couple of years ago now.'

Even though she was exposing herself to a fresh tirade about her future with Gabriel, she asked, 'Is she married?'

'No. As far as I know, she had a boyfriend, a German man, but he left her. I think she's a pretty difficult character. So you see, there she is, fortysomething and alone.'

It wasn't a harangue, but rather a latent threat. But allusions have the advantage that you can ignore them. She decided not to ask about the man with black leather gloves, and continued enquiring about Beatriz Noguer.

'Do you know where she lives?'

'Darling, where does this sudden interest in the family come from?'

'Curiosity.'

'She lives along the Rambla de Cataluña.'

'Along, or on? Walking along the water and on the water isn't the same thing.'

Come on, laugh a little, she thought after uttering this gentle blasphemy. Her mother did laugh, although she feigned reluctance.

'On the Rambla de Cataluña, next to the Alexandra Cinemas.'

'Would you like another coffee, Mama?'

She ordered two more from the waitress.

While her mother related Salvador Noguer's life story, Ana decided that she would go to the Rambla de Cataluña the next day to meet someone she found much more interesting than Salvador Noguer: Beatriz Noguer, who must be some sort of cousin.

Perhaps Beatriz would be able to help her.

22

The room was growing dark. Beatriz rubbed her tired eyes and switched on the desk lamp. The bulb blinked out its death throes before it blew.

Once again, she needed money. Her *Introduction to the Dialects of the Iberian Peninsula and Their History* was required reading in many Latin American universities, but the cheques from her Argentinian publisher arrived irregularly and were far from lavish. Ask her brother for money? It wasn't only her pride that held her back, but the fact that he had already been quite generous when he'd given her his part of the family flat.

She glanced at the bookshelves in her office. They looked like a set of teeth riddled with cavities. She counted the gaps. Twelve.

She was sure that the bookseller would buy her edition of Ovid's *Metamorphoses*. That would be the last casualty. But she had to be careful that he didn't take advantage of her situation. She got up and surveyed the bookshelves slowly, stroking the spines with a finger. She could live for quite a while off the books and the remaining silver in the house, like a squirrel surviving the winter on its reserves. Except that in her case she had no way of knowing when the winter would end, especially now that her one-way ticket had turned out to be a pipe dream.

Truth be told, she couldn't afford the dictionary she had left on hold at the bookstore. It was pretty absurd to sell valuable books and spend the money on other expensive ones, even if she needed them for her work. It wasn't pretence, like that of the starving squire in *Lazarillo de Tormes*, who scattered crumbs on his shirt front to make it look as if he'd eaten. Someday, when the winter this country was plunged into ended, she would write about that book to make it crystal clear how much she abhorred the glorification of Lázaro de Tormes as a representative of the national idiosyncrasy. Worshipping the picaresque, putting deception on a pedestal. What poverty of spirit!

She took down the copy of the *Metamorphoses*, a lovely illustrated edition printed in Venice in 1521.

It would be even better if, instead of buying the dictionary, she tried to negotiate with the bookseller to give her a cheaper edition of the book she was thinking of selling him. She had already done that at other times, but she had never put those inexpensive editions in the place of those she'd had to sell. The words were the same. What was lost, in the case of the *Metamorphoses*, was the thick paper, the leather binding, the initials on a black background. And the engravings. She ran her fingers over the ribs of a small treatise on emblems as if it were a sleeping kitten's back. Her heart shrank at the thought of selling it.

Just then the doorbell rang. Encarni had gone out. Beatriz thought that she must have forgotten her keys, so she opened the door without glancing through the peephole. In the doorway was the young woman she had seen at Aunt Blanca's funeral procession, the one who had been arguing with her mother right behind her. Since Beatriz didn't say anything, the young woman introduced herself.

'I'm Ana Martí, Patricia Noguer's daughter.'

Beatriz stared at her, confused. Patricia Noguer? She tried to figure out how they were related; the girl told her before she had a chance to.

'We're cousins, second cousins, I think.'

Even though she had no idea what this second cousin was doing here, it didn't seem right to leave her in the doorway like a beggar. She invited her in with a wave of her hand.

'I wanted to consult you about something.'

Beatriz was unsure as to which room she should lead her to. Then Ana added, 'It's a linguistic consultation.'

She led her to the study. She turned on the ceiling light and took a small lamp from a pedestal table between the two windows to replace the one on the desk with the blown bulb.

'Make yourself at home.'

She sat in front of her newly discovered cousin and gave her a professorial look.

'How can I help you?'

'Well, I work for *La Vanguardia*.'

She noted a tinge of pride in her voice. It was justified; it was very difficult to get a position on the editorial staff of a newspaper, especially if you were a young woman.

'Ana Martí,' she repeated out loud, and suddenly realised who she could be. 'So you are the daughter of Andreu Martí?'

'Yes.'

'I'm so sorry about what happened to your father. He was a good journalist.'

'He still is, although he doesn't practise.'

She was right. Wasn't that her situation, too? She wondered if Ana Martí was aware of the parallels, if she was also referring to her with that comment. Just in case, she smiled at her. The young woman understood it as an invitation to return to the subject that had brought her there.

'I write about criminal cases. Right now I am reporting on the murder of Mariona Sobrerroca.'

She remembered that Encarni had mentioned it to her.

'Mariona Sobrerroca? Is she the one who was killed in her house on Tibidabo?'

'Have you read my article?'

Beatriz shook her head. She had to disappoint her; she wasn't among her readers.

The young woman didn't seem to mind, since she ploughed on with her account: 'She was strangled. Brutally beaten beforehand.'

Beatriz thought that if she asked whether they had also ripped out one of her eyes she would sound very morbid.

'And the body, how shall I put it . . .? Was the body intact?'

Her cousin looked at her, taken aback. This wasn't surprising; the question had come out sounding quite odd.

'Well, they tore off her right earlobe.'

'Nothing more?'

'Not that I know of.'

'I heard that she was missing an eye.'

Ana's eyes widened, her shock growing ever deeper.

'No, not at all. Where did you hear that?'

'Rumours.'

Beatriz hoped that she sounded contemptuous enough that Ana wouldn't ask anything more. Where had the rumour about the eye come from? Something like that usually had a solid basis in fact. The details were exaggerated, or left out; sometimes the nuance was changed, but there was always a basic structure that ran through each retelling.

Then Ana burst out laughing.

'Now that I think about it, there was an eye, but it was plastic, it fell from one of those skeletons that doctors have, where you can see the bones, the veins and all that.'

Beatriz nodded. Well, there was the basis of the rumour. But surely that wasn't why Ana had come.

'You said you needed my help . . . '

Ana drew some pages out of her handbag and placed them on the table.

'In the Mariona Sobrerroca case, some letters were found. Love letters, with no return address. No one knows who the author could be. The only thing that seems clear at this point is that they were written by a young man.'

Beatriz tilted her head with interest. Ana pointed to the letters.

'These are copies of the originals. The police let me make them.'

'The police?'

'Yes. I am working with them.'

Beatriz recoiled in her seat. A reflex that her cousin didn't notice, because she was speaking with her eyes glued to the papers.

'The author signs himself Octavian, like the character in Richard Strauss's opera. Which is to say, a young man courting an older woman. That's all I've been able to glean. If we could get more out of them, it might be important to the case ...'

She paused. Beatriz stared at her, waiting for more information. Ana continued, 'Since I happened to hear something you said yesterday, about how the way someone writes is like a fingerprint, a clue that someone leaves ...'

Beatriz arched her eyebrows.

'You happened to hear?'

'Well, I was having a smoke behind the mausoleum when you were talking to that young man.'

'And you didn't feel the need to clear your throat so that we knew you were there, or leave so that you wouldn't be eavesdropping?'

'To be honest, no. Your conversation was too interesting.'

'I can imagine,' answered Beatriz curtly.

Ana gave her a timid smile of apology and, with a few taps of her fingers, pushed the letters towards her.

'I thought that perhaps you could read the letters and tell me something about their author.'

Her cousin was asking her for help in a matter related to a police investigation. Just what she needed. The fewer dealings you had with the police, the better. What business did a linguist have with police matters?

'I'm sorry, Ana, but I prefer not to have anything to do with these things.'

'But you could really help. I have the impression that the investigation is heading in the wrong direction. And until now, no one has thought of consulting a specialist.'

A specialist. If she was a specialist in anything, it was medieval literature and the dialects of the Iberian Peninsula.

'Really, I don't think I can help you.'

She couldn't, and she didn't want to.

Although, who knows? Maybe she could take a quick glance, out of professional curiosity, and see if she was able to extract any information from them. She tried to glance at them stealthily. Maybe she could tell Ana where the author was from.

She realised that Ana had seen her surreptitious glance because she launched another offensive: 'I was very impressed by everything you said in the cemetery about the letter that the young man showed you. Perhaps you could do the same with the author of these anonymous letters.'

Beatriz shook her head. Even if she found something, it was unwise to get mixed up in police investigations.

Ana was silent for a moment before saying, almost in a whisper, 'I saw photos of the victim. Someone capable of abusing another person like that cannot go unpunished and walk the streets a free man.'

Beatriz stared at Ana. There were all kinds in her family: supporters of the Republic, Falangists, priests, liberals, even a couple of anarchists. What side was Ana on? They had purged the father, and now his daughter was working for a newspaper that continued publishing under the Regime; therefore she had adapted. What's more, she admitted collaborating with the police. Beatriz answered, also in a very soft voice, 'This country is swarming with people who have abused many others with impunity.'

She looked Ana in the eyes. Would she now remind her of her duties as a citizen of 'new Spain'? What did she care, anyway? They had already branded her a Red, so she had nothing more to lose by speaking her mind. She felt bold, with a sudden desire to provoke Ana. 'And some are even paid to do it. They've been given a post and honours. They have been promoted because they have been particularly efficient at liquidating their fellow countrymen. Taking them out of their beds and putting them up against a wall.'

She shot a defiant glare at Ana, expecting her rebuttal, a fist on the table, a threatening tone. Instead she saw her sink into her chair, eyes downcast, biting her lips. The energy with which she had entered the house, the vivacity that shone in her gaze, had disappeared. Beatriz remembered the rest of the story too late: that Ana's brother had been executed in prison by firing squad. Her own lack of sensitivity left her so stunned that she couldn't say another word.

Ana pulled out a handkerchief and dried her eyes. Then she stood up and made to collect her papers. Beatriz placed a hand on top of them to stop her.

'Leave them here. I will take a look at them.'

Ana still hadn't let go of the papers, and gazed at her with a mix of surprise and scepticism. Beatriz didn't want to tell her that she considered it her moral obligation after her obvious tactlessness.

'Out of scientific curiosity. Perhaps I can find something out about their author. But, if I do find something, I don't want anyone to know I helped you. I don't want to have anything to do with the police. Understood?'

Ana let go of the letters.

'I appreciate it. And you have nothing to fear; I won't reveal where I got any information you might give me.'

'Then I'll see what I can do.'

'When might you know something?'

Beatriz looked at her. She had recovered a hint of her previous sparkle, but she squeezed the handkerchief in one hand.

'I don't know. Right now I have a lot of work, but I will try to find some time for it.'

She escorted Ana to the door.

'Why don't you call me tomorrow?' said Beatriz. She searched for a slip of paper and jotted down her number.

'At what time?'

'Around midday.'

'At twelve noon on the dot.'

'Sure, like the Angelus.'

Ana smiled again. Beatriz closed the door with relief.

After Ana had left, Beatriz began to read the letters.

Love letters. The spelling throughout was correct. Ana had told her she'd copied the texts word for word. Mariona's lover wasn't a bad writer.

While she was at it, the best thing to do would be to work systematically. She spread out the papers over her desk, ordering them chronologically.

The first one began with a very formal address:

Dear Madam,

Please forgive my urgency. Don't think me impertinent if, mere hours after leaving your company, I pick up the pen to be able to be close to you again, even if only through words. The echoes of our conversation still resound within me; I still see you before me, graceful bearer of the white standard, and I feel the magic of your presence. Your intelligent words, both keen and so feminine, have made chords vibrate inside me that I thought had grown mute long ago.

Perhaps I shouldn't speak to you of this and offend your tender ears with the halting expression of my feelings. No, I shan't reveal how much I enjoyed our conversation; to what point, after long years of grief, I now feel alive again, as if my tired heart has come back to life, freeing itself of the cold arms of the night in which my soul slumbered for so long. As you can see, I can barely contain my feelings long enough to organise my ruminations and I foresee that I shan't be able to conclude this letter without stopping occasionally. But perhaps (it is merely a faint hope that I have no right to express), perhaps someday you may feel something similar.

The author had made prolific use of motifs from Spanish literature, but his great inspiration was undoubtedly the Vicomte de Valmont. What could she tell Ana about him? The author was very well read, and seemed to be having a lot of fun. The torrent of words that supposedly flowed directly from his ardent heart onto the page was a collage of literary quotes.

The third letter in particular caught her eye: the author was now addressing her familiarly and in a bolder tone. He no longer praised Mariona Sobrerroca's spirit and charm from a respectful distance; rather, he launched into a description of her physical charms:

I still see you before me, your magnificent figure, your blonde
hair whose shine outstrips burnished gold, your graceful neck that
triumphs with glowing disdain over shining crystal, the snow-
white silk scarf, the beloved standard that once guided my steps
towards your arms, your rose lips, the blue irises of your eyes
whose gentle clarity reminded me of the shimmering of the
morning reflected in the sea.

Beatriz raised her eyebrows. How vain, lovestruck and, most of all, dim-witted does someone have to be to fall for such compliments, which were obviously cribbed from an anthology of Spanish love poems!

Except for that 'standard'. Why had the scarf been a standard? Because he had taken it off her, fondled her neck that shone brighter than crystal, and the rest had just happened naturally? Or what? Hadn't he also mentioned it in the first letter? He had.

Beatriz thought it over. She tested her hypothesis. It held up.

23

Surely Ana would be late. Beatriz glanced at her watch. She had arrived at the Athenaeum ten minutes early. As she almost always did, since she calculated that the trams could be running late, or so full that she'd have to wait for the next one, or that one of the frequent power outages would leave them stranded, immobile in the middle of the street.

Ana's call the day before had already been behind schedule. She had said she'd call at noon, and she'd called three hours later. She apologised, and Beatriz accepted her explanations reluctantly. She hated being made to wait; it bothered her because she knew that if she used that waiting time to get something done, it might be interrupted at the worst possible moment.

'Have you found out anything?' Ana asked when she called.

'I think so.'

'Are you going to tell me, or do I have to guess?'

'It's a bit involved to go through over the telephone. Why don't we meet tomorrow at the Athenaeum and I'll explain it to you?'

'Tomorrow is Mariona Sobrerroca's funeral.'

'And?'

'Nothing: just that it's better if we meet up afterwards. That way I can tell you what I saw.'

She wasn't interested in what Ana might see at the funeral. She had other things to do. In fact, she had suggested the meeting place because once she had resolved this business with the letters, she could consult some books in the library there. The Athenaeum was located in an eighteenth-century palace in the old part of the city. She liked to work there, in one of the reading rooms with its green leather-topped desks and its tall bookshelves. She was still a member; a former school friend had made sure she didn't lose her affiliation after the war. The library's collection had grown during that time, bolstered by the private libraries of various scholars who had been forced into exile. At first she had found it difficult to work with volumes whose bookplates showed the names of their previous owners. With time she'd grown used to it, as with so many other things.

The leather sofas in the café were the same as before the war. Unlike the watered-down coffee. On the table there was a copy of that day's *La Vanguardia*, with a photo of the *Santa María* at anchor in Barcelona's port and another of the Director of Prisons visiting the workshops at the Modelo prison. The third photograph was of a reservoir in Badajoz. She leafed through the newspaper. The announcement of an homage by the army to the Blessed Sacrament during the International Eucharistic Congress; an article by Tristán La Rosa about the novel *La noria*, which she didn't want to read. Who wants to read about the reality of life in Barcelona? Wasn't it enough having to live it? She noticed a long headline that trumpeted the end of food rationing. Thanks to the abundance of consumer goods that would be available in Spain from now on. So when you didn't have to use ration cards to buy bread, you were living in 'abundance'.

She took a black notepad from her bag, jotted down the word 'abundance' and wrote in the margin: 'When there is barely enough of something'. In recent years many words had changed their meaning. Like 'red', which was used vehemently to single out communists and enemies of the state. Little Red Riding Hood was now called Little Crimson Riding Hood. She had found a book of stories with that title in a bookshop a few days earlier. They had also changed the names of streets and squares, in the typical way that regimes take possession of places. The Library of Catalonia had been rebaptised as the Central Library. Some words disappeared, the meaning of others shifted and yet others became omnipresent, such as Spain, destiny, manhood, holy. She took notes on it all in her little book, without knowing if she'd be able to make use of her observations one day. Then, her gaze landed on the article about the most recent speech given by Barcelona's Civil Governor.

The crime rate in the new Spain is low. Precisely because our government is tolerant and humane, precisely because the rights of citizens are respected, precisely because we are not a police state, we value our security forces' tireless work even more highly. They are men who are as patriotic as they are capable, who watch day and night over the well-being and peace of our citizens.

Beatriz made a surprised face. Tolerant and humane were relatively recent additions to the list of qualities the Regime used to characterise itself. They were new labels, to be hung on the chest like medals. She turned a page in her notebook and took down the words and the quote, adding a brief commentary. Then she glanced at the photo illustrating the article and the text accompanying it.

His Excellence, Señor Acedo Colunga, Civil Governor of Barcelona, accompanied by his personal secretary, Señor Sánchez-Herranz Robles.

The Civil Governor was in uniform, his semi-bald head surrounded by a halo of curls. Beside him stood a young man, dressed in civilian clothes, with sloping shoulders and a doughy face.

She continued reading and wrote down the reference to 'the highly modern methods used by our police'. Modernity was another of the new labels. In the second half of his speech, however, the governor began to threaten the press. He had nothing, he declared, against open criticism; that was healthy and appropriate. Beatriz shook her head as she read. How much of that supposedly healthy criticism got through the censors? Soon the Civil Governor got to his real target, the journalists who wrote with apparent correctness but who underneath that smooth, polished surface hid arrogant, when not treacherous, judgements on the well-intentioned actions of the Regime. The message was quite clear: 'Be careful that even the slightest hint of critique of the Regime can't be found in any of your copy'. Beatriz looked away from the newspaper in disgust. Then a shadow fell over the table.

It was Ana. The girl had been running, and a lock of her hair had slipped out, which she'd tucked pell-mell behind her ear. Beatriz invited her to sit down, pointing to the sofa beside her and waving to the waiter.

After they'd ordered, Ana picked up the newspaper and made a scowl of displeasure. She pointed to the young man in the suit.

'Acedo Colunga and his lackey. He's the one who writes all his speeches.'

Beatriz said simply, 'Dreadful.'

She didn't say that she wondered how she could work under such conditions, because to do so might put her cousin in the position of having to justify herself and she didn't think that was right.

Ana folded the newspaper so the article couldn't be seen.

'Yes, the man is terrifying, a really evil character. He was at the funeral too, standing in for his boss. All of Barcelona society was there. All of them very worked up and demanding that the murderer be arrested without delay. All in their finest black clothes.' Her voice darkened as she added, 'The article will appear in the society pages.'

The waiter arrived with a coffee and poured in the hot milk. Ana said it was plenty just as the milk threatened to overflow the cup.

'Will you have sugar, madam?'

The waiter was already extracting one of the cubes that filled the sugar bowl with a pair of tongs.

'Leave the sugar bowl there, I'll serve myself.'

She waited until he had gone and, to Beatriz's surprise, managed to dissolve two cubes into her coffee without spilling a drop.

Their eyes were still on her cup as they both started to talk at the same time.

'I have the letters.'

'I'm dying to know what you've discovered.'

Beatriz put on her glasses and brought the letters out of her handbag.

'Let's see, where do I start? The first thing that caught my eye was that our author uses a lot of literary models. In the earliest letters he puts a great deal of care into winning over his beloved. At times I was reminded of epistolary novels in which the only thing the characters do is write letters to each other.'

Ana eyed her expectantly. Beatriz enjoyed the attention.

'He is a cultured, well-read person. The letters are a mosaic of quotes. That makes it difficult to say much about the author. He could be said to be wearing a mask.'

'*Der Rosenkavalier.*'

Beatriz shrugged. 'It's a very well-known opera; I'd say it forms part of the general culture of the well-educated bourgeoisie. And the decently educated. So it's a banal choice that doesn't tell us much about the writer.'

She gazed at Ana.

'But there is something that the letters do reveal.'

She moved aside Ana's coffee cup to put the copy of the letter on the table. She pointed with her finger to a few lines.

'Here he describes her.'

She gave Ana a little time to read the passage in which he compared Mariona's blue eyes with the shimmer of the sea at dawn. The source of his inspiration was widely known and she expected her cousin to recognise it straight away.

'He's taken fragments from Bécquer's *Rhymes.*'

'Right. But I'm referring to something else. He mentions a silk scarf that showed him the path, calling it a standard.'

'Surely that's a metaphor. He is the lost wanderer who finally finds his way, thanks to Mariona.'

'No. I believe that here it refers to something literal. I think they used the scarf to recognise each other.'

'You mean, they made a date without having met?'

Beatriz nodded in satisfaction. Ana was proving to be clever.

'And they met through an advertisement and then they set a date? He wore a carnation in his lapel and she wore a white silk scarf?'

'That's my theory.'

'But why don't we have any letter where they introduce themselves and make a date to meet for the first time?'

'Good question.'

Which wouldn't be any use unless they found some answer to it. It didn't have to be definitive or complete. Half a reply is often a starting point. So she ventured, 'Perhaps Mariona Sobrerroca threw it away because a beginning like that didn't fit with her image of a romantic relationship. When someone heaps praise on your golden hair and shimmering blue eyes, you surely don't want to think that you met him through an advert.'

In her head she added, *And when someone promises you the moon and stars, you lap it up. Until he leaves you.*

Ana shook her head.

'I don't think Mariona threw anything away. The boxes the police have from her house were filled with souvenirs. Letters, old postcards, theatre tickets, train tickets ...'

'But there was no advertisement.'

'Not that I saw.'

The waiter came in carrying a tray with the empty cups left by a group of men who had been sitting at one of the tables in the courtyard garden. One of them had abandoned a copy of the Falangist newspaper *Arriba*. The waiter made sure the men couldn't see him and then threw it into the bin with an expression of disgust. She and Ana saw him. Her cousin turned towards her and said, 'Maybe Mariona organised her keepsakes, the good ones in drawers so she could look at them, and perhaps she made the others disappear into an attic or behind the shelves.'

Beatriz had to laugh, because this made her recall the pile of papers into which she had jammed the letter from Oxford.

Ana went on thinking aloud. 'If they met through an advertisement, the newspaper or magazine where it appeared would have the address of our Rosenkavalier. If he was the one who placed the ad, he would have had to leave an address where they could send the replies.' Ana took another lump of sugar. Her fourth. 'But if he was the one who answered her ad, that complicates things,' she added after putting the cube onto her spoon and letting it soak up coffee. The spoon and the sugar disappeared into her mouth. She closed her eyes for a moment.

Beatriz observed her. She realised that she had come through: she had read the letters, as promised, and she had even given Ana a useful clue. Her part was done. Still, she asked her, 'What are you going to do now?'

'I don't know.'

'What do you mean, you don't know?'

She was disconcerted. She had given Ana a clue, she had a thread to pull on and still she didn't have any idea as to how to proceed.

Ana beamed at her.

'But I'll think of something.'

Having contributed one of the pieces of the puzzle, Beatriz realised that she wanted to identify the other pieces. She asked her, 'What magazines publish that type of advertisement?'

'Mostly women's magazines: *¡HOLA!*, *Mujer Actual*, *Luna y sol*, *Astra* . . .' Ana thought for a moment. 'Each one has a specific audience. An article for *Mujer Actual* is very different from one for *¡HOLA!* You have to look for other adjectives, adjust the length of the sentences, because you are addressing a different public. Women like Mariona usually read *Mujer Actual*, but perhaps she saw the ad in *Luna y sol* and answered it.'

'Then, in my opinion, the best thing would be to check the back issues of the magazine you think is most likely.'

She made a huge effort to suggest this in such a way that it didn't seem intrusive, but she couldn't conceive of letting Ana leave without a concrete plan. Since she seemed rather interested, and certainly not put out or irritated, Beatriz carried on, 'Taking into account the dates on the letters, you could assume that the period to look at would probably be the first two weeks in January, maybe the final week of December last year.'

'When almost two years had passed since her husband's death. It could be that Mariona Sobrerroca considered her mourning over.'

'Could be. The letter describing their meeting is the third one, and it's dated 29 January. The others are dated one and two weeks later respectively. I don't have much experience in these matters, but I imagine that between the advertisement and the first meeting not more than three or four weeks passed.'

Ana nodded.

'Then we would have to look at those weeks before to see if any advertisement was published with the name Octavian or The Knight of the Rose.'

At that point her cousin interrupted her. 'He might have used another name. Young Lonely Heart, or something like that.'

Ana picked up her coffee cup and immediately set it down again on the saucer. Beatriz thought that it must be empty. Ana said, 'It could also be that Mariona was the one who placed the ad.'

'It's possible, but I would look first for Octavian or The Knight of the Rose. And I'd start with the magazine you think it's most likely Mariona would read, and if you don't find anything there, try the next one on the list, and so on.'

She trailed off. Ana laughed. 'OK! Understood. But your plan has a lot of "maybes" and "perhaps".'

'Of course; but many of those can be eliminated if you give your plan a thorough review.'

'All right.'

Ana didn't sound enthusiastic, exactly, but Beatriz felt it was a solid working plan. It was true that if she started with the wrong magazine, the search would be a long one. And if she had bad luck, it would be in vain. But then at least she would know that this path didn't lead anywhere, and she'd have to look for another one.

With a rapid movement, Ana swiped her finger through the remains of the coffee and sugar at the bottom of the cup and licked it. 'You know what? This plan of yours is pretty laborious, but I'll think about it. First, I have to go to the newspaper office.'

She smiled at her. She got up, took her by the shoulders and gave her a loud kiss on each cheek.

'Thanks so much for all your help. You are amazing!'

Beatriz didn't know how to respond to such effusiveness. She picked up the packet of letters and held it before her with both hands as if it were a protective shield. 'I could analyse them further, if you'd like.'

'Do you think you can find out even more?'

'Perhaps.'

The letters didn't stop Ana from hugging her.

'Be careful! You're going to crease them.'

'Sorry. I have to go. I have to hand in the article about Mariona's funeral.'

She grabbed her bag and coat and gave her a last quick peck on the cheek.

Beatriz watched her leave. She wondered if Ana would get in touch with the magazines right away. Beatriz didn't have the impression that she was planning to make a list of publications and check them one by one. But, really, it was none of her business. Was it?

24

The Knight of the Rose.

She could imagine Mariona feeling like the Marschallin of Strauss's great work, in love at fifty-three with a younger man like the lover in the opera. Was he as young as Strauss's Octavian, who was seventeen?

They had already seen, from the dates on the letters, that she had waited quite some time after her husband's death before answering a 'friendship' ad. The guardians of the nation's morality couldn't be so innocent as to believe that such a thing existed as friendship between men and women. Or did they think those 'gentlemen' were making innocent dates to escort women to concerts of the Montserrat Boys' Choir? Where had she got that part about the boys' choir? She realised that the music from the radio had infiltrated her thoughts. The host had announced the musical interlude after saying something about the forthcoming Eucharistic Congress. She turned off the radio.

A 'friendship' advert, a euphemism constructed with forced words to suggest honesty. Mariona saved any slip of paper that reminded her of moments in her life, even the most routine meeting of the Ladies of Charity; how was it possible she hadn't saved that ad? In some well-protected place, because it was also somewhat shameful, but she wouldn't have got rid of it. It was still in Mariona's house.

So, once again, she set off running out of her own house. She took the stairs two by two on the way down and three by

159

three when she reached the first floor, because Teresina Sauret had just scrubbed them. She came face to face with her on the last flight, still on her knees on a foam pad.

'Some people have great timing,' complained the door-keeper.

'If you had got to the fourth floor, I would have realised and waited,' she responded wickedly and with the poise that being up to date on the rent gave her.

It was mean and she knew it, a retaliatory 'money talks' after having avoided her for several weeks, but her remorse lasted only as long as it took to come up with her plan on the way to the newspaper, the waltz from *Der Rosenkavalier* echoing in her head.

She went straight to Sanvisens's office. 'Would you be interested in some photos of Mariona Sobrerroca's house?'

'Of course. Especially of the scene of the crime. Is there a possibility?'

'Castro told me that I can go with him to see the house. If you lend me a camera.'

'Wouldn't it be better to send a photographer?'

'No. I don't think they want any more journalists.'

'All right. Do you know how to use one?'

'Please!'

'Then tell Ramoneda to lend you one. Don't forget to put a film in it.'

'Come on, boss!'

She left the office in such a hurry that she hardly paid any attention to the last thing that Sanvisens told her: 'Carlos is coming back on Monday, Tuesday at the latest.'

Twenty minutes later, she turned up at Castro's office.

'I was expecting you this afternoon.'

'We had a meeting at the paper, and my boss has asked me for some photos.'

'You aren't taking any photos of me, I can tell you that now.'

'No, not of you. They would be photos of Señora Sobrerroca's house, to go with the article.'

'What article? There's nothing new to report.'

'Another point in my favour. A couple of photos, a brief description of the crime scene and, since it's new information, people will be satisfied.'

There it was. She'd played her bluff card. There was no turning back.

The tightening that preceded one of the inspector's rare smiles started to be visible on his face. He had unmasked her. Once again he had read what she hadn't wanted to tell him.

Or had he?

The words that followed were spoken in an unequivocally admiring tone: 'You would sell your own grandmother for a good article!'

She gave him a flustered smile in return for his unflattering praise.

Castro rose, opened the door to his office and called for Officer Sevilla. He pulled the door behind him. Castro and Sevilla's voices were so muffled that she couldn't make out what they were saying. At one point they almost disappeared. The inspector must be giving him instructions about her. She imagined that he was asking him not to take his eyes off her, and to be discreet, not tell her anything about the case. If only he were also asking him to be kind.

It seemed he had told him not to speak to her. Sevilla barely said a word on the way there, just gave instructions in the form of orders: 'Sit down, you can get out of the car now, follow me, it's this way, go in.' And when they were inside, 'Don't touch anything.'

'Relax, I won't.'

To avoid raising the officer's suspicions, she said out loud everything she was supposedly doing: 'I am going to go through the house to get an overall idea. I'm not touching anything . . . I hope you don't mind if I take some notes. I'm not touching anything . . . I'm just taking a look in that corner to see the details. I'm not touching anything.'

She did everything slowly. Soon she found three places where Mariona Sobrerroca could have hidden the advertisement. Did she need to hide it? Of course, she had a maid.

From the occasional dealings she'd had with her, she knew that Mariona was a bit of a romantic. Ana had met her husband. Jerónimo Garmendia was like his name, solid and dour; she couldn't imagine him capable of outpourings of love or awakening any sort of passion. She imagined that, after being widowed, Mariona had given free rein to her desires. She had already seen several bookcases filled with romance novels. That was one of the possible hiding places. Another was the significant collection of records lined up underneath a very modern record player. The third was among the programmes from the Liceo Opera that Mariona kept perfectly in order on a sideboard in the parlour.

Sevilla, bored, decided to go out into the garden to smoke a cigarette.

'Don't touch anything.'

She pretended to be absorbed in her notes and didn't look up as she replied, 'Of course not.'

The officer went out.

Ana didn't have time to look in all three places. Which should she choose? Mariona, so romantic ... in love with a younger man ... sporadic visits ... days of waiting ...

Her first impulse was to go over to the novels. She read the titles, hoping that one of them would suggest that it hid what she was searching for; but from *I'll Wait for You For Ever* to *Spring in Autumn*, any one of them could contain the advert. When you enter into the parallel dimension of allusion, every interpretation is possible. Even *Sacrifice for Love* could be the key. And there were so many novels! Sevilla would have to smoke his way through an entire packet of cigarette papers to give her time to browse all the books. She gave it up as an impossible task, and took it on trust that the books weren't the hiding place. The waltz from *Der Rosenkavalier* played again in her head. On another shelf the opera programmes were lined up chronologically. When had they performed Strauss's opera at the Liceo? She couldn't remember. She really didn't know and she didn't have time.

She went towards the records, getting on her knees to see

them better. Thank you, wonderful alphabetical order! O, P, there was no Q, R, S. Strauss, Johann, Richard. *Der Rosenkavalier*. Mariona, enthralled, listening to the final tercet but, unlike the Marschallin, she didn't have to renounce her young lover so he could go with someone younger. Mariona would listen to the tercet in triumph.

Ana also felt triumphant. There it was! The clipping of the advertisement was carefully placed between two of the records.

She heard the creak of the door to the terrace. She stuck the advert between the pages of her notebook before putting the record back. She wouldn't have time to get up and move away from the record player, so she sat on the floor and pretended to be taking notes.

'What are you doing on the floor?'

'I didn't want to sit on the chairs in case they still needed to dust for prints.'

The officer seemed convinced.

'Have you taken the photos?'

'Not yet. I only need to jot down one thing and then I'm ready.'

She photographed the room where the crime had taken place: the exact place where they had found Mariona's body, her husband's desk, also the skull, which was still missing an eye; someone had left it to one side.

'What's going to happen to the house?'

'I think it will go to a nephew or a brother. I don't know,' replied Sevilla.

Then, as if he regretted having given her any information, no matter how insignificant, he asked in a surly tone, 'Have you finished now?'

'I have.'

They left the house.

In the car, Ana wondered if she had put the record back in the right place, or if she had mixed it up with those by Johann Strauss. She assessed Officer Sevilla out of the corner of her eye and relaxed. They weren't going to notice if she had.

*

Reading the advertisement that had caught Mariona's eye, Ana wavered between compassion and laughter, with a hint of embarrassment for the other woman in the mix: 'A young heart, disillusioned by the fickleness of blossoming girls, unripe fruits who have filled him with remorse and darkness, seeks correspondence with an understanding lady leading to friendship. The Knight of the Rose.'

The target of his words was clear: the protective instinct of the mature woman, a little past her prime, who would be willing to heal the wounds of the Knight of the Rose. If the reader of the advert was an opera fan, the promise of possible romance was more than evident behind the 'friendship'. It was the perfect bait for Mariona Sobrerroca.

For the first time she also voiced to herself a suspicion that she'd been turning over in her head since she had known about the advert. What if the 'Knight of the Rose' was a professional? Someone who specialised in extracting money and a lifestyle from older women? The idea made her feel a combination of aversion and sadness.

The piece of paper, just a few centimetres square, was neatly cut out; on the back of the advert there were three lines of an incoherent text, almost random words, few of them useful; the articles and prepositions weren't much help. But the two imperatives 'make', and 'then make a sa'. A what? A sack, a saddle, a sandwich? A sauce!

It was a recipe.

Recipes, friendship advertisements. She thought of a few publications that the clipping could have come from. She had to get copies of each of them.

Yet again, she hurried out of her flat. Just as she was congratulating herself for having avoided the doorkeeper's usual commentary, she ran into her at the street door. Broom at the ready, like a brigadier, Teresina Sauret was keeping watch over the house. Her eyes swept the ten or twelve metres of pavement that she considered her territory, although the bustling pedestrians walking on it were oblivious to that fact. Ana uttered a brief greeting; too bad she didn't wear a hat like men did, allowing them to resolve such matters with a simple touch of the brim. She heard Teresina's reproving murmur and joined the flow of people to her right, heading towards the Ramblas.

She bought all the women's magazines she could find, even some like *Medina*, the magazine of the Falange's Women's Section, where it was highly unlikely they would accept such advertisements. But an investigation was an investigation.

Back home, she started to search, with the advertisement she had found in Mariona's house in front of her. *This I'll save for later*, she told herself when she came across a feature story on Mario Cabré and Ava Gardner. It seemed they were having a romance. Some people have all the luck!

She found a couple more articles she wanted to read 'later', and got lost for a few seconds gazing into Tyrone Power's eyes, but she kept up her search. Until she found it, in *Mujer Actual*. The classified section had the same typography. *Mujer Actual*, a magazine with fashion, recipes, some practical tips for the home and feature stories on the entertainment world. Another one. Maybe the difference lay in what there wasn't: she didn't find any articles that touched on religion or morality, at least not explicitly. The classifieds filled an entire page. She was in luck; the magazine was produced in Barcelona.

Ana had never been much of a planner. At least not in her writing – her best ideas always came to her while she was working. On the way to the newspaper office she had come up with the idea of taking photos in Mariona's house. She would have to write some copy to accompany the photos, or she'd have to do some explaining to both Sanvisens and Castro. She would do that 'later', too. First, trusting that the strategy would come to her in a similar way, she decided to go to the magazine's headquarters.

She found herself on the Vía Augusta. She took the bus. On the way she tried to think how she could obtain the address where the replies to the 'Knight of the Rose' were being sent, but without knowing what the place was like or what kind of people she would find there, she felt unable to come up with a plan.

The magazine's offices were on the main floor of a stately building with a reception area.

She went in. The receptionist looked up with his eyes but didn't lift his head. The little novel he was reading seemed to have him completely captivated.

'If you're here about the job, you're too late.'

'What job?'

'Doesn't matter; even if you knew, it's already taken.'

'Well, all right. I'm visiting the magazine *Mujer Actual*.'

'On the main floor. But the job's taken.'

'Fine, I understand.'

'I don't want them getting angry with me later for having sent another one up.'

'Another what?'

'Another one looking for work. It's taken.'

'I'm not looking for work. Can I go up?'

'Nobody's stopping you.'

He said all this without looking at her, his eyes glued to the book *Merciless Duel in Carson City*. What a title!

She went up to the first floor. A small bronze plaque screwed to a heavy dark door announced the offices of *Mujer Actual*. Nothing that could help her with a plan, *the* plan.

Perhaps another less conspicuous, handwritten sign taped beside the doorbell would be helpful. *During office hours, enter without ringing.* She did.

She entered a wide vestibule with an empty counter behind which there was a table with a typewriter, some pigeonholes for correspondence and issues of the magazine in neat piles. There was a sheet of paper in the typewriter. So the post had only been temporarily abandoned.

To one side of the door she saw a rack where men's and women's coats hung. She heard voices and the sound of typewriters from behind the closed doors. From a hallway to the left, footsteps approached. They belonged to a man of about fifty, who greeted her with an angry expression.

'That Cesáreo has a brain like a sieve! Another one! Didn't he tell you that the cleaning lady job is taken? That guy lives on the moon, I'm going to have to talk to the owner . . . '

'Yes, he did tell me,' interrupted Ana.

'Then what are you doing here? Aren't you a cleaner?'

'No. I'm a journalist, from *La Vanguardia.*'

'Excuse me, pardon the confusion.' The man was visibly embarrassed. 'How can I help you?'

A bad conscience is one of the most powerful motors behind human actions. She would think that later, on the bus home, seated beside a woman who was sniffling noisily, though she didn't dare to offer her a handkerchief so as not to draw attention to it. That maxim clearly explained her strategy.

But at the moment the man realised his mistake, Ana's reaction was instinctive rather than planned: 'A very delicate matter has come to our attention.'

The man indicated that it would be better if they went into his office. His name was Joaquín Muñárriz, and he was the magazine's director. When Ana entered his office the first thing she saw were the portraits of José Antonio and Franco hanging on the wall flanking a large wooden cross. The usual. But it was the first time she'd come across an exhibition of framed photos such as the one she saw on the right-hand wall. Muñárriz must already have been aware of the surprising effect it had because, although he offered her a seat, he escorted her towards the wall and gave her time to look, one by one, at the images that completely covered it. All of the photos were dedicated, from the ones of Lola Flores, Celia Gámez and Luis Miguel Domínguin, to those of Gary Cooper, 'for my friend Joaquín'; Charles Boyer and Ava Gardner, 'Kisses, kisses, kisses for Joaquín'. Ana's eyes leapt from Antonio Machín to Cary Grant.

'You are a man of the world. That makes it a bit easier for me to explain the situation to you,' began Ana with her eyes still on Burt Lancaster's clear gaze.

The actor's mocking half-smile approved of her deception. 'Tell me.'

They moved away from the photos and sat face to face at Muñárriz's desk.

'A few days ago a woman got in touch with us. She told us she had been deceived by a man she met through one of your friendship advertisements. The man, after asking for her hand in marriage, had carnal contact with her, and . . . '

'She's pregnant.'

'That's it. How did you know?'

'Why else would she be looking for him?'

'That's true. I wanted to ask for some information about this individual: his name, his address . . . '

'She doesn't know his name?'

'She knows the name he gave her, but who knows if it's real, seeing that he's disappeared? He said his name was Octavian.'

'And did he use some sort of code name? That's usually the case.'

'The Knight of the Rose.'

'Miss, what did you say your name was?'

'I didn't, but I'm Ana María Martí.'

'Look, Señorita Martí, as you yourself said, I am a man who's seen something of the world, even though I've ended up here. Don't think you can fool me.'

Ana shot an alarmed glance to the right. The eyes of Bette Davis, beneath high, thin brows, interrogated her in return.

'You write for the society pages, don't you? And you aren't here as a journalist for *La Vanguardia*, are you? This is a private matter and, correct me if I'm wrong, the person you are talking about, if it's not you, is someone very close to you. Or am I wrong?'

The sigh that Ana couldn't contain was understood by the director of *Mujer Actual* as an expression of relief at finally being able to tell the truth.

'You're right. It's my sister. I'm sorry to have to resort to that trick, but she's desperate.'

'Not another word! We journalists have to stick together. What was his name?'

'The Knight of the Rose.'

Muñárriz got up and left. He seemed to have grown several centimetres. When he returned a few minutes later, he still seemed tall but he'd lost some of his heroic height.

'Here it is, but unfortunately I can only give you the number of a post office box.'

'Here in Barcelona?'

'In Martorell.'

'Well, it's something, at least.'

She thanked him. Muñárriz accompanied her to the door. The secretary, an older woman with an old-fashioned updo, a style called the 'Arriba España', stopped writing when she saw them come out. Before saying goodbye, Muñárriz told her, 'If you are ever looking for work, I want you to know that our doors are always open for someone as honourable as you.'

'Thank you very much.'

She suddenly felt mean. She decided to leave the doors to *Mujer Actual* closed behind her.

She went downstairs. The receptionist was still absorbed in his *Merciless Duel in Carson City*.

25

The ringing of the telephone echoed in the flat and the silent Sunday afternoon shattered like a crystal goblet hitting the floor. Beatriz put down her fountain pen and picked up the receiver. She heard a crackling and her cousin's lively voice.

'You were right.'

She needed a moment to remember what she was referring to.

'And I've found out more things,' she heard from the other end of the line.

'Really?'

She heard herself and thought she sounded like Mercè, one of her aunts, in some never-ending cocktail conversation: 'Really? So he has a lover and keeps her in a flat on the Diagonal?' *Really? The novel is the hit of the season?* Her Aunt Mercè always seemed friendly and interested, but an hour later she didn't even remember what the conversation had been about.

'Beatriz, are you still there?'

'Of course.'

There was a brief silence at the other end of the line.

'Do you have some time this evening?'

The truth was that she didn't have time. On her desk was a half-written article in which the ideas were just starting to come together. On the other hand, she wanted to know what Ana had found out.

'Goodness gracious! Señora Sauret, must you mop right here, right now?'

Although she could tell that Ana was covering the receiver with her hand, Beatriz heard her irritable exclamations and the sound of a metal bucket clanging against the floor tiles. Then a disagreeable voice whose words she couldn't make out. A pause, and Ana picked up their conversation in the same friendly tone she'd had at the start.

'I'm going to have to go. Can we get together this afternoon? That way I can tell you all about it.'

She didn't respond. She was still considering whether to beg off with some excuse when Ana spoke again.

'Come on, my treat. To thank you for your help, all right? You know Pastís? It's at the end of the Ramblas, on the second to last street on the right.'

Beatriz hesitated. Then her cousin added, 'At nine thirty?'

If she didn't want to go, she should probably say something.

'I really have a lot to do, Ana ...'

'Would you prefer to meet later?'

Beatriz sighed.

'No. Nine thirty is fine.'

'Brilliant.'

Again, crackling was heard in the receiver and finally Ana hung up.

Beatriz was peeved. Ana could have told her over the phone. Now she would have to meet up with her to find out what parts of the mosaic she had unearthed. And in a bar with a reputation for being bohemian.

The bar was small, not to say minuscule. It was one room, more or less half the size of Beatriz's study. There was little light, and on the walls hung paintings by the owner himself, besides many photographs. The paintings were so gloomy that they were barely distinguishable from the dark walls.

Ana was already sitting at a table by the wall and waved to her.

She could barely wait for Beatriz to take a seat before she started telling her, 'You were completely right. Mariona Sobrerroca answered a lonely hearts ad.'

She was clearly very satisfied, proud of her findings.

171

In tribute to the name of the bar, they ordered pastis. The waiter left the glasses and the jug of water for them to mix it themselves.

Ana took her first sip and related how she had found the advertisement. Her procedure wasn't exactly what you'd call systematic, but it had been successful. Beatriz finished off her drink and gestured to the waiter for a refill. The owner of the bar had changed the record. The sound of a saxophone filled the place. It was a little warm, and the alcohol relaxed her shoulders.

She smiled at Ana and asked, 'And now? What are you planning on doing?'

Ana furrowed her brow.

'I don't know yet.'

Again. Did she always have to play it by ear?

Ana traced the edge of the glass with her finger.

'I suppose, first, I should talk to Inspector Castro, who is in charge of the case. I imagine he'd be able to find out the Knight of the Rose's address from the central post office. If he deigns to consider what I tell him.'

Beatriz didn't have the slightest idea about how collaborations between journalists and the police worked. Maybe 'collaboration' wasn't the right word. It was clear that Ana was in a patently hierarchical situation and that she was on a lower rung. On the other hand, perhaps it was a game of deceiving and being deceived. Or some mix of the two.

'Does this Castro expect you to tell him what you've discovered?'

'Of course.'

'Does he know that you've been investigating on your own?'

Ana took another small sip of her anise and said, 'No. But I'm a journalist, not the police; I'm not accountable to him. He's not my boss.'

Despite the force of her words, Ana didn't sound terribly convinced by what she was saying. 'Accountable'. Another expression Beatriz wasn't entirely sure was apt.

172

'You're not so sure about that, are you?'

Before Ana could respond, the waiter filled their glasses again.

'Not really. Castro doesn't take me very seriously; I think I amuse him, so he lets me carry on. I find it . . . '

She searched for the word. Beatriz wanted to lend her a hand: 'Degrading, humiliating, offensive, insulting . . . '

'Stop, stop! That's enough. Yes. All of those things. More or less. But I would like to show him my worth, even though I know that's a childish reaction. On the other hand, I'm afraid that if I go too far, he'll take me off the case completely. To tell you the truth, I'm afraid of him too. He's a violent guy, coldly violent, the kind that punches you without warning, you know?'

Beatriz saw Ana's left hand close into a fist on the table. She tapped it a few times with her index finger and said, 'You've got something.'

Ana opened her hand. Her empty palm shone despite the dim light in the bar. Ana's gaze, already somewhat muddied by the alcohol, showed confusion.

'What do I supposedly have?' She turned her hand over and looked at the back of it.

'You know things that could be useful to him. Bits of information. You could swap them.'

Ana looked at her before answering. 'Do you mean I should swap information instead of handing it over?'

Beatriz shrugged. 'More than swapping, I would present it so that it seems as if you are offering it to him generously. I don't know how journalists collaborate with the police in this country; I don't know this Castro; really, I know precious little about all of this. Which is why I am not going to give you any advice; I don't even dare make any suggestions. I simply wanted to point out a possibility.'

'Pointing out possibilities to someone isn't very different from giving them advice.'

She wasn't wrong. Sometimes Beatriz got lost in hair-splitting speculation. But Ana didn't seem to mind too much.

Her thoughts had already moved on. 'So, it's better to give him the whole story, and not just the beginning. Don't you think? I have to find out who the post office box in Martorell belongs to. There must be some way of knowing.'

Let's see what her cousin would come up with now, after the stunt at Mariona's house and the visit to the magazine.

'I have a plan,' she said, after polishing off her drink and making a sign to the waiter to fill them both up again, prompting Beatriz to finish hers. 'The best thing would be to go to Martorell, to see him.'

Clearly she and her cousin didn't mean the same thing when they talked about having a plan.

Martorell was about two hours by car from Barcelona. Perhaps Ana had the rather innocent idea of going to the post office and asking. Beatriz didn't say anything.

'Maybe they'll give me the address at the post office.'

That was unlikely. Especially since she wouldn't be going there with a police escort. Once again, Beatriz kept her musings to herself.

'They aren't just going to give it to me.'

Beatriz remained silent. Ana kept talking.

'I have the day off tomorrow.'

She could see her face perfectly, but the wall behind was blurry. Was it because of the increasingly dense smoke? Or was it the pastis?

Meanwhile, the waiter had changed the music. Edith Piaf was singing 'La Vie en Rose'. The record had been played so many times that the music emerged amid much crackling. The waiter approached and refilled their glasses. Beatriz mixed the anise with water while murmuring along with Piaf. The liquid turned a milky colour; both women contemplated it as if they hadn't already repeated the ritual several times that night.

'It's really an aperitif, and it's typical of Marseille,' said Beatriz.

'You are a bit of a Francophile, aren't you?'

'Yes, you could say that.'

'Have you been to Paris?'

'Yes, a couple of—'

'Well, I want to go to New York. France is fine, but America is the future.'

Hearing Ana's somewhat condescending tone, it suddenly dawned on Beatriz how young she was.

'Do you speak English?'

'When I have some money, I'm going to do a correspondence course. With records, for the pronunciation.'

She was having more and more trouble with her Spanish pronunciation with each drink. Ana's eyes rolled as she tried to speak over Piaf's singing. 'I could go to Martorell tomorrow. Are you coming?'

The question didn't surprise her as much as hearing herself reply, 'We could go in my car. We'd get there faster, and we wouldn't be dependent on the train.'

'You have a car? You drive? Brilliant!' Ana was slurring slightly. 'What time should we leave?'

'When did you want to go? You do want to go, don't you?'

'Pick me up at my house tomorrow at nine.'

She ordered another drink.

26

Muffled sounds at the door. Rustling, voices. Then a dull thud, as if a sack had been dropped against the door. Encarni sat up in bed. No one had ever tried to break into the house. Besides, one imagined that burglars didn't make such a racket. Unless they were new to the job. Clumsy and nervous. The kind that end up killing you simply because they are so nervous.

'Bed is the worst place to die,' her grandfather used to say. So she forced her feet out from under the covers. The floor was freezing. She felt around for her slippers. They had been her employer's, and were lined with sheepskin, with a ridiculous pink pom-pom. But they were warm. The bad thing was that the heels made a noise as you walked. If she wanted to move stealthily along the hallway, she'd better not put them on.

The tiles seemed colder with every step. She got to the door without making any noise. On the other side she could hear the voices more clearly, and the metallic jangle of keys. They weren't thieves. Two women's voices, one speaking loudly, the other in whispers. She knew the one speaking loudly. She opened the door. A gust of anise entered the house. Sweet, intoxicating, repugnant. On the threshold was the missus and a taller woman with dark hair and the keys in her hand, although she still hadn't made contact with the lock. The missus was staggering and leaning on the doorframe.

Encarni had never seen her in such a state. She'd have to see how she handled her alcohol. She had experience with drunkenness. Sometimes it made people aggressive, like her father, who would curse the Caudillo and his riff-raff, then he cursed the treacherous anarchists and wished them the plague, cholera and impotence, and finally he beat his wife and children. When her mother was drunk she got weepy: 'Holy Mother of God, what have I done to deserve this life?' Although she had to admit that she was right. The Mother of God hadn't treated her too well, despite all her prayers and offerings.

The woman with dark hair glanced at Encarni's bare feet; the maid looked her in the face. Then the woman turned towards the missus and said, 'Beatriz, we don't need the keys any more.' Then she turned to Encarni again. 'I don't think she's feeling very well.'

'I understand.'

She took Beatriz by the shoulders. She murmured, 'I had a lot of fun, cousin. Maybe we could do it again sometime. I'd really like that.'

The woman with the dark hair responded very seriously, 'Of course, but now you need to rest a little bit. Come on, two more little steps and you'll be home.'

The missus obeyed. The young woman, it seemed, was her cousin. Of course; that was why she spoke to her like that.

'I can take care of putting her to bed,' said Encarni.

'Do you need help?'

'Don't worry about it.'

'Very well. Good night, then. Good night, Beatriz.'

The missus was leaning against the wall. She lifted her right hand in a farewell, but quickly let it drop, as if it were too heavy.

The woman grabbed the doorknob and addressed her, 'Do you want me to . . .?'

Encarni nodded and the woman closed the door behind her.

Señora Beatriz took two steps and knocked into a sideboard; the pieces inside crashed together. She had hit one of the corners; it must have hurt, but she didn't react. Encarni saw that she was struggling to walk upright. It would be best to get her into bed straight away.

With gentle prods she guided her towards the bedroom.

'Encarni, I'm afraid I'm not feeling very well.'

That was obvious. And tomorrow she'd be feeling even worse.

'You have to go to bed, Missus Professor.'

'I'll be the one to decide that.'

'As you wish,' said Encarni, as she sat her on the edge of the bed with a last shove, gentle but resolute.

It would be enough to take off her shoes and her suit jacket. Then she could go back to her own bed, nice and warm. Her feet were frozen. She stood on one of the little rugs. Much better.

'Come on, missus, take off your clothes, I'll hang them up for you.'

'Why?'

'So they won't wrinkle. Tomorrow I don't have time to iron.'

'Well, you can do it the day after tomorrow.'

'Fine, you can sleep in your clothes if you want. I've heard that the elegant ladies in Paris do that too.'

Her employer's gaze was murky when she tried to focus on Encarni.

Encarni turned to leave. It worked; she saw out of the corner of her eye that the missus was taking off her shoes, and that she had started to pull down her skirt with difficulty. Encarni helped her to get her jacket off. The missus lay down on the bed and, with her last bit of strength, she pulled the sheet and blankets to cover herself up to the shoulders.

Now all she needed was the pail. Encarni dragged over the enamelled metal bucket with barely a sound and put it to one side of the bed's headboard.

27

She was awakened by the carousel that turned squeakily inside her head. Every turn was a stab of pain. Some furry animal had got inside her mouth. Her face felt rigid; surely some of the nerves that moved the muscles of her face were paralysed. The French call that feeling *gueule de bois*, wooden face. It was reassuring that there was a name for it. That had to mean it occurred frequently, that it wasn't a singular case of facial paralysis that had just struck her and that at some point it would pass.

Her stomach had turned into a mollusc that contracted at the mere recollection of the anise, like an oyster when you squeeze a few drops of lemon onto it. Why hadn't she been a little more careful with the drinking? It occurred to Beatriz that the mollusc would react with wild convulsions to the painkillers her head so urgently needed. The doctors of King Alfonso X 'the Learned' would have rubbed her forehead with one of the stones with curative powers that appear in his *Lapidary*. But in the thirteenth century they were unfamiliar with the anise hangover, of that she was sure. The best thing to do would be to start with water: clear, room-temperature water. Then some well chewed white bread, to form a cushiony layer on the walls of her poor stomach. Finally, soon, when it was feeling safe, the painkillers. In half an hour she would surely be feeling much better.

She sat on the bed. That wasn't a good idea. Her stomach showed its displeasure immediately with a heave. Luckily someone, maybe even she herself, Beatriz couldn't remember, had put a bucket beside the bed and she reached it in time. The bitter stench of vomit mixed with that of the anise. She could barely hold herself upright. If she let herself fall back into bed the situation was not going to improve in the slightest. She got up, wrapped herself in a robe and walked hesitantly towards the kitchen.

She opened the door. The music drilled into her head like a brace and bit. Encarni had the radio turned all the way up while she bustled about the kitchen, humming something through her teeth. Beatriz grabbed a jug and poured some water into a cup, before turning down the volume. Encarni indicated with a nod that she had seen her, but continued her litany. As she drank in short sips she understood what it was that Encarni was murmuring: the Lord's Prayer. When she got to 'for ever and ever. Amen', she started all over again.

It seemed that her stomach wasn't rejecting the water.

'What are you doing?' Encarni made it clear that she wasn't going to answer her yet and continued mumbling. 'Are you praying for my health? People will think I'm on my deathbed!'

Encarni started laughing, opened the door to a pantry, pulled out a bottle of powdered aspirin and put it on the table without interrupting her prayers.

When she reached the 'amen', she pulled the pan off the flame and put two eggs under the stream of cold water.

'They need three Our Fathers to be perfectly cooked, the whites hard, the yolks soft. That's how we always do it at home.'

Beatriz shot her a pathetic look and said in a pleading voice, 'I hope they're not for me.'

'Don't worry, ma'am.'

Beatriz sighed. It was the moment to move into phase two.

'Do we have any bread?'

'Just bought. Perfect for dipping.'

Beatriz shook her head. She chewed the bread at a rumi nant's pace, with her eyes closed so she wouldn't see Encarni drowning her slice in the yellow, perfectly cooked yolk.

Then she dared to embark on the riskiest part of her plan, though she started with just a teaspoon of powdered aspirin in a glass of water. She watched hopefully as the cottony clouds formed, beneficent clouds that would soon put an end to her suffering. As she was bringing the glass to her lips, the doorbell rang.

Encarni wiped her lips with a napkin and went to open it. Soon voices reached her in the kitchen; an argument.

'We made arrangements.'

'It's not possible. The missus isn't well.'

'Not well? Let me speak with her.'

'No, she is quite poorly.'

She got up – not without difficulty – and approached the door. On the threshold she saw her cousin dressed in a comfortable pleated skirt, a short-sleeved blouse, a jacket over her shoulders and a beige scarf on her head, all of which gave her the look of someone going on a trip, which couldn't be a good sign. Vaguely she began to recall some plans. Martorell. She had agreed to go there with her, and what's worse, she had promised to drive. And there she was. But honestly, she was ill. Well, she wasn't really ill. She was indisposed. Extremely indisposed. The mollusc moved again; the aspirin had just reached it. Beatriz ordered the mollusc to be still. Then she said to Encarni, 'Please, take our guest to the library. And make us two coffees.'

'Holy Mother of God! Coffee, for you?'

'Of course.' Beatriz tried to put as much dignity as she could into her voice. 'With milk and sugar.'

An offering for the mollusc. Which she hoped it would accept kindly.

She went to dress. Slowly, making sure to move her head as little as possible. Then she filled the sink with cold water and dunked her face for as long as she could hold her breath. She repeated it twice more until she felt that her facial muscles were obeying her again.

Fifteen minutes later, she was sitting in front of Ana in the library.

After a couple of sips of coffee, Ana asked her, 'When do you think we can leave?'

Even though she felt quite a bit better, thinking of the pot-holed road to Martorell made her feel dizzy.

'I don't think I can drive today.'

Ana was clearly disappointed.

'Oh! But I was counting on it.'

Beatriz closed her eyes.

'Really, I can't.'

Ana leaned towards her.

'This type of illness comes and goes. I'm sure the fresh air will do you good.'

Maybe. Why not try it? The day before the trip to Martorell had seemed attractive to her, promising. Today she saw it more as a crazy scheme dreamed up over drinks.

But why not give it a shot? She glanced around her: the shelves with their endless rows of books and their gaps. The collected past. Usually she loved bringing them back to life, but today she wasn't in the mood. She looked up at the stuccoed ceiling. The sky remained closed above her.

'Why not?' she said, to convince herself. 'Give me a few minutes to get ready.'

28

'Do you always drive this slowly?'

Beatriz didn't turn her head as she answered, 'Only when my head is about to explode, every pothole is a whiplash and the sun is my worst enemy. *Non aveva Febo ancora recato al mondo il dí.*'

'What?'

'Ottavio Rinuccini, *Lamento della ninfa.*'

They were passing through apple orchards. The trees were covered in flowers. Beatriz had the window open a little so that the cold air would reach her temples and forehead. Ana could imagine that, some time ago, this was where the chauffeur had sat. It was an old Hispano-Suiza, as black as a cockroach, which her cousin kept in a garage on Valencia Street. The caretaker had checked the tyres, put in some petrol and taken it out onto the street. They had gone through the city very slowly. Many pedestrians stopped to stare; it wasn't common to see a woman driving.

'When did you learn?'

'While I was in Buenos Aires.'

'Well, you didn't pick up Fangio's style,' joked Ana sarcastically.

'Whose?'

'The Argentinian who won the world motor-racing championship last year.'

'Don't know him.'

That wasn't surprising, given what she'd learned about her cousin.

A truck loaded with crates of vegetables passed them on the inside, riding up on the verge. The driver, a farmer with parchment-like, weather-beaten skin, pulled the cigarette from his mouth and shouted at them as he shook his arm violently out the window. 'Win your licence in a raffle, did you? This isn't a cart race!'

'Ignore him,' said Ana.

'I intend to. "Hearing, seeing and keeping quiet, were an aid, / in times when eyes, ears and tongue could be expressed, / and not seen as offending crimes and forbade."'

'Who is it this time?'

'Quevedo.'

'By the time we get to Martorell I'll have brushed up on all my university reading.'

Beatriz burst out laughing. The pain this caused made her wince.

'"Laughter makes me free, gives me wings. Takes away my loneliness, smashes my jail cell."'

'Another one?'

'Yes, I took the liberty of slightly changing some verses by Miguel Hernández. I doubt you read him at university. Not Hernández, who died in prison; not Lorca, nor Salinas, nor a number of others.'

Beatriz's face grew dark. They travelled several kilometres in silence until she asked, 'How do you picture the Knight of the Rose?'

'I don't know. Young, handsome.'

'What does handsome mean to you?'

Gregory Peck in *Duel in the Sun*, she would have said, but she didn't want to give such a trivial answer after her cousin's displays of erudition; she chose to change the subject.

'Do you have a map?'

'In the glove compartment.'

Ana opened it, and for the first time in her life recognised one that did justice to its name: inside there were three pairs of white cotton gloves. Each pair was joined at the palms, as if praying, and held together with a metal clothes peg.

'What's this?' she asked Beatriz.

'They're gloves.'

'I've guessed that much on my own. What do you use them for? They aren't for driving.'

'They are library gloves. I always carry them with me because in some libraries out in the provinces they aren't prepared for visits, and I don't want to touch the manuscripts with my hands.'

'So you don't dirty them.'

'So I don't dirty them.'

In all that time Beatriz hadn't turned her head towards her; that seemed to be the most difficult movement for her, and Ana took advantage of the fact to keep poking around. She found a small bottle of perfume, a comb, a compact and a map. As she pulled it out, a small flat packet wrapped in tissue paper came out with it.

'What's in here?'

She forced Beatriz to look.

'Spare stockings. Be careful that the wrapping doesn't come undone; I don't want them to run.'

Ana placed them carefully on the bed of white gloves as her cousin returned her eyes to the road ahead.

Ana spread the map across her knees. She couldn't help comparing her cheap wool stockings with Beatriz's very fine silk ones.

'At this speed it's unlikely we'll miss the turn-off.'

And so it was. They reached Martorell without incident, parked the car near the train station and sought out the post office.

When they got there they still didn't have any concrete plan.

'Observe,' said Ana. 'The first thing we have to do is observe.'

'Fine.'

'*The Manual of the Perfect Detective*,' she added, mimicking her cousin's tone when revealing poets' names.

'And what do we have to observe?'

'First, an overall inspection of the space, and then the staff and where the boxes are and who is in charge of them.'

Beatriz nodded.

'Then,' continued Ana, 'it would be best if we divided up the task: first one of us goes in alone, observes and then the other goes in and notices other details.'

Beatriz entered first. Ana waited for her, sitting on a bench in the sun. A few minutes later, her cousin came out of the post office.

'That's it?'

'There isn't much to see. Do you have any paper?'

Ana pulled a notebook and pencil out of her handbag. Beatriz took them and started to draw.

'This is the lobby. Here, to the right, there is a counter for parcels. A man of about forty is stationed there. I noticed he limps slightly with his right foot. Across from that there is another counter with a window where they do money orders; I saw a sixtysomething man with glasses there. To the left side of the office, in a hallway, are the PO boxes. There are twenty. At the end of the hallway, there is a small counter. The girl who works there seems to be the one in charge of the boxes. She is young, about your age, I'd say.'

For the first time Beatriz looked up from the paper with its neatly drawn sketch. She hadn't had to correct a single line.

The door to the post office opened and they saw a young woman come out. Beatriz elbowed Ana to get her to take a look at her.

'She's the one in charge of the post office boxes.'

She passed by without seeing them; her gaze was fixed on a man about her age who was leaning against a car, waiting for her. He wore a chauffeur's uniform, including a hat, which he removed when he saw her approaching. They kissed each other on the cheek, but the way they held hands gave them away.

'She only came out for a moment to meet her boyfriend,' said Ana.

'And without permission.'

The door to the post office opened again. A man emerged and, not caring that there were onlookers, shouted at the girl,

'Elena! Who do you think you are? Come on, inside, and enough carousing. That's for Sundays.'

The girl jumped and drew away from her boyfriend. She said something that Beatriz and Ana couldn't hear, turned and headed back to the post office. The man was waiting for her with the door open.

'He's the one in charge of money orders,' said Beatriz. 'He must be the boss.'

When the girl passed by again, Ana saw that she wore no stockings, that the lines travelling up the backs of her legs were drawn on. The girl entered the post office.

Ana had a brainwave. 'Beatriz, you have to give me your stockings.'

Her cousin looked at her, bewildered.

'We need something that we can offer her in exchange for information. Some stockings would be a good swap.'

'We'll have to go back to the car.'

'That would waste time. We could give her the ones you're wearing.'

'Used stockings?' She pulled a face.

'I don't think she'll mind. I wouldn't either. Do they have any runs?'

She examined her legs. Beatriz hid them beneath the bench.

'If you move like that, you'll end up breaking a stitch!'

'No, I'm not taking these ones off. Let's go and get the others.'

They returned to the car and fetched the stockings from the glove compartment.

'Are you sure they have no runs?' asked Ana.

'If you haven't made any.'

They returned to the post office. Ana entered the building with the little packet in her bag and went straight to the PO box counter. The girl's eyes were red; she had been crying. She still hiccuped a little as she spoke to her.

'How can I help you?'

She ignored the question and said quietly, 'What an ogre your boss is! All over nothing! And in front of everybody.'

The girl nodded with an afflicted expression. She was about to burst into tears again.

'You've no idea how much I can relate to that,' continued Ana. 'I'm in a similar situation.'

The girl's sorrow began to be tinged with curiosity.

Then she went into the most daring and perhaps the most contemptible part of her plan, a complex story of forbidden love worthy of a romance novel. A friendship via correspondence that had led to love. She added parental prohibition and the man's sudden silence.

'I'm afraid that my parents wrote to him and forbade him from writing to me any more. But if I knew the address that the post office box belongs to ...'

The girl understood. 'That is not allowed.'

'I know. But it's my only hope. There are things that are above the rules. If you can't understand that, I don't know who can.'

The girl hesitated.

'I also have a little thank-you gift for you.'

She drew the tissue paper packet out of her bag, opened it carefully and showed her the stockings. The girl's eyes sparkled. *She must*, thought Ana, *be imagining her boyfriend's response to seeing them on her.*

'Which box is it?'

'Number Thirteen.'

The girl's face showed a sudden sorrowful expression that Ana didn't know how to interpret. She left for a moment and returned with a little piece of paper on which she had written down the address.

'Thank you.'

Ana handed her the stockings. She took them, thanked her and looked at her again sadly. She didn't say goodbye; merely turned and went into the back room again. Ana supposed it was to examine her trophy in privacy.

29

'I can't see anyone. There's uncollected post behind the door.'

Ana stood up. She had been looking through the letter slot. To keep it from making a noise when it closed, she lowered it slowly with her index finger. Then, as if to make full use of the finger she had already extended, she rang the bell.

They waited a moment.

'The owner doesn't seem to be at home,' said Ana.

She covered her hand with her coat sleeve and turned the knob. Surprisingly, the door opened with a gentle creak. She turned towards Beatriz with triumphant eyes and disappeared into the house. Beatriz entered behind her, trying to stop her and to keep from stepping on the letters scattered across the floor.

'What are you doing?' she whispered. 'What are you going to do if the owner comes back and finds us in his house?'

'Talk to him.'

Ana knelt down, picked up one of the envelopes and showed it to her.

'And his name is Abel Mendoza, by the way.'

'Would you talk to someone who had entered your house like this?'

'I'll tell him I'm a journalist.'

'Would you talk to a journalist who had entered your house like this?'

Ana didn't reply.

'Hasn't it occurred to you that this man could be Mariona's killer?'

'I haven't stopped thinking about it since we discovered he existed, Beatriz.'

But she was already inside the house as she was saying these words.

'Well, since we're here, we can have a look around,' conceded Beatriz. They continued speaking in whispers.

They had to turn on the light because the interior was darkened both by blinds and by thick curtains that reached the floor. They were in a hallway that had two doors on the left and another two on the right. It smelled of damp, mould, closed rooms. Beatriz took the first door on the right.

'Don't take off your gloves,' Ana said.

She still wore her leather driving gloves, although they had parked the car a street away.

'I should wear some too. I should have grabbed a pair from the glove compartment.'

Beatriz opened her bag and took out some cotton gloves. She tossed them to Ana. 'I used them last week when I was in the manuscript section of the Library of Catalonia. See if they fit you.'

They flew towards Ana like a limp, rather awkward dove.

'You still call it the Library of Catalonia, too?'

'Of course.'

Fifteen minutes later they had covered all the rooms in the two-storey house. An old kitchen with a refrigerator even older than Beatriz's. The dining room furniture was worn but clean. The upholstery on the armchair in the small adjoining parlour was darned, and the china plates and the crockery were piled up neatly behind the glazed doors of a display cabinet.

On the first floor there was a study, also small, whose window opened on to the Llobregat River, which flowed by a few metres away. One of the walls was taken up by an enormous wardrobe, disproportionate and rather absurd in that room. The rest of the space was filled with a desk, dominated by an old typewriter, shelves of books and an office cabinet used to store files and folders.

'A good place to work,' she said, acknowledging the place's

tranquillity. "'What a restful life has he who flees the noise of the world!'"

'Fray Luis de León!' interrupted Ana. 'Am I right?'

Beatriz sat at the desk. On the polished wood surface, the rings from many cups of coffee and glasses of wine sketched a pattern whose only regularity was that it avoided the writing area. Yes, that was the desk he worked at. She opened one of the drawers. Inside they found perfectly organised piles of different types of paper, thick letter paper in various shades and also cheap writing paper. To the left of the desk there was a shelf with an old edition of the Royal Academy of Language's dictionary, countless anthologies of love poems and romantic novels by Carmen de Icaza, Concha Linares ... What does one write with a reference library like that? Obviously not a scholarly study on Spanish epic poetry.

She turned towards Ana.

'I think he writes his Knight of the Rose letters here.' She pointed out the bookshelf to her cousin. 'He has everything he needs to write love letters: dictionaries, and little books like *Your Social Correspondence* by Teodoro Inclán and *The Words of Lovers. Love Letters to Touch the Heart* by Angelines Peñarroya del Río and the *Outline of Spanish Grammar.*'

'In case his "beloved" minds errors.'

'Some literary models. Look, here is a complete edition of Bécquer's *Rhymes.*'

Beatriz got up from the desk, went over to the bookshelf and pulled out the volume.

'In case his memory fails him as he's writing and he forgets a verse. We don't all have your incredible memory.'

Again Ana leaned over the filing cabinet she'd been fiddling with for a little while. She had pulled out a hairpin and was trying to pick the lock.

'At last.'

She smiled victoriously. She went over to the bureau and lifted the rolltop cover; the wooden slats creaked a little, but it opened easily. Behind it were five neatly labelled folders. Ana grabbed the one whose spine read 'Pi–Su' and put it on the desk. Beatriz stood next to her as she opened it. Their eyes immediately fell on the archive page where it read 'Sobrerroca, Mariona. Barcelona.' Beside that, the address and a date. Inside the card file there were approximately twenty letters, some written on light violet paper; between them were very thin white sheets.

'Copies. Made with carbon paper.'

Ana went through the sheets.

'Here is their entire correspondence. It starts with the advertisement in *Mujer Actual*.'

She continued to page through.

'Look, here is where he does his accounting.'

His expenses and income were listed in two columns.

'Train to Barcelona. Two coffees and tea biscuits in the Mauri Bakery.'

'That was their first meeting, the one with the white standard.' Beatriz pointed to an entry that showed two coffees and two glasses of cognac at a place in Sants.

There were two more mentions of cafés; a meal in a restaurant. Then just train trips. Perhaps they were already meeting at Mariona's house. Or she had started to take care of all the expenses.

The column of earnings showed fewer figures, but much higher ones. A thousand pesetas to get him out of a financial jam. Twenty thousand pesetas, investment in a plot of land.

'I don't make that in two years,' said Ana.

'The last entry is on 20 April, a week before Mariona was killed.'

The 'Sobrerroca, Mariona' file was only one of the many that filled the filing cabinet. They didn't need to say out loud what that meant. Beatriz remembered Mariona Sobrerroca. The last image she had of her was the photo accompanying her obituary in *La Vanguardia*, a woman in her fifties, attractive, maybe a little plump. She had bought a lover, even though the payment was hidden beneath the euphemism of loans. It was one way to combat loneliness; there were worse ways.

Ana seemed more interested in the other aspect of the, what

should she call it? business? She showed her the previous page in the archive. 'Palau, Carlota' it read. The address was in Tarragona, the date two years earlier. There was also an advertisement and a lot of correspondence. At the end, the list of income and expenses.

Beatriz calculated the earnings.

'Nine thousand pesetas from Señora Palau.'

Ana checked the dates of the first and last letter.

'This relationship lasted at least a year. And here is the previous page.'

Another woman from Barcelona. The components were repeated: the advertisement, the correspondence, the chart of income and expenses. And, they saw, the dates partly overlapped with those of the woman in Tarragona.

'So he had two at once,' said Beatriz.

'At least. Now I understand why the girl at the PO box office looked at me with pity. She knew that Mendoza received letters from a lot of women.'

Ana pulled out another folder, the first one; she rested it on the cabinet and started to write down names and dates. Beatriz wanted to read the letters.

'To this one, Carlota Palau, he also signed himself The Knight of the Rose and Octavian.'

She read the complete correspondence, the initial sounding out, the letters in which he set out the bait with which, evidently, he managed to reel her in and – the part that she was morbidly fascinated by – the skill with which he got rid of her.

'He gently snuffed out the flame. In one letter he claims he can't live without her and she, of course, is flattered. But then come the direct demands. He wants them to live together, to make their love public; he wants to meet her family, her friends, he wants to go to Mass with her on Sundays.' Beatriz can't hold back a giggle. 'Too much for poor Carlota.'

'You don't think he said it seriously?'

'No, not at all. If you look at the evolution of the correspondence and you compare it to the income chart, you can see that there is a certain correlation between the passion and the sums of money.'

Ana left the filing cabinet for a moment and went over to the desk to see what Beatriz was showing her.

'Imagine if Carlota Palau had said yes.'

'I don't have that much imagination, a middle-class lady from the provinces marrying a young arriviste. It wouldn't even work in a novel.'

'And Mariona? What point was the relationship at?'

'Judging by the letters, a crucial one.'

Beatriz went back to the correspondence; Ana, to another of the files.

Mendoza had cut out the ad that had brought them into contact and had glued it to a thick piece of paper along with its publication date. So he kept a meticulous record of everything he was doing; if he maintained several relationships simultaneously, he needed to do that in order to avoid mistakes. After the advert followed Mariona's letter, very contained, feeling out the situation. The Knight of the Rose had responded with identical caution. He told her that he was looking for a cultured woman with experience of life. He gave the impression that he didn't have much interest in young girls. 'Butterflies that flutter in the sunlight, fleeting beauties, nothing more.' Mariona had agreed to meet up, and she had suggested wearing a white silk scarf around her neck so he could recognise her.

Beatriz was pleased with herself. She had been right. She didn't read Mendoza's other letters; they were carbon copies of the ones Ana had showed her. She was interested in Mariona's replies. She was clearly the one setting the pace and determining how far to take the frivolous allusions. If he were Hansel, she wrote in one of her letters, the only thing she wanted was to lick his lollipop. Beatriz already knew his response; his only desire was to lose himself in Little Red Riding Hood's forest. Beatriz blushed with embarrassment over such direct and pitiful metaphors.

Fortunately Ana wanted to show her something. She went to stand beside her.

'Look. It's a reply to the same advert. And here, too.'

The correspondence that Mendoza had maintained with those other two women who had responded to the advert in *Mujer Actual* was relatively brief. In one of the letters they saw that he had noted in pencil 'Not worth the trouble'. In another he put 'Distrusting nature. Too much work'. The last letters before the next woman arrived were of farewell. The content was the same in both cases: the Knight of the Rose explained to them that he had to go to Argentina. The tone was adapted to the recipient. Sentimental and stuffed with romantic verses for one. For the other he had mostly used Quevedo and Lope de Vega to lament life's ups and downs. Beatriz couldn't help but be reminded of a fellow student at university who had been purged by the Regime and now made a living writing romance novels. He had chosen the wrong type of text; writing love letters was much more profitable. She put the letters to one side and looked out of the window. The view wasn't bad: a garden surrounded by a low wall and behind that, the river. On the other side, fields that were beginning to burst into life. If the study were hers, she would have put the desk right in front of the window.

Ana's voice brought her back to reality; they were intruders in someone else's home. 'We should leave. We've been here for a long time.'

'Really! You don't say.'

Beatriz grabbed one of the files. The material was fascinating; she wanted to read more. 'We can borrow this, can't we? I suppose this must be very interesting to a journalist.'

'What are you saying? That would be concealing evidence.'

'At this point they aren't evidence of anything.'

'They're evidence. Leave them where they are.'

Beatriz didn't let go. Ana went on, 'I don't know what Castro would do to me if he found out that I'd taken something from the house.'

Of course. She would have to tell the police about her discovery. She put the folder back in its place, along with the others, and they closed the cabinet.

They went downstairs. As they were opening the door to leave, a voice came from the other side of it.

'Abel? Señor Abel, are you at home?'

It was too late for Ana to stop mid-motion; she opened the door and found that the voice belonged to a woman in her thirties. It was obvious that she had come running – her wide skirt was still swaying and a lock of hair had slipped out of the white ribbon she wore around her head.

Ana, with Beatriz standing behind her, replied, 'No, he's not at home.'

Several different expressions crossed the woman's face: disappointment, confusion and curiosity.

'Who are you? I haven't seen you around here before.'

'Relatives. We're his cousins.' Ana smiled. 'And may I ask who you are?' The woman smoothed her skirt.

'Montserrat Rius, I live over the road. Sometimes I take in parcels that come for Señor Abel. But I haven't seen him for a few days, and I was surprised because he usually lets me know so I can watch for the postman. And when I saw you ...'

Beatriz held back a smile. The neighbour was obviously fishing to find out more about these women who were visiting Abel Mendoza. She gave them an apologetic smile.

'And, tell me, how did you get into the house?'

'With this key.' Beatriz turned the key in the lock, pulled it out and displayed it in the air for a moment before dropping it into her handbag.

Three deep wrinkles appeared on Montserrat Rius's forehead.

'That's odd. Señor Mendoza never gives out his key. Not even to me. When he leaves the house, he leaves everything well locked up, the blinds lowered, the shutters closed. He doesn't even let me go in, and we've been neighbours for ever.'

Beatriz smiled with extreme friendliness. 'But we are family.'

She had just found the key hanging from a small hook behind the door. She couldn't imagine what it was doing there, but that was the least of her concerns; it had got them out of a real fix.

Ana addressed the neighbour again, 'Goodness. What a shame cousin Abel isn't here! We were passing through, and hoped to find him at home. You don't have any idea where he could be, do you?'

'No, but it's not the first time he's gone away for a few days.'

She gave them a brief stare before saying goodbye and starting back to her house.

Ana followed her with her eyes as she headed off. Beatriz took her by the arm. 'We'd better leave. I don't think she believed us. If we're not careful, she might even call the police.'

As they went to the car, she took a last glance at the house. Something on the first floor had made her feel uncomfortable, something strange. She mentioned it to Ana as they got into the car.

'It must have been nerves,' her cousin replied. 'You don't uncover something like this every day, do you?'

It was true. Although, given the choice, she would rather be unearthing the animal symbolism in *The Book of Good Love*.

30

They were barely out of Martorell when it started to rain hard.

Beatriz had driven with exasperating slowness on the way there because of her hangover, and now she did so because of the poor visibility.

'You have to drive according to the weather conditions,' she justified herself to her cousin.

And according to your age, Ana was about to add spitefully, but she held her tongue. She was aware that her irritation was due to nerves. They had made a real discovery, and she was dying to shout it from the rooftops; she was euphoric. Beatriz took it upon herself to burst her bubble: 'How sad!'

'Why?'

'All those letters from abandoned women.'

'True,' she said, hoping to nip the subject in the bud. Too late. Many of the abandoned women had responded to his ending things in letters. Letters that oozed desperation, regardless of the tone they adopted, from the proud spite of 'it's your loss' to the absolute humiliation of 'I'm willing to do anything for you. Just ask and I'll do it'. There were threats, pleas, offers. All of them from lonely women who now felt twice as alone after being duped by that Don Juan.

'Fear of being alone makes us easy targets,' Ana murmured. She caught a painful wince on Beatriz's profile when she added, 'It seems we aren't meant to be alone.'

'Or we haven't been taught how,' responded her cousin, putting her foot down for the first time during the drive, as if she felt a pressing need to reach Barcelona. 'But everything can be learned. Trust me.'

She was talking about herself, thought Ana. It was the first time Beatriz had done that. Ana didn't ask any questions, although she wondered what scab she had unintentionally scratched.

After a few minutes of silence, Beatriz said, 'He must be really heartless. When he couldn't get any more dough out of them, he would leave them or get them to end the relationship themselves.'

'What was different about Mariona Sobrerroca?'

Beatriz immediately understood. 'Do you think he killed her? Really?'

'Doesn't it seem probable to you?'

'It seems absurd to me, Ana. It's killing the goose that lays the golden eggs. It's stupid. And the man may be many things: unscrupulous, contemptible, cruel . . . '

'Beatriz, you sound like a thesaurus.'

' . . . but he's not stupid. Someone capable of deceiving so many women and adopting different personalities, simultaneously even . . . You shouldn't think that these women were stupid, either. We aren't talking about naive teenagers, Ana, but grown women, with experience, who surely had some good times with him.'

'I didn't take you for such a liberal, Beatriz.'

'Is that a criticism?'

'No, no.'

They were skating on thin ice. Better get back to the case.

'This Mendoza is someone who is always putting on and taking off masks, with the constant threat of being discovered. He's someone who could one day lose control. Perhaps he turned up without having studied his role thoroughly enough and Mariona found him out. How would you react if you found out you were the victim of such a humiliating scam?'

'I would report him. Despite the shame of airing the story, I would shop him, no doubt about it.'

'You see? Can't you imagine the scene she would make,

insulting him, telling him she was going to call the police? Then he lost his cool and killed her.'

'Possibly. There was a fight, no doubt about that.'

'And then he strangled her.'

Beatriz didn't answer. In profile her expression was one of extreme concentration, her brow furrowed, her lips tight. After a long silence and without turning, she said, 'But imagine if he had come home while we were in his house? What would he have done to us? From the looks of it, he's a murderer.'

'We don't know that. I was speculating, Beatriz.'

'Perhaps. But still, I think you've got me into something that is even uglier than I thought.'

'I got you into? Except for your hangover this morning, I have the feeling you did it willingly.'

Beatriz let out a weary sigh before answering, 'You're right, but I think this is where I bow out.'

For a few miles all that could be heard was the tapping of raindrops on the car roof. As they were waiting at the gate of a level crossing, Beatriz searched for something in her handbag. She took out her cigarette holder.

'Mind if I smoke?'

Ana shook her head. 'Did you learn that in Argentina, too?'

'No. Just the holder.'

The gate started to rise. Since there were no cars behind, Beatriz lit her cigarette unhurriedly. Then she pulled away.

'Can I ask you something, Ana? Why do you want to be a crime reporter?'

'I don't want to be a crime reporter, I want to be a reporter of serious news. I'm sick of fashion and society.'

'But isn't it a huge leap from parties to such gruesome subjects?'

'They are two sides of the same coin,' she started to say.

Beatriz gave her a look of admiration that she found so flattering she was almost tempted to conceal her real reasons. But, checking in briefly with her conscience, she was forced to admit, 'I'm writing about this case because it's the one they assigned me. I'm not fooling myself. I know that I have my name to thank for being able to work and that, on the other hand, because of my name, there are stories that will remain out of my reach, just as there are others they won't let me near because I'm a woman. So, when the chance to write about something important came up, I jumped at it.'

Beatriz nodded in approval as she brought the cigarette holder to her lips.

Ana kept only one motive hidden: her growing fascination for this kind of thing.

The rest of the trip passed in silence, and soon they were back in Barcelona.

'Where should I drop you?' Beatriz asked Ana.

Beatriz had to be tired. Ana was, too: the lack of sleep, the trip, everything they had discovered was enough for one day. She imagined Beatriz would put the car back in the garage, take the lift up to her flat and find dinner prepared, but Ana still had an unpleasant formality to deal with. Because she wasn't kidding herself – she knew Castro wouldn't be pleased with what they had done. Her tiredness had given her the clarity she had lacked in the last few days. Her actions had been a mistake. Suddenly she saw herself and Beatriz like two amateur detectives in a British popular novel. They were amateurs, but instead of the Sussex countryside, they were nosing around Martorell, and the policeman they had to report their findings to wasn't a rather grumpy but essentially friendly inspector. He was a detective in Barcelona's Criminal Investigation Brigade; he didn't wear a tweed suit or smoke a pipe and he certainly wasn't friendly.

She asked Beatriz to drop her off at the Plaza Universidad. Her cousin, stricken by her own tiredness, didn't notice Ana's sudden low spirits; nor did she insist on taking her along the Ronda to her door. She was in a rush to get to her own house.

'Come on, now go and sleep it off.'

The awkwardness of Ana's words of farewell as she climbed out of the car was further evidence of her growing anxiety.

She walked towards Riera Alta Street, pondering what her opening gambit might be. She'd work the rest out later, but what she needed were a few phrases to get started, and she was struggling to find them. She prayed her only instrument – her tongue – wouldn't leave her in the lurch.

She couldn't make the call from her house. She didn't want to be spied on by Señora Sauret. She needed a more discreet place to call from. She went into several cafés pretending to be looking for someone until she found a place where the telephone was in a booth. She asked for permission; the waiter set the meter to zero and gave her a line. She dialled Castro's number. No answer. Maybe he had already gone home, she thought with relief after the sixth ring, but then someone picked up at the other end.

'Hello?'

She recognised him, but she bought a little time by asking, in a tremulous voice, 'Inspector Castro?'

'Yes. Who is this?'

'Ana Martí.'

No reaction at the other end. No greeting, no snort of irritation.

Castro sensed something. Or was she only imagining it, out of a bad conscience?

'Speak.'

Yes, he had sensed something. In his case, 'speak' wasn't an invitation; it assumed that she would tell him what she had to tell him. So it was best to get on with it.

'I'm calling because I wanted to give you some information that might be useful in the Sobrerroca case.'

'Very well. What is the information and where did you get it from?'

'I discovered that Mariona Sobrerroca was corresponding with, and was almost definitely in a romantic relationship with, a man named Abel Mendoza, of Martorell. They met through an advertisement in the magazine *Mujer Actual*. In my opinion, this man could be a suspect in her murder.'

'How did you find this out?'

She told him that she had had the clue from the letters she'd copied in his office, explaining how she had found out where

202

the advert came from and how she had obtained the address in Martorell.

She wasn't expecting applause, but the silence that followed her explanation was ominous.

'Did you touch anything in this Mendoza's house?'

'I read some of the letters. That's how I know how his scam worked.'

Silence again. She knew that Castro could tell she was hiding something, but she didn't want to implicate Beatriz. She had been careful not to let a single 'we' slip out during their exchange; she had to resist that distrusting silence at the other end of the telephone.

'You aren't keeping anything from me?' enquired Castro.

'No.'

She didn't say anything more. She didn't fall into the trap of trying to underpin her denial with more words, like every typical liar.

'We'll see. Tomorrow I'll see you at the station at ten. Then you'll tell me the whole thing again.'

He hung up.

Castro hadn't raised his voice once in the entire conversation. Ana would have preferred it if he had. She was exhausted. Her feet dragged heavily, the walk home seemed never-ending. She opened the door and walked right past the postboxes. She still had four flights to climb.

31

That night Ana didn't have nightmares because she could barely sleep. *Tomorrow I'll see you at the station at ten. Then you'll tell me the whole thing again.*

She woke up with those words echoing in her mind and, as she made coffee, she repeated them out loud, trying to imitate Castro's tone.

'Tomorrow I'll see you at the station at ten. Then you'll tell me the whole thing again.'

She finally got Castro's tone, and all of a sudden felt intimidated. She would tell it all to him again and then she'd see what happened. At the very least he would get angry. That she thought she could take. But he could also throw her off the case, and she wouldn't be able to object and say she had given him information, the generous exchange that Beatriz had mentioned at Pastís. What nonsense! She imagined the inspector's dry laugh if she dared to raise the notion, and she was ashamed at the ridiculousness of the thought that she, Ana Martí, a novice journalist, could negotiate with that volatile man.

She drank another cup of coffee, trying to think of the person she wished she had sitting across the kitchen table from her right then. Gabriel, no: he had his own worries. She couldn't go to her father either. Only bring successes home, that was her motto. She'd rather not make Beatriz nervous. She was hoping she hadn't got her into any trouble. Besides, she didn't need any poems that morning, just moral support.

Sanvisens, she would talk to Sanvisens. She finished off her coffee.

It was eight in the morning. Sanvisens would already be at the office. She had time to talk to him before she went to the station.

The day was going to be sunny; the morning fog beat a retreat, not without leaving a souvenir of its visit in the humidity that impregnated the air. She wrapped a jacket around herself. She noticed she was the only person taking her time amid the flow of people that passed her on the pavement. Heavy legs, sombre faces, occasional voices. A porter pushing a metal cart loaded with boxes of vegetables said as he passed her, 'Reciting the rosary at this hour? I'll slip you something you can worship.'

Ana hadn't realised that she'd been repeating the policeman's words in a low voice. She sent the porter to hell, but he didn't mind much; he was already several metres past her, swerving obstacles. When she stepped into the newspaper office she heard a familiar but unexpected, voice, 'A rookie! A girl!'

Her heart skipped a beat. Belda was there. She suddenly remembered that Sanvisens had told her last week, but at the time she'd been so excited about her plan that her boss's words reached her now like a lost letter finally arriving at its destination.

She stepped back, out of view of the two men. They hadn't noticed her presence. Even though the scene seemed absurd, like something out of a bad spy movie, she stayed glued to the doorframe to eavesdrop on their argument. She sensed that what would come next was going to hurt her and yet she didn't want to miss a single word.

Carlos Belda was beside himself.

'This is unheard of! It's as if, instead of being off sick for a week, one day I've woken up a hundred years later, like Sleeping Beauty. A rookie! A girl!'

'I know, and you don't have to shout,' replied Mateo Sanvisens.

'It's the case of the year. You could at least have given it to Roig.'

Tomás Roig would have passed it straight to Belda as soon as he asked. Not only because he was on the staff, but because on more than one occasion they had saved each other's arses. Carlos had written Tomás's articles when his wife had died and he had spent several days out of the loop. Everyone knew that Tomás – who was more fond of the Regime – was his first censor; his red marks had spared Belda more than a few problems. 'YRY' Tomás would write when Belda didn't manage to hide his pro-Catalan ideas, an abbreviation for 'You're revealing yourself'.

'Why *didn't* you give it to Roig?'

'Can you imagine Roig moving in those circles?'

Since he had become a widower, Roig's natural slovenliness knew no bounds. Sanvisens had asked him at least to come to work in a suit, and he did. A suit that gradually became covered in stains, until Carlos would have pity on him and take him by the arm after work and say, 'Today, Tomás, time for a touch-up.'

This little alliteration meant that they were going to a small dry cleaner's in the Barrio Chino, on Unión Street, which shared its back courtyard with a brothel. While the dry cleaner took care of his suit, they would spend several hours in the adjoining establishment. Tomás Roig left with a clean, ironed suit and a soiled conscience.

'All right,' conceded Belda, 'Roig isn't the best choice, but that novice? Who does she think she is?'

Sanvisens gave him an answer: 'She's doing a good job. And the police have accepted her readily.'

'Who's in charge of the case?'

'Castro.'

'Castro? Castro is mine!'

'Calm down, Carlos.'

'For God's sake, Mateo. I'm out for a week, and you replace me with the first person you bump into.'

'Don't be so unreasonable.'

But Carlos was too furious, and the Sobrerroca case was too alluring, so he kept at it. 'If she wasn't his daughter, would you have given it to her? Ever since she showed up one fine day, you started giving her little jobs. She writes well, I'll give her that, but there are a lot of people who write well and they don't all get to work at *La Vanguardia*. She's freelance, OK, but if we're not careful, soon she'll be asking for her own desk and then a contract. Will you give it to her?'

Sanvisens turned his back as he said, 'Carlitos, don't push me. We'll talk later.'

'Yes, we will. This subject's not closed.'

Ana hadn't been wrong: eavesdropping on that conversation did hurt. Carlos Belda's words stung. Those belittling adjectives held such power over her! And the accusation of favouritism hurt her even more. Even though Sanvisens had dismissed it.

She still had more than an hour before her meeting with Castro. That must be how the defeated feel on their way to sign the surrender agreement. What do you do with the hours, the days, between being declared a loser and when the document is signed and sealed? How do you kill that time? Now she knew: reviewing all your mistakes, one after the other, time and time again.

She entered the station on the dot of ten and asked for Castro.

'He's not here. He had to go out on urgent business. He'll be back later.'

32

Isidro Castro loathed ambiguity, especially when it affected his judgement. Ana Martí's call had disconcerted him. On the one hand, it made him angry, no, furious that she had dared to investigate on her own; on the other, he had to concede that, if what she had told him was true, it radically shifted the course of the investigation. It wasn't, as they had supposed, a break-in, at least not in the first place, but rather a scam artist specialising in wealthy widows. Not a negligible discovery in the least. And he owed it to her. So instead of calling her in immediately, he chose to see her the next morning. Besides, he was exhausted; as on every day recently, he had spent more than twelve hours working and he wanted to have dinner at home. Even so, before leaving he had sent two officers to keep watch on Mendoza's residence in Martorell.

Once he got home, he regretted not having spoken with her earlier, because he couldn't get what she had told him out of his head. His dilemma could be summed up in two alternating phrases: 'Who does she think she is?' and 'Boy, is she clever!' He only thought them though. He never spoke to Araceli about work. Really, he didn't talk about much at all with her; she, on the other hand, talked a lot. That was fine; it distracted and relaxed him. His wife's life was tinged with a sedating grey, her daily triumphs and defeats were so innocuous that he thought of her life as ideal, the closest to a state of peace that he could possibly imagine. Araceli's words and the children's stories over dinner distracted him from his dilemma over Ana Martí. Daniel barely coughed.

Before going to bed, they listened to the comedy programme on the radio. Araceli enjoyed Mary Santpere's humour. Isidro closed his eyes and listened to the comedienne's voice and his wife's laughter as if they were both coming out of the device that presided over the parlour from the sideboard. He forgot about the case during that time, but when he put his head down on the pillow his thoughts returned to his conversation with the journalist. Who did she think she was? His body tensed up and he clenched his fists.

'Is something wrong, Isidro?' his wife asked him.

'Nothing, just a cramp. Sleep, sleep.'

He heard a giggle from the children's room.

'Boys! If I have to get up, you'll be sorry. Come on, put down the comics!' he shouted at them.

Reading past their bedtime again. Those boys were clever. Like Ana Martí.

The next morning, while he shaved, he thought of the call once again. At that point in the day, he was more grumpy than anything else, and that gave him the solution to his dilemma: he would thank Ana Martí for her help and then he would put her in her place. Who did she think she was? First of all, and therein lay the root of this whole mess, she thought she was a journalist. A lady journalist. Absurd. Crime reporter. They should have left her in her society pages, talking about outfits and cocktails. As soon as she arrived, he was going to come down heavy on her. She was lucky he hadn't complained to the newspaper . . .

Shortly afterwards, he left the house and headed into the city. He lived in Collblanc, a neighbourhood in Hospitalet de Llobregat.

He jumped off the tram at the Plaza Universidad. He would walk the rest of the way. He took Pelayo Street. First he passed by a lingerie shop where it was rumoured there were trapdoors in some of the changing rooms, and they kidnapped the good-looking girls to sell them to harems; then he passed by the offices of *La Vanguardia*. Was Ana Martí already working? As soon as she showed up at his office he was going to give her a dressing-down she'd never forget. Then he would send her back to her newspaper. Definitively.

But as it turned out, the dressing-down would have to wait. When he reached the police headquarters, a colleague in the CIB came out to meet him.

'Isidro. Where have you been? They've found a dead body in the Llobregat.'

'So?'

'It's yours.'

'Mine? I've got another case.'

'Don't tell me that. Verdejo is in Saragossa, Prim is in court, Manzaneque I don't know about, and that's all Goyanes told me. So it's yours.'

'Where did they find the stiff?'

'On the edges of Prat del Llobregat. Near the railway bridge.'

A well-aimed stare saved Isidro from having to ask any more questions.

'A man, about thirty years old, fully dressed. The car's been waiting for you outside for half an hour.'

The car reeked of the driver's sweat and the aftershave lotion of the man who was already seated in the back. They crossed the city in silence, three men in an unmarked car. Even so, when they drove close to the pavement on the Paseo de Colón, past the main post office, he had noticed a few fearful looks of recognition. Maybe it was their faces, maybe it was the vehicle, maybe both. It didn't matter; the only thing that mattered was that their mere presence was intimidating.

'They're shitting themselves,' said Olivares, the driver, as if he had read his thoughts.

They reached the Prat. Curious onlookers were following the police progress around the corpse that lay on a piece of fabric spread out on the bank of the Llobregat River.

Some of the nosy parkers were crowded around the nearest end of the bridge and were watching the scene from there, ignoring the trains that passed behind their backs, making the entire structure vibrate. Some lads took advantage of their mothers' distraction to place coins on the tracks for the passing trains to flatten.

'Have you looked to see if he was carrying any ID?' Isidro asked the policemen who'd been keeping watch over the body since a fisherman had found it trapped in the reeds and informed the police.

'We haven't touched anything.'

'Well done.'

But this meant he had to do it. It really repulsed him to touch dead bodies that had been in the water. He had always avoided them, even in his village when the sea coughed up some drowned sailor's body. It was their scent, and the feel of their skin.

He knelt down and for a moment he thought he caught a whiff of saltpetre and putrefaction, but the body hadn't come out of the sea. It smelled only of decay. He brought his hand to it, opened the jacket and pulled out the wallet with his fingertips.

'Here.'

He passed it to one of the policemen, who understood that he had to examine the contents. As he dried his fingers on his mackintosh, Castro watched the officer who had taken the wallet without flinching now open it up and list everything he found: 'A five-peseta bill, a faded bus ticket. Look. He even had his ID on him.'

Castro grabbed it from his hands. The document was still wet, but the name was perfectly legible: Abel Mendoza.

He lifted his head and said, 'Mariona Sobrerroca's murderer.'

His colleagues gawped at him. Castro enjoyed the moment immensely.

33

It was four in the afternoon when Ana stepped inside Castro's office, the third time she'd called at the police headquarters. She had spent the day wandering the city.

The inspector received her in shirtsleeves behind a pile of folders. She recognised them. She knew the ones filling another table and piled up on two chairs; they were the files that she and Beatriz had seen in Mendoza's house in Martorell.

Castro had to beckon her in a second time because she was still in the doorway. She obeyed. The long wait and her two prior attempts to speak with him had chipped away at her. She felt fragile, porous, like a sand sculpture that would disintegrate as soon as Castro applied the slightest pressure. Sometimes waiting for a blow is as hard as receiving it, and she had spent so many hours speculating how and in what form it would be delivered that at first she was unable to understand what the inspector said to her.

'I have to congratulate you, Señorita Martí.'

'Well, I ... the truth is that ... '

'But, don't just stand there.'

Castro stood up and extended his hand to her. They shook hands firmly.

'Good job. You saved us many hours of investigation, and there are a few poor wretches who have you to thank for being released from a state-subsidised cell and bread and water rations.'

She responded to his congratulations with a disconcerted smile. She didn't understand what he was talking about.

'The case is solved.'

'What?'

'We know who killed Mariona Sobrerroca. Thanks to your discovery in Martorell, we know the relationship between the victim and the criminal and we can imagine the motives.'

'So, it was Abel Mendoza?'

'That's right.'

'The motives?'

'We suppose that, after striking up a friendship with Señora Sobrerroca and establishing an intimate relationship with her, he discovered that the victim had valuable objects in her home and tried to rob her. She surprised him in the act and then Mendoza killed her.'

The inspector responded easily this time, even though the question that followed his statement harboured some doubt.

'You suppose? What does he say?'

'Nothing. And he won't. This morning we found him dead in the Llobregat.'

The next remark came unprompted by a question.

'Suicide, by all indications. We don't yet have the autopsy results.'

'Then the case is definitively solved?'

'We're waiting on the autopsy, as I said, but the visual inspection points to suicide.'

'When can I ...?'

'The day after tomorrow. We don't want anything to come out in the press until we are sure. Then we will give you the pertinent information, although your colleague has already been by this morning to tell us that he is back on the job.'

'My colleague?'

'Carlos Belda. But don't worry, this case is yours. Obviously!'

Again Castro demonstrated what Ana had come to think of as his telepathic powers, saying, with his gaze distractedly in a file folder, 'I don't like Belda either, but I suppose my reasons are very different to yours.'

She didn't want to go into her reasons. Erasing Belda from her thoughts was starting to become common practice, and she found it most pleasurable.

As would be the conversation with Sanvisens, where she explained her role in solving the case, when she showed him that having given her the opportunity hadn't been a mistake. It had been a good move, and an act of justice. Not some sort of recompense, as Belda presumed, but professional justice.

34

Beatriz was aware of her own restlessness. There was something, she couldn't even call it a thought, more like a hunch, that stirred deep in her mind. Had she really been so deeply affected by what they had discovered in Martorell? Why hadn't she been able to get all of those women who had trusted Abel Mendoza out of her head, women he'd abandoned when he grew tired of them, or when they didn't give him enough money? She thought of Jakob.

One shouldn't be so stupid as to aspire to be happy with someone. Sharing nights talking in a bar in Madrid; drinking wine and discussing literature; plans for the future; trivial things, too. And then, intoxicated by shared affinities and timid touches, walking along the city streets to reach the small flat in Cuatro Caminos where she lived while she wrote her doctoral thesis under the guidance of the old master. One shouldn't give oneself over to such stories ... Only to end up even more alone later. When Jakob's scholarship ended, he returned to Frankfurt. They wrote to each other often. Once he visited her in Barcelona, shortly before the war. She showed him the city and even introduced him to her parents. Her mother tore her eyes away from the French novel she was reading for a moment and asked her, 'Are you going to get married?'

'Why?' she had responded in a tone that made it clear how absurd the idea seemed to her.

They were kindred spirits who didn't need papers.

Jakob went back to Germany, but shortly afterwards, he and his parents had to flee the country. He obtained a post as a professor of Spanish literature at the University of Edinburgh. At that point she no longer found the idea of getting married so absurd. Neither did he, from the looks of it, because he married a rich Scottish woman. He even sent her an invitation to the wedding. Now, every once in a while, he would send her his latest book, or the offprints of his publications. Depending on the mood she was in, she would either throw them out immediately or leave them in some corner where she couldn't see them.

No new Jakob would come. There had been the odd fling; a couple of times they had ended up in a discreet love hotel or in a motel room in one of the cities where she had attended conferences. She got up out of the chair in which she had been trying, in vain, to read and headed to her desk. The best thing would be to work a little.

She sat down and put on her glasses. A fellow student had sent her a doctoral thesis in which the author presented further arguments to pinpoint Gonzalo de Berceo's origins in La Rioja. Nothing new. She didn't want to admit it to herself, but at that moment she couldn't care less about the vicissitudes of an eighteenth-century cleric and poet and his Alexandrine verses. She shot a glance at the small pile of Abel Mendoza's letters. A melancholy look that turned playful as she wondered, why not try to work out where he was from? It would be funny if he were from La Rioja, too. Mendoza had to be a surname with Basque roots. She checked it in one of her books of heraldry. She was right: from Llodio, in Álava. It pleased her immensely to be right. A last name from Álava, but Abel Mendoza lived in Martorell, in the Baix Llobregat region. She would have to find out if he was Catalan or from somewhere else. Plunging into a fresh rereading of his letters, she found that they had completely lost their ability to make her sad. They were no longer fake love letters, they were first-hand linguistic material for reconstructing a story she was fascinated by. Her work in the field was beginning to bear fruit.

It was a shame that they were typed copies. Were they medieval manuscripts, she would analyse the way each letter was drawn and the colour and detail of the illumination, to be able to attribute them to a particular monastery or school of scribes. But she only had fourteen letters copied on an old police station typewriter that would soon need a ribbon change. They were all written correctly; there were no spelling mistakes, real or faked, as in the anonymous letter denouncing Pablo.

The subjects of the letters were all the same: his love and admiration for Mariona, quotes, allusions to their meetings and occasionally words of gratitude for the money she had 'loaned' him.

But something didn't fit.

She read the last letter again carefully. That was it. There was something in it that was off; something in the tone was different. But why? Then she hit upon the answer. The key was in the more neutral words, the ones that didn't transmit content: the adverbs, the conjunctions, the tag words that gave the letter its particular tonality. In the last one, the text was filled with connectors such as 'really', 'truly', 'somehow', 'in other words'. There was also the imperative 'look', three times. The other letters didn't contain any of those expressions.

In her head she heard the voice of the old master repeating, 'Check everything systematically. Science isn't based on impressions, but on facts.'

She sketched a chart on a sheet of paper and started to write down which words appeared in which letters. The results were surprising. In all of them except one she found elements of connection such as 'surely', 'finally', 'in any case'; in the last one, those elements had been replaced by others such as 'really', 'truly', 'somehow', 'in other words', more in keeping with a new eagerness to reinforce his argument than merely to present it. All the letters except the last one displayed complex, sometimes elaborate, syntax and the vocabulary was more sophisticated.

She took off her glasses.

The last letter must be by a different author. She had to let Ana know.

35

'No,' Ana refused fervently. 'It can't be.'

Beatriz sighed. For more than fifteen minutes Ana had been insisting that the case was solved. That Abel Mendoza had been Mariona's lover and her killer. That he had met Mariona through an advert, had extracted a lot of money from her and had finally strangled her, perhaps because she had discovered his dirty dealings or because he had tried to burgle her house and she had surprised him in the act. Afterwards, perhaps remorseful over his crime, he had thrown himself into the river. And thanks to her help, the inspector had solved the case.

Beatriz persisted. 'I am absolutely sure that the last letter was written by someone else.'

'And what does that matter?'

Ana frowned and let her head fall in a gesture that showed dismay and impatience in equal measure. Beatriz didn't allow herself to be deterred. 'Well, it matters quite a bit. There are two possibilities. The first is that Mendoza is the true killer, as you and your inspector affirm. Which, pardon my frankness, is very convenient, since Mendoza is dead. But the fact that the letters were written by two people shows that at least one other person knew about his relationship with Mariona, and that that person pretended to be him in order to make a date with her. The last few letters of their correspondence all have the same structure; they talk about how wonderful their last meeting was, and set up the next one. The killer copied the model, went to Mariona's house to rob her and killed her.'

'And Mendoza?'

'He committed suicide when he found himself without a source of income and the suspect in a murder investigation. Or the other guy killed him.'

'And how did your mysterious author gain access to the previous letters?'

Beatriz soon found herself replying.

'Perhaps it was someone close to the victim who found the letters. Her maid, for example.'

'Impossible!'

'How can you be so sure?'

'Don't forget that I was there when Castro interrogated her, that I was watching her face. She wasn't lying.'

'Some people are very cunning. She left, supposedly to visit family outside of Barcelona, so that she would have an alibi and the accomplice did the rest.'

'Not that woman. Besides, in that case there was no need for a letter. She could have told her accomplice when Mariona would be out. Actually, if the letter really is by someone else, it exonerates her even more.'

There was a tense silence. Beatriz looked out of the café window. It was getting busier out on the street. From here they could see the building that housed the offices of *La Vanguardia*, where she had gone to inform Ana of her discovery. She had found her in a large room where fifteen other people were banging on typewriters, talking on the telephone or yelling from desk to desk.

She turned to her cousin, who seemed to be examining her coffee cup very carefully. She ventured a joke.

'Are you expecting to read the right answer in the coffee grounds?'

Ana glared at her furiously.

'Beatriz, the matter is completely resolved. The only thing that doesn't fit is your theory about the two authors.'

'That's true. And since that theory is correct, the whole solution to the case collapses like a house of cards.'

'Not at all. It only shows that perhaps, *perhaps*, there was a third person who was aware of the situation. And not even that seems to be proven by your absurd little chart.'

Ana pointed to the paper that was still on the table, the chart where Beatriz had written down in detail all the stylistic deviations of the last letter, which had reminded her so much of the controversy over the possible double authorship of the medieval classic *La Celestina*.

'Maybe he was just having a bad day, and that's why he used other words.'

'No.'

'Or he was in a hurry and wasn't as careful in his composition.'

'No.'

'You're so stubborn!'

'Yes, because I'm right.' She paused briefly. She almost didn't dare to say what was going through her head, but she said it. 'Ana, I'll remind you that, without any sort of evidence, you were the one who was already thinking, on the way back from Martorell, that Mendoza had to be the killer. I'm afraid that your presumption influenced you. That type of procedure is not scientific.'

'We aren't dealing with science; this is a police investigation.'

'Shouldn't they go together, without prejudice or interest? That's how I've worked. I don't think anything has clouded my judgement.'

Ana scowled angrily.

'And you're saying mine is clouded?'

'Yes. If you write the article as you are planning to, your boss at the paper will be thrilled, Castro will want to work only with you and your career will take off. Don't you think that could cloud your vision?'

She had struggled to say it as gently as possible. Ana made as if to grab her jacket while gesturing to the waiter that she wanted to pay. Beatriz continued, 'I'm not saying that my theory explains what happened, I'm merely asking you to accept that there is reasonable doubt, there are loose ends, which means that . . . '

'That the case isn't solved, you don't have to repeat it. God! I'm not surprised no one can put up with you.'

Beatriz felt the violence of the jab, but she didn't want the rage that had dictated Ana's words to overcome her too. She resorted to one final argument.

'I'm talking about doubt, Ana. The mere suspicion that Mendoza wasn't the killer should be enough. Remember that you yourself told me, to convince me to help you, that we couldn't let Mariona Sobrerroca's killer go free and not receive the punishment he deserves.'

'The afternoon shift is about to start. I should be at my desk.'

Beatriz put her hand on Ana's arm and said, without raising her voice, 'I think you know that I'm right. Knowing something and not being able to say it is the norm in this country. But not wanting to know something, intentionally shutting your eyes because it doesn't suit you to say what you know, that's opportunism.'

Ana got up and put on her jacket. 'You don't know when to stop, do you?' She turned on her heel and left.

'See you soon.'

Beatriz wasn't sure that Ana had heard her; she went out of the café without looking back. From the window she saw her cross the street, but she wasn't heading towards *La Vanguardia*'s offices, rather to the Plaza Cataluña.

Beatriz bit her lip. Arrogance. Wanting always to be right was a form of arrogance. Her particular mortal sin. Ana had left furious, and didn't want to listen to her any more. Being right doesn't get you very far if no one will listen to you.

36

Ana crossed the Plaza Cataluña briskly. Even though she had to write the article, she also needed to walk a little to clear her head.

She was confused, and increasingly irate with Beatriz for having plunged her into this confusion. 'The seeds of doubt,' she formulated to herself. More than a seed, she corrected herself: her cousin's words had grown like the legendary magical beans. 'Very witty. And now what?'

You can't write an article when you're in a bad mood, or in a state of euphoria. That was a lesson from her father. She wandered up the Rambla de Cataluña. She noticed a man sitting on a bench reading *La Vanguardia* and soon she passed another who carried a copy folded under his arm. 'Tomorrow they'll be reading my article,' she thought proudly. Immediately she felt a blow to the stomach, as if she had swallowed a stone. She had doubts. Did she have doubts? She shook her head, but couldn't soothe the discomfort in her stomach.

She stopped short. What would those who bought her newspaper be reading tomorrow?

She felt a strange relief when she saw a third man, who was reading *El Noticiero Universal* and leaning on the doorframe of a barbershop. They wouldn't publish anything about the Sobrerroca case. Would that be better or worse?

She sat on a bench at the corner of Aragón Street.

She thought about going over to the Paseo de Gracia. Sometimes window shopping helped her think, but not today.

Looking at store windows is contemplating the imperfect past, in static displays. That wasn't what she needed just then. She needed movement, action, drama if possible.

Her feet led her to Caspe Street.

There was the Novedades jai alai court, which hid its splendour and beauty behind a modest facade. She was received by the doormen's discreet greetings, the arching motion of an usher indicating where she should sit and, already in the stands, the sound of the ball hitting the wall, the voices of the players and the audience, the shouts of the bookmakers. The bookmakers at Novedades were the most elegant in Barcelona, with their white jackets and red berets.

She sat down and followed the first match attentively.

By the second round, she already felt at home and accepted a spectator's bet.

'Two hundred to one hundred.'

For the blues. The runner threw her the ball and she caught it securely. She was proud of her reflexes, which allowed her to catch it with a single firm motion. There are things that, once you've learned them, you never forget. She had acquired that skill as a girl, going to the pelota court with her father and her brother Ángel on Sunday mornings. She had been fascinated by the names there, which sounded like dynasties: Artamendi II, Atano III, Urrutia, Olaizola. She had also learned all the rituals of the game and grown used to its sounds. Without looking, she could recognise the blunt thwack of a hand, the spongy, elastic blow to the basket, the dull thud of the bats.

That had been before the war.

Afterwards, her father never set foot on a jai alai court and Ángel never returned to Barcelona. She went back to Novedades shortly after they were notified of his execution by firing squad. She would sit in the stands and describe the game to her brother, as he used to explain the rules to her when she was little. Soon it would be nine years since his death. In a few years she would be the same age Ángel was when they killed him, twenty-seven. But she hadn't gone there to think about him. She focused on the game.

The blues finally lost, even though they had been making a good comeback.

She could quit and simply watch the next match, or play a little more of the money her father had sent her.

The next match was about to begin.

A murmur of admiration ran through the stands. It was the debut of a young player, sixteen years old, on the red team. Someone beside her said, 'They say he is the reincarnation of Erdotza.'

Erdotza, the best player ever, capable of beating two opponents alone, had died on that court. In 1942, ten years earlier, he threw himself to the floor for a drop shot. He managed to return it, won the point and then died right there from a heart attack. A legendary play. But his reincarnation . . . What rubbish!

In an appeal to reason versus rubbish, she bet against the reds.

She won. She took it as a sign. She was aware of the irony that her conclusion was as irrational as the image of the player's spirit searching for someone to reincarnate into on the jai alai court. But she was grateful to have been able to clarify her thoughts.

She walked back to her house. She already knew what she was going to do. She would write the article with the official version of the case's resolution, but measuring her words, so that, as Beatriz had done, an attentive reader could harbour some doubts about whether the case really was closed.

She didn't think of herself as superstitious, but, just in case, she gave thanks to Erdotza's spirit.

37

Joaquín Grau didn't ever openly admit it, but he liked what he saw when he looked in the mirror. The silver shine at his temples, far from ageing him, made him look dignified. He turned his head slightly; he had a large, aquiline nose that gave him a regal air. He was also tall and svelte. He definitely had good presence, he confirmed with satisfaction.

Nothing like the squalid little boy who had once stubbornly sat with his homework at the kitchen table of the flat over the family's hardware shop in Gerona, his mother's voice repeating, 'Joaquín, make an effort. You have to make something of yourself in this life.' And he had made an effort, although not as much of one as he led her to believe, because his lessons came easily to him. A Jesuit took care of him, Grau supposed at the behest of his mother, who was always keenly devout. Father Leonardo got him a modest scholarship and a bookbag so he could study in Barcelona. Later, the war took care of paving the way for him.

He ran the comb through his hair once more and made sure that his suit jacket was well buttoned up. Then he closed the mirrored door to the wardrobe in his office. He was ready to start the day.

On his desk he found the morning editions. His secretary had left a copy of *La Vanguardia* opened to the page where the bold headline 'Mariona Sobrerroca Murder Solved' immediately caught his eye. He extended his arm to grab the paper but the ringing of the telephone shifted his motion towards the receiver.

'Good job. Very good job.'

Fernando Sánchez-Herranz imbued his voice with a laboured seriousness. Grau knew that Fernando did it to try to compensate for his round fleshy face and droopy cheeks, which gave the impression of a lack of character.

'The Civil Governor is very satisfied with the work done by the police and the public prosecutor's office, and asked me to convey his congratulations.'

He had taken note of his achievements in the matter. Good. On the one hand. On the other, the Civil Governor could have called him personally instead of delegating the task to his personal secretary.

'Thank you.'

His gratitude had come out sounding somewhat cool, since Fernando said, 'Really, Joaquín. Acedo is most satisfied. The police did an exemplary job. They are even more effective since I sent Goyanes from Social to the CIB. With this success we can show up all those who say that our country is backward and our police force is brutal. And I think much of the credit is yours.'

Grau was astounded. Praise came from above. Bestowing praise was a privilege that *he* had enjoyed in relation to Fernando, for over a decade. He had praised him, criticised him and advised him. He had supported him and got him the post he now held as secretary to the Civil Governor. And now Fernando was the one praising him.

Fernando continued speaking. 'We are very proud of you.'

We. Us. The Civil Governor and I. Grau noticed how the rage began to rise up his neck, a tide of lava, of burning red fury. Over his forty-four years he'd learned to control it, to channel it in the right direction. That was how he knew that this was a moment when he had to keep it contained. He changed the subject.

'How are things going for you in the Civil Government?'

'Well. A lot to do. A lot of responsibility. These are complicated times.'

It was true. The new government named by Franco had

227

produced seismic shifts in the Regime, and it remained to be seen how far the shock waves would reach.

Fernando's tone grew confidential.

'This damn city needs an iron hand. A hand that inspires fear, so much so that no one will dare to pursue their subversive impulses. The fact that, with the Eucharistic Congress, the eyes of the world are now fixed on us doesn't make it any easier. It's our international endorsement. The world can't keep on ignoring us.'

It irritated him no end that Fernando thought it was necessary to give these explanations, but he held his tongue.

At some point, Fernando's voice had lost all trace of energy; it sounded gentle and trusting when he said, 'I've thought of you often in these last few weeks, of your advice, your support.'

Had he remembered that the person he was talking to was his mentor, his promoter? Or was he trying to manipulate him with strategies learned at the private school his well-to-do family had sent him to in Ávila? Perhaps Fernando had forgotten that he too had studied with the Jesuits.

Grau's rage had faded to anger. He responded in a friendly but distant way. After the obligatory courteous exchanges, he hung up the phone.

The article in *La Vanguardia* didn't improve his mood. That Ana Martí had words of praise for the police, and named him and Castro several times. Yet he still didn't like it.

It had been decided – the impersonal wording didn't hide the fact that he was the one who had made the decision – that the Sobrerroca case would be dealt with delicately. He could have taken advantage of the situation to throw a negative light on part of the city's bourgeoisie, but it wasn't in his best interests to fall out with people he might need. The iron hand that Fernando had been going on and on about began in a smaller framework, more home-made, if you will, of daily policies. And the Sobrerroca affair was a perfect example. How should the relationship between Señora Sobrerroca and this Mendoza chap be presented to the public? Some would portray it as fair punishment for the vices of the upper middle class. Barcelona: Gomorrah itself in the boxes at the Liceo, at the cocktail receptions, at the private parties, behind the velvet drapes of its mansions. This was true, in part; but telling the truth at all costs wasn't always the smartest option. Señora Sobrerroca had to be presented as the innocent victim of an unscrupulous criminal. Up to that point, everything was fine. The author had stuck to the guidelines. Why, then, had the text made him so uneasy?

He read it again and hit on the cause of his disquiet. The journalist presented the results of the police work with kid gloves. 'Inspector Castro made clear that the case was solved', 'The public prosecutor affirmed that ...', 'According to the investigation report, the killer was ...'

Grau had nothing against her quoting him, but here the results of the investigation and the resolution of the case were presented as something that the police and the prosecutor's office were announcing, as opposed to being facts. A version put forth by the police. That was what it was. Grau was sure now: the author was writing as if she herself wasn't entirely convinced by the investigation. It wasn't openly critical, but her desire to distance herself was evident.

Ana Martí.

Grau decided to make two phone calls. The first one, to Mateo Sanvisens.

The second call would be to an old friend in the Political-Social Brigade, to find out what he knew about this Ana Martí person.

38

The next article that Abel Mendoza read about the Sobrerroca case declared him dead. 'Abel Mendoza, the presumed murderer, committed suicide by throwing himself into the Llobregat River.' Well, well. From fugitive to corpse. Reading and rereading those lines he felt cold, with a terrible prickling at the back of his neck, and terribly hungry.

He went into a bar. He had got some money out of Mercedes, and he allowed himself another slice of potato omelette. It hadn't been cooked in good-quality oil, or even clean oil, but having been confronted by the news of your own death, being able to taste even something rancid is cause for celebration.

He needed a calm place to think. The brothel was still closed and Mercedes had kicked him out of bed because it was her time of the month and she wanted to be alone.

Fine. He couldn't think there anyway, not next to a woman who complained and sighed every time he shifted in bed and tried to ease her pain with absinthe. Abel was disgusted by the smell of absinthe; the taste repulsed him too, and after a bad night he had come to associate it with Mercedes's nausea and vomiting.

A police siren sounded in the distance, and made him think that the street wasn't a safe place for him. He couldn't go back to the brothel until nightfall and he couldn't go from bar to bar with the little cash he had on him. But he needed a place to take shelter, a place where he wouldn't be seen. A dark place.

A dark place in the middle of the day. Such as a cinema. The Argentina Theatre.

The ticket cost him three pesetas.

Once inside the cinema, he realised that he hadn't even looked at the posters to see what film was showing. It didn't seem to matter much to most of the other patrons either, he deduced from the deep breathing and snores he heard as he walked down the dark aisle. Many were, like him, simply looking for warmth and darkness.

He sat on the left side with his jacket folded over his legs. Then he glanced at the screen. In a tavern, Lola Flores was speaking, her deep black eyes opened very wide, to a group of avid listeners. 'Soon she'll start singing and dancing,' thought Abel. Waiting for the music to start, he didn't realise that a woman had approached him. He noticed her presence when he felt a hand on his thigh and the tinkling of her bracelets. A handjob harlot.

'No, thanks,' he said to her.

'Only two pesetas,' she replied, her hand creeping towards his fly. His jacket hid her movements.

'Thank you, I'm fine. What I want is to take a little nap.'

'I'll help you sleep better. That bloke up there is sleeping soundly after my services.'

'I appreciate it, sweetheart, but please, let me sleep.'

Abel pulled her hand from his crotch and gave the woman a kiss on the cheek. Now that his eyes had got used to the dark, he could see her face. She was about fifty years old and the half-century had dragged down her features. She smiled at him sadly.

'You're a sweetheart; good-looking too,' she replied with the shyness of a teenager. 'I'll make sure they let you sleep.'

She headed off as silently as she had come.

Lola Flores was finally about to sing 'La niña de la venta' up on a stage. Abel curled up in his seat and rearranged his jacket so that it covered him better. The newspaper rustled in his pocket, reminding him that the article in *La Vanguardia* had been written by a woman, somebody named Ana Martí. A woman, a journalist, not the police. As the flamenco hand-clapping began on the screen, he thought that anyone else in his situation would have rushed to call the newspaper to refute the news of his death. Several rows behind him, the whore's bracelets shook to the rhythm of the handclapping. The clapping accelerated and revealed the firm thighs of the dancer for a few seconds. The bracelets sped up as well. Lola tucked up her skirt and her foot-stamping increased its pace, as did the metallic tinkling of the bracelets. The scene ended with the stamp of Lola's heel, a moan from the man in the rows behind and Abel's sigh as he remembered that he was dead. Fine. It's good to be thought dead when you're hiding from the police. Actually it was better than fine, it was perfect for him to be able to do what he had planned. And then finally to be able to flee the country. But reading the news of his death had given him a superstitious fear that he couldn't shake off. It was like dreaming about his own funeral. Was it a sign? A warning? What had his brother told him that one time? That you can't witness your own death in dreams, that everybody wakes up before seeing themselves as a cadaver. Was it true? He didn't remember ever having seen himself dead in a dream; he hadn't ever dreamed of his burial either. That was the absurd romanticism of poems, of romantics like Bécquer and Espronceda. The kind of thing that poor Mariona was so fond of. And his poor brother.

Thinking about the two of them brought him back to reality, to the newspaper article.

What if he tried to talk to the author of the article? He could call her. And say what? She was a journalist; journalists are interested in information and he had plenty of that. He could give her some bits of information in exchange for her telling him what the police knew, something that would let him know how safe his position really was. Tit for tat.

What would he tell her? Most importantly, that he hadn't killed Mariona. Would she believe him?

And what if she turned him in? That was the risk, but he could hold out the bait that he had even more interesting information for her. Or maybe it would be better to use another tactic. One of the ones he used with the women. The women liked to protect him, even though they didn't really know what from. Maybe Ana Martí would want to protect him too. Ana Martí was her name. Where did he know that name from? Of course! Aneta Martí, the one who did those society write-ups that Mariona enjoyed so much. He would talk to her.

He suddenly felt he was being observed. He turned and saw the whore sitting at the end of the row looking at him, watching his profile. She gestured to him. Come on, come over. The night before, Mercedes hadn't let him touch her; she wasn't in the mood. The woman sat beside him, stuck her hand beneath his jacket and nimbly opened his fly. It was done properly, though he was disappointed by two things: her routine efficiency and the fact that she charged him. His handsome profile hadn't earned him a free handjob, not even a discount.

Didn't matter; at least it had relaxed him and he trusted that the darkness, the voices and the music from the film would help him to forget his situation for a while.

A few minutes later, in the left-hand block of seats of the Argentina Theatre, one more man was sleeping like a baby.

Before ringing the bell, Abel had checked his outfit one last time. He had undone one button on his shirt, just one, the way she liked it, and he had run a hand through his slicked-back hair.

'Like Valentino. No, better, like Ramón Novarro,' Mariona had once said to him before ruffling his hair with both hands.

'The way she liked it,' he repeated to himself, looking at his compressed reflection in the shining copper plaque that bore the name of Mariona's husband. *Dr Jerónimo Garmendia. General Medicine.* Dr Garmendia, physician to the best families in Barcelona, had died two years earlier, on Three Kings' Day in 1950, but the plaque remained there to remind anyone who wished to know that Mariona Sobrerroca was Garmendia's widow.

Abel always turned up well groomed, with his white shirt well ironed, his trousers impeccable with a perfect crease and his shoes shined by the expert hands of the bootblack in the Plaza Real, so that she could ruffle his hair, unbutton him and wrinkle his clothes.

He rang the bell and waited. Nothing. He rang again and put his ear to the door. He couldn't make out any footsteps or sounds. Although he wasn't wearing a watch, he was sure that it was the time they had agreed on. Mariona had left the wrought-iron gate open so she wouldn't have to go out to the street to receive him. He waited a few seconds and pressed the bell again as he knocked, as if the buzz he could hear perfectly as he held the black button down needed the reinforcement of percussion.

Again, silence.

He could think of only one explanation: she had fallen asleep in the garden. That had happened once before; she had been sitting in her double swing seat with the satin cushions beneath the pergola and within minutes he saw her nodding off, victim to drowsiness, in a languid pose she surely imagined was very romantic.

Abel smiled. Mariona was sometimes quite twee.

And when she slept, she slept soundly. So banging on the door wasn't going to do him any good; the only thing he'd achieve was to attract the attention of someone in the neighbouring houses.

He pricked up his ears to make sure that no one was approaching the house. Then he pulled out a picklock he carried in his jacket pocket and, since it wasn't locked with a key, he had the door open in less than a minute.

He headed towards the terrace with sure steps, convinced he would find her asleep in some ridiculous pose on the swing. She wasn't there; only the point lace cushions. One had fallen to the floor; he picked it up and tossed it back with the others. In case she was spying on him from the gallery, he corrected his gesture and plumped it up with feigned care. Then he turned with a smile. He was expecting Mariona's blonde head,

234

and he gave a slight start when he saw his own reflection in one of the panes of glass.

This must be a new game.

He started to move through the house with exaggerated slowness.

'Mariona, where are you?'

He repeated the question like children playing hide and seek, dragging out the 'o' of her name.

'Mariona, it'll do you no good, the wolf is going to find you and he's going to eat you up.'

He leapt into the bedroom. Empty. The bed was unmade, the coverlet hung crumpled over it, the mattress somewhat out of place. The doors to the wardrobe and drawers stood open. What had Mariona been doing?

He went into the dressing room. Empty. Clothes and shoes lay strewn over the floor. What ensemble had she chosen that day?

He went into the dining room. Also empty, like the maid's room – it was her day off – and like the parlour, which he gave just a quick glance, and like the kitchen. There was only one room left. Her husband's office. She kept it intact, like a sanctuary. Abel trembled with excitement as he opened the door.

'This is what you want today, you naughty girl?'

There lay Mariona. Pale, blonde, voluptuous . . . and dead.

Fortunately, he had found what Mariona had hidden and what the person who'd killed her had surely been searching for. Mariona had kept it very well concealed. Once it was in his possession, he hid it even better, using a technique his brother had learned from his comrades in the resistance.

That night, worn out from another day of erratic wandering, he took refuge in Mercedes's bedroom. While she slept, drunk on absinthe, Abel wrote two letters. One he sent to *La Vanguardia*, to the attention of Señora Ana Martí. The other he put into the inner pocket of his suit jacket. He would send it after he'd spoken with the journalist.

That was the most dangerous step. He was afraid. Over the

course of the day, the apprehension brought on by the news of his alleged death had become fear. Now he felt those words like a latent threat. *Abel Mendoza, presumed murderer, committed suicide by throwing himself into the Llobregat River.* An icy wave travelled up his spine, and he felt the cold, dark waters closing around his body. You can't dream of your own death, but you can imagine it as you lie trying to fall asleep. The body dragged downriver, battered by branches, nibbled by fish, wrapped in a cold blanket of water. He hugged Mercedes's feverish body to keep from drowning in that image, and submerged himself in sleep.

39

It was almost ten thirty when the telephone rang in Mateo Sanvisens's office.

'Hello, Mateo. It's Joaquín Grau.'

Sanvisens unconsciously pushed his back up against the chair, as if he were on a mountain climb and searching out a solid wall to protect him.

'Yes?'

'I just want to know one thing. What are you playing at, Mateo? What? Tell me.'

'I'm sorry, I don't understand what you're talking about.'

A moment of silence hung at the other end of the line, the kind you hear in the mountains before a dry crunch announces an avalanche. It wasn't a crunch, but rather a weary, irritated sigh that preceded Grau's words.

'Why is the article you published about the Sobrerroca case so lukewarm? Or did you think we wouldn't realise, because you butter up the police and the public prosecutor?'

'Realise what?'

'Well. I can see that the situation is worse than I thought. I am speaking with the editor-in-chief of *La Vanguardia*?'

Sanvisens wasn't going to fall into the trap of answering. Grau realised that and continued speaking.

'Supposedly every article goes through your hands before it's published. Isn't that right?' Since he already knew that he wasn't going to respond, Grau forced him to. 'Isn't that right? Answer me.'

'It is.'

'Then I have to infer that you don't agree with the resolution of the Sobrerroca case either.'

While Grau was speaking, Sanvisens had searched for a copy of the newspaper and opened it to the page with Ana's article, being careful not to make a noise with the paper. As soon as his eyes fell on the first 'according to the police version', he knew what Grau was talking about.

The day before he hadn't been feeling very well. Digestive problems had given him an acute headache. For the third time that year, he hadn't reviewed the articles. He had got away with it the first two times; this third one was going to cost him. He couldn't let the authorities accuse him of questioning the job the police had done. Not again, like the time they cast doubt on the official version of the Carmen Broto murder. So he interrupted Grau to keep him from doing what he usually did: getting worked up into a fit of rage.

'I overlooked it. I read the text too superficially. I admit that it was my mistake, and I apologise. What do you want us to do? Issue a correction?'

Grau was slow to respond. Sanvisens waited with his back glued to the chair.

'I accept your apology because I know you. A correction doesn't seem to me to be the right solution. It calls too much attention to the article that's already been published. What I want is another article. And I want it in the proper tone.'

'I understand.'

'That's better. I want it tomorrow, and I also want you to make it clear to the author of the text that these slip-ups won't be tolerated. Why do you send a woman to do these things?'

It was a rhetorical question. Grau had been pacified by his concessions and was now going on about the importance of the press in the attainment of the Movement's objectives. Sanvisens agreed just enough to make it clear that he had been listening to the five minutes of monologue.

After hanging up, he sat for a moment, defeated. From his chair, he glanced sadly at the framed photos of mountains that covered the wall. Montblanc, Everest, Kilimanjaro, Aconcagua. The best ones were outside of Spain. The highest, in Nepal. The most dangerous, Nanga Parbat, in Pakistan. The most beautiful, in Africa. 'And we're here.'

Had he made a mistake about Ana Martí? She had quickly outgrown the society pages, and ghostwriting for her colleagues had given her experience. He had thought that her ambition would be compensated for by her womanly compliance, that her eagerness to follow in the family profession would make her more reasonable, more pragmatic. She had made a mistake, but it was only a mistake in that place and time. In other circumstances, he would have sworn that she was a good journalist. No, he hadn't made a mistake about Ana.

Even so, he had to punish her. In order to protect her.

Half an hour later, Sanvisens glimpsed a burst of colour. A deep red jacket. Ana had just arrived. He rose, stepped out of his office and called to her.

'Ana, can you come here for a minute?'

40

If there is such a thing as a time machine, it exists in words, she thought. *Ana, can you come here for a minute?* Her boss's voice transported her with dizzying speed back to her childhood, when her parents would ask her that same question, almost always when she was about to get a scolding.

She didn't have time to take off her jacket. She crossed the typewriter-filled room and went into Sanvisens's office.

'Close the door. Sit down.'

She remembered having sat on that side of the same desk after an 'Ana, can you come here for a minute?' when it was still her father's. She was very young, and sometimes he would bring her to the newspaper. What age was she then? Six, seven? What had she done that time? Didn't matter. That was before.

Sanvisens immediately explained his crestfallen expression. 'I got a call from the public prosecutor, from Grau. About your article. Not so much about the content, but about the tone.'

Ana already knew what her boss wanted to tell her, but she let him repeat his conversation with Grau; otherwise she would have been admitting that she had done it on purpose, which she ended up doing anyway when he asked her, 'Why did you put in that layer of distance?'

'Because I'm not sure I believe what the police are saying.'

'What reasons do you have for that?'

Since she was already on the subject, she explained to him how she'd decided to consult with her cousin Beatriz about the letters and, despite the growing disapproval she saw in Sanvisens's face, she also told him that they had travelled to Martorell together. Here she left out the visit to the Bar Pastís, instead highlighting that the police owed the discovery of the connection between Abel Mendoza, his love letters and Mariona Sobrerroca to her and her cousin. Finally, she reached Beatriz's latest discovery, and confessed that it had made her doubtful.

At that point her boss began to shake his head.

'You should have kept it to yourself.'

'Why? The more I think about it, the more convinced I am that the police have left loose ends. And that gives rise to doubts. Reasonable doubts.'

She was repeating Beatriz's words.

'That's their job. Investigating in Martorell was their job too. Interfering was a mistake.'

'Even if I were to give you that point, at least you can admit that I have a right to express my scepticism.'

The word 'right' caused Sanvisens to wince. 'Scepticism' made it worse.

'Another mistake.'

'But our job is to tell the truth.'

'It used to be, Ana, it used to be.'

'So what are we doing here?'

'Don't act the innocent with me. I'm not buying it. What are we doing? We're doing what we can.'

'What they let us do, you mean.'

'If you want to hear it that clearly stated, yes, what they let us do.'

Ana bowed her head and bit her lower lip. Sanvisens got up, went around the desk and rested his hand on her shoulder.

'That's just the way it is. Take it or leave it. We aren't in a position to negotiate.'

She certainly wasn't. A woman, and a rookie. As soon as she was married, if she married, her husband could forbid her from working. No, she wasn't in any position to demand, or even expect, anything. So she just asked, 'And now?'

Sanvisens seemed relieved to move on to something less delicate and talk about action.

'Now we have to do two things: first, you have to write a proper, unequivocal article, for tomorrow ...'

'Proper?'

'Don't start, Ana. And tonight you are going to put on your best dress and you're going to go to the Italian consulate. Today they are introducing the new consul and there is a reception.'

'A society piece? But ...'

'But what? Can't you see that I'm helping you?'

'Thank you,' said Ana, trying to sound as if she meant it.

41

At eight in the evening, walking up to the first floor of the modest palazzo that was home to the Italian consulate, Ana felt out of place. Not because her dress was second-hand, a gift from one of her rich cousins. And not because her high-heeled shoes had already visited the local 'while you wait' shop, and certainly not because her earrings were the ones she always wore, the only ones she owned. It was because she was entering the hall lit by sumptuous Venetian glass chandeliers as a crime reporter, and not as a society columnist.

Even so, before going in, she pasted on a wide smile that soon found its reflection in a familiar face, Conchita Comamala.

'Aneta Martí!'

The woman's strange habit of always calling her by that name restored a certain order to her thoughts. Aneta Martí, society; Ana Martí Noguer, crime. Two names for a double life that still couldn't erase the displeasure Sanvisens had caused her by sending her to cover the event. No, finding names for her two characters didn't disguise the bitter taste of punishment in the assignment, but it gave her the courage to face up to it. She began to pay attention to the clothes the guests were wearing.

Conchita Comamala wore a tailored sky-blue satin dress, which opened into a sweeping floor-length skirt; her dark hair was swept up in a chignon that revealed her neck, from which hung a platinum and diamond choker. She gripped Ana's arm with a gloved hand, as if taking possession of her.

Ana was surprised by the gesture of familiarity and, searching for something to say, she pointed to her dress and ventured, 'Balenciaga?'

'Your incursion into the underworld hasn't clouded your keen eye.'

'Mariona Sobrerroca didn't exactly belong to the underworld.'

'She didn't, no, for God's sake. But those policemen ... and the killer, a brute from Martorell ... '

Comamala led her into the main salon. It seemed that all of Barcelona society was there that night, squeezed into the embassy's three reception halls. Even though the balcony doors were open, she already noted a faint aroma of sweat mixed with various ladies' perfumes. On a platform to the left of the room, a small string orchestra played, too timidly, fragments of Italian baroque pieces, adagios and largos. No *vivace* that could interrupt conversations.

Several heads turned as she passed. Ana understood that she was a coveted person, the object of morbid curiosity about her experiences in the 'underworld', where policemen and criminals mingled in the mind, and not only of Conchita Comamala.

Finally they reached a pedestal table that held a sculpture of two mythological figures whose carefree eroticism had made it a talking point for a group of women.

'We'll have to ask the consul to put it somewhere else. This hall is used for the celebration of public acts,' one of them said vehemently.

Other voices seconded her half-heartedly. The five women stared at the faun's hands on the nymph's body and tried to imagine what was happening in the parts the sculptor hadn't made visible.

Conchita Comamala and Ana arrived as their displays of moral indignation were reaching a climax.

The youngest of the women was the one who seemed most bothered. Ana had seen her before. She was Dolores Antich, the wife of Fernando Sánchez-Herranz. Just then she addressed Isabel Mira, appealing to her in her role as a patron of the arts and president of several foundations: 'You have to talk to those degenerate Italians; it's hard to believe their capital is the home of the Pope.'

'Of course, Dolores. I will convey our indignation and I will ask them, kindly but firmly, to remove that indecent little statue from view.'

Ana's appearance shifted the attention of the small group of women who, rather than focusing on what was going on between the nymph's legs, were now more interested in knowing what had happened between Mariona's.

'Is it true he was a swindler?'

'A widow scammer?' said the widow of Solsona, earning herself a couple of suspicious looks.

'Did you see him?'

'Did they take you to see the body?'

'Whose? Mariona's or the killer's?' asked Ana. She was starting to enjoy the attention. Maybe it wouldn't be such a bad night after all.

'Mariona's,' said one of the women.

'No, the killer's,' corrected another.

'Is it true he was black?'

'Where did you get the idea that he was black?' interjected Comamala.

Ana smiled as the spiral of conjectures became more and more absurd. But she kept quiet, not even nodding or shaking her head. She knew that any information she gave them would give rise to new speculations that would have her name attached to them; so she kept quiet and smiled enigmatically.

'Very young is what he was, that's why Mariona was looking so well,' declared Comamala.

'What's it like, working with the police?'

'It must be unpleasant, dear girl, just thinking of the lout who was with you ... ' declared Isabel Mira.

'Did you notice his suit?' said Comamala. 'His tailor hates him.'

That was the first time Ana made her opinion known. 'Yes, it even makes you wish he wore a uniform.'

245

'Do you have something against uniforms?' The barb came from Dolores Antich.

'No, no. Why would I?'

'Because I know who you are. Your family isn't exactly distinguished by their fondness for the Regime.'

The steely tone of her words cut short the other women's frivolous curiosity. Two of them suddenly realised their cava glasses were empty and melted away. Isabel Mira returned to the sculpture of the faun, trying to divert the attention of the woman with the icy voice whose dour countenance hid the fact that she was not yet thirty years old. She spurned Isabel's efforts and marched off. Her dark blue organza dress revealed a pair of stiff shoulders.

'Party pooper!' said Comamala between gritted teeth.

'Why did she act that way towards me?' asked Ana.

'How do I know! She went and married a man from Castile, from Ávila. What can you expect of such people!'

With that explanation, apparently losing interest in Ana, she abandoned her there beside Isabel Mira and the statue of the faun.

Before Isabel could try to recruit her to her moral crusade, Ana trotted away. She looked for one of the waiters serving drinks and grabbed the first glass she came upon, just to have something in her hand.

Dolores Antich had gone over to her husband, Fernando Sánchez-Herranz. Ana was aware that behind Sánchez-Herranz's soft, gluttonous face there lay a ruthless officer, a representative of the Falange's hard line. His wife interrupted the conversation he was having with a tall man whose back was to Ana. She whispered in his ear. Then Fernando Sánchez-Herranz looked openly in Ana's direction. The man he was speaking to also turned and Ana instantly forgot about Dolores Antich and her husband. Framed by silvery temples, two dark eyes, very close to his nose, shot her a predatory look. It was Joaquín Grau, the public prosecutor. He made a gesture for her to approach them, a mere motion of his fingers towards the palm of his hand that he repeated twice. *Come here.*

246

The hand that tirelessly signed death sentences. Now the hand was ordering her to come over.

She took a step in his direction. Before she could take a second, a waiter with a tray loaded down with drinks stepped between her and the prosecutor and quickly turned towards the trio. They hadn't been talking about her, and Grau hadn't gestured towards her; it was the waiter he was calling over. She immediately turned around and looked for a place where she could get out of Dolores Antich's sight.

At that point she would happily have left the party and gone home, but she was there to work, so she had to stay and observe. Perhaps there was a spot near the orchestra where she could mingle among those who pretended to be listening to the music, seated beside pedestal tables filled almost entirely with bouquets of flowers. Gathered there were a girl who was possibly fleeing her parents' watchful eyes, an older woman whose feet were surely hurting, as she sat on a low armchair, concealing the fact that she'd slipped her shoes off underneath her long skirt. There too was the eightysomething banker Lluch, who everyone knew was almost completely deaf, but who followed the movements of the violin bow with the demented look of a cat watching a mouse's tail.

In the corner, between the orchestra and the wall, sat a man of about fifty who wore a very well-cut tuxedo that was starting to be tight on him. Although he moved his foot to the rhythm of the music, his attention was on the people filling the main salon of the consulate. He had a glass of wine in his hand. As soon as he set it down in the tiny space left by the floral centrepiece on the table beside him, a waiter rushed over to refill it. Ana saw that behind the flowers there was a half-hidden chair, and she decided that she would sit there and disappear for a little while.

Dolores Antich's words were echoing in her head: *Because I know who you are. Your family isn't exactly distinguished by its fondness for the Regime.*

*

247

The orchestra embarked on a new piece, with little enthusiasm. Ana sat behind the enormous bouquet of flowers and polished off her drink, which turned out to be red wine. The vase, a pot-bellied piece of porcelain, hid her from direct view, and the flowers made sure that those standing in the room couldn't see her, such as Dolores Antich and the two men with her. She sighed with relief. She leaned back in the chair and discovered a bottle of wine hidden behind the vase. She touched it. It was a white, and still cold. She discreetly filled her glass. This time she drank in short sips as she observed Prosecutor Grau, who was still conversing with Fernando Sánchez-Herranz and his wife.

Grau had complained to Sanvisens. Again she remembered the conversation they'd had that morning. If she had to give it a headline, it would be 'His Master's Voice'. Actually, now that she thought about it, she could attach a similar headline to herself, since after leaving her boss's office she had applied herself to writing the article he had asked for exactly the way he'd asked for it. As she wrote it she felt as if he had his hand on her shoulder, as if he were behind her, controlling every word.

'I will not talk in class. I will not talk in class. I will not talk in class. I will not talk in class. I will not talk in class.' Copy that a hundred times in your notebook, Señorita Martí. That was how she had felt while writing the article.

'I will not talk in class,' she repeated in a soft voice a couple of times, following the orchestra's melody.

She was starting to feel the effects of the wine. She had barely eaten anything since breakfast; the conversation with Sanvisens had destroyed her appetite. What was she doing there, taking cover behind a vase? Paying for her mistake, that's what. Punished and in a corner, not with her face to the wall, but surely the two fronds of gladiola sticking out from the bouquet looked like donkey ears emerging from her head. She lifted her cup as if toasting Grau and exclaimed, 'Yes, sir. His master's voice.'

'You are absolutely right, señorita.'

The words came from her right, on the other side of the

vase. She craned her neck and looked through the flowers. It was the man in the well-tailored tuxedo.

'There's no need for you to get up, señorita, we can introduce ourselves like this.' The man in the tuxedo's voice sounded jovial and a bit tipsy. 'Jaime Pla.'

'Ana Martí.'

'Ana Martí Noguer, I presume. Would you like a little more wine? Put your glass on the table and I'll pour you some. But never again do what you did before.'

'What did I do?'

'Mix it with red.'

'Do we know each other?'

Jaime Pla filled her glass. 'We do now.'

'How do you know my name?'

'A little bird told me.'

'Señor Pla! I'm not five years old.'

'That's true, forgive me. I have to confess that this isn't the first bottle the waiter "forgot" here. The young man to the right, near the door, talking to Aurelia Montané, told me.'

Ana looked to where he had indicated. Aurelia Montané, middle daughter of Augusto Montané, owner of wine cellars and caves, patron of the Palau, among other things. And ugly. Toothy, horse-faced; those were the adjectives Ana mercilessly applied to her, because the young man she was chatting to was the good-looking one with the leather gloves whom she had seen at Blanca Noguer's funeral. Toothy, horse-faced, flat-chested ... She turned towards the vase and asked Pla, 'And how does he know me?'

'Suffice it to say that his name is Pablo Noguer.'

She hoped that the sheltering bouquet also concealed her disappointed face from Pla. A relative. The only attractive male Noguer.

'Getting back to the beginning of our little conversation, Señorita Martí, I wanted to tell you that you are absolutely right.'

'Ah, yes?'

'Sánchez-Herranz is the voice of his master, but of his new master.'

Ana listened closely as she kept her eyes glued to the little group that had been joined by a fourth person. Pla added, 'Grau met him during the war and considers him his pupil. It was he who insisted he be sent to Barcelona, and it was his influence that placed him in the Civil Government.'

'Well, he is a very conscientious pupil. From what I understand, he is making a career for himself.'

'That is quite true, señorita. Sánchez-Herranz is quite ambitious. I can't stand people without ambition, and please take that as a compliment. He has it in spades, and now he revolves around a larger star, Acedo, the Civil Governor.'

Ana turned to her right.

'Why are you telling me all this, Señor Pla?'

'I thought it might interest you.'

'Thank you.'

'No need to thank me. Would you like a little more wine?'

His insistence that she drink, worthy of a bad spy novel, put her on her guard. She held out her glass and he filled it, but Ana didn't bring it to her lips.

'Do you know what I'm thinking, Señorita Martí?'

Ana gazed at him. Pla composed a melancholic expression before speaking. 'About how much Mariona Sobrerroca would have enjoyed this party.'

'Yes, I suppose she would have. Did you know her?'

'We all know each other here, as people do in small towns. I also know that you covered the sad case of poor Mariona Sobrerroca ... What are they saying about it?'

So that was what Señor Pla wanted. First he tells her a little bit about Sánchez-Herranz, one of the new stars in Barcelona's society circle, and in exchange he expects she'll give him what she knows about the case. She can't help telling him, in a falsely innocent tone: 'That she was an excellent hostess, and that her tennis backhand had improved tremendously ...'

'Don't be snide. Don't you think it's terrible what happened?'

'Of course. What do you want me to say?'

Pla's voice no longer sounded as slurred as it had at the

beginning of the conversation. He interpreted her ambiguous question in the way that most suited him.

'Perhaps you could tell me a little more about the police investigation. Those things that aren't published in the papers, you know?'

'And why would I do that? It is a police investigation. You must already know that I can't go around telling people such things.'

'Come on! You aren't going to tell me that it's a professional secret.'

'Well, it is, of course. In a way.'

Pla didn't raise his voice, but he sounded peeved. 'What foolishness! Who do you think you are? All I'd have to do is call the examining magistrate to find out.'

'Well then, go ahead.'

Ana stood. Pla took her hand to keep her from leaving, but she pushed him away curtly, as if flicking off a piece of lint.

She couldn't walk across the room if she didn't want to run straight into Grau. She knew that Pla was following her movements. She searched for an escape and found it to the left, in a small side room that mostly held clusters of men smoking. She saw a balcony at the back and headed over to it. She went out, leaned on the railing and exhaled in relief.

'Are you running away from my boss? So would I.'

It was Pablo Noguer.

'If you're here to ask questions too, I'm leaving.'

'No, you can relax. I won't give you away.'

'But you gave him my name.'

'Because he read your articles and asked me if we were related. Because of the Noguer name.'

'And how did you know what I looked like?'

'I saw you at the funeral. Don't you remember?'

'No,' she lied.

'Oh.' Disappointed, Pablo made a face and took a drag on his cigarette.

Ana regretted having denied it; it was an adolescent reaction.

She really wanted a smoke.

'May I have one?'

'What will people say?'

'We can move out of sight a bit.'

They went over to one side of the balcony. No one could see them there. Pablo produced a cigarette and held it out to her.

'Well, I remember you.'

Ana looked at him. His dark eyes, his long lashes, his straight nose, the shape of his face ... 'Are you really a Noguer?'

'What a strange question! Of course. My father is Salvador Noguer.'

'My mother is Patricia Noguer. How are they related?' She consciously avoided asking, 'How are we related?'

'Your mother is, if I'm not mistaken, my father's cousin.'

Ana's mind leapt like a squirrel from one branch to the next on her family tree. Before she reached the conclusion that the son of her mother's cousin was something like a distant relative, Pablo planted a kiss on her cheek, dangerously close to the corner of her mouth.

'It's a kiss between cousins, for the record. Anything more and we'd have to ask for dispensation from Rome.'

'Oh, really? Well, we're not cousins; you would be something like a third cousin, and dispensations aren't needed for that degree of kinship.'

'Is that so? Well then it's a shame you have a boyfriend.'

The journalist in her took note that, first of all, he was very well informed; then she allowed that the flirting on the part of her non-cousin was not disinterested.

'You're a bit of a libertine, I think,' she replied, but her tone was more tongue-in-cheek than insulting. Pablo picked up on it and smiled with false shyness.

'I have to leave before Pla comes looking and finds me here. See you soon. And I hope the next time we meet you'll remember me.'

42

She awoke in surprise, because her last memory before falling asleep was of thinking 'I can't sleep'. On the way home, and as she undressed and climbed into bed, she hadn't been able to stop going over what had happened that day and, especially, the encounters she'd had at the Italian consulate. Her mind leapt in no particular order from Sanvisens's words to Dolores Antich's furious looks; from Pla's questions to Pablo's kiss. The kiss was the leading candidate for keeping her awake, but wine and exhaustion were close on its heels.

Eight o'clock. She had missed only two hours of rest but she was feeling them. She washed quickly and hung the dress she had worn to the reception in front of the open window to air. It smelled of tobacco, but she had made it home from the party without picking up any stains; 'Immaculate,' she mused, thinking of Pablo, first, and then, immediately, of Gabriel.

She chased them both away by drafting her society piece: 'The salon of Barcelona's Italian consulate, with its opulent Murano glass chandeliers, was the setting for the presentation ...'

Then she went to the newspaper.

On arriving, she shot a glance at Sanvisens's office. The door was closed, but she could see him through the glass. He was talking to someone. She went over to the desk where she worked and glanced towards his office again. She saw that the person Sanvisens was talking to was Carlos Belda.

Was he complaining about her covering the Sobrerroca case

again? Did he know about the Civil Governor's objections? If he did, it wouldn't be because of her boss. But Belda knew everyone in those circles, just as she had come to know so many society people. She remembered Belda's irate reaction, his 'Castro is mine'. She had reached the conclusion that Carlos Belda's rejection of her wasn't due to the fact that she was a woman (although that was his usual argument), but because she was Andreu Martí's daughter. Her father had been his mentor. Her father had had many disciples, but few that he had thought of so highly as Carlos Belda.

'My outstanding student,' Andreu Martí would say proudly.

Maybe he was in terms of his writing, but not as far as his integrity was concerned. After the war, Belda had jumped on the winning bandwagon, and from there he watched his former mentor fall without lifting a finger to stop it, or even to cushion the blow. He had repudiated him.

Belda could perfectly imagine the pain that this had caused her father, and there she was, her mere presence reminding him of it day after day. That was why he hated her so much, thought Ana. That was why, knowing that she was a constant, albeit unintentional, instrument of paternal revenge, she tolerated Carlos's aggression and mockery with relative stoicism.

She made a clean copy of her text, her eyes darting from time to time towards Sanvisens's office. What were they talking about for so long? She couldn't see Belda's face, but she could see his vehement hand gestures, which shot up and down and arched through the air. Sanvisens didn't move his hands as he replied, but his face showed his tension. Their voices couldn't be heard in the writers' room; more than the closed door, it was the incessant clacking of typewriters that drowned them out. Suddenly, there was what one of the veterans called 'the passing of a journalists' angel' and all the sounds stopped at once. Ten heads raised and looked around to celebrate that strange silence. Before a telephone, typewriter key or the rasp of a cigarette lighter had the chance to put an end to it, there was a thud from Sanvisens's office, the dull blow of a fist on a desk. All ten looked in that direction while the editor's voice said, 'I already told you, no!'

Carlos Belda burst furiously out through the office door and found all of his colleagues' curious eyes upon him.

'What? Don't you have anything better to do?'

He headed over to his desk, passing Ana's on the way.

'And what are you looking at?'

He grabbed the typed page with a version of her text that Ana had left beside the typewriter.

'Hey! What are you doing?'

'Reading a bit about the topics that make the world go round. So, the wife of the consul wore a dress of raw silk? What would become of mankind if such a detail were over-looked?'

The other nine journalists watched the scene, frozen in shock. A telephone rang on one of the desks, but no one moved to answer it.

Ana felt her face burn. Although rage was squeezing her throat closed, she managed to answer Belda. 'When you need it for your first society piece, I'll give you some lessons on fash-ion and style.'

Her words made him even more furious, but they also thawed out Roig, who, before Belda could say something even more tactless, stepped in front of him.

'Relax, Carlos. Live and let live.'

Belda dropped the page onto the desk. His lips were trem-bling with fury but he didn't speak again. He settled in his place, lit a cigarette and, clenching it between his lips, started to bang away on the typewriter.

Half an hour later, a porter came up with the post. Ana never got any. Notifications of social events were addressed to the newspaper; as were the scarce thank-you notes from people mentioned in her pieces, and the fortunately even more scarce complaints. Still, she looked distractedly at the limping, grey-bearded man who went from desk to desk, always plac-ing the envelopes in the left-hand corner, the stub of a Celtas cigarette stuck at the side of his mouth. He would have put them in order twice: first, alphabetically by the recipient's last name; then by the size of the envelope. Once he had them all prepared, he went up to the first floor of the building and began his delivery, also in alphabetical order. He didn't care if Francisco José Aparicio was seated next to Ramón Fonseca. Before he gave Fonseca his letters, he would cross the entire office to give Carlos Belda his, as he was second in the alphabetical order. He couldn't do it any other way; he didn't know how.

'A bit fuddled from the bombs,' one of the journalists had said once, after another failed attempt to make him grasp a more efficient way of distributing the post.

'Leave him alone,' said another. 'Besides, why do you care how he does it? The results are the same.'

'And his obsession with the clear corner, what about that?' replied the first in a more than half-hearted defence, but he really didn't care.

But you had to comply, and always leave the left corner of the desk clear so that the porter could place the envelopes there with the words 'Today's post,' wait for an acknowledgement of receipt and only then go on to the next desk.

The desk that Ana was sitting at wasn't prepared; the left corner was buried beneath old copies of *Noticiero Universal*. The porter stayed standing before her with an envelope in his hand and an incredulous expression on his face. Ana extended her hand to take the envelope, but the porter squeezed it against his chest and his eyes went to the pile of newspapers. The other journalists were looking on. She rushed to remove the newspapers and the porter put the envelope down, aligning it perfectly with the edges of the desk.

'Today's post,' he said with relief.

'Thank you very much.'

The porter continued his route. After Martí came Roig. The other writers went back to work.

She picked up the envelope. Yes, it was addressed to her, and there was no sender's address. She opened it up.

Dear Madam:

You don't know me, although I'm sure my name will be familiar to you. I am Abel Mendoza. I am the person you and the police think is dead. It is all a terrible misunderstanding and I want to tell you the truth. Can we meet? You will understand that I find myself in a delicate situation, and so I sincerely beg you not to inform the police — let me tell you the truth first. I suggest Friday the 16th, at three in the afternoon at the Estación de Francia.

Which is to say, today. In a few hours. She kept reading.

Please sit on one of the two benches beside the main door that leads to the platforms. Carry a copy of La Vanguardia *and wear something blue. Please, do not try to trick me. We will be watching you, and remember that I have interesting things to tell you.*

It was signed Abel Mendoza. If the letter was real, and Abel Mendoza was alive, then who was the dead man in the Llobregat River? What was their relationship, if there was one? But there had to be some link, because the dead man was carrying Abel Mendoza's ID. There was also the possibility that the dead man really was Mendoza, and that the person who wrote the letter was setting a trap for her. Although she couldn't imagine what motive he would have for doing that.

'What? Getting fan letters already?'

She hadn't realised that Carlos Belda had approached her desk and was standing over her, arms crossed over his chest.

She quickly turned the letter over and then saw that on the back there was a clumsy drawing of a rose. The Knight of the Rose. She covered it with her hand, but she was sure Belda had seen it. He burst out laughing, with loud, forced guffaws that sought to win him an audience. Several of the journalists looked up at him and Ana.

'Our new reporter is getting letters from admirers. Who could it be? A murderer? A conman?'

Since a few of the others laughed at his joke, Belda returned to his desk satisfied. He had finally got what he wanted, and he set to work. Still, Ana felt as if she was being watched for the rest of the time she was in the office.

She looked at the letter again. That handwriting; she knew it. It was the same as the original letters she had copied in Castro's office. Was it the same as the last letter, as well? It must have been, because if the handwriting had been different, she would have noticed it as she was copying them. Or perhaps not. Was she so focused on copying the content that she didn't compare the handwriting? She hadn't looked carefully. Why would she have? When she was copying them she was working under the assumption that they were all by the same author. But if the handwriting was the same, how could there have been two authors? And what if the handwriting was a scrivener's? She couldn't come up with a reason that might explain why two different authors would have dictated their letters for Mariona to the same person.

The more she thought about it, the more confused she was about the letters.

After considering it carefully, she decided that she would keep the rendezvous with the man claiming to be Abel Mendoza, but that she wouldn't tell anyone, not Sanvisens and not Castro. Should she tell Beatriz? No. Mendoza, dead or alive, was the main suspect in Mariona's murder. She had to be very careful. She might be meeting up with a killer. But they were meeting in a train station, a crowded public space. There was no way she would go with him anywhere that wasn't full of witnesses. She grabbed the pointed, dagger-shaped letter opener that lay on the desk and put it in her handbag.

An hour later, she rose to go to the rendezvous; Belda had his eyes glued to her. His mocking little smile had disappeared.

43

The Estación de Francia was so called because it was where trains heading north departed from; but a couple of years back it had become the destination for immigrants from the south of Spain fleeing a famine that didn't officially exist. Since the police monitored the passengers, and sent those who had no work contract back whence they had come, many jumped out of the cars as the train was making its final turns, just before the metal structure of the station's two naves came into view. Those who weren't literally hunted down by the police discovered that the promised land still offered a few dingy holes for them in the shanty towns that rose up on the slopes of Montjuïc and in the Somorrostro and Can Tunis.

Arriving at the station, Ana was met by a stream of people loaded down with suitcases, cardboard boxes tied with string and cloth bundles. She went up the stairs and crossed the lobby, dodging near collisions and trampled feet. There were two benches *beside* the main door to the platforms. Really, the author of the letter should have written *flanking*, she said to herself, immediately retorting, 'How pedantic, I'm acting like Beatriz.' She was nervous.

Both benches were empty. She chose the one on the right and instantly thought that maybe she should sit on the left-hand one. She switched benches. It seemed more uncomfortable. That wasn't possible; they were identical. Yes, she admitted, she was nervous.

She unfolded her copy of *La Vanguardia* and made sure that

her blue jacket was visible. Sky blue, the bluest thing she could find. She had had to buy it at the El Águila department store before heading to the rendezvous at the station. Unquestionably blue: not too close to green, like turquoise, nor imitating purple, like indigo. She had also taken into account that navy blue could look black if the lighting was bad.

Someone sat on the bench. Ana glanced to the right. The man by her side was strikingly handsome, with a well-proportioned profile: high forehead, straight nose, full lips without looking feminine, with the corners slightly upturned by the beginnings of a smile, a strong chin. The man turned and looked at her with intense blue eyes. He was meticulously shaved and his dark hair was carefully combed back, but the violet shadows under his eyes and his gaze gave a hint of something despicable in that lovely face. A few hours later, in a moment of calm, Ana would think of how the halo of danger he radiated had only added to his attractiveness. She even laughed at herself for imagining she was a saint resisting temptation, first Pablo and then Abel. But that came later. At that moment, on the bench at the Estación de Francia, her wonder at how handsome the supposed Abel Mendoza was, was overlaid by her astonishment when he addressed her.

'Are you Ana Martí?'

She nodded.

'Thank you for coming. I needed to speak with you.'

'Why?' she asked, and immediately regretted it.

The man looked at her in some confusion.

'Because you are the one who writes about Mariona Sobrerroca.'

'True, true,' she hastened to say.

'And because, according to your article, I'm dead.'

'According to the police, as well.'

'But as you can see, here I am.'

'And who are you? The body found in the Llobregat had Abel Mendoza's wallet on it.'

260

'Yes, I know. What if we take a little walk around the park? We'll end up drawing attention to ourselves here.'

Ciudadela Park was a safe place. There were always people strolling, and wardens. They turned right out of the station. As they passed through the park gates, the man began to speak again.

'I don't know where to start.'

'Perhaps, if you'll allow me, with the most awkward question: did you kill Mariona Sobrerroca?'

'No.'

'Then is the man in the river the killer?'

'No.'

'How do you know?'

'Because that man was my brother Mario, and I killed him.'

Ana stopped short.

'Please, let's keep walking,' he implored.

This would have been the moment to ask why, but she was struck dumb.

'I suppose I should keep talking,' said Mendoza.

'Please,' Ana managed to say in a thin voice.

'My brother and I had a kind of . . . business.'

Abel Mendoza explained how he and his brother had started answering lonely hearts adverts from older women. He spoke in a confusing rush, with the urgency of someone who knows he doesn't have enough time to tell her everything he wants to.

'Mario was in hiding at the Martorell house. He'd escaped from jail. They put him there after the war. They were going to execute him. He was a Red, you know? He wrote a lot of pamphlets. When he escaped, he found me in our town, in Monzón, and since they would eventually have found him there, we went to Martorell to the house of an aunt who had emigrated to Mexico. Mario lived there in a false room behind the wardrobe, in the room where I wrote the letters.'

Then Ana remembered how Beatriz had pointed out the wardrobe in the house in Martorell, and how she'd seemed uncomfortable. What she had attributed to nervousness at their trespassing was also due to her somehow sensing that the two storeys of the house didn't match up.

'He was always the clever one in the family; he had studied, he wanted to be a literature professor or a librarian and spend his days reading. He studied here, in Barcelona. And, even though he was a bookworm, he got into politics. He was highly intelligent. The letters were his idea. He wrote them; he was quite good, he always knew what they wanted to hear. And I was the face. At first we did it all very quickly. A couple of meetings, we'd take money from them, or they would give us some, and then, well, that would be that.'

'And you? You, with the women . . .?'

'You want to know if we were intimate? Less than you'd imagine. Most of them were real romantics. Mario was the one who did most of the work, writing the letters, finding the poems and telling me how I had to talk to them. He wrote the words and I, well, shall we say, added the music.'

She tried to laugh, but failed.

'Why did you kill your brother?'

Mendoza tried to button up his jacket but it was too small for him. 'It was an accident. We were fighting; I pushed him, he fell, hit the edge of a table and died.'

'Why were you fighting?'

'Over a disagreement.'

They turned right and took one of the paths that led to the lake. Suddenly, Mendoza stopped short. A park warden was striding towards them. Ana froze, too. The guard, dressed in a uniform and with a nasty face, stopped in front of a bench and violently shook a woman who had lain down there to sleep.

'Hey! You! This isn't a bedroom! Sit up!'

The woman was about forty years old. She was wrapped in a dirty blanket. With sleepy eyes she looked at the guard while she struggled to sit up.

'Yes, sir. Forgive me, sir.'

'If I see you lying down again, I'll call the police.'

'No, no! I'll sit up.'

Meanwhile, Abel Mendoza and Ana recovered from their shock and walked on. They didn't speak again until they reached the lake.

'Why did you fight with your brother?'

'Mario didn't agree with the way my relationship with Mariona was progressing.'

'Why? Did you fall in love?'

'Please! Not another romantic! Well, I think Mariona did, but what really bothered my brother was that we had a plan to go away together, just me and her. We wanted to go and live on the Côte d'Azur. As soon as we had enough money.'

He shot a sad look at the Ciudadela Park's pathetic lake.

'We had it all planned.'

'What did you have planned?'

But Abel Mendoza was lost in another moment, with his gaze on the water. 'When I told Mario about it, he was furious. I told him that there would be money for him too, plenty, but he criticised me for abandoning him.'

Abel covered his face with his hands. 'Then the accident happened. Since the house overlooks the river, I threw him into the water at night.'

'And you put your wallet on him to hide his identity?'

'No, I put his jacket on him because, even though I'm sure it seems absurd, I couldn't just throw him into that cold water with so few clothes on. I didn't think he had his wallet in the pocket, with a copy of my ID.'

'Why was he carrying a copy of your ID?'

'It was a fake he carried when he went out for a walk sometimes at night. He went along the river where no one would see him, but if he ever had the bad luck to run into a Civil Guard patrol, he carried those papers in my name. And now look, I'm officially dead. That's why I'm going to finish what Mariona and I started.'

'Why don't you tell me what it's all about?' asked Ana, testing the waters.

Mendoza smiled at her.

'No. Not that. You'll find out later.'

'Why not now?'

Mendoza looked straight ahead as he spoke to her. 'Because it's not the right moment. Don't ask me any more about it, please.'

'Why did you tell me all the rest?'

'Because I thought it would interest you. It does interest you, doesn't it?'

Her 'yes' came out weakly. She didn't like the situation, the veiled words after his confession. She was afraid, but not of the man she was speaking with. Despite not having proof, she believed him when he said that he wasn't Mariona's killer. What she didn't understand was why he had sought her out – what did he expect from her? What Mendoza said next made her even more uneasy.

'I'm convinced that the person who killed Mariona is after me, too. If she gave him my name before she died, now he thinks I'm dead. My only option is to disappear for real, but first I have something I must do.'

'What?'

'I'm sorry, but I can't tell you. It's too dangerous.'

'Why don't you go to the police? The thing with your brother was an accident, and—'

Mendoza's expression couldn't have been more eloquent. 'Do you honestly think that makes any sense?'

He was right.

'That's why I'm asking you not to go to them either. Give me a little time, Señorita Martí. Don't talk to anyone about me. Least of all the police.'

'What makes you think I'll accept?'

'Because in the end you will have a good story, I promise you that.'

'A good story with two dead bodies. My duty is to inform the police. Just talking to you incriminates me, because, even though your brother's death was an accident, you have committed a homicide, and—'

'Maybe because you are a good person.'

Ana looked at him, astounded. Mendoza kept talking. 'I'd

heard about you. From Mariona. She said that you were an honourable person, who came from a line of journalists.'

He didn't fool her with those words.

'I can see you've learned a lot from your brother about knowing what women want to hear.'

No, he hadn't fooled her. Nevertheless, he almost had her trapped.

Mendoza ignored her sarcasm.

'Look, Señorita Martí, the only thing I want is to get away from here. But first I have to do a couple of things. I have to meet someone.'

'The person who killed Mariona?'

'That's just speculation.'

'Who is it?'

'I'm not going to tell you. It is someone extremely dangerous, which is why the meeting will be, like this meeting with you, in a public place where it will be easy to get away. But in case something goes wrong ... '

Mendoza noticed Ana's frightened expression.

'Don't worry, no one knows that we have seen each other.'

They had already walked all the way around the lake. Mendoza headed towards the exit that opened on to the Salón de Víctor Pradera.

'In case they want to get me out of the way, I left important information hidden in a safe place. I'm meeting this person on Sunday. Afterwards, if everything goes well, I'll need a few days to prepare for my departure. Before I leave, I will get in touch with you. If you haven't heard from me between now and next Friday, that means my meeting ended very badly.'

'And then?'

'Then you have to go to the La Cruz de Malta bar on Conde del Asalto Street. Ask for "Ears" Amancio, and tell him that you came to pick up Abelín's gift.' Abel stopped and turned to face her. 'I'm not going to ask you if you'll do it. I believe you will, and that's enough for me.'

Ana was about to speak, but he wouldn't let her.

'No, I don't want to know. You have the information. I hope that Mariona wasn't wrong. Wish me luck. Goodbye.'

In a flash, he set off running and left her in the middle of the Ciudadela's main path.

Shortly afterwards, she too went out of the park. At the end of Víctor Pradera boulevard, near the Arco de Triunfo, she thought she saw the disappearing back of a man. A tweed jacket. Like the ones Carlos Belda usually wore.

44

She had been sitting in front of a blank sheet of paper for half an hour, chewing on a pencil. The image of the monastery of San Millán, with its monks meticulously writing and its manuscripts, kept slipping from her mind, despite her efforts to concentrate. Instead, she saw herself arguing with Ana and being, as always when she knew she was right, stubbornly uncompromising. Ana had been less obstinate and had left room for 'reasonable doubt' in her article. What had her boss said to her about that? She hadn't talked to her since their meeting at the Zúrich café.

When she had returned home that day, she had told herself that it was for the best. That way, she could go back to her work. But the words that had been said insisted on getting between her and her books. She stroked the cover of one of the volumes of the etymological dictionary that, after arduous negotiating, she had got from the bookseller for a good price. That was one time when she appreciated her inflexibility. She had been working with it for two days, and already had several rows of index cards on the table. What she had to do was concentrate on her work, on summing up all the ideas and getting them down on paper. That was what she must do.

The pencil broke in her mouth. Suddenly she was spitting out bits of wood, varnish and lead, accidentally splattering the page she'd been trying to write on.

She got up and went over to the kitchen. She heard Encarni's voice singing along softly to the radio.

'Juanito Valderrama sings so well!'

'You're not so bad yourself.'

'Did you know that on Radio Juventud there is a programme where they give prizes to people who turn up and sing?'

'You and your competitions, Encarni.'

'If I ever decide to go and sing, I'll dedicate a song to you, ma'am. To you and my mother, of course.'

'Thank you very much,' she replied distractedly. 'I'm just going out for a moment.'"

'Will you be back for lunch?'

'I think so.'

Encarni returned to her song.

Beatriz put on a jacket and went out. In the street she was met by a cold breeze. It was mid-May, but it didn't feel like spring yet. Going down the Rambla de Cataluña, she passed groups of Sunday walkers, many of whom were already carrying little parcels from one of the local bakeries; they supported the cardboard tray with one hand while a finger of the other went through the bow of the string that held the wrapping closed. Beatriz stuck her hands into her jacket pockets.

She walked at a good pace, and about twenty minutes later she was in front of Ana's house on Riera Alta. She opened the front door and went into a rather decrepit front hall. The chequered tiles were good ones, and at some point had gleamed; now many of them were cracked. To the right, twelve rusty postboxes were laid out in two rows; then came the staircase, whose railing ended in a marble pilaster. Beneath each step metal brackets meant to hold the carpet stuck out uselessly. They too had seen better days.

She started to mount the stairs. Halfway up, she heard a voice behind her. 'Can I help you with something?'

She turned. At the foot of the stairs was a short, stout, middle-aged woman. Despite the distance between them, she could smell a mixture of stew and sweet wine coming off her. The woman's face was red; she must have run to catch her from the flat on the lower floor, whose open door was almost hidden opposite the staircase, as if it were more a storage room than a flat.

'Señorita Ana Martí?'

'Third floor, second flat.'

She thanked her and continued walking up. She didn't hear the woman, who she reckoned was the famous Teresina Sauret whom Ana had complained to her about, close the door. Surely she had been lying in wait. Typical doorkeeper. Someone would have to do a study on whether such traits were nature or nurture, because the one at her house would have done more or less the same thing, except with a bit more discretion owing to the difference in neighbourhood.

She reached Ana's flat and rang the bell. As the door opened, Beatriz saw surprise on Ana's face. She invited her in and led her to a sitting room.

Beatriz had been preparing her speech the whole way over. As soon as they were both sitting down, facing each other on two sofas, she began.

'Listen, Ana, I wanted to apologise for being so stubborn and for ...'

'You were completely right.'

'... for not having listened to ... What? I knew it! I was right. What made you change your mind?'

'Abel Mendoza.'

Ana watched her reaction carefully.

'Abel Mendoza?'

'I spoke to him.'

'When?'

'On Friday.'

'Why didn't you tell me? It doesn't matter. Tell me now, what did he say?'

Ana explained how she had received a letter signed by Abel Mendoza, how they had met up and walked around the Ciudadela and Mendoza had told her about his brother Mario.

'So,' said Beatriz, 'Mario was the one who wrote the letters, and Abel took care of ... of the rest.'

'That's right. And it was Abel who wrote the last letter asking to meet up with Mariona. He waited a day, and when he arrived at her house, he found her dead.'

'And he confessed to having killed the other guy, his brother?'

'Yes, during a struggle. It was an accident. So you see, you were right: there were two authors.'

Beatriz didn't feel at all happy about having been right; instead she felt a strange feeling of loss. Again she pictured the house in Martorell – the study, the books, the filing cabinets – and reflected that the author of those letters, who had shown such linguistic sensitivity, such an accomplished style, was dead.

Ana told her that Mario Mendoza had, since shortly after the war, been living secretly in the house. That's why there had been that absurd wardrobe in the study. Beatriz had noticed that there was something strange about the house. Now she understood that it was missing a room on the first floor, the room where he hid. The blinds and thick curtains made sense as well. That way, no one would see any light in the house when Abel was out.

'Why were they fighting?'

'He says that Mario didn't agree with the direction his relationship with Mariona was taking.'

'Had they fallen in love?'

'He laughed at me when I asked the same question, but perhaps he had. It seems he didn't want to continue with the business. They wanted to move away together, to the Côte d'Azur.'

'To France, the mature woman and her young lover, like in a nineteenth-century romance novel. Can you imagine the scandal, here?'

She could indeed imagine.

'Did you say he's very handsome?' she asked Ana.

'Like a film idol.'

'Do you think he is the killer?'

'I don't know what to think. I would say no, but sometimes I wonder if he isn't playing with me and using me for something I don't understand. Although honestly, it's hard for me to believe that he is Mariona's killer.'

'Then who killed her, and why?'

'It could have been a break-in, as the police originally thought.'

'Perhaps someone was after the house,' ventured Beatriz.

'What house?'

'Mariona's. It's worth a small fortune, and at Aunt Blanca's funeral I heard some comments about it.'

'Well, well, well. So when you were shooting looks at me and my mother while we bickered about my veil, it was because we were preventing you from eavesdropping on more interesting conversation.'

She burst out laughing. She was glad that Ana was starting to talk to her like this again. She had missed it.

'Inheritances are one of the biggest causes of family strife,' continued Ana.

'You're telling me. My brother Salvador has made a lot of money out of that kind of dispute. Literature is filled with fights over inheritances, starting with Cain and Abel. Not to mention Esau and Jacob. Or King Lear, to get away from the Bible. Greed is one of the great motives in the history of crime.'

'That's all well and good, but Mariona didn't have children, and, as far as I know, the house will go to her brother, who is much wealthier than she was.'

'Love is, too; love scorned is an important motive, not only in literature.'

'Maybe, maybe.' Ana seemed to have an idea.

'What are you thinking?'

'That maybe one of the women Abel broke up with found out about his relationship with Mariona.'

'How?'

'Claudia Pons said that Mariona was planning to bring someone to her daughter's First Communion. What if she wanted to go with Abel? I can imagine that she would talk it over with a friend she trusted. Just think if it was one of Abel's "lovers", or that she knew someone who had been? And then that woman . . . '

'Too incredible, too many coincidences. It's not a good story; it wouldn't work in a book.'

'Exactly! Because this is real life, Beatriz. And in real life stranger things happen than in books.'

Beatriz didn't share that opinion in the least, but it wasn't the moment to explain to Ana that, in her view, literature exceeded life in every aspect.

Ana related the rest of her conversation with Mendoza, that he had plans he hadn't wanted to reveal, and he had instructed her to go to some bar called La Cruz de Malta and ask for someone named Amancio, alias 'Ears', to pick up a parcel from 'Abelín'. It was all very confusing.

'Let's say he isn't the murderer. What do you think it is he wants to do?'

'I haven't stopped thinking about it since our meeting. I've been over his words, in case he somehow gave himself away, but I've come up with nothing. Just that he has an idea of who it was. Maybe he saw him; maybe something in Mariona's house gave him a clue. But I don't know what he's looking for.'

'Revenge.'

'*Vendetta, tremenda vendetta di quest'anima solo desio . . . Di punirti già l'ora s'affretta,*' sang Ana softly. 'Sorry, you reminded me of *Rigoletto*. Revenge, you say, because he really did love Mariona?'

'Or because her death deprived him of what promised to be a good life, at least for a few years.'

'You're no romantic, Beatriz!'

'I'm afraid not.'

She knew they could end up fighting again, yet she had no choice but to take that risk. She said, 'Ana, I know I have the habit of telling people what to do, and that I can be somewhat demanding, but I have no alternative. Get yourself out of all this.'

'Out of what?'

'You don't owe Abel Mendoza anything. You yourself realise that he set a trap for you when he said that Mariona valued your journalistic integrity. But don't forget that he is a murderer. And what if he kills again? Or, even worse, imagine if the police arrest him and they find out that he spoke to you. You'll be an accomplice.'

Ana chewed her lip. She got up and stuck her head out of the sitting-room window. Since her back was to her, Beatriz couldn't see the effect her words had caused. After a brief silence she said, 'You're right. I have to talk to Castro. He isn't going to like this.'

'He'll only like it less the longer you wait to tell him.'

'Yes, but he thinks he has the case solved, that the killer is dead. He is pleased, the public prosecutor's office is pleased, everyone is pleased. Even Abel Mendoza is pleased.'

'But the case isn't solved. Not really.'

'You and your inconvenient truths, Beatriz.' Ana turned around, smiling. 'Tomorrow I'll speak to Castro. It's his business. This is too big for you and me.'

Those final words came as a huge relief. They meant that she and Beatriz were giving it up. That all of this was no longer hers to deal with. They would go back to their daily routines. For the first time in a long time, that last word glowed with positive implications.

45

Although Isidro claimed to read only the sports press, it was true that he read the newspapers – when, as was now the case, they were talking about him.

He wasn't an experienced reader, or as touchy as some, which was why he had even enjoyed the mitigating features that had tempered Ana Martí's first article on the resolution of the case, because they meant his name was featured more prominently: 'According to declarations by Inspector Isidro Castro, who headed up the investigation', and 'In the opinion of the police officers investigating the case', which was to say, his opinion and his alone.

'Of all the deadly sins, pride is the least reprehensible because it is so very Spanish,' he said to himself as he put down the newspaper with the new article on the table and gave it a few approving pats, like an obedient little dog. He was in a great mood.

Now all that was left was the paperwork.

They were going to bring the evidence they had gathered at the house in Martorell to the guys in the Social Brigade, who wanted to go over Abel Mendoza's correspondence with the ladies to see if there were any paid carnal relations. He preferred not to know much about that, although he had trouble imagining how a man would do it – a male whore? It's easier for the women, because they don't have to do anything. But the men?

Several boxes were filled with letters, books, drafts ... He was a real professional in his craft, that was clear. One of the slippery ones, like Boira, and maybe even better, because they didn't have Mendoza in their records. Who knows how long he'd been carrying on that business, or other, similar ones, without them having the slightest clue? He was smart; he chose a type of victim who, mostly out of shame, wouldn't turn him in. Maybe that was Señora Sobrerroca's fatal mistake, threatening to shop him. They would never know. It was the sole blemish on an otherwise perfect investigation. Perfect? Something was keeping him from seeing it that way, the shadow of a doubt that he couldn't manage to catch hold of, whose reason escaped him and which tinged the resolution with uncertainty. It wasn't perfect, then, and not only because he owed one of the key clues to a rookie journalist.

'Gratitude is a sign of a good upbringing.'

That was what his father had taught him, and he'd taught it to his children. Pride was a sin, gratitude a virtue. One compensated for the other. And the two went hand in hand a few minutes later, when he got a call.

'Inspector Castro? This is Joaquín Grau.'

Castro sat up straight as a rod, as if the prosecutor could see him. They dispensed perfunctorily with the usual greetings and Grau got to the point.

'Castro, we here at the public prosecutor's office want to congratulate you on your excellent and prompt resolution of the Mariona Sobrerroca murder case.'

'Thank you very much. It's my job.'

'Of course, and your duty, but it is only fitting to praise a job well done, to laud the fulfilment of duty, which is the foundation of the new Spain.'

'...'

The good thing about receiving praise from a lawyer is that it contains more words, and goes on longer.

Isidro didn't have the eloquence to offer in return.

'Furthermore, I must commend you again, as I said, for the speed of your work at such an important and delicate moment, just before the Eucharistic Congress, when the eyes of the world will be on Spain and on Barcelona in particular. We want them to see a clean city.'

After Commissioner Goyanes had mentioned it, Isidro could no longer ignore the Eucharistic Congress. They talked about it on the radio, they mentioned it in bars, in newspapers, in the shops his wife went to. The guys over in the Social Brigade were going to be short-handed if they tried to get rid of all the indigents tarnishing the city's image. But that wasn't his problem. Because of the Congress, they had asked him to solve the case urgently. And now he was being congratulated for it. And still Grau wasn't finished.

'Castro, I consider you one of my best men, I've always trusted you and once again you have proved me right. Therefore, I want to express my deepest respect and my gratitude. Your sense of duty and your loyalty are worthy not only of praise, but of a tangible reward. Which is why I want you to know that I am going to nominate you for a promotion to Inspector, First Class. What do you say?'

'Well ... I ... this ... thank you so much, but ... '

'No buts allowed. You must accept.'

'Of course. I am very honoured.'

'That's what I like to hear.'

Grau paused, cleared his throat and switched to a less solemn tone.

'On a separate issue, I've read your preliminary report. Where is the material found in the house in Martorell currently located?'

'Here, in an office.'

'The prosecutor's office is interested in inspecting it again. In a few hours, two of my assistants will come and pick it up.'

'It's just that Social have asked me for it as well.'

'Social? What do they want it for? I'll talk to them. Can I send my men right away?'

'Yes, fine ... But what is it you want?'

'Well, as far as I'm concerned, mostly to be able to write a documented recommendation. I would also like to inspect the material found in Señora Sobrerroca's home. Not all of it, only what's there that has to do with her relationship with Mendoza.'

'Of course; I will leave it ready for your men.'

'One last thing. I suppose that Mariona Sobrerroca's house is still sealed?'

'Yes, of course, until the order comes ...'

'Well, I am going to inspect it this afternoon.'

'But, is there a problem? Is something missing?'

'No, there's nothing. But you do realise that it's a case with many facets, one of which has caused a stir in the higher echelons of Barcelona society, and we have to be careful. Even more so with the impending Eucharistic Congress. Do you understand?'

The truth was, he didn't, but he didn't want to answer back. Politics. His motto was, don't get mixed up in politics.

'You can have your men come and pick up the keys any time.'

'Thank you, Castro. First-class Inspector Don Isidro Castro.'

But half an hour later, Isidro was knocking on Commissioner Goyanes's door, not to tell him about his imminent promotion, but to give him the reason as to why it might not happen.

46

'There's material missing from the Sobrerroca files!'

'What?'

'Grau asked me to give him the documents, and when I went to look for them I saw that some things were missing.'

Goyanes stood up and went over to him. Even so, they couldn't help practically shouting at each other.

'Grau? What does he want them for?'

'For his final report.' Isidro didn't dare mention his promotion, not under these circumstances.

Goyanes shot him a strange look. Isidro chose not to pursue that line of discussion.

'But that's not what's important now; evidence has disappeared.'

'Are you sure?'

'I checked carefully.'

'What's missing?'

'The letters Mendoza wrote to Mariona Sobrerroca.'

'Just those?'

'No, mostly those, but also two packets of postcards and a bundle of family letters. I checked the inventory list.'

'Where was the material?'

'In my office the whole time.'

Goyanes looked increasingly worried.

'Nasty business, someone stealing important papers out from under our noses. Best if this doesn't get out. Not a word, not even to your trusted men, understand? We have to clear this up discreetly.'

'And what do I say to Grau?'

'I'll take care of that.' He paused before telling him, with a grin, 'Don't worry about your promotion.'

'You knew about it?'

'Of course. I'm not the Commissioner for nothing.'

With a hand on his back, he steered Castro towards the door.

'Watch your men carefully. I will pull some strings, too. This looks like an inside job. Who would dare to come and burgle police headquarters?'

But as he walked down the stairs, Isidro remembered that there was someone who had had an opportunity to stay in his office, alone, and steal the papers: Ana Martí, while she was writing her articles.

He sent Sevilla to find her. 'Go to her house, to the newspaper, wherever you have to, but bring her to me as soon as possible.'

'Can I take a motorbike?'

'Whatever you want, but get on with it.'

Sevilla rushed out of the door.

47

Blue sparks flew as the tramcar screeched to a halt on Balmes Street. First an elderly woman emerged, carrying a parcel from the Quilez grocery, one of the best in the city. She was followed by a young woman who looked like a maid and carried a shopping basket. Then the doorway was clear and Ana could get on. As she bought her ticket from the conductor, she spotted a seat free by the window and reserved it with a glance. Ticket in hand, she sprang over to it before some of the standing passengers noticed it. She sat down and smoothed her skirt. The tram got under way with a jolt. She looked out of the window, over the hats of the pedestrians walking by on the other side of the glass. Most of them went at a swift pace, as if they were trying to reach a better, safer, cleaner place.

She went over in her head what she wanted to say to Castro. It wouldn't be easy to convince the policeman. And, if he did believe her, he most probably wouldn't do anything about it. The case was solved, and they all seemed satisfied.

But Beatriz was right, what other option did she have besides talking to Castro?

At Plaza Cataluña, the tram braked abruptly. Ana had to hold onto the seat in front of her. Through the window she saw a boy running across the street with a pile of newspapers under his arm; that was what had made them stop short. The driver shouted at him angrily and the boy shot him a contemptuous look.

The tram took off again. Ana couldn't help imagining Abel Mendoza putting a jacket on his dead brother before tossing his body into the river. 'Cold is worse than hunger. Hunger makes us savages; the cold dehumanises us.' Her father had told her that on one of the few occasions when he'd talked about being jailed on Montjuïc, knowing both hunger and cold. That was the root of his obsession with bundling the family up in warm clothes.

She alighted at Plaza Urquinaona and continued on foot to the police headquarters. Would she ever get used to that building? She wasn't sure she wanted to.

She went up to the first floor where Isidro Castro's office was. On the stairs she passed two men loaded with cardboard boxes that they held steady with their chins as they felt for the steps with the tips of their shoes.

She reached Castro's office. The door was closed. Before knocking, she took in a deep breath, filling her lungs with smoke from Celtas cigarettes. She went in as soon as she heard the inspector's voice. She was greeted by a look of fury.

'Where were you? Sevilla is looking for you.'

'I went to run some errands . . . Why is he looking for me?'

'Close the door and sit down here.' Castro pointed to the chair in front of his desk. She obeyed, somewhat frightened.

'Is something wrong?'

'Where are the letters?'

'What letters?'

'Mariona Sobrerroca's letters. What other letters could I be referring to?'

'In my house. What did you expect?'

Castro's right hand began to quiver threateningly.

'What are they doing there?'

The wrong reply in the wrong tone would surely earn her a slap, but Ana didn't know which reply would be the correct one.

'I have them carefully put away.'

Wrong answer, although the desk took the blow, a hard, heavy punch that preceded the inspector's words: 'How can

281

you answer me with such impudence? Don't you realise the situation you are in?'

'What are you talking about?'

Castro looked at the ceiling impatiently.

'I'm talking about the fact that you removed material from my office, evidence in a murder case, Mendoza's letters to Mariona Sobrerroca, which, as you just confessed, you have in your house.'

A terrific sensation of déjà vu came over her as she replied, 'I didn't confess anything, I only said it.'

Hadn't those been the words that had earned Carmen Alonso, Mariona's maid, her first slap? Her gaze went from the inspector's eyes to his right hand, but more than any possible blow it was the look in his eyes that was beginning to frighten her.

Castro struck the desk again.

'Señorita Martí, you are trying my patience! Why did you take the letters?'

'You gave me permission!' The policeman looked at her with such surprise that she added, 'Yes, you told me I could copy them. I asked permission, through your officer, Sevilla, and you said that I could copy them. Did you forget?'

'You only took the copies?' Castro shook his head.

'Why would I take the originals?' added Ana.

'I shouldn't have let you touch that material.'

'You're being unfair. Following that lead, we went to Martorell and discovered the relationship between Mendoza and Mariona Sobrerroca.'

'And do you think we wouldn't have worked it out for ourselves, sooner or later?'

The scorn in Castro's reply was meant to derail her, but she wasn't going to give in. Not with what she knew, what she had come to tell him. She wanted to launch into her explanations, but Castro's attention had seized on another detail.

'Did you say *we* went?'

A single oversight, a slight slip of the tongue and Castro was all over her like a hawk swooping on a mouse in a wheat field.

'Er, yes, I didn't go alone. I showed them to Beatriz Noguer, a renowned linguist, who—'

'What! You showed confidential material to another person? Who is this Beatriz Noguer? A relative?'

'Something like a second cousin, but I consulted her, as I said, because she is a language expert, to ask her for her opinion, you know? To find out things about the author of the letters and—'

'This is unheard of! Who do you think you are?'

Ana knew that she had to keep talking, that she shouldn't allow herself to be intimidated.

'But Beatriz Noguer found something very important. She found out that there is at least a third person implicated in the letters, because the last letter, supposedly written by Abel Mendoza, was actually written by someone else.'

An expression of disbelief was frozen onto Castro's face.

'What is this madness?'

'It's not madness. The two authors theory was confirmed when I spoke with Abel Mendoza, the real Abel Mendoza.'

'What are you saying?'

'That last Friday I spoke with the real Abel Mendoza.'

She waited for her words to have their effect on the policeman. It came quickly: his fist clenched again, his lips tensed into a thin line.

'What are you getting at?'

Ana explained her meeting with Mendoza, from the letter that arrived at the newspaper to the plan he said he had. She didn't tell him about the bar La Cruz de Malta. The cold stare with which Castro met her story threw her off course.

'Do you know what this means?' she asked him in the face of his silence.

'Yes. That once again you have been snooping where you don't belong.'

'And, as I did last time, I've brought you important information. Abel Mendoza is alive and he didn't kill Mariona Sobrerroca. The killer must still be on the loose. Do you see?'

'What do I need to see?'

'That the case isn't solved.'

'Why? Because some guy who claims to be Abel Mendoza says so? I'm afraid, miss, that you've fallen for the oldest trick in the book. Wait.'

He got up, headed to the door and shouted, 'Is Sevilla back yet?'

He waited in the doorway. As always, Sevilla appeared instantly. He looked at his boss with a questioning gaze, then saw Ana.

'But, she's here! I've been hunting for her all over Barcelona!'

Castro interrupted him.

'And when were you planning on telling me that you hadn't found her? Or were you going to take another spin on the motorbike?'

'It's just that—'

'Forget it. Listen, Sevilla, when did the last of Calvo Sotelo's murderers turn himself in?'

'About a month back.'

'How old would you say he was?'

'Twenty-five, at the most.'

Castro let her work it out. Former finance minister Calvo Sotelo had been assassinated in July 1936.

'You can go, Sevilla.'

The officer left. Castro stood, leaning on a filing cabinet. Ana understood that he considered the conversation almost over.

'Look, there are always people who do these strange things. Some because they aren't right in the head, others because they want to spend a few days eating and sleeping indoors at the government's expense,' he grinned. 'You don't know how many confessions we get for petty crimes when it gets cold.'

She gazed at him incredulously. 'Now it's you who's trying to pull my leg.'

Castro shot a look towards the door, but she got there first. 'You don't need to call Sevilla again.'

Castro accepted that the conversation wasn't over, and he sat down.

'The man I spoke to knew a lot about the case. He knew things that didn't appear in my articles.'

'Criminals talk about crimes with each other, too; they brag about their accomplishments and their feats, especially when they've been drinking. They don't need the newspapers – in their world, information circulates along different channels.'

'And what about the letters?'

'What do you mean?'

'The last one wasn't written by the same person.'

'Yeah, sure. Your little partner put that story in your head.'

'It's not a story. It's a fact, linguistically proven.'

'I think it's wonderful, and I hope you two have had fun playing detective, but that's enough nonsense. Let's get serious now.'

'I've been serious the whole time.'

'I'm sorry, but no. And since I'm not in the mood for any more nonsense, I'm going to spell it out for you, and for the last time. If you want, take notes: the Sobrerroca case is closed. The killer, Abel Mendoza, is dead and soon to be buried.'

'But—'

'The bloke you talked to is a fraud. Are you following me? All right, on to the next thing.'

Castro hadn't raised his voice, but with each point he enumerated, his tone grew slightly darker. He was speaking very slowly, as if he were actually dictating.

'Finally, I strictly forbid you to take any sort of action in this matter. You can thank the fact that I attribute all this to naivety, and not bad intentions, for my not calling the paper to complain. But this is the last time I will tolerate something like this. One more misstep and I will arrest you for obstruction of justice and contempt. Are we finished?'

He picked up a piece of paper and a pencil.

'Give me Beatriz Noguer's full name and address.'

Ana gave it to him.

'Is something going to . . .' she couldn't find the right word, 'happen to her?'

'Not if you two stay nice and quiet. And tomorrow I want

the copies of the letters here,' he pointed to his desk. 'All the copies you have. Understood?'

Ana fought back tears of rage. She nodded her head, but said, 'She has the carbon copies from the Martorell files.'

Castro glanced at the table that held the material, then turned towards her. 'Are we finished or not?'

'Yes. May I go?'

'No one's stopping you.'

She left. He didn't say goodbye; she wouldn't have been able to reply anyway.

She left the police headquarters in tears. No one paid much attention; it was all too common a sight.

48

On Wednesday morning Carlos Belda visited the morgue at Montjuïc. No sooner had he parked outside the mortuary grounds than he lit a cigarette to cover up the odour.

Now that the Sobrerroca case was closed, he had got Sanvisens to agree that the next interesting case would be his and, in a macabre kind of droit de seigneur, he had first dibs on the investigation, which in this instance meant finding himself at the morgue with Inspector Manzaneque of the CIB.

Manzaneque was waiting for him at the entrance to the morgue. They greeted each other with a firm handshake. The policeman was a hale man of about fifty. The only button on his jacket that was done up was heroically resisting the pressure from his prominent belly. His hat covered a dense head of hair, white like his moustache. He was smoking too, but rolling tobacco. He pulled out a paper from the little packet, put just enough tobacco on it to make a reedy cylinder and closed it with a swipe of his tongue.

'Hey, Belda, you ready?'

They had known each other for years, and Manzaneque knew that morgue visits weren't the journalist's favourite thing.

'Depends. What have we got?'

He pointed into the morgue with his cigarette.

'Bloke in his twenties. They found him in the slums, all done up in make-up and women's clothes.'

'How was he killed?'

'Strangled.'

287

'When did they turn him up?'

'Yesterday. Better give me your handkerchief,' said the policeman, jabbing a finger in the direction of Belda's jacket pocket. 'According to the forensic doctor he's been dead since Sunday.'

Carlos pulled out a white monogrammed handkerchief and held it out to Manzaneque so that the policeman could put a few drops of menthol on it.

'Shall we go in?' said the policeman.

'Let's go.'

They went in. They walked down a long corridor and then down to the basement.

'Did you hear about Castro?' Manzaneque asked.

'What?'

'They're going to promote him. For the Sobrerroca thing. They're making him a First-class Inspector.'

Carlos thought he should call to congratulate him.

They went into the morgue room. They were received by an employee dressed in a grey lab coat that was too long and too narrow on him.

'The one from Somorrostro,' the policeman said.

They followed the employee. He had one of his sleeves rolled up, the right one, and Carlos wondered while they were walking if there was something hidden under the left sleeve, which swayed with the employee's every step. That distracted him from the first wave of smells: damp mould and ammonia.

He hoped it was a case worth writing about, since he had to go through the unpleasantness of seeing the body.

There were a lot of dead people, but most of them didn't make the newspapers. Others were mentioned only in brief notes, which could be edited out if other articles grew or they needed more space for an advert for hair pomade, revitalising tonic or a fountain pen. They were those who'd died from the cold or illness in some alley. Second-class deaths that held no interest, that weren't important because they didn't serve to exemplify the punishment of evil nor glorify the police. Hopefully this cadaver wasn't one of those.

They had found him in an abandoned rookery in the Somorrostro, a 'historic' slum that had been there since the previous century and was right by the sea, near the Barceloneta. Yes, as Manzaneque had said, the body had definitely been there since Sunday: three days of rot.

They went into the room where the bodies were held.

'Have you already seen it?' he asked the policeman.

'And smelled it.'

Carlos squeezed the handkerchief in his palm to have it ready as soon as the employee opened the storage unit, which they quickly reached.

'Open it, will you,' ordered Manzaneque.

The employee struggled with the door; he did have a left hand after all. When he finally managed to open it and revealed the dead man's face, they saw that it still bore traces of make-up. His skin seemed covered by a thin mask, his eyes were shaded in blue and he wore fake eyelashes. His lips were slathered in a layer of cracked lipstick.

To Manzaneque the motives for the crime were obvious: 'A queer crime. This guy liked to dress up like a lady, but that's it. The other one wanted to take it further, he refused and the other guy raped him. From the way he left him from behind, the forensic doctor says it was his first time. So they busted his cherry and then they finished him off.'

He turned to the mortician's assistant. 'Why haven't they washed his face?'

The man shrugged before offering a hypothesis, 'They can't have done his photos yet.'

'You think?'

Manzaneque turned to Carlos, indignant, but he wasn't paying attention. His eyes were glued to the dead man's face. Manzaneque asked him, 'What's up with you? Did you know him?'

'I thought I did, but now, looking closely, I don't reckon I do,' he said, his mouth and nose covered by the handkerchief.

The policeman didn't even suspect that Carlos was lying to

him. The journalist shifted his attention by changing the subject. 'It could be something for us if your hypothesis pans out. Crimes between deviants are of interest to the public, and they also serve as a moral example.'

'That would depend on who did it,' the policeman replied. 'Remember the one with the son of the Civil Guard colonel?'

'But that didn't happen in the Somorrostro.'

'Well, that's precisely where some of these degenerate rich lads like to go. They find what they're after: excitement and bodies. There are fathers who sell their daughters, why can't there be ones who sell their sons?'

'You're right. And if someone from the top brass is implicated in this case, that's another someone who'll soon be sent to serve his country in Morocco.'

They continued their conversation as they left the room and the morgue grounds.

'So you're interested?' asked the policeman.

'At first glance, yes,' Belda said with feigned indifference.

'You don't seem very enthusiastic.'

He played the ambition card with Manzaneque. With Castro's promotion, there would be movements in the CIB and a lot of eagerness to stand out. The press was an appealing ally.

'I think we could do something,' he said. 'Can you send me a photo of the corpse? Without make-up?'

Manzaneque didn't ask what he needed it for.

'You'll have it tomorrow.'

Shortly after, they parted ways.

Carlos got into his car, but didn't start it. He had to think. He needed the photo of the face without make-up to be completely sure he wasn't making a mistake, that he had seen that man before. It had been last Friday, when he followed Ana Martí to the Estación de Francia. The dead man was the one he had seen her talking to in Ciudadela Park.

49

He arrived promptly at eleven.

Ana had spent all Thursday morning combing the flat, making sure everything was in place.

She had hidden her personal belongings, and hoped she hadn't missed anything.

That was the price for being able to live alone in that flat: not being able to make it her own, always being some sort of conservator, more so even than a guest. But since she had seen that her grandfather looked only fleetingly inside the closets and drawers, she had filled them with her things and covered them with some of his clothes. She had also acquired the discipline of not leaving anything of her own, no matter how small, in view.

As on his previous visits, her mother escorted him to the building entrance. Then she left to run errands in the neighbourhood and said that she'd be back to pick him up in an hour.

Grandfather opened the door with his own key, looked at Ana, surprised to see her there, and, after greeting her with a kiss on each cheek, began to go through the rooms. What she hadn't yet managed was to stop feeling guilty with each visit. *Usurper.* She imagined that was what her grandfather's disconcerted look was saying as he turned his key, opened the door and saw her there. Teresina Sauret's bowing and scraping when she saw him only further exacerbated the image of the dethroned king returning from exile for a day to look over his lost land.

In the sitting room, he stopped in front of a pedestal table.

'There was a vase here! There was a vase here!' he shouted, pointing to the place, a tabletop with a doily crocheted by his wife where, indeed, there was a vase missing.

'I broke it, Grandfather,' responded Ana in a childish tone that she had discovered placated him whenever he flew into a fit of rage.

'Do you forgive me, Grandpa?'

'All right, but you have to be more careful. Where is Rayo?'

The dog had died at least fifteen years before, but her grandfather mixed up the past and the present.

Ana would have to buy a vase similar to the one that had got broken because between one visit and the next, he would forget her explanations. That had been her only mistake. The rest of the visit went as always and, as always, left her exhausted and sad for the rest of the day. The entire house was impregnated by the scent of the Heno de Pravia soap that her mother washed her grandfather with before he left the house.

She pulled a text she had to edit for a publisher out of a drawer and began marking it up fiercely in red pencil. A few hours later she wouldn't remember what it was about, but she left it free of errors, repetitions, superfluous commas, clichés and imprecisions. A couple of innocent adverbs took the brunt of her bad mood, to which Sagrario Ortega, the second-floor neighbour, contributed with her radio. She had it going full blast, and the voices rose amplified and distorted by the interior courtyard. 'Coplas, coplas, coplas.' Failed love or, even worse, 'joy, joy'. She tolerated the metallic timbre of Concha Piquer in 'Tatuaje', but when she heard the first chords of a new song and realised that Estrellita Castro was about to start singing, she slammed her window shut and began to sing 'Suspiros de España' at the top of her lungs to cover up that high-pitched warble that set her teeth on edge.

She put on her jacket, still singing, grabbed her papers, singing, stuck them in her bag and went down the stairs. When she reached the front door, she rang her neighbour's bell several times before running off like a mischievous little girl.

She had planned on going to the newspaper after lunch to do more editing and, perhaps, get a new assignment. So she'd just go earlier.

She couldn't stop thinking about what she could do with what she knew. Her biggest doubt was over how to deal with what Mendoza – because she still believed that he was Abel Mendoza, despite Castro's mocking comments – had left at La Cruz de Malta. Wait another day, until Friday? She had promised him that. She had already gone against what they'd agreed by talking to Castro. Did that give her carte blanche to break her promise again, or did it require her at least to stick to the rest of it?

She reached the newspaper office, which was obscured by a cloud of her colleagues' cigarette smoke. She inhaled a deep lungful of the cleaner air in the staircase and headed towards her usual desk, which meant passing Carlos Belda's. He wasn't sitting there, but he was somewhere in the office. His tweed jacket hung on the back of his chair and a cigarette butt was still smoking in the tin ashtray that he'd pinched from the bar next door. CINZANO, it read around the rim. A lamp illuminated the surface of the paper-strewn desk. The light directed her gaze towards a photo. She didn't mean to stop and look at it – she didn't want to look as if she were snooping – but she pulled up short when she recognised the face in the image, its eyes closed. She had to lean against the desk. It was Abel Mendoza, and he was dead.

'An old friend?'

Carlos's voice at her right shoulder made her jump. Her left arm swept through the air and hit the lamp with the back of her hand as she whirled around to face him. Carlos looked at her quizzically. She didn't see the sardonic gleam in his eyes, or the scornful sneer he usually had when addressing her. But she hadn't forgotten them, so she shook her head.

'So, you don't know him?'

'No.'

'I thought you did.'

'Why?'

'Because of your reaction.'

'It's an unpleasant image. Or do you like it?'

'Well, I could swear I saw you with him.'

Asking when would have given her away. She merely widened her eyes and looked at him, incredulous. That made three times she'd denied Abel. She repressed her desire to escape his scrutiny, but she was feeling more and more uncomfortable, her mouth was dry and she needed to sit down because her legs were shaking.

'Is he your new subject?' she said in the most neutral tone she could manage.

Now he was the one who didn't answer. He forced her to move aside.

'Can I sit down at my desk, or do you want to keep adorning it for a bit longer?'

But as she was about to leave, he grabbed her by the arm, drew close to her ear and said, 'You'd do well to tell me whatever it is you've got up your sleeve. For your own good.'

He relinquished his grip.

Ana didn't make it to her desk. She left the newsroom and ran into the toilets. Locked in one of the cubicles, she remembered how she'd done that a few times before, at school, to escape punishment from a furious teacher. It never worked. The Sister would always wait; nuns have a lot of time on their hands.

Hiding wouldn't do her any good.

She came out of the cubicle and splashed some water on her face.

She already knew what she was going to do.

50

'Carlos, can you come here for a moment?'

Carlos got up from his desk and went into Sanvisens's office.

The editor-in-chief greeted him with a glass of water in his hand, into which he put a spoonful of Eno fruit salts.

'Stomach again?'

'This is pure habit. I've bought into that advert we run. Care to try it? It's very refreshing.'

'Some other time. What did you want to tell me?'

Sanvisens drank the contents of the glass in one gulp.

'They called me from the Civil Government.' He covered his mouth with his hand to hide a burp. 'About the notice yesterday, about the dead guy.'

'The queer from the Somorrostro?'

Sanvisens nodded with a hiccup.

'What about him?'

'They don't want any more coverage of the subject.'

'Why not?'

'All these questions!' He hiccuped again. 'Because they don't.'

'But they didn't say whether it's because of the nature of the crime, or the victim's identity?'

Sanvisens shook his head and changed the subject. 'I shouldn't have drunk that so quickly, now I've got hiccups. But I have something else for you. Yesterday there was an attempted break-in at a jewellery store on the Rambla de Cataluña. Three armed men went in, but the owner confronted them with a pistol. There was a shoot-out. They wounded the owner, but he in turn wounded one of the three robbers, and it seems that he was a member of the resistance.'

Carlos was barely paying attention, not just because Sanvisens's hiccups were getting on his nerves, but because he was already plotting his next move. He wasn't just going to forget about the dead guy from the Somorrostro.

'So, go over to the jewellery shop and prepare something for tomorrow.'

'Yes, that's good.'

They went their separate ways. Sanvisens held his breath and counted to thirty; Carlos mentally paged through his little black book of useful phone numbers.

The first call Carlos made was to Inspector Manzaneque.

'Thanks for the photo,' he said.

'What did you want it for?'

He gathered two things from the policeman's curt tone as he put to him the question he had forgotten to ask the day before: that he wasn't going to be able to count on his collaboration, and that Manzaneque too had received orders.

'To get into the case. You know how I usually work,' he said as if he were oblivious.

'Well, since the case isn't going to be published, you'd better send it back to me.'

Carlos continued to feign ignorance.

'What do you mean, it's not going to be published? Why not?'

'Orders.'

'Who from?'

Perhaps Manzaneque's resentment at having been stripped of the opportunity to see his name in print would make him more talkative.

'I don't know.'

'You don't know, or you don't want to tell me?'

'The end result is the same, isn't it?'

'Does it have to do with the victim's identity? Or with the murderer?'

Manzaneque sighed at the other end of the line.

'Since we've known each other for years, I'll tell you: we'll never know. The public prosecutor's office has ordered the case closed at the request of the Civil Government.'

'But . . . what about the stiff?'

'Going into a mass grave. He'll be buried tomorrow.'

'I get it.'

'Good.'

'Cheers, Manzaneque. I owe you one.'

'At the dry cleaner's, OK?'

'OK.'

'And give me back the photo. Don't forget.'

As they said goodbye, Carlos was already looking up another phone number in his little black notebook. He had other contacts in the force. Before dialling the number, he shot a fleeting glance at the desk Ana Martí usually used. It was empty.

51

The La Cruz de Malta bar on Conde del Asalto Street was squeezed between a narrow doorway with a broken metal grille and a shop whose window displayed a small stack of bars of Lagarto soap beside a few feather dusters that seemed to have attracted every speck of dust in the neighbourhood. The place was a long tunnel traversed by a bar festooned with stools. At the back, there were some tables – the general murkiness meant that she couldn't see how many. Behind the bar, the wall was obscured by casks of wine with taps and a pitted mirror that, instead of making it wider, only reflected the narrowness of the room.

There were barely any customers: two women sitting at a back table and an old guy leaning on the bar. All three stared at her openly when she came in; she supposed and hoped that it was because she was new to the place. Her simple clothes shouldn't attract attention in that neighbourhood.

For the length of the walk there she had avoided looking back to check whether someone was following her, but she kept feeling the ghostly pressure of a hand falling abruptly on her shoulder before an authoritarian voice said, 'One moment, señorita.' In her head she heard another voice, the voice of common sense asking her to turn around, warning her that she didn't know what she was getting into and, above all, that she might not be able to get out. But Mendoza's dead face was dragging her towards that foolish undertaking. She had promised him. She was going to make good on the promise. Finally she reached the bar and stepped inside.

The landlord had his back to her, but he turned when he saw his three regulars looking towards the door. He was a fat man in his forties. At first she thought he was giving her a fierce glare, but when he came over to her end of the bar, she realised that the smoke from the cigarette stuck between his lips was irritating his left eye. When she got her first glimpse of him face to face, she immediately knew that he was Amancio, otherwise known as 'Ears', because he had none; in their place were two scraps of shrivelled flesh. She brought her hand to her mouth. The man understood why and explained in the routine tone of a museum tour guide: 'In Seville, when Queipo de Llano came in, instead of giving me his famous coffee.'

'Give him coffee' was the coded phrase with which General Queipo de Llano sent someone off to be shot by firing squad. The old man at the other end of the bar let out a sly, high-pitched cackle and, looking into his glass of wine, said, 'Fucking Moors, fucking Moors.'

The barman ignored him.

'What do you want to drink?'

'Nothing,' stammered Ana. 'I've come to pick something up.'

The man didn't react.

'Can you hear me?' She pointed obliquely with her index finger towards where his ears should have been.

'Of course, I'm waiting for you to tell me what you want.'

Ana moved closer to the bar and heard a crunching beneath her shoes that she chose not to scrutinise.

'I've come to collect something someone left here.'

The barman was beginning to understand, and he drew nearer to her.

'I was sent by Abelín.'

Ears glanced around him.

'Be careful. That one sitting over there is Mercedes, his girl-friend. Well, his girlfriend around here.'

He winked at her. Or was it the cigarette smoke in his eye?

'I imagined you'd be older, from what he told me. And already widowed.'

Another wink. She then understood that he had taken her for one of Mendoza's 'lonely ladies'. She decided to play along.

'My husband was much older than me.'

Ears moved the cigarette from one side of his mouth to the other, then leaned even further over the bar so that he could speak without the regulars hearing.

'I'm sure Abelín gives you more joy than the old man, may he rest in peace. Tell him, before he leaves, that he must stop by and give me a couple of classes. I want to know what he gives you ladies to get you like this. What he does to have even Mercedes letting him sleep in her room.'

As if she had sensed that they were talking about her, the woman who must have been Mercedes interrupted her chatting and shouted at the barman, 'What, Ears? Neglecting the customers?'

'What the hell do you want, Mercedes?' he yelled without turning around.

'Give me another little glass of wine.'

'Wait a minute, can't you see I'm talking?'

'Up yours, Dumbo!'

She held her tongue then, but Mercedes and the other woman didn't take their eyes off Ears or Ana. Their hostile looks were robbing Ana of her confidence.

'If you'll just give me what I came for, I'll let you get back to work.'

'Bah! They're in no hurry. Whores don't have many johns at this time of the day.'

But he turned around and disappeared swiftly into a back room separated from the bar by a beaded curtain.

Mercedes got up and came over to her then.

'Are you looking for work?'

'No.'

'You're ashamed, ain't you?' Her voice softened a bit. 'You'll lose that quick enough, you'll see. But, even if ol' Ears tells you

300

to, don't sign on with The Colonel's Wife. Her pimp beats the girls, even when they haven't done anything wrong.'

'What are you telling the lady?' Ears' voice came through the beaded curtain.

'What's it to you?'

The barman re-emerged carrying a dark-coloured envelope. He tucked it into his armpit, grabbed a little glass and filled it with red wine from one of the casks.

'Here. Now sit down and leave me alone.'

'You're a nasty one!'

But Mercedes picked up the glass and returned to the table.

'And I won't say what you are because there's a lady present.'

'And what am I?'

'Mercedes, don't start with me!'

During the entire exchange, 'Ears' Amancio and Mercedes had their backs to each other. The barman came over to Ana and held out the envelope. There was a damp stain where it had been under his arm.

'Thank you.'

She slipped it into her handbag.

'Tell you-know-who to come by before he leaves town. Just a couple of tips . . .'

'If you want, I'll give you one myself.'

The man looked first at Mercedes, who, as if she were waiting for it, gave him the two-fingered salute.

'That whore needs a couple of good slaps,' he grumbled. Then he addressed Ana, 'Go on, I'm all ears.'

'Simple. Be considerate to her.'

'But she's a—'

'You don't need to remind her of it all the time. I'm sure she likes it about as much as you like not having ears. Well, I'm off.'

'Say hi to Abelín for me.'

'I will,' she said with a lump in her throat, already on her way out of the bar.

Closing the door behind her, she stood for a moment, looking up and down the street. If someone had been spying on her movements inside the bar, they would've had to do so from outside. If they were to catch her, it would have to be now and she would rather see it coming; she didn't want to feel a hand on her shoulder. There were plenty of people on the street, but no one approached her and the only pedestrian who looked at her twice was a woman whose expression indicated that she was in the way, standing there on the pavement.

She could start walking.

The envelope in her handbag weighed on her as if it were full of lead. Her visit to the La Cruz de Malta had drained her, and she was plagued by the question of whether Abel Mendoza's friends would ever know that he was dead. From the way they spoke about Abelín, they clearly knew that the article about his death published in the newspaper was false. Would they believe it if it appeared in the news again? From what she had overheard when she passed by Sanvisens's office as she was leaving *La Vanguardia*, that wasn't going to happen.

Along with the envelope, she had taken on a responsibility and an obligation; she had to get to the bottom of the matter. But she didn't want to drag Beatriz into it again. By insisting that she help her with the letters, she had already got her so mixed up in the case that she had even revealed her identity to the police. Maybe at the very least she should try not to implicate her further.

She decided to go home with the envelope and go on alone. She would call Beatriz at some point from a discreet telephone and explain. She couldn't do it in her building, not with Señora Sauret spying from behind the door.

She found her not behind the door but in front of it when she arrived home. She tried to slip past her with a hurried greeting, but when she was barely two steps up the stairs, the doorkeeper caught up with her and cried from the other side of the banister, 'Señorita Martí, this has always been a decent house.'

She stopped, disconcerted by that inexplicable statement.

'OK,' she answered.

'Because of your grandfather, there has never been too much gossip about you living alone at your age.'

Even though the 'not too much' was attractive bait, she chose to keep quiet and wait for the 'but' that was peeping out at the end of the statement. It soon showed itself.

'But I find it very improper that you let people into your home. Men. I don't think Señor and Señora Serrahima would approve.'

'Men? In my home?'

'Don't try to deny it. An hour ago two men came into the building. As it is my duty to keep an eye out, I asked them where they were going and they said to your flat. I told them that you weren't here because you had gone out a while ago and they said it didn't matter, they had the key and would wait for you inside.'

'What were the men like?'

The doorkeeper eyed her suspiciously.

'Where did you get the money to pay two months' rent at once? This is a decent house, I won't allow—'

'What were these men like?'

'I won't allow—'

'What were the men like, you horrid old witch?'

Teresina Sauret was petrified, but she moved her lips as if they were under someone else's control. 'Tall. Well built. I couldn't see their faces properly because they were wearing their hats down low, and—'

She was cut short by a noise on the staircase. A door opened and footsteps were heard. They both looked up. Two shadows peered down the stairwell.

'That's them!' said the doorkeeper.

They were four flights up and the light kept her from seeing their faces, but when one of them shouted, 'Señorita Martí, come up, we're waiting for you,' she understood that it wasn't in her best interests to get to know them, so she turned tail and ran out of the building.

'Señorita Martí, stop!'

With Teresina Sauret's voice screeching at her back

demanding an explanation, she locked the front door behind her to gain a little time. Those guys didn't have her house keys; those guys had broken into her apartment with a pick-lock.

She tore down the street and round the first corner. She didn't stop until she'd reached the Ronda de San Antonio, where she leapt onto an overcrowded number twenty-nine tram that was already making its way to the Plaza Universidad and hid among the passengers. She pretended to drop her handbag so that she could crouch down for the first few metres, then she stood and paid her fare with her head bowed, as if she were having trouble finding the coins. She didn't dare to look out of the tramcar for fear that she would find the two men running after it. She glanced out only when she reached the university. As the tram braked, approaching the stop, she scanned the faces of the passengers waiting to board. The only person who was panting from running was a woman. The passengers got on and soon the tram resumed its route.

'Mind your bags!' warned the conductor. He had recognised a pickpocket among the new arrivals.

Ana pressed her handbag tightly to her side. Despite her intention to leave her cousin out of the whole business, she realised that the only place she could go was to Beatriz's house.

52

Two different smells had been wafting into Beatriz's study from the kitchen. One reminded her simply that she needed to eat; the other actually made her mouth water. The first was the rather acrid whiff of the mixed vegetables that Encarni boiled until there wasn't a single fibre left to chew in them, until the chard or cabbage took on the consistency that Beatriz imagined seaweed had.

'Vegetables that aren't well cooked are hard to digest,' Encarni had argued the first time she showed signs of protesting.

You don't argue with someone who worries about your health, so she kept quiet and ate, as if she were a little girl again. The second aroma was rice pudding, the white paradise that followed the green purgatory. A nice plate of rice pudding. That brought out her real appetite, once her more essential hunger was sated.

The dishes Encarni prepared revealed her efforts to satisfy both of the houses she fed, since she always took two containers of food home for her family. So, now that Beatriz thought about it, the digestion Encarni was tending to with the overcooked vegetables was her mother's, not Beatriz's. At least it could never be said that she was a stingy boss, like so many who made their servants endure greater hunger than the teacher Cabra in Quevedo's *The Swindler* did his pupils. She and Encarni ate the same things. When there was more, they ate more; when there was less, less. She laughed, remembering the passage in Quevedo's novel, in which Don

Pablos describes the broth the teacher served them as 'so clear that it posed more danger to Narcissus than the pool'. Not in her house. Encarni took dinner home for her family, and she made a rice pudding unlike any Beatriz had ever eaten.

'My grandmother's recipe,' Encarni would say proudly when she complimented her on it.

There was still half an hour to go before lunch. She didn't think well on a full stomach, and not on an empty one either, she confirmed when she realised that she had turned the page of the article without having really read it. Antonio Marichalar wrote well; being close to the Regime didn't necessarily imply that one was a bad writer. It was one of the last issues of the magazine *Escorial*. It seemed that the Falangists were running out of steam in their service to 'the new Spain'. She had already formed the impression from reading previous articles that some of the early Falangists, such as José Luis López de Aranguren and Gonzalo Torrente Ballester, were starting to grow less fond of a totalitarian ideology and Franco's Regime. Even the fanatical Laín Entralgo, with his inquisitorial gaze, had softened. Perhaps something was changing. Her stomach growled. She closed the magazine. 'Food first, then morality,' as Brecht would say.

How had she got to Brecht from Quevedo? Via hunger; her desire and her need to eat.

Erst kommt das Fressen, dann kommt die Moral. She remembered it perfectly in German. She got up from the desk and went to the bookshelf where she kept volumes in that language. She always thought that the notorious Spanish ignorance of other languages would protect her collection if they ever searched her home. Among the classics – Goethe, Schiller, Kleist and Herder – who, due to a general lack of knowledge were mistakenly assumed to be harmless, she had Brecht, one of the authors she had shared with Jakob. *The Threepenny Opera*: banned by the Nazis, banned by Franco. Why not translate it? It could be her next project. Perhaps then she could send it to Jakob. It would be a good way, if not the perfect excuse, to get back in touch with him.

She and Jakob had corresponded a lot. He wrote in German, with some phrases in Spanish, which were the ones she best remembered. Sometimes he made mistakes, such as when he wrote 'once on a while' instead of 'once in a while', something she never corrected because, for some inexplicable reason, she found that construction, so peculiar to him, very sweet. She couldn't bear the thought of someone reading the letters she wrote to or received from Jakob. She guarded her privacy so closely that Jakob used to say she was more German than he was. She hoped that, after their break-up, he had destroyed all her letters. She had fulfilled her part of their tacit pact and burned his.

From Quevedo to Brecht, and from Brecht to Jakob. She was getting sentimental. If she didn't eat soon, she would end up reciting one of Ramón de Campoamor's trite poems, and that would be the last straw.

She heard the sound of the doorbell. Whoever it was, the visit was welcome, because it banished from her head one of the moralising verses she so loathed.

Encarni opened the door. Beatriz heard Ana's voice. She waited for a moment. Why wasn't she coming to her study? She stepped into the hall. Encarni had taken Ana to the kitchen; she followed. Seeing Ana's expression, she realised that they were facing a more serious problem than having some bad poem stuck in her head, or her lunch being late.

'Abel Mendoza is dead,' Ana managed to say before her voice cracked.

Encarni crossed herself. Then she picked up a glass, filled it with fresh water and offered it to Ana. She drank it eagerly and was able to continue speaking.

'What happened?'

'He was murdered.'

'How? When?'

'I don't know exactly. But I saw a photo of him on the desk of one of my colleagues at the newspaper. It was a police photo, from the morgue.'

'How do you know he was murdered? Couldn't he have had an accident?'

'No. The police don't send photos of accident victims to the press. In yesterday's newspaper, Carlos Belda, the one who had the photo, published a brief note about a man found dead, dressed as a woman, in the Somorrostro. It had to be him.'

Beatriz remembered how Ana had described Abel Mendoza as one of the most handsome men she had ever seen, a leading man type, she had said. And a swindler.

'Then maybe he was killed by the person he said he was going to meet up with.'

'That's what I'm afraid of. Whatever it was he was trying to do, it played out very badly.'

'Have you gone to the police?'

'No.'

'Why not?'

'I don't dare. Castro threatened me if I even thought about getting involved in this case again.'

'But now, with what's happened, you would have evidence that you were telling the truth.'

The sentence sounded wrong. 'The truth' was an increasingly slippery word to define. It was always up for manipulation. Every regime distorted the truth to suit them; this Regime used it as if it had been tailor made for their purposes.

'I'm afraid,' responded Ana, 'that the police don't want to hear anything more about all this. Least of all Castro. I heard that, thanks to his work on the case, they are going to promote him. Do you think he would risk an opportunity like that just to establish a truth that no one seems interested in? Besides, we've been forbidden to write about the dead body found in the Somorrostro.'

'Why?'

'Because someone must know who he is, and they don't want it made public, despite the police having the corpse of the man they say is Mariona's murderer.'

'And you are convinced that he isn't the one?'

'Completely.'

'That would mean that Abel Mendoza was killed by the same person who killed Mariona.'

'That's what I think. But that's not all. When I got home, there were two men waiting for me.'

'Who were they?'

'I don't know, but I have the feeling that I'd seen one of them before. I don't know where.'

She had calmed down a little, but she was still frightened. Her story was very disturbing. Beatriz took a deep breath.

'Maybe they wanted to sell you something, some cold cream or the Espasa encyclopedia.'

She tried to make a joke, recalling Ramón, the door-to-door salesman who turned up every year at her parents' summer home in Castelldefels to sell them 'the books that belong in every cultured home'. Her parents had never bought a single volume, but she and her brother Salvador would wait for him in front of the house to buy a few of the little booklets of adventure stories he also carried.

'Travelling salesmen don't come in twos, ma'am.'

Encarni set another glass of water in front of Ana. The abruptness of her movements told Beatriz that her awkward attempt to reassure Ana had made Encarni angry. Because it had been Encarni who had let her in, who had brought her into the kitchen when she was completely beside herself. She had also been listening to her attentively, and she was the one who, even though she was unfamiliar with the story, was taking charge of the situation. Beatriz felt a bit of an idiot for her comment. It was no time for levity.

Now it was Encarni who had something to say, but first she very deliberately placed two cups and a sugar bowl on the table. She had put the coffeepot on the stove when Ana arrived, and she served the coffee before adding, 'Only the police come in twos.'

Ana started spooning sugar into her cup. Her hand was trembling.

'He had a lisp! I know where I know him from. He lisped when he spoke. I saw him once at the Vía Layetana headquarters – he's a policeman, some guy named Burguillos.'

Policemen. In desperation, Beatriz suggested an idea that

309

offered a plausible, but above all harmless, explanation. 'Perhaps they wanted to give you a message from Inspector Castro.'

Ana shook her head.

'Then they would have called me at the newsroom.'

'And why send two men to deliver a message?' added Encarni.

Beatriz sighed. Her hypothesis had come up against two irrefutable arguments. She always had a hard time backing down when she was clinging to something that showed itself to be a dead end and she had to start her reasoning again from zero. She wasn't fooling herself; she had tried to minimise the real danger because she still refused to accept that, contrary to her expectations and her wishes, they were mixed up in all this. Not only that, but they were in deeper than ever. It was Ana who came up with the worst possible explanation of all.

'They were Castro's men. Only he knew about my meeting with Abel Mendoza, only he could suspect that I know something more about this business.'

'But what? You've already told him everything you found out, and he didn't want to hear it. Why would he come looking for you?'

'Because I have this.'

Ana pulled the envelope out of her bag.

Beatriz immediately guessed what it might be.

'You didn't go looking for whatever Mendoza left at the bar?'

'La Cruz de Malta. Yes.'

'But, Ana, what were you thinking? Don't you realise the danger you put yourself in?'

'Mendoza left it there for me to pick up if anything happened to him.'

'And what if he ended up telling that to the person who killed him?'

'He was prepared to keep quiet.'

'How can you be sure? You didn't know him. In such an extreme situation, they might have given him the option to save his life.'

Beatriz saw that her objection made an impression on her cousin.

'He knew all too well that he was dealing with someone very dangerous,' she argued after a few seconds. 'He was prepared.'

Beatriz wondered what she would do in a similar situation, with no hope of salvation, when keeping quiet or speaking out led to the same outcome. What would she have done? Kept quiet and died with the hope that later the guilty would be punished? To die with the only consolation being posthumous revenge. Yes. That's what she would have done. Was that what Mendoza had prepared himself for? Did the envelope contain his revenge? His will? It didn't matter, since it was not the contents but the mere fact of having it that implicated them irretrievably.

'We've been reckless, Ana.' The envelope lay sealed on the table. 'Who did we think we were? Roberto Alcázar and Pedrín?'

'Surely not those two, they're fascists.' Now it was Ana who was trying to make her laugh.

Encarni, on the other hand, standing between them, remained sombre.

'Ana, please. Imagine Mendoza had talked about La Cruz de Malta. What would have . . .?'

'But he didn't, or the envelope wouldn't have been there.'

'And those two men? What were they doing at your house?'

Beatriz was silent. That was the question: what were those two men doing at Ana's house? Why were they waiting for her there, and not in the bar? She answered the question herself: 'Because they didn't know about the bar.'

Ana and Encarni looked at her expectantly. She continued, 'That's it. The two policemen weren't on Mendoza's trail, they were on yours.'

'Why did Castro send two men to look for me? What does it have to do with Mendoza's death? Why have they forbidden us to talk about him?'

'I'm afraid, Ana, that Castro hasn't been upfront with you,

311

that he has other interests in this case beyond a promotion. That's why he didn't want you to know the truth.'

She couldn't imagine what Castro's involvement might be, but nevertheless, Ana may have become a danger to him. Which meant that Ana herself was in danger.

'Do you think they followed you here?' she asked.

'I can't say for certain, but I am fairly positive that they didn't see me get on the tram. I don't think they even knew what direction I was heading in.'

Beatriz had to approach the window and look down at the street below. On one of the benches on the central pavement she saw a plump, well-dressed woman trying to soothe a child who was having a tantrum. The other passers-by were ordinary pedestrians walking to and fro along the Rambla de Cataluña. Even so, she felt an urgent need to draw the curtains and bolt the front door. Then she went through the entire flat to make sure that all the windows were closed.

When she returned to the kitchen, she found Ana and Encarni attentively examining a piece of paper. They had opened the envelope.

'And what's that?' said Encarni.

'I don't know what it is, but we can rule out a couple of things. It isn't a postcode and it isn't a locker number.'

'It's not an address either. At least, not one here, in Barcelona.'

'You know what it could be? A bank account number. Or a cryptogram.'

Encarni looked at Ana, her eyes wide.

'What's that?'

Encarni didn't get a chance to find out because Beatriz had drawn near. When she saw the combination of numbers and letters written on the piece of paper she said at once, 'That's a catalogue number for a book. A book in the Library of Catalonia.'

53

The library smelled as it always did, of dry paper and dust. Yet Beatriz inhaled the air with gusto. The library had always been a refuge for her, her entrance into the Middle Ages, into the Renaissance, the periods she escaped into when the present became unbearable.

She headed straight to the area where the large wooden card catalogues stood. The books' file cards were ordered into strict, tight rows stuffed into dozens of tiny drawers with handwritten labels. In some drawers you could see that the cards had a little breathing space. That was where the censors had come and removed authors who were banned. Freud's name was among the missing. As were the names of Marx and Bakunin, and those of Huarte de San Juan and Vives. A simple, effective procedure: cards disappeared; books didn't exist.

Beatriz grabbed one of the request slips and wrote the catalogue number that they had found in Abel Mendoza's envelope on it. The problem was that they didn't have the name or the title of the book to go with the number. But she knew how to solve that problem. She had already seen that Pilar was at the service desk, and she was one of the librarians she knew best there. She approached the counter and waited for her to finish speaking with a visitor who was complaining about not being able to take a book home.

'It can only be read in the reading room.'

'It's just that the damp isn't good for my rheumatism.'

Beatriz grinned. She had grown used to wearing an additional light jacket when she went to the library and, in the winter, fingerless gloves to be able to write while keeping the rest of her hands warm.

'Well, I'm sorry. But those are the rules.'

The man left, grumbling under his breath.

Pilar greeted her. 'Dr Noguer, I haven't seen you all week.'

'I've been working at home.'

'I'm not surprised. With the damp here ... And spring seems to be dragging its heels.'

'It'll be one of those years without a spring. One day we'll go out on to the street and all of a sudden it'll be summer. I have a little problem, Pilar. It seems that the last time I was here I jotted down a book reference so quickly that all I have is the catalogue number. I don't know what it is, but I underlined it, so I think it must be something interesting. Do you think you can pull it out for me so I can give it a quick look? Ever since I saw the number, I've been wondering what book it is and why I wrote it down.'

'Of course. That kind of thing can drive you up the wall, can't it? It happens to me when I can't remember a title or an author; I can't rest until I find it out.'

Pilar glanced at the catalogue number.

'It's in storage.'

'Can you get it for me now?'

'Of course.'

The librarian beckoned one of the employees, a young lad who was pushing a little cart from which he slowly distributed the books that the readers had requested. On one of the final tables he left a pile of books for an older man who was frenetically scribbling away on small sheets of paper.

'Old Montoliu,' said the librarian.

'He's still at it?'

'It's what keeps him alive. The day he finishes it, he'll die.'

The boy came over and the librarian gave him the slip of paper.

'Miguel, can you bring this? Quickly?' she said in a firm tone.

He took the paper and hurried off.

'The boy confuses fetching things silently for fetching them slowly.'

'How is your daughter?'

The last time Beatriz had been in the library, Pilar had told her that her young daughter was sick again.

'A little better,' she said resignedly.

Beatriz nodded. The librarian's daughter was ten years old, a delicate child whom all the bacteria that Barcelona was swarming with seemed to have ganged up on.

Another reader had approached the counter and was demanding the librarian's attention.

'Forgive me, Doctor, we forgot to write on the slip where you are sitting. Where should I send Miguel?'

'To the reading room.'

She wrote down the number of her favourite table, trusting that no one was already using it. Then she remembered Ana.

'Pilar, I forgot, I brought a student who wants to see the library.'

She pointed to Ana, who had been waiting the whole time near the entrance.

'That's fine. Bring her in.'

Pilar was already focused on the card that the other scholar was showing her.

Beatriz thanked her and headed to the reading room with Ana. How she loved that room! It was hard for her to imagine that the nave had been built to hold a hospital and that instead of tables and shelves along the wall, there had been sick and dying patients. On rainy days like this one, the silence of the room was disrupted by the rhythmic drumming of raindrops falling from the leaky roof into metal pails spread about below, but, even so, it had a secluded atmosphere that bordered on the monastic.

Her favourite spot was free. Tonet, the least friendly of the librarians, was the one who enforced silence and order in the room. Seated behind a raised counter, he had the gift of making everyone who entered feel like an intruder.

She sat down with Ana and waited for them to bring the book. The other readers lifted their heads for a moment and then returned to their texts.

The boy arrived a few minutes later, dragging his feet, placed the book on the table and moved off just as slowly. She and Ana stared at the volume, a thick edition of the first part of *Don Quixote*, folio-sized and leather bound. The binding wasn't original; rather, it was the kind the library used to replace those that had been worn out from use.

Finally Beatriz picked it up.

'Why would he have written down the catalogue number of *Don Quixote*?'

She was hoping at least for a title that would give them something they could interpret as a message. What was there in that copy of *Don Quixote* that could represent Mendoza's posthumous revenge?

Ana was thinking the same when she said, 'Maybe he underlined some passages of the book.'

They began to turn the pages, more and more quickly until the person sitting at the next table looked up furiously to ask could they stop making so much noise. They reached the end of the book without having found a single underlining or annotation.

Beatriz checked the index. She thought that in front of some of the chapters she could make out traces of pencil marks. There were unscrupulous people who wrote in library books; there were others, like her, who erased such marks if they were in pencil. It would be ironic if someone had erased Mendoza's message in order to clean up the book.

She mentioned it to Ana in a whisper. She peered at the slight remains of what could have been marks to signal certain chapters. She lifted the page, turned on the little lamp and held it up to the light. Beatriz wrote down the chapters where she thought she could make out one of the marks. There were five.

'Start reading. I'm going to request another copy for me.'

Beatriz went over to Tonet.

'How can I help you, Doctor?'

'Are there copies of *Don Quixote* available on the open shelves?'

'Of course!' The librarian looked at her derisively. She ignored him.

'Where can I find them?'

He pointed them out. She headed to the bookshelf and pulled out the book. She returned to the table with it and sat beside Ana, who was already absorbed in the text.

They didn't know what they were looking for, and the chapters didn't have any common connection. Nor did the titles give them patterns they could link, and they couldn't seem to find any clues in the plotlines.

They had been rejecting one hypothesis after another for more than an hour.

'Should we go to the courtyard for a moment and get some fresh air?' said Ana.

They went out, both silent and frustrated.

'Do you know what doesn't make sense to me?' said Ana. 'I can't imagine Abel Mendoza leaving secret clues inside *Don Quixote*. That wasn't how he did things, from the little I knew of him. The one who wrote was his brother.'

'Didn't Abel tell you that his brother had wanted to be a librarian? I imagine he knows perfectly how this library works, then. It must have been his brother who had the idea.'

'Yes, but the idea to do what?'

'I don't know, but I have the feeling we're trying too hard. That we're missing something obvious.'

'Then let's start from the beginning.'

They went back to the reading room and examined the book afresh, as if they had just been handed it. Then they saw it. The book seemed to be awkwardly bound. The endpapers were made of normal paper, and they were somewhat off-kilter. In fact, once they checked, they realised they weren't endpapers at all: they were flyleaves that were strangely springy, sort of puffed up. No bookbinder worth his salt would deliver a book in that condition, and much less to the National

317

Library of Catalonia. The book had been tampered with. They glanced at each other.

'There's something inside here,' said Beatriz. 'How do we open it?'

'Wait. I'm going to look for something.'

Ana got up and went to the cloakroom where they had left their jackets and bags. She came scurrying back, panting from exertion. She showed Beatriz a sharp nail file. She stuck the tip beneath the endpaper and lifted a corner.

'Not yet, they can see us. We should cover ourselves a little better.'

She hastened to the shelf that held the reference books and grabbed a few: the Real Academia dictionary, another Latin one and two thick volumes of an etymological dictionary. And just then Tonet, the gruff, rather unhelpful librarian, had a fit of gentlemanly behaviour, got up from his throne and came over to help Beatriz carry the books to the table.

'Allow me to assist you, Doctor.'

Ana turned her back to them. Thank heavens she hadn't gone on separating the endpaper and had hidden the nail file. If Tonet caught her, not only would he throw them out of the library and perhaps ban her for ever, but also, and at that moment this seemed much worse, they wouldn't find out what was hidden in the cover of that copy of *Don Quixote*.

Luckily, Ana had seen them and, pretending to look up from her reading, greeted them with a smile. They placed the books on the table, forming a wall that hid them from indiscreet looks and obscured their movements. Then Ana began to separate the paper from the cover with the utmost care. Beatriz sneaked glances around them. The readers were still absorbed in their books and Tonet, recovered from his fleeting bout of friendliness, was complaining about how poorly a visitor had filled out the request form, forcing him to rewrite it. With the file Ana made a slight scratching noise and, even though it was almost inaudible, it seemed to her that the vaulted room amplified it. The person seated in front of them might have heard because he shifted in his seat. Beatriz put her hand on top of the file to stop Ana. When the man turned a page of the book he was reading, they resumed. False alarm.

Finally Ana managed to separate the endpaper enough to venture a look inside. There were some very thin sheets of paper between it and the cover.

They had found what they were looking for.

They pulled out the paper delicately. They were octavos of India paper, fragile as butterfly wings.

'There might be more beneath the other cover.'

They repeated the process, and again extracted several pages.

Beatriz was impressed by the cleverness of the hiding place. Without having met either of the brothers, it was clear to her that it was Mario Mendoza's idea. She wanted to understand the scheme well before reading the papers. She got up and went to the card files. She searched in Authors. The card for that edition of Cervantes' work wasn't there. There was no card with that number in the Titles catalogue either. Brilliant. They had made the cards disappear. Without a catalogue number, the book couldn't be requested, so no one had touched it since they'd hidden the papers there. The book existed only for someone who had the key.

She went back to Ana, who was making a pile of the little papers.

'Don't you want to read them?' Beatriz asked her.

'Here?'

'You don't think this is a good place to read?'

'What I don't think it is, is safe.'

54

Beatriz organised the papers carefully on the polished table of the small room. Pilar had opened up one of the reserved rooms, the Cervantine room, so that they could work in peace; that afternoon, no one had requested any of the volumes from the special collection. Ana rested her head on her hands while she read various pages written in tiny script on cramped lines.

Beatriz leaned back in the chair and contemplated the little pile of papers. Fragments of medical records from the military hospital at Vallcarca, and numerous handwritten notes. They were from Mariona's husband.

She had read all the pages in the packet. She glanced at the one on top. In the mid-1940s, Dr Garmendia had given a young woman an abortion. Garmendia had neatly recorded the date, time, the anaesthetic used and that the patient had returned to his office three weeks later for a follow-up visit, in which he had discovered symptoms of a syphilitic infection that he had treated with penicillin.

The patient, Dolores Antich, had been luckier than other women in her situation, who ended up resorting to a back-street healer who dealt with their problem with knitting needles and infusions of rue. And as for the venereal disease, she had also had it better than most Barcelonians. In the mid-1940s, penicillin could only be acquired on the black market and cost a fortune. Reading up to that point, it could seem as though Garmendia was the saviour of wealthy women who had got into trouble, except for a little handwritten note that was stapled to the medical report: *Baby's father, Josef Kuczynski. Supposedly a Polish nobleman, but Dolores doesn't seem entirely convinced. Lives at the Ritz.* Beneath, a later note in the same handwriting, which Beatriz presumed was Dr Garmendia's: *Not Polish – Argentinian.*

It seemed that Garmendia had done some investigations of his own and had discovered that Dolores Antich, daughter of a good family and the future heiress of several textile factories, fell pregnant by an Argentinian chancer who, to top it all, had given her syphilis. There was a similar story involving Carme Rius, but instead of the fake Polish count it was a friend of her older brother and, to further complicate the situation, a descendant of grandees of Spain. In this case it wasn't syphilis but some other venereal disease; something that also appeared in the notes about two more patients. All well-known names, to the point that even Beatriz knew who many of them were.

It appeared that the good doctor had been in charge of discreetly mitigating the unexpected consequences of the sexual activity of the city's upper class, whether they were infections or unwanted pregnancies. She'd counted eight of the former and five of the latter. All with names, dates, treatment. Several of them with additional information. Much of it came from the patients themselves. People reveal a lot of things to doctors, benefactors par excellence.

Ana passed her one of the papers. 'Look, on this page of his visiting log it says to whom and when he prescribed cocaine. Quite a list.'

'Let me see.'

Ana handed her the sheet of paper. It was definitely a succulent list of names. One in particular caught Beatriz's eye. Jaime Pla. What a snake in the grass! For a moment she felt the power that possessing shameful information gives one. She let out a giggle.

'What is it?' asked Ana.

She told her, without giving his name, what had happened to Pablo, 'A nephew of mine.'

'I can imagine what I would do in his place, knowing that about my boss,' replied Ana before returning to the papers.

Minutes later, she looked up from her reading and showed her two pages darkened by Garmendia's tiny handwriting. They looked like pages from a private diary.

'Look, this is serious. It's not just a scandal, it's a crime.' She was irate. 'These are notes by the doctor where he writes that someone named Rodero offered him penicillin. But when he compared it with the other shipments he'd acquired earlier, he saw that the colour wasn't the same. Since he knew from a colleague that there had been several batches of adulterated penicillin going around on the black market, he didn't buy it, and instead demanded an explanation from this Rodero character.'

'From the way he freely made use of penicillin in his treatments,' Beatriz said, pulling out two more fragments with information about gonorrhoea treatments, 'he needed a reliable source on the black market. He couldn't run the risk of tainted penicillin.'

'That's why Garmendia wanted to know where Rodero had got that shipment of adulterated penicillin. Apparently it came from the Vallcarca military hospital; someone there was regularly making large quantities of penicillin disappear from the military pharmacy.'

Beatriz raised her eyebrows.

'And?'

Ana slid a page across to her and pointed to a column with her finger.

'Our Dr Garmendia managed to get – who knows how, maybe he knew someone – copies of the pages of the pharmacy's medication registry where the diverted amounts are recorded.'

Beside the amounts, Garmendia had noted that it was striking that the flow stopped when they changed the public prosecutor who had been in charge of the investigation. The doctor had jotted down a question: 'Did they take him off the case, did they suspect him?'

322

'Can you guess who that prosecutor was?' Ana asked her.

Beatriz shook her head.

'Joaquín Grau.'

'Isn't he the same one in charge of the investigation into Mariona Sobrerroca's death?'

'The very same.'

'And the doctor had evidence against him?'

'No. Only conjectures. In the notes, Garmendia speculates on the possibility that it was a pharmacy employee who stole the penicillin, adulterated it and sold it on the black market. The doctor also bought it through an intermediary. His suspicion was that Grau didn't put much effort into the investigation, if not impeded it as much as possible, because he was getting a cut.'

'You mean, he accepted bribes from the thieves? And when they transferred him, he could no longer "protect" the business and they gave it up?'

From the notes one could infer that Garmendia had tried to get in touch with the employee at the military pharmacy through other doctors, but had had no luck. It wasn't clear, however, what his intentions were.

'It could just as easily be that he was looking for a direct source of penicillin, without intermediaries, as that he wanted to confirm his theories about the prosecutor's dealings,' said Ana.

'When you think about it, even though he didn't have conclusive evidence, it looked bad for Grau,' murmured Beatriz.

'Yes; it would be enough for someone to continue investigating. In the hands of a political enemy, that information could be very damaging.'

'But Garmendia wasn't a political enemy of Grau's, was he? Why was he saving all this information?'

'Because it's highly sensitive information.'

'But it doesn't make sense that he blackmailed his patients. If he had done that with the abortions, not only would he have lost all his patients, but he would also have incriminated himself,' objected Beatriz.

'But perhaps, thanks to these secrets, he was able to obtain certain favours. To keep him happy and quiet for ever.'

Beatriz nodded. *Manus manum lavat.* Coming from a family of lawyers, she knew the system well. Ever since she was a little girl she had witnessed occasions on which her father acted strangely, arriving home in a fury and shouting in the parlour. Her mother would try to calm him, but he would be beside himself. Later, she understood that those were moments when one of his clients, important manufacturers and bankers, afraid that his professional confidentiality wasn't enough to keep their dirty dealings secret, offered him favours and benefits, bits of business that weren't terribly legal in themselves and which, in turn, bound him even more tightly to the network of mutual interests. In a third – and disappointing – stage of these discoveries, she had understood that her father, despite his shouts and pronouncements against the 'moral decadence of our times', had on most occasions ended up accepting the favours.

Ana's voice pulled her from her memories: 'Perhaps he collected them to exchange when he needed something. For example, if he required the help of a prosecutor, or the economic support of a powerful manufacturer, like Arturo Sanabria, who had beaten a prostitute to death, or the counsel of a cocaine-addicted lawyer ... '

'And after his death,' added Beatriz, 'Mariona found the papers and started to use the information. She tried to profit from them. With her husband dead, she no longer had to stand on ceremony. She began to blackmail people.'

'Conchita Comamala insinuated that recently Mariona had seemed more flush with money. She was wearing a pair of earrings again that she'd had to pawn before.'

'Which means someone was paying up.'

Blackmail. So that's what it was. Some of the pieces of the mosaic were fitting into place. Mariona not only had money, but she had found someone to share it with. What had Abel Mendoza told Ana? That they wanted to leave the country and go and live on the Côte d'Azur.

'I would never have thought that Mariona had the character or the personality to do something like that,' commented Ana.

'You see, human beings are surprising creatures.'

Beatriz would have liked to tell her cousin that some of the best authors had been despicable people, that Villon was a criminal and Quevedo surely abhorrent. And to explain to her how much she hated Garcilaso for having let himself be killed so young due to his eagerness for the glories of war. So stupid. But it wasn't the moment; she'd save it for some other time.

Ana continued putting the pieces together: 'Abel and Mariona had hit on a real gold mine if they were thinking of running off together.'

'But it seems that the owner of the gold mine got tired of paying and preferred to put an end to it all with a bloodbath. There are so many names in those papers! And one of them is Mariona's killer.'

'And Abel's.'

There were a lot of names, it was true, but only one person had the means and the power to manipulate even the investigation of his crime.

'Grau,' she said.

Ana nodded.

It was all making sense: the way the investigation had been handled, Castro's interest in presenting it as a common break-in, the way they had used the press, hiding the murder of the real Abel Mendoza.

'That was the man he told me he was planning on meeting. After Mariona's death, Abel must have tried to blackmail Grau on his own. He needed money to disappear.'

'And he ended up like her.'

'He wasn't wrong when he said he was meeting an extremely dangerous person.' Ana's voice had a bitter taint to it.

She got up, went over to one of the room's towering shelves, returned to the table and, gesturing at the papers with a mixture of disdain and sorrow, said, 'And this must have been his life insurance!'

'Why?'

'He was so naive; he must have thought that, by threatening to make it public, he had an unbeatable advantage. That's why he sought me out. How could he have been so ingenuous? How could he think any of this would be publishable? It's one thing for those involved not to want it made public, but for it to appear in the press is quite another. None of this would ever make it onto a newspaper's pages.'

'But now we have to think about what we are going to do with these papers and all that they imply.'

Beatriz felt the familiar pressure of the chair's backrest as she reclined. She had sat there many times reading. Reading and thinking. Literature showed the abysses in human behaviour: the greed, the stupidity, the jealousy, the evil, the eagerness for power. It was all in there. But you could close the covers of the book and go back to being by yourself. She stared at the papers.

Those papers were very much alive. They couldn't remain stuck between a book's covers; they couldn't be kept on a shelf. They had cost two lives. One of the people whose names appeared on those pages had killed twice.

Now the papers were in their hands.

'What do we do now?' Ana was both asking her and wondering aloud at the same time.

Beatriz didn't know. But she was beginning to understand that it wasn't about what they could do, but about ensuring nothing happened to them. They had material in their hands that was too delicate.

'I don't know. If even the police are after this ...'

Ana nodded.

'To start with, I'll talk to my boss, Mateo Sanvisens.'

'Is he trustworthy?'

'I hope so.'

'You hope so?'

'Yes, I hope so. Sanvisens is like a tightrope walker who manages to stay a few centimetres above the daily quagmire without muddying himself too much. He gets splattered, but keeps himself up there on the tightrope, watching. The question is whether he'll come down from his position for me.'

'But we won't give him the papers, will we?'

'No. I mostly want his advice. And I need to get out of here. Get out of here and do something. I can't stay in this reading room any longer; I'm starting to feel as though I need oxygen.'

Beatriz could understand that. But she would have asked to stay in there for the rest of her life.

'Be careful, Ana. If the police are looking for you ... '

'And what if I was mistaken, and it wasn't Burguillos's voice?'

'Then perhaps we are wrong about Grau. But whoever it is, someone very dangerous is after these papers.'

'What are you going to do?'

'I'll stay here a little longer. Then I'll go home and wait for you there.'

'Take the papers with you. Hide them.'

'Of course. The Mendoza brothers gave us a masterful lesson in that. Poe, with his purloined letter, looks like a mere intellectual exercise next to their pragmatism.'

They said goodbye. Ana went out into the street.

55

On Carmen Street she plunged into the flood of people. They even filled the road, and had to squeeze together on the pavements every time the occasional car passed by.

She was trying to keep from looking around to see if she was being followed, but it was hard not to. Men in twos. Tall men. Men who were coming in her direction and looking right at her. Men in dark mackintoshes and hats pulled down low. She held her breath when she passed them. Only two streets. She was almost there. She was pulling it off.

Suddenly she felt a hand on her shoulder. She let out a scream.

'Pardon me, young lady. I didn't mean to scare you.'

The hand gave way to an entire arm that surrounded her shoulders. From her right side appeared Tomás Roig, who embraced her. She let him do it, as much out of relief that he wasn't a cop as guessing that if the police were pursuing a single woman, she and he would be more inconspicuous together.

Tomás Roig released her after a few paces. They entered the newspaper together. There she had to solve a second problem. She didn't want Carlos Belda to see her. She didn't know how, but she was sure he was mixed up in the whole business.

'Aren't you coming up?' Roig asked her.

'I have to speak for a moment with the porter who brings up the post.'

Roig went up the stairs, grappling with his lighter flint that wouldn't spark.

Ana looked for the porter.

She found him behind a small counter, leaning over the desk. He was filling in an illustration in a children's colouring book. When he noticed she was there, he lifted his head, two green pencils in his hand, one light and the other dark.

'Five is green. But which green?'

'Let me see. Where does it go?'

The porter pointed to a girl's jacket. He had already coloured her hair yellow and her wellingtons orange.

'This one.' Ana chose the lighter one. 'Trust me; you know I cover fashion.'

The man smiled in gratitude. Before he began to colour in the jacket, she said, 'I have an errand for you.'

That was the formula usually used to get his attention.

'Please go up to the newsroom and see if Señor Carlos Belda is there. But just look. Don't say anything to him if you see him, is that clear?'

The man got to his feet. A few minutes later he came down the stairs shaking his head.

'He's not there.'

'And Señor Sanvisens?'

'I don't know. I didn't look. I only looked for Señor Belda. Do you want me to go up again?'

'No. I'll go up myself.'

She thanked him and praised the precision with which he had filled in the spaces for the first four colours. The porter beamed proudly.

She headed up. She saw Sanvisens in his office and went in, even though he was talking on the telephone. The editor-in-chief understood that it was something important and cut the call short.

On the way there she had thought about what she was going to tell him. Everything. Now, before Sanvisens's anxious gaze, she realised that the question was how. So she began with a headline.

'Mateo, I'm in danger.'

She gave him the subhead as he sank into his chair: 'It's

about the Sobrerroca case. I have some very sensitive documents and they are after me to get at them.'

She then plunged into her story, beginning at the very beginning. First came Isidro Castro and the police investigation, which Sanvisens listened to with modest anticipation; it was already familiar. The appearance of Beatriz and the letters was received with shock and perhaps some rebuke, but that disappeared completely when Abel Mendoza entered the tale in person and exited dead. Sanvisens was astounded.

'But . . . but, my dear girl, what have you done?'

The last feature of the story, the discovery of the documents, left him literally struck dumb because a coughing fit prevented him from getting a word out. He rose and took a drink from a little glass that held the dregs of a white coffee that must have been sitting for at least two hours waiting for some errand boy to remove it. Then he turned towards her.

'How did you get yourself into this mess?'

'I've already told you.' She intentionally ignored the fact that his 'how' was really a 'why'. 'What I need is for you to help me think of a way out of it.'

Sanvisens paced back and forth behind his desk. Curiously, Ana noticed, he took three steps to the left, but needed four to go to the right.

'And Castro?'

'That's the worst of it; I'm afraid he's in on it. I think his task was to carry out a fake investigation in order to close the case without revealing the names of the people behind it. That was why he was so focused on the break-in theory. And the same reason why he refused to pay any attention to me when I insisted that Mariona had a lover.'

'And the dead guy in the river?'

'That was an unexpected twist. When they found the body in the river with Abel's ID, they thought it was him. He wasn't in their records. I imagine they didn't try too hard with the autopsy; besides, the blow to the head could have been from the fall into the river. That corpse was a godsend for them.

They had killed Mariona, and the person they needed to pin it on went and committed suicide.'

'But soon after, the real Abel Mendoza turns up and talks to you.'

'And I, like an imbecile, talked to Castro. I gave him away to the police, Mateo; it's my fault they killed him.' Her voice cracked as she spoke.

Sanvisens came out from behind his desk and hugged her.

'How could you have known, Aneta?'

He was right, but she couldn't help feeling responsible for his death. He had asked her not to talk to anyone and she had put the police on his trail when they'd given him up for dead. Sanvisens stroked her hair like a father consoling his daughter. But now it wasn't about that. She wasn't a girl who had come running for comfort after grazing her knees. She would cry when it was the right time; this wasn't it. There were still many loose ends.

She moved away from Sanvisens.

'I can't believe that Castro is heading up this inquiry; I think he's only carrying out orders,' he said then.

'And I'm afraid that we also know who is giving the orders.'

'Who?'

She hesitated enough that Sanvisens noticed it.

'Ana, where does this sudden distrust come from?'

'It's just that everything is so complicated. Knowing things has become dangerous.'

'Not knowing things. It's saying what you know that's dangerous.'

'That's why I think it's better if I don't tell you anything more.'

'I've spent years deciding what to say and what to keep quiet. It's one of the survival tactics I'm best at.' Sanvisens accompanied that last sentence with a weary smile.

If there was something she had learned in the past few days, it was indeed that distrust was another of the basic survival strategies. But, on the other hand, she needed to trust someone; she needed to in order to keep on believing that they had some possibility of getting out of this situation.

'The one pulling the strings is Prosecutor Grau.'

Hearing the name hit Sanvisens like a bolt from the blue, and he couldn't disguise it.

'Are you sure?'

'Not entirely, but there are a lot of arguments pointing to him: he has the motive, Mariona's blackmail over the penicillin trafficking; he had people to carry out the murder, policemen of his ilk or some of the thugs that work for them; and he also has the means to manipulate the investigation.'

'I always took him for a merciless fanatic and, because of that, the first one to comply with the morality he preaches.' Sanvisens sounded dismayed.

'Well, now you see. What this story shows us – the moral, if you want to call it that – is that too many people aren't who they appear to be. Castro, for one. Then there's Carlos.'

'Carlos who?'

'Carlos Belda.'

'What does he have to do with all this?'

'I think he's been spying on me. I think he followed me that day I met Mendoza at the Estación de Francia, and that he somehow knows the meeting had something to do with Mariona Sobrerroca's murder.'

'That's a very serious accusation. What brings you to that conclusion? I know he isn't your best friend, but—'

'He threatened me – indirectly, but he threatened me. And now, because of one of those two, I've got the police after me.'

Sanvisens, who had started pacing again behind his desk, stopped and rested his hands on the back of the chair.

'What can I do, Mateo?'

'The only thing I can offer you is information. I'll do everything I can to find out who knows what, and what they know about you and your cousin.'

'It's always useful to know who you're running from.'

'Now it's best if you get out of here and lie low. Do you have somewhere to go?'

'Yes.'

'Not your parents' house. If they're looking for you, it's the first place they'll go. Is there anywhere else?"'

'Yes, I think so.'

The walls of Beatriz's house, in a reversal of the story of the three little pigs, were no longer made of brick, but of wood.

'And the documents?'

'Well hidden.'

The walls turned to straw.

'How can I get in touch with you?' Ana asked.

'Call me here, at the office. I will tell you what I know, whatever it is.'

Ana rose. Sanvisens came over and hugged her again. At that moment her fear almost turned to panic. Was he saying good-bye to her?

'Be very careful. I could never forgive myself if anything happened to you. I gave you the assignment.'

'I got myself into this, don't blame yourself.'

She left the newsroom. She went down the stairs and waved to the porter, who showed her the light green pencil with a satisfied expression. She lifted her thumb in an approving gesture. Turning to leave, she suddenly came smack up against a wall comprised of two strapping men who blocked her way through the door. She recognised Officer Burguillos.

'Where are we off to in such a rush?' said the other man, grabbing her by her left arm.

'What do you want?'

She yanked her arm out of the man's grip, but Burguillos already had a hold of her too.

'What do we want? Nothing. To take a little stroll.'

'And have a little chat,' added the other man, grabbing her left arm again. 'It's always pleasant to stroll and chat with a pretty girl.'

'While she's still pretty and can still walk.' Burguillos's lisping, raspy voice was right in her ear.

They began to drag her. Ana tried to resist by gluing her feet to the floor, but they lifted her bodily. She thrashed wildly between the two men, who grasped her even tighter. Just as they reached the door to the street, all movement stopped and Burguillos, on her right, crumpled strangely. She turned to him and saw that a green pencil was sticking out of his ear. The other man, gobsmacked, dropped her and turned towards the attacker – the porter, who was threatening him with his coloured pencils.

'Run, señorita, run.'

'And you?' she cried as she took off.

'Doesn't matter. They can't leave me any stupider.'

The last thing Ana heard were confused shouts.

'Son of a bitch!'

'Get away from the door!'

'Run, señorita, run!'

56

'How about I buy a chicken? Mercader, the man from the poultry shop, has a brother-in-law that brings them from his farm in Granollers.'

Beatriz smiled somewhat absently. Encarni made an excellent chicken in *sanfaina*; it always came out tender, even the breast meat.

'Fine. If they're good, bring two.'

Who knew what would happen in the coming days? Eating well doesn't protect you from the unpleasantness of life, but it makes it somewhat less disagreeable. And besides, part of the chicken would be wrapped up and taken to the slum where Encarni's family lived. She was thrilled with the generosity of the order, but that didn't mean she'd lost her pragmatism.

'Only if they're really good. You never know with Mercader, you always have to watch him.'

Encarni would undoubtedly make sure, pushing her thumb in to see if the meat was fresh, carefully checking the colour of the chicken's skin, comb and even its feet. And she'd only buy two whole chickens if she was convinced.

'Anything else, ma'am?'

Encarni waited one more moment before stepping out of the house with the shopping basket in her hand.

She had just closed the door when the telephone rang. Beatriz picked up the heavy black receiver and heard Ana's voice. 'I only escaped by the skin of my teeth.'

'What happened?'

She was calling from a bar. Beatriz could hear the shouting of the regulars in the background, the banging of cups and plates, the voice of a waiter ordering dishes.

'Two men were waiting for me at the door to the newspaper and they tried to force me to go with them. If it hadn't been for the porter, who intervened, I don't know what would have happened.'

'Calm down. Where are you?'

'In a restaurant on Caspe Street.'

'Then come to my house at once.'

'No, that's not possible.'

'Why not?'

'They were policemen. One of them was Burguillos, as I suspected. As soon as they tell Castro that I got away from them, they'll work out that, since I can't go home, I'll get in touch with you. I'm afraid your house is one of the places they'll be looking for me.'

Ana paused. Beatriz understood that she was giving her time to reach the conclusion that she couldn't stay in her house either. She looked around her, at her desk, her Persian carpet, the shelves filled with books. Her refuge, her home. She felt it slipping away from her.

From the other end of the line came Ana's voice urging her, 'Do you get the situation?'

'I'm afraid I do.'

'We need a safe place to meet.'

In her mind, the word 'safety' was always associated with books. Places with books were safe places. They had just snatched her most precious one – her personal library – but that wasn't the only one.

'Go to the Athenaeum. We'll meet there.'

'OK, but be careful. They might already be looking for you.'

She heard Ana hang up. The house was deadly silent. If what they were imagining was true, she would have to leave for a few days. She still didn't know where they could go.

But the important thing was to get out of the house as soon

336

as possible. And Encarni? How could she warn her of the danger? She didn't have any idea where Mercader's poultry shop was; maybe Encarni had told her at some point, but she hadn't paid attention. What would happen if the police came looking for her and found Encarni? They might try to pressure her, thinking that the maid could give them information as to her whereabouts. She decided that the best thing would be to demonstrate Encarni's innocence by leaving her a note. She scribbled.

Encarni, I have to leave urgently due to a serious family matter. I will be gone for at least a week. Don't worry. There's money in the drawer of the little table in the hall for your weekly shopping.

She signed it, making sure her name was completely legible. She placed the note on the kitchen table, held down by the salt shaker so it wouldn't blow away.

There was no way she could leave the copies of Mariona's letters in the house. She bundled them into an envelope and jammed that in her handbag along with Mendoza's papers.

She was about to leave when the telephone rang again. She picked it up thinking that it was Ana, who'd forgotten to tell her something. But the background noise was different.

'Is this Señora Beatriz Noguer?' asked a smooth male voice.

'Yes.'

'This is Inspector Castro, from the Criminal Investigation Brigade.'

The receiver almost fell from her hand. She said nothing. The man continued speaking.

'I wanted to make sure you were at home. I am going to come by in half an hour to speak with you. I would also appreciate you returning the copies of the letters that Señorita Martí gave you. Do you still have them?'

'Yes. No.'

'Yes or no?'

'Yes,' she had to admit.

'Good. I'm glad to hear it. Wait for me at your house.'

His tone was imperious. He hung up.

Beatriz glanced furtively at the window. What if Castro was already having her watched? She cautiously approached the window and looked out at the street, half hidden by the curtain. No one seemed to be watching her. But if they were, she supposed they would be discreet enough not to allow themselves to be seen.

How could she get away without attracting attention? The building's inner courtyard led to a house on Balmes Street whose back door was always open, but to get to it she'd have to climb over a wall.

She sighed. She hadn't climbed a wall in more than thirty years, and it was obvious that today, however terrified she was, she wasn't going to manage it. She had to go through the front door. Suddenly, absurdly, the name of the playwright Tirso de Molina popped into her head. Why had she thought of him now? Don Gil! *Don Gil of the Green Breeches*. Disguises. A woman disguised as a man.

She raced to the old wardrobe she had at the end of the hallway. There it was. Her Uncle Lázaro's magnificent cassock, and he hadn't been much taller than her.

A few minutes later she was appraising herself in the mirror. Despite the danger she was in, she couldn't help but think, like Don Fermín de Pas, the confessor of *The Regent's Wife*, that she looked good in a cassock, although it was a bit long for her. Even better; that way it hid her shoes. She threw a black cape over it, and succeeded in hiding her hair well beneath Uncle Lázaro's black hat. Its wide brim covered a good part of her face.

She looked at herself once more – this time objectively – and saw that she was quite inconspicuous. Anyone seeing her dressed like that would see only a priest. If her movements and her way of walking weren't particularly masculine, they would undoubtedly attribute it to the fact that she was a member of the clergy. They would see a small priest, who walked somewhat curved inward and carried a large bag.

She took a last glance around the house. A farewell, she

hoped not for long. She closed the door and walked slowly down the stairs, controlling her gait.

Ana burst out laughing when she related how she'd managed to get out of the house.

'I would like to have seen that.'

Beatriz shrugged it off.

'I changed my clothes as soon as I could. Luckily no one noticed that the priest never reappeared after going into one of the confessionals at the Santa Maria del Pino church.'

Ana had to laugh again. Then the gravity of their situation came sharply back to her and her face grew serious once more, the way Beatriz had found her when she arrived at the Athenaeum. By this point, Castro already knew that Beatriz had fled her house. The police would be looking for them with even more determination.

'What can we do now?'

'Maybe hide in some cheap hotel. I brought money with me.'

Ana shook her head.

'Too dangerous. They have to keep a register of their guests.'

'But aren't there hotels that are a little less painstaking about that?'

'Sure, in the Barrio Chino, for example. But I think that the two of us would attract a lot of attention there, and some informer might be minded to mention it to the police.'

Ana stirred another teaspoonful of sugar into her cup. Beatriz realised how tired she was; she saw her fallen shoulders, the slight tremble at the corner of her lips and the violet circles around her eyes.

'We can't go to my parents' house, it will be the first place Castro looks for me.'

Beatriz nodded. She had no one who could shelter them. Some of her old friends no longer lived in Barcelona; others had emigrated, or simply disappeared from her life. She thought of her brother. Salvador. He would definitely take them in, but it could create a lot of problems for him and he'd already done enough for her. Ana seemed to have read her thoughts because she murmured, 'We're like a ticking time bomb. Anyone who takes us in will end up with problems.'

'We are exiles, like El Cid, and no one can give us shelter.'

She began to recite some verses from *The Poem of the Cid*: 'Take him in they would gladly, yet none so much as dared: / the malice of King Alfonso had them rightly scared. / Before nightfall in Burgos entered the royal decree, / sealed by the King and brought carefully: / that to The Cid Roy Díaz, no man must offer shelter.'

As she recited the lines, she felt her mood improving. Ana looked at her, surprised. 'What are you so happy about?'

'It's just occurred to me where we can go.'

57

Pablo had arrived home little more than half an hour ago. He was tired. He had spent the morning in court and the afternoon dealing with paperwork at the office. He had a slight but persistent headache, a pressure on his forehead that he hoped wouldn't spread. He sat on a sofa in the small sitting room of his flat and rubbed the area with his fingertips. *Maybe it's my vision*, he thought, *maybe I need glasses*. He leapt up, went over to the window, opened it and looked out at the street. First at the window across the way. *I can see everything*. Then two floors down, at the first-floor balcony of the same block of flats. He could perfectly make out all the pieces of clothing hanging from the line. Another flat. The street. He could see the number painted on the wall; he could see the geometric design made by the bars in the door. He could even, despite being three storeys up, make out details on the clothes of passers-by. He could make out their faces clearly as they approached. He looked up and down the street. Then he recognised a familiar figure rounding the corner. It was his Aunt Beatriz. She was carrying a bag or a small suitcase. Who was the woman walking beside her? To his dismay, he had to squint to see her better, but when he recognised her, he forgot all about the indication that his sight was slightly waning. It was Ana Martí, his 'non-cousin', the one from the funeral, the one from the party at the Italian consulate. He was pleased to see her again.

They were drawing closer. He couldn't imagine that they just happened to be passing by his street; they must be coming to see him. Since he didn't want them to catch him spying on them if they happened to glance up, he pulled his head back into the sitting room and closed the window.

As he waited for them to arrive, he wondered what his Aunt Beatriz wanted. She didn't often visit him, usually quite the opposite – he was the one who normally dropped by her house to chat, or to consult her over some problem. And why was Ana Martí with her? He didn't think it had to do with the anonymous letter he had pilfered from Pla's safe. The matter wasn't completely closed, but he had certainly buried it. Or had she discovered something new? In that case, what could Ana have to do with it?

Finally the bell rang. He opened the door. The expression on the two women's faces left no doubt that it was something serious. His aunt's question alarmed him even further.

'Pablo, can we spend the night at your house?'

'Of course, of course. But, what's going on?'

He waved them inside and led them to the sitting room.

'I'm afraid we are in danger, Pablo.'

His aunt's use of the plural allowed him to look at Ana openly. He found her even more attractive than he had at the consulate party, but the seriousness in her face left no room for him to expand on his appreciation. He scooped a pile of news-papers from an armchair and offered them seats.

'What's happening?'

It was his Aunt Beatriz who began laying out the whole scenario, in which he played a small opening role thanks to their conversation in the Montjuïc cemetery. Then came Ana's visit and Mariona Sobrerroca's letters. There Ana intervened and told him about the trip they had made together to Martorell and how they had discovered a love-letter workshop.

'Aunt Beatriz, I didn't take you for someone so adventurous.'

'I'm not. The situation has turned very ugly.'

'When we discovered the whole business of the letters, it

'never occurred to us that there were two Mendoza brothers and that Abel had accidentally killed his brother and thrown his body into the river,' continued Ana.

The story got darker the longer it went on. The real Abel Mendoza was dead, murdered; the police were looking for them and they had material in their possession that incriminated many of Barcelona's society figures.

'And you think that one of the people whose names appear in those papers is Mariona Sobrerroca's and Abel Mendoza's killer?'

'We don't think they did it with their own hands, but they ordered their deaths,' clarified Ana.

'Do you suspect any one of them in particular?'

'Joaquín Grau.'

He couldn't have been more shocked.

'And the others?'

'They aren't powerful enough to have the police doing their dirty work,' said Beatriz.

'Those would be the ones who paid up religiously,' added Ana.

They showed him a few names, almost all of them well known, including a magnate who owned warehouses and wharves down at the port.

'This one,' commented Pablo, 'wouldn't have sent the police, exactly; more like union thugs.'

Then his eyes fell on a name: 'Pla! Not Pla too?'

Ana's reaction surprised him. 'Now I understand. The letter in the cemetery. Yes, I couldn't help overhearing your conversation. You are the nephew in a sticky situation.'

'Not any more.' He smiled at Beatriz.

Then he remembered that she and Ana were there about an infinitely more serious matter.

'Do you think my house is a safe place?'

'For the moment, yes. The police will first look in circles closer to me, but I doubt they'll think I'm at a nephew's house. They will look for people my age.'

His aunt continued to surprise him, not only for her

343

unexpected adventurous side, but also because, as a person he'd always presumed lived more in books than in the real world, she was all of a sudden showing astonishing practicality.

'But we won't stay long,' clarified Ana. 'Just until we know what to do.'

That phrase plunged all three of them into a vexed silence. They had no idea at all what they should do.

Every one of the authorities that, even in this country, they could have turned to – the police, the public prosecutor's office, in a word, the 'law' – was implicated in the matter. And who were they? A bookworm and a rookie journalist. And he? A two-bit lawyer. The harshness of these labels proved to Pablo that he was succumbing to low spirits as well.

Ana was leaning slightly on the arm of the chair and looking towards the window with her chin resting on the back of her right hand. His Aunt Beatriz was sitting very upright with her hands together on her lap. If he didn't know better, he would have said she was praying. And yet, if it wasn't prayer, it had to be something similar, because Pablo saw her slowly lift her head and rest her gaze absently on the ceiling. He knew then that she was reverting to her true religion. He imitated her. A minute later Ana also began contemplating the same vague point on the ceiling. Out of the blue Beatriz glumly named the divinity to whom she had appealed.

'Lope. *Fuenteovejuna*. The people cry out for justice against the Commander and, in the end, the King and Queen deliver it. Something similar happens in *Peribáñez*. Also in Calderón's *The Mayor of Zalamea*. In the face of a powerful person's injustice, the villagers appeal to a higher authority. What a utopia! Not to mention that it's a sad irony of the times, in which we have to run away from those who should protect us from abuses.'

It wasn't exactly a comforting or encouraging comment.

'A higher authority,' said Ana, who was still looking up at the ceiling. Pablo searched for the point her eyes were fixed

344

on. It wasn't a higher authority, but rather a five-petalled flower that decorated the moulding. He and his aunt looked at each other, then back up at the ceiling and then at Ana. 'We have to go to a higher authority.'

'Who do you want us to go to, Ana? They're all involved, from Castro to the public prosecutor.'

Beatriz's voice sounded so hopeless that Pablo was quick to defend Ana's idea, even if only to have the feeling that he was doing something.

'Don't write it off so fast. Let's think about it. Really, what we need is someone who would take care of this matter for us so we could stay out of it. Isn't that right, Ana?'

'You know the police structures, Pablo. The commissioner in charge of the section where Castro works doesn't come from the CIB but from Social, right?'

'Yes, Commissioner Goyanes. He is a hardliner, a son of...' he restrained himself after a glare from his aunt, '... his mother. They put him there to control the guys in the CIB, who some believe are too modern in their methods and their contacts with foreign police.'

'Yes, and so?' asked Beatriz.

'Well, he and Castro don't get on, I've noticed when I've worked at the headquarters.'

'Of course, they have different ideas. Castro is one of Grau's men. The prosecutor didn't look favourably on the Civil Government putting Goyanes at the head of the CIB. The Commissioner has never been a real member of the CIB, nor will he ever be. He's Social all the way. I don't think he's mixed up in this.'

'You don't think he would take advantage of the opportunity to strip the CIB of its prestige, even if he is now one of its commissioners? If we gave him information that he can use against Grau...'

'And how are we going to do that, Ana?' asked Beatriz. 'We can't turn up at headquarters and tell him all this.'

'You can't, but I can,' said Pablo.

'How would you do it?'

345

'First of all, by feeling out the territory. I will tell him that I've got information that's so juicy, I find myself forced to break partly with professional confidentiality in order to set him on the trail of some serious accusations against people in his Brigade. I'll tell him what we know about Mariona and Mendoza's business and about the blackmailing and . . . '

'And what if he wants to know where you got all that information?'

'Simple, Tieta; I'll tell him that Abel Mendoza came to me to see if I could help get him out of the country, and ended up telling me much more because he was desperate and he trusted my confidentiality.'

'And how did Mendoza find you? Your firm isn't exactly the first one a poor wretch like him would think to turn to,' objected Beatriz.

'He met me the same way Goyanes did: a spell of court duty. For your information, I have quite a good reputation, although only in certain circles.'

He seemed to be convincing them. Ana had laughed at his last comment, and his Aunt Beatriz had given him a look of admiration. Then she grabbed one of Garmendia's papers. 'You'll have better luck convincing him if you show him this.'

'But, Tieta, surely you don't want to hand them over? Even though they are after you for them, these papers are, unfortunately, your life insurance policy.'

'Just this one.'

'And what do we expect him to do?' asked Ana.

'What you and Pablo said. He'll take down Castro, and Grau will fall with him.'

'If he does accept, we'll only give him the material relating to Grau. We can't give him the rest. Goyanes would have a lot of people in his power. What do you think someone like him will do with the information about the abortions, for example?'

'It's true.'

Pablo interjected, 'For the moment I think the important thing is that we see how Goyanes reacts.'

He shot a look up at the ceiling stucco, at the flower with five petals. It was a preposterous, desperate plan, but it was the only one they had.

The next day he would go and talk to Goyanes.

58

Carlos Belda was already putting on his freshly pressed suit jacket when Mateo Sanvisens came into the dry cleaner's.

'Are you alone?' he asked.

'I came with Roig, but he's going to stay for at least another hour. He really needed it. His suit was covered in big grease stains and he needed the company.'

Sanvisens didn't get the joke.

'Have you paid?'

'Wait.'

Carlos paid for the services rendered. The owner of the dry cleaner's and brothel gave him his change while he kept shooting looks at the gaunt man who hadn't taken his hands out of his trouser pockets. He must have been worried he was a cop. Carlos tried to take the fellow's mind off it.

'If my friend asks for some extra service, put it on my tab and I'll pay for it next time, Adriano.'

'Whatever you say. Are you satisfied?'

Carlos patted the trousers of the perfectly pressed suit and gave a couple of little tugs on his jacket sleeves.

'Impeccable. As always.'

Sanvisens was growing impatient. He opened the door to the dry cleaner's. Carlos followed him out.

'Is it something urgent?' he asked.

'It's something serious. Let's go somewhere where we can talk.'

Santa Ana Street was already crowded at that hour of the

morning. They passed the Jorba department store. Carlos searched for something or someone that would give him the chance to break Sanvisens's silence. Maybe a funny crack about the Latin motto that decorated the sculpture on the department store's facade, *Labor omnia vincit*, work conquers all; but considering that Sanvisens had come to find him at an illegal brothel, it seemed counterproductive. How had he located him? Who had told him where he was? Had he called his house? Carlos had told his wife that he was heading to the newspaper early because he had a long feature to write. He'd have a scene when he got home, but the ticking off that might be waiting for him weighed less on his mind than Sanvisens's silence, which he found more unbearable with each step. He was searching for some topic to break it with: an eccentric pedestrian, an odd hat, a little lapdog wearing a bow, the weather. The weather!

'Did you know they want to put a giant thermometer at the bottom of Portal del Ángel Street? It'll be the largest thermometer in the world, more than twenty metres high. It'll go along the entire front of Cottet Optician's, and will work with lights. Each degree of temperature is a red lamp that lights up.'

Sanvisens acknowledged receipt of the information with a nod of his head.

They continued in silence, dodging passers-by and beggars, more common in that part of town with its shops and churches. They took Los Arcos Street on the left, which led them to the cathedral square. Carlos filled the silence with recollections of his old aversion to the facade of Barcelona's cathedral, its neo-Gothic arches, its neo-Gothic columns, all fake. They headed towards it.

The beggars became more numerous. The entrance was completely surrounded. He counted and classified them so that he could go past them without feeling as afflicted. Seven in total. Three old women swathed in clothes from head to toe, a man with only one hand, a man without legs, a girl and an ambiguous bundle coiled over itself and leaning against a wall.

Inside, the air was heavy with wax, incense and the sweat of the faithful who'd filed out only ten minutes earlier. He trailed Sanvisens, passing several chapels on their right. In the middle of the nave Sanvisens pointed him to a pew. They sat down. The rest of the people remaining in the cathedral were a fair distance off, absorbed in their devotions. No one turned to look at them.

'Why did you bring me here?'

'So I could talk to you,' he responded in a whisper.

'We could have talked on the street.'

'But I want you to tell me the truth,' he replied, as his gaze flickered around the cathedral nave. *You wouldn't lie to me here, would you?* said his movements.

Sanvisens was projecting his ethical code onto others, which was, in Carlos's opinion, sometimes his greatest defect or, in this case, his greatest virtue.

'Carlos, have you interfered in any way in the Sobrerroca case?'

He wasn't looking at him; he kept his eyes straight ahead, and his expression left no room for doubt: he knew something, and there was no point in lying to him. He would never forgive him for it.

'I've just made a few enquiries, asked some questions . . . '

'What questions? Who did you ask?'

Sanvisens sat bolt upright on the bench and, although he was muttering, his voice had an imperative, curt tone. Carlos leaned closer and began his confession, in a reedy whisper: 'The truth is, one time I followed Ana Martí and saw her talking to a man in the Ciudadela. It was after she'd received some letter that had got her all wound up.'

'You spied on a colleague?'

'I'm not proud of it, if that's what you want to hear. But it would only have amounted to a less than glorious moment in my career if I hadn't happened to recognise the same man on a slab in the Montjuïc morgue a few days later.'

'Why didn't you come to me?'

'Because you would have thought I was jealous of that girl.'

'Would I have been wrong?'

Carlos was silent.

'Who did you go to with your questions?'

Belda leaned even closer to Sanvisens. His tone was contrite. 'I called a contact I have in the police force.'

'Who?'

'It's just that—'

'Who?' shouted Sanvisens.

Several people turned to look. One of them got up, surely on her way to tell a priest.

'Commissioner Goyanes, of the CIB.'

'To tell him what?'

'That I knew the dead guy at the morgue because I'd seen him once, talking to somebody who worked at the paper, the one who was writing the articles about the case.'

'Why? To what end? Are you aware that you've put Ana Martí in danger? Do you know they came looking for her at the office and that, if it weren't for the porter, they would have taken her on one of their walks?'

'The retarded bloke?'

'That's the one. He took care of the thugs all on his own. Those guys were policemen.'

They both knew what that meant: that someday, when they were least expecting it, the police would be lying in wait for them around a corner or in a doorway.

'Why did you do it, Carlos?'

At that moment, Carlos was unable to give a reason beyond his professional spite and how unbearable he found the presence of his mentor Andreu Martí's daughter in the newsroom. His silence led Sanvisens to a different conclusion. He turned to him with a forlorn expression, and when he spoke, his voice was full of sorrow: 'Are you an informer, Carlos?'

Belda rubbed his forehead with his hand several times before saying, 'No, I'm not an informer. I'm just an imbecile.'

59

'Isidro.'

'What is it?'

'Jesus, you're in some mood,' chided Manzaneque before getting to what had brought him to his colleague's office. 'We've got a dead lady.'

'Well, how about that! How original! A dead lady! It's not even nine and we've already got our first stiff. Where?'

'In the Ensanche, on the Rambla de Cataluña. Come on, let's go.'

They left the office and headed towards the car. No words were exchanged, but it was clear that Manzaneque was going to drive. They got in and drove off.

'Want a smoke?'

Manzaneque held out a packet he pulled from his shirt pocket without taking his eyes off the traffic. Bisonte brand.

'Black tobacco? No thanks.'

'You smoke blonde now? Are you getting queer on me?'

'I'm trying to give it up.'

He couldn't stand how his wife moved her face away involuntarily when he approached to kiss her. But he wasn't going to tell that to Manzaneque, who continued with his mocking, 'Oh, fine. I get it. Black, blonde, then you start with menthols and once you end up using a cigarette holder like a showgirl on the Paralelo, your life's complete.'

'Fuck off!'

'Aren't we touchy! It's great to see how much you're

enjoying your promotion. If they ever make you Commissioner, you'll probably blow your brains out with happiness.'

He couldn't explain to Manzaneque – he couldn't explain it to anyone – but his euphoria over his promotion to First Class Inspector had been snuffed out. Ana Martí's visit hadn't been a bucket of cold water, but it had prompted an insidious drip-drip in his mind that had eventually extinguished his enthusiasm. The solution to the Sobrerroca case was a fraud; his promotion, nothing more than a bribe, a juicy bit of meat to keep the dog from barking. He wouldn't bark, he wasn't that stupid, but he couldn't stop growling at everyone, starting with Manzaneque.

They reached the Rambla de Cataluña. As the car approached the huddle of onlookers that had formed in the street, Isidro's heart shrank. He knew the building; he had been there the day before only to confirm that Beatriz Noguer hadn't waited for him, that she'd fled.

Manzaneque whistled to get the crowd to part and drove the car up on the central pavement. When they climbed out of the vehicle, everyone fell silent. That was the immediate effect of the policemen's presence.

The officer who was keeping the nosy parkers out of the house told them that the dead woman had been found in the first-floor flat by the doorman's son. Isidro glanced at the boy, about eleven years old, who was watching him fearfully from a stool inside the doorman's cubbyhole. Beside him stood a man in dark blue overalls, who put a hand on the boy's shoulder in a protective gesture that identified him as his father. Seeing the policeman's gaze on him, the man began to speak.

'I sent the boy up to deliver a letter from abroad, from England, that had just arrived. The boy collects stamps, and Señora Noguer always lets him have them. He knocked on the door and then he realised that it wasn't closed and went in.'

'But I didn't touch a thing!'

He didn't need to hear any more.

Isidro went upstairs without urgency. If Beatriz Noguer was dead, there was no reason to rush.

Another policeman was posted in front of the partly open door to the flat to keep out the indiscreet looks of the fellow residents gathered on the landing. Just like at a wake, there was a murmur of voices beneath which the occasional nervous giggle could be heard. And just like at a wake, the appearance of a new person shut down all the voices at once, and one or two seconds later someone let out a sob.

Isidro entered the flat and closed the door behind him.

He oriented himself by the voices of the officers he heard to his right. Following them, he found the kitchen. He went in. A woman's legs covered in dark stockings stuck out from behind a table. On the kitchen floor, potatoes and vegetables had scattered. The first red stain that caught his eye wasn't blood but a tomato someone had stepped on. The woman who lay on the floor, face down, her head twisted to the left in a puddle of blood, was not Beatriz Noguer. She was a young woman.

'It's the maid, Encarnación Rodríguez Alarcón,' said the officer who was inspecting the kitchen.

Isidro carefully approached the area where the woman's head was, dodging the vegetables that had fallen onto the floor, as well as the dark pool of dried blood around her head. He knelt down and touched her face. It was cold and bore dark patches that weren't from the blows that'd killed her, indicating that she had been dead for more than twelve hours. She must have been murdered a few hours after he had knocked on the door in vain. It seems they had surprised her in the kitchen as she returned loaded down with groceries. That meant that her killer had entered the house before she did. Was whoever it was there when he rang the bell? He knew it was a useless speculation that served only to accentuate the crushing feeling of failure that now seized him.

'Found anything suspicious in the flat?' he asked the officer.

'Everything is suspicious, because the whole place has been turned upside down. Have a look for yourself, if you want.'

He left the room and went through the flat. They had emptied every drawer in the house, from the dresser where the owner had kept her clothes to the sideboard with napkins and silverware. But where they had really vented their anger was in the room that must have been her study. The shelves were empty, books heaped open on the floor, the drawers had been ripped from the desk and their contents scattered on a rug, of which only a small triangle could be seen under all the paper. He was beginning to understand that it wasn't a break-in; that they had been looking for the owner of the flat. In reality, they wanted something that she had in her flat or that they thought was there. The letters. That damn Ana Martí hadn't given him the copies! Why? And where was Beatriz Noguer? Had she fled, or had she been kidnapped? Again the big question: why? The fact that they'd searched with such determination might mean that they hadn't found Beatriz Noguer and so they couldn't get what they were looking for out of her. Whatever it was, it was so important that they had killed that poor maid over it and – he now saw clearly – the man Ana Martí had told him was Abel Mendoza. What did Mariona Sobrerroca have to do with all this? Ana Martí had told him that Mendoza was her lover. Why had they been bumped off? Seeing the way the killers had gone through the flat, it was clear they were looking for papers. What did Señora Sobrerroca's letters have in them that unleashed such violence? Who was in a position to exert such violence?

He heard voices at the front door. He recognised that of Coroner Soldevila, who was coming to remove the body. He went back to the kitchen to inspect the crime scene once more, making sure that the officers had taken note of everything important and that they had taken all the necessary photos.

'Castro! This is an extremely unappetising scene! And forgive the remark, it's in poor taste. What do we have here?'

'It seems to be a break-in, Coroner.'

'And the poor girl, in the wrong place at the wrong time, is that it?'

'Unfortunately.'

It was the only time that morning that he didn't lie or hide information from Coroner Soldevila. Since Isidro was known to be a man of few words, no one found it strange that he remained almost mute while the body was removed. When Manzaneque came upstairs after interrogating the doorman and his son, Isidro asked him for a cigarette.

'Your good intentions don't last long, son,' he said, pulling out the packet of Bisonte.

By this time, Soldevila was preparing to leave the flat.

'Congratulations, Castro. I heard about your promotion.'

'Be careful, sir, you don't know how badly he takes good news. If one more person congratulates him, he's going to bite someone's head off,' said Manzaneque, alluding to the painful grimace that had appeared on Isidro's face on hearing the coroner's congratulations.

'Well, I don't understand why,' Soldevila commented. 'You should be very proud.'

Isidro almost stalked off before he'd finished his sentence. He felt a lot of things: above all, fear at what could happen to Ana Martí and Beatriz Noguer. And he felt so many things in addition to fear: concern, rage, impotence . . . Everything but pride.

In the car on the way back, Manzaneque went on with his speculations but received only tepid comments in response.

'In my opinion, they killed the girl because she surprised them in the house.'

'That's what I think.'

'Something must have gone wrong . . . these gangs that burgle flats observe the habits of the people who live there and, when they have them well studied, they break into their houses when they're all out. They only steal things that they can get out without attracting attention to themselves: jewellery, money, gold or silver cutlery, watches . . .'

'The doorman didn't see a thing.'

'Doormen are easily distracted,' replied Manzaneque. 'One

356

of the accomplices makes a scene on the street and the doorman's out there, seeing what's going on.'

'Useless. They're all useless.'

'Another ciggie?'

'Yeah.'

Manzaneque passed him one, then drew a box of matches
from his jacket pocket. They were already crossing the Gran
Vía.

'Something up, Isidro?'

'No.'

'If you say so.'

Isidro shot him an incredulous look. Who did he think he
was? His father? His older brother? Manzaneque didn't catch
it; he was lowering the car window to toss out his cigarette
butt. Then he turned to Isidro. 'We'll have to find the owner,
Beatriz Noguer.'

'Yup.'

However, another question had begun to take shape in
Isidro's head. It was the reason behind the creeping irritation
he'd been feeling since he entered the flat. Who, besides him,
knew of Beatriz Noguer's existence? Who could link her to
the copies of the stolen letters?

60

Pablo had struggled all morning against his impulse to leave the office and return home. Early that afternoon he had an appointment with Commissioner Goyanes, whom he had called and asked to see, saying he wanted to discuss a case. He had taken the precaution of disguising his voice and not giving his name.

'When we meet, I will identify myself properly,' he had replied when Goyanes insisted.

Anonymous tip-offs and informants were the order of the day, the Commissioner accepted, albeit reluctantly. The bait that Pablo had offered him had been persuasive. In a tone somewhere between indignant and conspiratorial he had revealed that he had some evidence in his possession that was linked to 'a murder case affecting top brass', while stressing that he couldn't be more explicit.

'Because, unfortunately, I'm afraid that one of your men didn't honestly fulfil his obligations. You do understand?'

Of course, the Commissioner had understood and agreed to the meeting. What Pablo hadn't managed to get him to agree to was to meet outside of police headquarters, so he had to be careful not to run into Castro.

He was nervous, both wishing and fearing that the moment would arrive. The routine work he had on his desk wasn't helping to make the hours pass quickly, but he had to keep up appearances. His absence from the firm would draw attention; he had never missed a day of work, not even after the liveliest nights or with the worst hangovers, whose ravages were still evident on his face when he turned up at work the next morning. Even though they hadn't come right out and said it, he had the feeling that Pla and Calvet even appreciated his arriving at work punctually despite his lack of sleep and his pounding head. Cocaine had been a godsend for those mornings, until his bosses had set him up and he realised how vulnerable it made him. This morning he was relying on the help of coffee alone.

Now that he knew about Pla's addiction, he felt his resentment growing, but his revenge, in whatever form, was a secondary matter. Helping Ana and his Aunt Beatriz took absolute priority. So he'd have to wait and play it cool.

He pulled it off. He went running out of his office at midday and said goodbye to Maribel. When he was already reaching the stairs, he heard her cry, 'Pablo! Telephone!'

'I'm late for an appointment,' he shouted without stopping.

He started down the stairs.

'It's your father.'

He slowed his pace a little, but kept going. 'I haven't time right now.'

He reached his house just over half an hour later. As he went in he was surprised to find his Aunt Beatriz sitting in the hall-way, on one of the stools that flanked the little telephone table.

'It hasn't stopped ringing in the last half-hour,' she said, pointing to the phone. She was agitated. 'But I didn't answer it.'

As Pablo was taking off his jacket, the telephone rang again. Beatriz jumped. Ana appeared at the other end of the hallway. He couldn't see her face because she was backlit, but he noticed the tension in her bearing. He snatched up the tele-phone and answered it.

'Hello, Papa,' he said, and grinned at his aunt.

Immediately the distress disappeared from Beatriz's face. She leaned back on the stool and rested herself against the wall.

'I've been trying to track you down for the last hour,' said his father. 'I called you at the office but you had already gone.'

'I left the office on time today.'

'They told me. That's why I've been calling you at home.'

'Ah! You must have been calling while I was on my way here,' he said so that Beatriz and Ana would hear.

He looked up at the ceiling and composed a resigned expression. Beatriz shot him a complicit look that said 'my brother can be so controlling', and got up to let him speak in private. She was even smiling. Pablo couldn't return the smile because his father had come to the reason for his call: 'Son, something horrible has happened at your aunt's house.'

Pablo put a hand on Beatriz's shoulder to keep her from leaving. Ana had come closer.

'What happened?'

Beatriz turned. The smile was wiped from her face as she heard the following words from her nephew: 'Encarni, dead? How?'

'Someone broke into the house. It looks as if it was an attempted burglary, and she surprised them. They hit her over the head.'

Pablo had enough presence of mind not to be distracted by the two women's shock.

'And Aunt Beatriz?'

'That's the worst of it, son, we don't know where she is. No one has seen her in two days. I'm so worried. I'm afraid they've ...'

His father couldn't go on. Beatriz was making urgent gestures for Pablo to pass her the receiver. He shook his head and warned her to stay silent by bringing his index finger to his lips. He had the telephone pressed tightly to his ear and he could hear his father struggling to stifle a sob. He didn't know how long he would have been able to hold out, between Beatriz's silent pleading and his father's barely contained anguish, if Ana hadn't steered his aunt inside the flat.

'What are the police saying?'

'Nothing, of course. They have no idea. I spoke with the coroner, who is an acquaintance of mine, and he told me that it's being handled by the best man in the CIB, Inspector Castro.'

'I've heard of him.'

He had to remind himself how crucial his discretion was to keep from giving the game away to his father.

'What if they've kidnapped her?' his father conjectured.

'Why would they kidnap Aunt Beatriz?'

'I don't know, perhaps to pressure me. I'm involved in a big property deal where there are a lot of interests at stake. I'll just mention one name: Julio Muñoz.'

Muñoz was the king of Barcelona's black market, a man as powerful as he was unscrupulous.

'What can I do? What can I do?'

His father, who had always maintained his composure, even when, as a young child, a group of militiamen had burst into his family home and threatened to shoot him in the library, was falling to pieces.

Pablo had a flash of inspiration: 'Wasn't Aunt Beatriz wanting to spend a few days in La Rioja looking for some manuscripts? Don't you remember her mentioning that at Aunt Blanca's funeral?'

'La Rioja?'

'Yes. I remember distinctly. You were talking with somebody about some property, but she told you about it.'

His father clung to that impossible memory. Pablo wondered if the words he'd just invented weren't already echoing in his father's head.

'Where could that sister of mine be ...'

The expression Pablo had heard him say so many times in a disapproving tone now sounded filled with affection. His father was beginning to regain some of his calm.

'I'll let the police know. Poor thing! She's going to be so upset when she finds out what's happened! And now she's in the library of some monastery, engrossed in a dusty manuscript.'

The more he talked, the more convinced he seemed by what he was saying. They spoke only a little longer because his father was in a rush to call the police.

He found Beatriz and Ana on the sofa in the sitting room,

361

holding each other, both in tears. Ana was caressing her aunt's hair and trying to console her.

'I should have waited for her,' repeated Beatriz in a litany.

'They would have killed you too,' Ana said.

'But not her. They were looking for me. Not even that. They were looking for these damn papers.'

She lifted her face to speak to Ana. Her eyes were flooded with tears and two locks of hair fell over her forehead.

Pablo sat on her other side and took her hand.

'Ana is right, Tieta. These people are extremely dangerous and, it seems, deranged.'

They sat for a long time until Beatriz was calmer. She had her head resting on Ana's shoulder, who lulled her to sleep as she stroked her hair. Pablo held her hand. At one point he felt her grip loosening. She gradually fell silent too, stopped saying over and over that it was her fault. Pablo looked at her. She had her eyes closed, as if dozing. Ana had her eyes closed too, which allowed him to gaze at her with complete impunity. For a second the image of the two women resting on each other, breathing steadily, made him forget that they were in a situation that looked to be a dead end. He would have liked to preserve them like that, offer them a refuge that would keep them out of danger.

But it was merely an illusion. He couldn't protect them from anything, and they couldn't allow themselves to mourn Encarni's death.

As if she had read his thoughts, Ana's eyes sprang open with such force that Pablo thought he could hear it.

'We can't stay like this, waiting,' she said.

In her face, Pablo recognised the determination of someone who knows there is no way out.

'How long before your meeting with Goyanes?'

'An hour.'

'Well, let's go over everything you have to say. Beatriz, you should lie down for a little while.'

'How can I lie down?'

'You have to rest a little, to get over the news of Encarni's death.'

'I don't want to get over it. I don't want to.'

Pablo noticed that Beatriz's expression had shifted from sadness to rage. He was young, but he had been to enough funerals to know that this was the flip side of mourning, as necessary and human as the grief.

Encarni's death didn't change their plan; in fact, it only made it more pressing. They went over it together.

Soon afterwards, Pablo left the house and set off towards the Vía Layetana.

61

As soon as Isidro arrived at headquarters, he ordered Sevilla into his office. In the blink of an eye, the officer was standing before him.

'Did anyone assist you when you made enquiries into Beatriz Noguer?'

'No.'

Sevilla told him that he had followed the normal procedures to check if a person had a criminal record, that this was how he'd found out that she'd been purged, that she had lived in Argentina . . . The information that he had given to Isidro.

In order to get it he had had to make a few calls and request details in writing. All of which left a trail. An internal trail, but that was exactly what had been worrying Isidro since the disappearance of the letters and other materials on the Sobrerroca case: the thief was among them, on the force.

'Why do you want to know?' asked Sevilla.

Isidro was faced with a dilemma. Could he trust Sevilla, or was he the mole? He couldn't imagine it was him. And he urgently needed someone he could confide in. In a matter of seconds, as the officer stood on the opposite side of his desk shifting his weight from foot to foot, Isidro made a decision: he would trust him. And if he was making a mistake, he'd damn it all to hell. He'd take his wife and his kids and they'd all go back to his village in Galicia.

'Sit down, Sevilla.'

The officer obeyed.

'What I am about to tell you is serious. Some very strange things have been going on here in the last few days.'

Then he revealed the disappearance of the letters, his suspicions, his questions. Sevilla's face darkened as he listened.

'Well, there is something I have to confess to you, boss,' he said finally.

Sevilla didn't know that his words were practically giving Isidro an attack of vertigo; that, in his burning desire to flee, he was clearly envisioning his family home in Galicia. The officer went on: 'A few weeks ago I saw something strange too, but I chose not to tell you because I didn't think it was important.'

The inspector's mind returned to Barcelona.

'What did you see?'

'One time when that journalist from *La Vanguardia* was here, while you were talking to the Commissioner, Burguillos went into your office and I caught him poking around in the Sobrerroca papers.'

For a moment, Isidro was stock-still. Then he slapped his forehead with the palm of his hand.

'Burguillos! That bastard! It has to be him!'

Suddenly a lot of things became clear. Burguillos had stolen the letters. Burguillos.

Burguillos, Goyanes's lackey, his boy for everything. Hadn't Goyanes got him out of his office on some excuse? Now he understood why: so that Burguillos could get in there and swipe the letters. Now, too, he understood why Commissioner Goyanes had asked him to treat the theft with such discretion. He had ordered the theft. He was the one who was looking for the two women. His men, therefore, were the ones who had gone into Beatriz Noguer's house. The ones who had killed that young woman. Why? Above all, for whom? Goyanes, like Burguillos, was just a subordinate. The question was, subordinate to whom?

'Fucking brilliant,' he said to himself and also partly to Sevilla, who was waiting in silence for him to explain what was going through his head.

Finding out who Goyanes was working for was secondary; the most pressing thing was to find the women before the Commissioner's men did – before his own colleagues did.

62

A few minutes after Pablo had gone, Ana called Sanvisens. She dialled the number and sat down on the left-hand stool, while Beatriz sat on the other.

She wasn't expecting much from the conversation. She was calling mainly to check that the line was still working, that she'd hear Sanvisens's voice at the other end. So she was surprised by his reaction when he picked up: 'Thank goodness you called! I need to speak to you urgently.'

'Why?'

'I've spoken with Carlos Belda.'

Sanvisens gave her a summary of their conversation.

'That cheat!'

Beatriz jumped.

'You're right, Ana, but the most important thing is that, if what Carlos has told me is true, it's not Castro who's after you, it's Goyanes.'

'No! Shit!'

Beatriz looked at her with fear in her eyes.

'I'm so sorry, Ana. What can I do for you?'

'Nothing, I'm afraid.'

She couldn't stay on the telephone with Sanvisens; she had to run, to try to find Pablo and stop him.

Hanging up, Ana turned to Beatriz.

'We've made a terrible mistake. It's Goyanes who's mixed up in this. I've got to catch Pablo before he talks to him.'

'I'm going with you.'

'No. You have to stay here in case he comes back.'

Reluctantly, Beatriz accepted.

Ana raced out into the street and hailed a cab.

She reached the Vía Layetana in fifteen minutes. Pablo couldn't be there already, unless he had taken a taxi as well. She trusted that he hadn't. It wasn't yet three o'clock. Pablo would be coming from Urquinaona Plaza. Ana ducked into a doorway on the opposite side of the street and fixed her gaze in that direction. Every once in a while she stole a glance at the entrance to the police headquarters, but discreetly. If someone asked her, she'd say she was waiting for her boyfriend. Why would anyone ask her anything? If someone came over and spoke to her, it would be because they had recognised her. She didn't know Goyanes's face, and he surely didn't know hers either, but Burguillos and the other cop did. With a bit of luck, the porter had pierced his eardrum and he was lying in hospital. She had forgotten to ask Sanvisens what had happened after she'd managed to escape their trap. She was hoping they hadn't retaliated against the poor man. And the other policeman? Every minute she waited added to the danger that she would be discovered.

Finally Pablo appeared around the corner. He was walking with determined steps. She didn't want to call his name; she had to approach him. She crossed the street, dodging cars. She hoped no policeman would feel obligated to pull her in for obstructing the traffic. Luckily no car honked, and her manoeuvre went unnoticed. She made it across the road; Pablo was so focused on his meeting with Goyanes that he didn't see her until she was two paces away from him.

Ana flashed him a big smile, looped her arm through his and dragged him to a stop. 'How lovely to see you, Pablo!'

Without letting go of his arm, she forced him to turn around.

'What are you doing here, Ana?'

'I'll tell you that as soon as I can, but first let's get out of here as quickly as possible.' They reached Urquinaona Plaza. 'It'd be best if we took a taxi.'

They flagged one down and gave the driver Pablo's address. They weren't quick enough to tell him to avoid the Vía Layetana. Still too disoriented by the danger they had just managed to escape, they didn't avert their faces as the cab passed by the police headquarters. There, Ana's eyes met those of someone she knew: Officer Sevilla.

63

Once Ana had left, Beatriz stayed sitting on the stool in the hallway.

Pablo's telephone had rung twice. She knew she shouldn't answer it, although she supposed it could be Salvador, concerned about her disappearance. *Wait a little bit, Tete*, she said to her brother in her head, using the nickname she'd always called him when they were little. In the gloom of the hallway she thought of Encarni, poor Encarni. She would never know what song she would have dedicated to her in the Radio Juventud contest. Her mood swung between crushing sorrow, guilt and rage that rose from her stomach and threatened to choke her.

One of Quevedo's sonnets came to her aid: *You, oh minister!, be sure to pay great mind / injure not the strong, injure not the despised; / when you take their gold and silver, be apprised / that you have left their burnished steel behind*. The first tercet failed to console her, but there were a few later lines whose repetition saved her from succumbing to the corrosive force of her impotent hatred.

> Those who see their certain perdition, abhor,
> more than their perdition, its underlying cause;
> and it is this latter that spurs their rancour.

She recited those lines like a litany until she heard footsteps on the stairs and a minute later the door opened. Ana and Pablo were home.

'Now what?'

It was Pablo who spoke, but any of them could have asked the question, and with the same bewilderment.

They put the paper Pablo had taken with him from Garmendia's collection back with the others. Pablo only dared articulate in fragments what could have happened if he'd arrived at his appointment with Goyanes. The Commissioner must already be wondering why he hadn't turned up.

'Thank goodness you didn't give him your name, Pablo.'

They were seated around the living room table. They had spread out all the papers on its surface and were looking at them as if in the hope that, suddenly, something new would leap out, abracadabra.

The window was open and they heard the voices of a small group of children who were playing Buck Buck in the street.

'Buck, buck, ya lousy muck, how many fingers have I got up, one, two, three or none?'

'One?'

'Two!'

Laughter and shouting.

Then a silence that matched their own, soon broken by more running steps and a voice, 'Buck, buck, ya lousy muck, how many fingers have I got up, one, two, three or none?'

'Two?'

'Yes!'

Shouts. Shouts and applause. And banging. Banging? The banging wasn't coming from the street, but from the door to the flat. The banging was just the prelude to the doorbell. Someone was hammering on the door.

Pablo got up. Beatriz and Ana sat paralysed at the table.

'Buck, buck, how many horns do I hold up?'

'Open up! Police! We know you're in there.'

64

Neither Pablo nor Beatriz knew that voice. Ana did. It was Isidro Castro.

Pablo opened the door. The two women had risen from their seats and saw him backlit in the doorway.

'Can I come in?'

'What do you want?'

'To talk to these two ladies.' Castro pointed in their direction.

Pablo stepped aside to let him in. The policeman's solid, stocky body seemed to fill the entire width of the hallway.

'Don't you think we've had enough of this cat-and-mouse game, Señora Noguer? And as for you,' he addressed Ana, 'whether I arrest you or not depends on what you tell me now.'

Pablo followed him into the sitting room.

'Make yourself at home, Inspector.'

Castro accepted the invitation and sat down at the table. The papers were still there, somewhat disordered in the panic at hearing him at the door.

The policeman glanced at them.

'If I'm not mistaken, there are a lot of people after these papers, isn't that right?'

Since he was looking at her, it was Ana who nodded.

'And are you going to tell me why, or do I have to read them?'

'Aren't you going to tell us how you found us?'

She wasn't particularly surprised by Castro's response:

'Señorita Martí, don't get ahead of yourself. I'll be the one who asks the questions.' Nor by the smirk that accompanied it. He was repeating something he'd said to her in their very first conversation. It was a wink, a sign that he wasn't the enemy, but that he wasn't openly presenting himself as a friend either. What Castro said next confirmed her interpretation.

'But if you must know, we made enquiries into Señora Noguera when you mentioned her part in your ... let's just call them *explorations*. And the doorman at her house told us that she received few visitors, but one was a nephew named Pablo. And a little while ago Officer Sevilla, whom you know, saw you jump into a taxi with a young man. So, as you can see, it wasn't that hard to work out. And now it's your turn. What do these papers say?'

They told him. From their discovery, to their contents, and how they were used to blackmail the people named in them.

'One of the names that appears in these papers is the person who killed Mariona Sobrerroca and Abel Mendoza,' said Ana.

'And Encarni.' Those were the first words from Beatriz since Castro had entered the house. 'In order to get these papers, they killed her, too.'

'I'm very sorry, ma'am.'

Ana began to see Castro as a possible way out of the situation they were in; an ally, perhaps, so she said, 'To tell you the truth, until a few hours ago, we believed that the person ordering the killings was Grau, the public prosecutor, and that you were mixed up in it too.'

'Forgive me if I don't laugh at your little joke.'

'I wasn't trying to be funny. We suspected Grau because he was implicated in a case of corruption and the trafficking of adulterated penicillin.'

'A crime that could cost him more than his job – it could get him the death penalty,' said Castro after listening to the details.

'And you, I hope you don't mind my saying it like this,' intervened Pablo, 'have the prosecutor's trust. He even promoted you. That was why we thought that you—'

'What made you change your mind?'

'The fact that we now know that Commissioner Goyanes is the one involved in the matter.'

'Then you can rule out Grau. He would never ask Goyanes for a favour. What other suspects do you have?' He said it in a tone that sounded rather cavalier, as if he were in a shoe shop trying on boots and asking for the next size up.

'We've got Arturo Sanabria,' Pablo said then.

Castro looked at him in astonishment and snorted before saying, 'Couldn't you find a bigger fish? What have you got on him?'

'Sanabria beat up a lover and took it too far. Dr Garmendia saw the woman and treated her at his house, where she died. Sanabria took care of getting her out of there and making her body disappear, but the doctor took down all her information. She was a prostitute named Estrella Machín.'

'Estrella Machín? Her real name was Virtudes Ortiz. Yes, I remember her disappearance, about five years ago. Everyone thought she'd taken off with one of her "protectors".'

'You don't seem very impressed by Sanabria as a possible suspect.'

'Because in my opinion, Sanabria doesn't have much to fear from those papers. Mariona Sobrerroca might have been able to get something out of him while his wife was alive, but Sanabria became a widower at least three years ago.'

'But he killed a woman.'

'No, he killed a prostitute.'

'And she wasn't a woman?' Ana shot Pablo a look. 'Doesn't the law protect everyone?'

Before Pablo could react, Castro did. 'I'll make it crystal clear: Sanabria, a Falangist industrialist with very powerful friends, supposedly killed a prostitute whose body was never found. Got it? Besides, it's not about reviewing each case; what we need to know is who is after these papers. And I can tell you that Sanabria isn't someone who has anything to fear. What else do you have?'

'Fernando Sánchez-Herranz.'

Castro snorted.

'Him too?'

'In this case it's his wife, Dolores Antich, who had an affair with a fake Polish count in 1945 and fell pregnant. Her parents brought her to Garmendia so he could give her a discreet abortion. She wasn't the only girl from a good home who ended up in his office for that reason. Two years later she married Sánchez-Herranz, who thought she was a good catch,' explained Pablo.

'Dolores Antich *was* a good catch,' replied Ana. 'He brought the ancient Castilian lineage and she brought the Catalan money. But she didn't turn out to be the virginal flower that Sánchez-Herranz imagined her to be. And while the abortion story is very dangerous for her reputation in Barcelona society, it's even more dangerous for Sánchez-Herranz's political aspirations.'

Not long before, the president of the Provincial Council of Barcelona had been disgraced because he had been seen in public in Madrid with a woman who wasn't his wife, a moral indiscretion for which he paid dearly. Even though it was common knowledge that many men had lovers, what was not tolerated was that it was done openly. It was a lesson she had learned well from working on society pieces, where all was known and everything was kept quiet.

'And, despite your ruling him out, there is still Joaquín Grau,' said Ana. 'It's odd. He is Sánchez-Herranz's political mentor, he owes all the power and position he has to Grau, but lately they've distanced themselves quite a bit. Both of them were in Mariona's hands.'

All four fell silent. Again the children's voices from the street came in through the window. They had changed games.

'One, two, three, nobody move without the King's say-so.'

Laughter, complaints, protests, clapping.

Castro's voice: 'Even though his crime could get him the death penalty, I repeat that Grau cannot be the one who ordered the killings.'

'Why not?'

'For the simple reason that I am certain it's Goyanes who's mixed up in this. I can't tell you why,' he said with a bitter smirk on his face. 'And Grau has never trusted him; they're not on the same wavelength. Goyanes is one of Sánchez-Herranz's men. That doesn't mean that Grau didn't benefit from Mariona Sobrerroca's death, but I think he doesn't know it yet. Nor will he. Your man is undoubtedly Sánchez-Herranz.'

'Our man? And you aren't planning on doing anything?' asked Beatriz. Her voice trembled.

'What do you expect me to do?'

'To solve the case properly, make sure that the people behind the murders are punished.'

'I'm very sorry, but this matter is out of my league.'

'Ours too,' said Ana.

'Nobody asked you to take it on.'

'But you can't leave us like this.'

'My hands are tied. Believe me, if I could do something for you, I would.'

Castro stood and made for the hallway.

'Then why did you come here?' asked Ana.

'Partly out of curiosity, partly out of . . . call it selfishness if you want to, I don't mind. For my own survival on the force, I need to know which way the wind blows. Now I know. And finally, because I really thought that maybe I could help you all out of this unharmed, but given the dimensions it's taken on, I don't see how. I think it's best I stay out of it.'

'And your duty?'

'My duty, Señorita Martí, would be to arrest you for obstruction of justice. So, as you can see, I'm turning a blind eye to everyone today. A word of advice: if you can, get out of the city, or better yet, the country, as soon as possible.'

Ana clutched the policeman's sleeve.

'You're abandoning us to our fate?'

'Don't be melodramatic.'

Castro roughly brushed her off, reached the end of the hallway in two strides, opened the door and left the flat.

They were alone.

65

Alone; and facing an enemy so powerful that even Castro feared having to deal with him. The tough guy at the CIB had almost run out of the house when he understood that it had to do with Sánchez-Herranz. How had Mariona Sobrerroca been so foolhardy as to blackmail that man!

Again, Beatriz felt as if rage was getting the better of her. However, this time it didn't blind her, but instead gave her a feeling of clear-sightedness.

A powerful enemy; a giant against whom they could do nothing. No, they weren't David. None of them was, not even the three of them together. No; it wasn't David against Goliath. Someone else would have to throw the stone.

'Do you remember what you said before, Ana? The master and the disciple, father and son. Joaquín Grau and Fernando Sánchez-Herranz, both in the hands of the widow of Dr Garmendia. Remember?'

'Yes. Why?'

'You said, didn't you, that they had distanced themselves from each other some time ago?'

'Yes, Sánchez-Herranz has been trying to undermine Grau's position for some time, despite all he's done for him.'

It was true. Sánchez-Herranz had arrived in the city under Grau's wing, but they represented increasingly remote positions. They were both in favour of the hard line. Grau in particular showed as much in his implacable police pursuit of 'common' crime. Many saw him as destined to become a minister in Madrid, based on what he'd achieved in Barcelona. Sánchez-Herranz, despite being younger, or perhaps because of it, belonged to the hard core of the Falange. He had got close to the Civil Governor, Acedo Colunga; his field was the pursuit of 'political' crime and, as Ana knew well from her work at the newspaper, he strictly controlled the press. Especially the newspapers edited in Barcelona: *La Vanguardia*, *El Noticiero Universal*, even the highly conservative *El Correo Catalán* were prey to all manner of suspicions, which were expressed in angry letters of caution that threatened severe punishment if whatever had earned his reproof were to be repeated. He was a crafty guy who had adapted himself to Grau, his protector, until he felt he was in a position that allowed him to reveal his true intentions. The tensions between him and Grau weren't public, but they were known.

'The son turns against the father, but he knows it and defends himself, like an old lion when a young rival tries to snatch his territory from him. The hatred provoked by the betrayal of someone he loved like a son knows no bounds.'

'How would you like to unleash that hatred?'

'With letters. It's a fitting end. This whole story began with a letter, and we can end it with another.'

'Tieta Beatriz, this isn't a novel.'

Pablo's tone was one of paternal indulgence, as if he were explaining to a little girl that it was her parents who bought and wrapped her Christmas gifts.

'Pablito, I'm not that unworldly. I wasn't born yesterday.'

'No. I don't want to offend you, but it's just that in real life stories aren't usually so neat and tidy.'

'But that's not what you were saying either, was it, Beatriz?' interjected Ana.

'Not exactly. What's clear to me is that we have a means to take the reins of this story and stop being its characters. I don't know if it will work, but ... '

'We can at least give it a try,' Ana finished her sentence for her.

Anything's better than just sitting around waiting for the

storm to pass, thought Beatriz, like those Republicans who had spent years hidden in secret rooms of their houses until they dared to come out, only to discover that the storm still hadn't subsided. Like Mario Mendoza, in whose way of life she saw a distorted reflection of her own.

'With letters?' asked Pablo.

'With one letter.'

'Ah! One letter. Easy as pie.' Pablo couldn't hide his disbelief.

'It won't be easy. But it is a strategy that has worked in other cases. When the threat is two giants versus someone without even the shadow of a chance, the solution can lie in pitting the two giants against each other.'

'And where did you say this has worked, Tieta? Because I haven't read it, but I know the giants in *Don Quixote* were windmills.'

'No, it's not from *Don Quixote*. It's the story of the brave little tailor.'

The smirk that had accompanied Pablo's sarcastic comments froze for a few seconds before melting away completely.

'Tieta, you're delirious.'

'Not in the slightest. I am, as you lawyers say, in full possession of my mental faculties.'

Pablo was about to say something, but Ana gestured to Beatriz to continue speaking.

'Do you remember the tale of the brave little tailor? It's by the Brothers Grimm. It tells the story of a tailor who one day killed seven flies with one blow.'

'Flies? That's more our speed.'

'Pablo!' reprimanded Ana.

Beatriz continued, 'He was so proud of his feat that he made a belt that read "Seven at One Blow", and since people thought it referred to men, they respected him but, all the same, they were constantly testing him.'

She saw that Ana was growing impatient, so she left out the tests and got to the relevant part: 'One day he arrived in a kingdom that was under the yoke of two giants. The people there asked him to free them, and in exchange . . .'

'They gave him at least half the kingdom and a princess, as usual. What are you getting at, Tieta?'

'At how he did it. What the little tailor did was pit them against each other. As they slept, he threw a rock at each of them so they both thought it had been the other. They ended up fighting and killing each other.'

'Very lovely and edifying,' said Pablo. 'I guess one of the rocks is the letter you were talking about, is it?'

'Yes. A letter from Fernando Sánchez-Herranz to Joaquín Grau.'

'And how do you plan on convincing him to write it?'

'I'm not. I'll write it myself.'

'And say what?'

'That I have the documents, and that I know he was involved in the adulterating of penicillin. I will make him think that I have him in my power, and that I am going to make use of my information.'

'And the other rock?' Ana asked then. 'Another letter?'

'No. Too symmetrical. In order for it to work, it's important that when the first giant asks the other, "Did you throw this rock at me?", he answers no, but that the first one still thinks he did. Which is to say, that when Grau alludes to the documents, he will sense that Sánchez-Herranz knows what he's talking about. So it is fundamental that Sánchez-Herranz has the documents in his possession. But they have to fall into his hands in such a way that he doesn't realise a trap is being set for him.'

Pablo shook his head, making clear how absurd he found the plan, but Ana was following her. She was thinking, racking her brains for a solution.

'Which is to say, that the Garmendia documents have to reach Sánchez-Herranz's hands via normal, official means. Or almost.'

'That's right. What are you thinking, Ana?'

'Castro.'

No. That wouldn't work. Her plan was precarious enough – not to say complicated. Counting on Castro, who had just

380

minutes earlier washed his hands of the whole thing and abandoned them to their fate, didn't make sense. Ana read as much in Beatriz's expression, but didn't give up: 'I'm already imagining what you two are thinking, but let me try. What do we have to lose? Nothing.'

'Well, we could lose one of the rocks,' said Pablo.

'Pablito, this is not the moment for more sarcasm, or defeatism. Do you have a better idea? If you don't, help us to keep thinking.'

Pablo got up, went over to her and gave her a kiss on the cheek.

'You're absolutely right, Tieta. And, as a lawyer, I suppose it's my job to look for cons. The first one. For the letter from Sánchez-Herranz to Grau. The handwriting?'

'We'll type it. Do you have a typewriter?'

'Yes, but what about the signature? Even if there is a typewritten name below it, we need a handwritten signature.'

'That is a problem,' said Beatriz.

Then she saw that Ana was staring at copies of *La Vanguardia* that Pablo had on a little table.

'Sanvisens.'

She and Pablo looked at each other, confused.

'I have to make a call.'

Ana made for the telephone in the hallway. They followed her.

'Mateo, there is something you can do for me.'

They couldn't hear Sanvisens's reply, but he seemed willing.

'You once told me that you received letters from Sánchez-Herranz complaining about articles he didn't like.'

At her boss's response, Ana grinned.

'I can imagine he complained about the article on the Sobrerroca case too. Thanks for not telling me that at the time. Yes, I would have been quite upset. Do you still have it? Can you lend it to me? Please, don't ask why. One moment.'

She turned away from the phone and said, 'The problem is how to get it as soon as possible.'

'I can go,' offered Pablo.

'But not to the newspaper offices. They must be watching. Wait, I know how.'

Ana spoke into the phone again.

'I have an idea: send an errand boy to fetch coffees at the Zúrich café and give him the letter. Tell him that he should deliver it to a man who'll have . . . '

'A double carnation in his lapel?' joked Pablo.

Beatriz admonished him with a look.

' . . . a copy of the *Noticiero Universal*,' replied Ana, 'and he'll be at the bar, drinking a white coffee.'

'*El Noticiero*?' was heard through the receiver.

Beatriz signalled to Ana that she wanted to speak with her.

'One second, Mateo.'

She put her hand over the receiver. Beatriz whispered into her ear, 'Tell him to bring several letters; that way I'll have more samples of the text so I can imitate his style.'

Ana gave him the message. Then she said, 'When you go to get the letters, Pablo, you can take a note to my father. I imagine the police have been to the house and my family must be worried. My father works in a grocery shop on Valencia Street. If you could swing by there . . . '

'No problem.'

'I'll call Castro later. Beatriz, I'd rather you didn't listen to the conversation, in case I really need to humiliate myself.'

'Of course. But maybe it will go well. We're like the mouse in the fable that appears in *The Book of Good Love*. Like the lion, he has spared our life, because we aren't even enough for an appetiser. "Sir, don't kill me, I won't fill your belly," says the mouse, but when the lion falls into a hunter's net, his claws are of no use to him. The mouse is able to gnaw on the net to free him and he says, "Thanks to my little teeth, you are alive today."'

It was irrational, it was absurd, but those verses filled her with optimism.

Unfortunately, it was only her they touched. Ana and Pablo couldn't hide their apprehension, but at least they had a plan.

66

She didn't know whether the call would end up being humiliating or not, but it would certainly be testing.

She took a deep breath and dialled the number. It rang three times before Castro answered. 'Criminal Investigation Brigade. First Class Inspector Castro.'

'It's Ana Martí.'

Castro seemed surprised.

'What do you want?'

'Your help.'

'I've already told you that for me the matter is closed.'

'And you can live with that?'

'I've lived with worse things, Señorita Martí.'

She had to land him before he took refuge in his cynicism.

'Then are you willing to work with someone, no, *for* someone who deceives his own men the way Goyanes did you? To work for someone capable of letting his men kill a young woman like Encarni, who's only ever known drudgery in order to support her family?'

'Look, Señorita—'

No, he wasn't going to interrupt her.

'Do you think that someone like that deserves to be in the CIB? And maybe, someday, thanks to his friends and his lack of scruples, to be heading up the CIB?'

'Don't try to manipulate me.'

'I wouldn't think of it. You said that you wanted to know what direction things were moving in; well, now you see. The

CIB, passing into the hands of one of Sánchez-Herranz's lackeys. And you think that Goyanes is going to leave you in peace? Sooner or later he'll realise what you know, because he'll keep pulling on the thread, a thread that, unfortunately, also leads to us. Do you think that when he knows about everything you are keeping quiet he'll leave you in peace?'

'And you want to offer me something to, let's just say, improve my situation?'

Ana thought that here Beatriz would have told him the fable of the mouse and the lion, but she lacked her cousin's imperviousness to the impatience of others. On the other hand, she was sharp enough to know that it was the moment to speak more clearly.

'Why else would I have called you? But I sense that you're still refusing to give me even a glimmer of hope. If I remember rightly, you claimed that if there was anything you could do for us, you would. Well, I'm calling because there is something you can do.'

There was silence at the other end of the line. Then, instead of Castro's voice, she heard footsteps and a door closing. She pressed the receiver against her ear. When Castro spoke again, the words sounded so clear in her head that she feared he could read her thoughts.

'Fine. Go on. But if at any point what you're saying isn't convincing, I'll just hang up. And then don't even think about calling me back, because in half an hour I'll have a patrol car in front of your door. Are we clear?'

Ana started to explain her plan to him. With each sentence she uttered, it seemed flimsier, and after each pause she expected to hear a click and the dialling tone. But Castro was still there. In absolute silence, without giving a single sign of acceptance, doubt or rejection. Nothing, as if there were a machine at the other end, a tape recorder. Ana got to the most delicate part: 'What you could do would be to put the papers that incriminate Grau in Sánchez-Herranz's reach, saying, for example, that you found them in one of Mendoza's filing cabinets in Martorell and that, given their sensitive nature, you chose to give them to him, since you know that Joaquín Grau is his mentor and that he will know what to do to avoid a scandal, one that would taint such a valuable institution as the public prosecutor's office . . .'

There was a sigh at the other end of the line. Had she gone too far? Was he going to hang up? Only the former: 'Señorita Martí, you don't need to write me a script, as if this was a radio serial.'

'Does that mean you'll do it?' she asked hopefully.

'But you do realise how crazy this is, what you're suggesting?' Castro burst out laughing.

'Then why did you listen to the end? To have a good laugh at my expense? Is that it? I amuse you?'

She was hurt, and she saw no reason to hide it. 'I see that I was completely wrong about you, Inspector. Oh! Pardon me, First Class Inspector. They told me not to get my hopes up about you, that you had only said you wanted to help us to ease your conscience, that you weren't going to lift a finger to solve the case or to help us, despite knowing that it leaves us in Goyanes's hands. I misjudged you. That's fine. It's a lesson I'll never forget for the rest of my life. Which doesn't look as if it'll be that long.'

'Jesus! More cheap drama. Fucking brilliant!'

They were both quiet.

Ana's heart was racing. Her pulse beat even faster when Castro said, 'I'll collect the papers tomorrow.'

He hung up without another word. He didn't even tell her when he would be dropping by. Why would he? He knew they wouldn't be leaving the house.

She remained sitting in the hallway beside the telephone for a few minutes. Then she went to look for Beatriz. Ana found her sitting on the sofa with her gaze fixed on the door, waiting for her.

'One of the rocks is in the air.'

385

67

'*El Noticiero*? Sold out.'

Before Pablo had time to curse Ana for saying he would be carrying that particular newspaper, the kiosk vendor knelt down and disappeared for a moment behind the little counter.

'Wait! I've got one left. If you don't mind it being a bit wrinkled ... Do you have any coins? I'm almost out of change.'

Twenty minutes after leaving the house, Pablo was at the bar of the Zúrich café with the newspaper. Soon the errand boy arrived with a copy of *La Vanguardia*. The letters were hidden in its pages.

'In the sports section,' he said, taking a sip of coffee.

Pablo didn't know what was appropriate in these situations, but for starters he paid for the boy's coffee and gave him a tip.

When he returned to the house with the letters from Sánchez-Herranz, Ana met him in the entryway. She had been waiting for him there.

'Were you able to give my father the letter? What did he say?'

'That a police officer came to the house asking for you, but refused to tell them why, and that they were very worried.'

'Did he read the letter?'

'Yes, in the back room. Afterwards he was somewhat relieved, but we couldn't say much because his boss was there. And he gave me this for you.'

Pablo produced a paperback from his jacket pocket. It was a small-format western novel, *Merciless Duel in Carson City*. He held it out to her. It had a note in it, in her father's hand.

'He pretended to dedicate it to me so he could write to you without anyone catching on. I didn't know your father wrote westerns.'

Neither did she. So that was why there was more money in her family lately. She opened up the little book and read:

My dearest daughter,
In your letter I read things that fill me both with fear for your well-being and pride in your courage. But everything that makes me proud of you as a journalist makes me frightened for my daughter, whom I fear I couldn't stand, we couldn't stand, to lose. Be very careful, Aneta. Come home soon.

She made a tremendous effort to control her emotions.

'Come on in, Beatriz is waiting for you too.'

When she saw him come in, his aunt practically ripped the newspaper from his hands. She shook out the letters and ignored everything else as she studied Sánchez-Herranz's style.

'She is furious,' said Ana to Pablo in a low voice. 'Furious and very sad about Encarni. While we were waiting for you she hid in the bathroom to cry alone.'

They looked at her. Beatriz was pencilling notes on a sheet of paper which she'd divided into columns in order to organise the characteristics of Sánchez-Herranz's style that she wanted to imitate in the letter: connectors, turns of phrase, adjectives.

'Are you hungry?' asked Pablo.

'No. We'll eat later.'

'Do you mind if I eat something?'

Neither woman answered him. Pablo went into the kitchen and prepared for himself one of the few things he knew how to make: rice boiled with a clove of garlic. He made enough for the three of them. It was a good idea.

Soon Ana came in, drawn by the aroma.

'My mother makes it the same way! Can I have a little?'

'As much as you like. Take Beatriz a plate too, so she eats something.'

Ana went out with a steaming plate of rice. She returned and sat at the kitchen table with Pablo.

'She says she'll eat it when she's finished. But between reading one letter and the next she ate a good spoonful.'

They ate in silence.

They had already finished and were listening distractedly to the radio when Beatriz came in.

'I've got the letter. I think I've captured his style well, but the signature needs work.'

She showed them the original and one of her attempts to imitate it. It was an obvious forgery.

'Let me try,' said Ana.

Her signature was only a little better, but you could still see the effort; it didn't look natural.

Meanwhile, Pablo had picked up a pen and, after two goes, he produced an impeccable imitation.

'Perfect!' exclaimed Beatriz.

'I'm good at drawing,' he explained, neglecting to mention that during his school years he had learned to forge his father's signature so that he could bunk off lessons.

'Well, now you have to type up the letter and sign it,' said Beatriz.

'And then what?' asked Pablo. 'We send it in the post?'

'No,' said Ana. 'It's about making Grau nervous, making him feel Sánchez-Herranz's threat. That threat has to reach him in the style that Sánchez-Herranz would use. It has to be something direct, brutal. Devastating.'

'What are you thinking of?'

'Grau must find the letter at his house, on a table. For him to see that they've entered his house without thinking twice about it, that Sánchez-Herranz's thugs have invaded his privacy and profaned it.'

'Grau, who is said to guard his privacy jealously,' added Pablo, 'for whom his house is, as the English would say, his castle, would be horrified by the idea of those brutes setting foot in his home.'

Beatriz interrupted him: 'Do you know what's good about there being three of us? At least one of us can ask the bothersome questions when the other two are getting all excited. How are we going to get the letter into Grau's house?'

Pablo saw in Ana's face that she had already thought of a way.

'I know someone who will do it if I ask him to.'

She was talking about Pepe the Spider, one of the people she read and wrote letters for.

'If we give him the address, he can get the letter inside.'

Ana started to type it up.

She remembered what Carmiña had always told her: *you don't type love letters*. The one she was typing up now was a letter filled with hatred.

68

'That's it,' she said.

Beatriz had retired to the bedroom. They found her immersed in *Don Quixote*.

'This is more helpful in life than the Bible. Pablo, I have to admonish you for the lack of Spanish classics in your library. Thank goodness I found this. A nice edition.'

'It was a gift from Papa.' Beneath Beatriz's scathing gaze, Pablo hastened to add, 'I promise I'll read it next summer. And I'm not saying this to change the subject, Tieta Beatriz, but we have something much more urgent on right now.'

Beatriz closed the book and left it on a side table next to the armchair where she had been reading.

'Are you ready?'

'Now we need to find Pepe the Spider,' said Ana.

'You know where he lives, don't you?' asked Pablo.

'I've seen the address many, many times.'

Pepe the Spider sublet a flat on Unión Street. He didn't trust the owner of the flat because she had once steamed open a letter from his girlfriend.

'The letter stank of cabbage ... she had opened it with the steam from a cooking pot,' he had told Ana.

That was why he received his post at an ironmonger's on Egipcíacas Street where a guy from his town worked. He had given that address not only because the guy was discreet: 'Now the letters smell clean.' It was true; the letters that she read to him from his girlfriend always carried the scent of soap. Getting a message to him wouldn't be difficult. The guy at the shop always let him know as soon as he got any post.

'There could be a problem,' said Ana. 'If he's been arrested. The last time I saw him, he was up to something, something big. If it's gone wrong and the police have got hold of him, our whole plan is sunk.'

Beatriz shook her head.

'Could be. Which is why we have to behave like you do when there's been a death.'

Ana shot a disconcerted look at Pablo, which Beatriz didn't catch because she was looking upwards, as she always did when stringing together an argument. With her gaze again fixed on one of the ceiling mouldings, she continued, 'When there is a death, the relatives and close friends are faced with an absolutely irreversible fact that is out of their control. They cannot do anything to change what has happened, so a whole series of rituals and activities have developed around the burial and the mourning. The idea is to do something, whether it's writing funeral notices, offering condolences, eating, preparing food . . .'

'You want us to make some cannelloni now?' Pablo tried to joke.

Ana put her hand over his mouth to keep him quiet; she wanted to know where Beatriz was going with this thought. Pablo took Ana's hand to move it away, but he didn't let it go, just brought it down to the space between them on the sofa, leaving it in his. Ana didn't turn – she had her eyes fixed on Beatriz – but she gently squeezed Pablo's hand in return.

'Go on, Beatriz.'

'What I mean is that we don't know if they've arrested this Pepe, but even if they have, we can't sit around and do nothing. Which is why it's important that we clear up the practical matters. The first of which is, where you are going to meet him.'

'It has to be in a public place. Where there are a lot of people,' said Ana.

'Beside one of the flower stalls on the Ramblas?' suggested Pablo.

'Too exposed. It would have to be near here,' she replied.

'The San Antonio market could work: it's open on Sundays and there are always a lot of people buying books and comics,' said Beatriz.

'What about the Apolo Amusement Park?' suggested Pablo.

It was a good idea. It was close by, so they wouldn't have to walk far and so risk being seen.

'Fine. Now that I've become your messenger, I guess I'll have to go back out into the street, won't I?' said Pablo.

'Leave him the message that we are going to meet on Sunday at noon in front of the entrance to the Autogruta ride at the Atracciones Apolo,' summed up Ana.

Once again, Pablo went running out of the house. They hoped that the ironmonger's hadn't closed for the day.

When he came back an hour later, he found the two women in the kitchen listening to the radio and he was able to give them at least one piece of good news: Pepe hadn't been arrested, and the guy in the shop was going to give him the message that very afternoon along with a letter from his girlfriend.

'Well, now there's nothing more we can do,' said Beatriz, getting up from the table. 'I'm going to go and read for a while.'

Pablo took her place.

They listened to the radio in silence. On the news was a piece on the preparations for the Eucharistic Congress. Ana thought about her mother. They weren't officially looking for her, though that didn't mean they wouldn't do anything to her parents, considering who was after them and the impunity with which he'd acted up until that point. Most likely, she told herself, they were watching over her parents in case she tried to contact them. The radio brought her back to Pablo's kitchen, the sound of the Montserrat Boys' Choir and a voice announcing the broadcast of a Mass.

'On Sundays,' said Ana, 'there are a lot of people at the Apolo. There is also more of a police presence.'

'Don't worry, I'll go with you. The people who are looking for you are after two women.'

Ana nodded without much conviction. She couldn't shake off the thought that her entire plan was hanging by very fine threads, like a delicate cobweb. It was almost ironic that at that moment everything depended on a thief named Pepe the Spider.

69

On Saturday night they went to bed very early, to shorten the wait. But not one of the three could get to sleep. Ana noticed that Beatriz was awake by her side, and she struggled to keep still so she wouldn't bother her. She heard Pablo's footsteps in the sitting room, as he got up several times from the sofa he was sleeping on.

She kept thinking about Castro's brief visit that morning. She reran the scene in her head, searching for signs, guarantees that the policeman was going to do what they had asked him to. The mere fact that he had come in person to pick up the papers was a good sign. And he had thought of how and when he would deliver them to Sánchez-Herranz.

'I'll call him on Monday. I'll go to the Civil Government offices to speak with him.'

That was good too.

The fact that he hadn't looked her in the eyes as he spoke made her uneasy.

Castro was perfectly capable of keeping the papers and using them for his own gain. The plan that might possibly save them also benefited him. If it went well, he would have Goyanes out of the way, but those papers would also allow him to call up other kinds of favours. They were depending on Castro fulfilling his promise, which is to say they were depending on the good will of a policeman. They were depending on The Spider being able to pull off what they would ask him to do. They were depending on Grau not uncovering the deception.

They were depending on Goyanes not finding them before any of it could take place. They were depending on killing several birds, and she wasn't even sure whose hand held the stone.

At some point, her tiredness got the better of her and she slept deeply but uneasily for a while before waking with a start feeling as though she were suffocating, like when she dreamed of her dead brother. She slipped furtively out of the bed so as not to wake Beatriz and headed to the kitchen to drink a glass of water. It was five thirty in the morning. She could already hear footsteps and vehicles on the street, but dawn hadn't yet broken. The floor was cold and she missed her old felt slippers. Remembering such a trivial object made her feel the first stab of pain for the life she felt she had lost for ever; she suddenly understood what it meant not to be able to return home: abandoned slippers, a pot that held a dying plant, a book she wouldn't finish.

She went into the kitchen and felt around for a glass.

'You can turn on the light if you want.' It was Pablo's voice. He was sitting at the kitchen table.

She jumped, but managed to repress the scream that was rising in her throat.

'I didn't mean to scare you,' said Pablo. 'You can't sleep either, eh?'

She shook her head. Her eyes had grown accustomed to the dark by then, and she was able to make out Pablo's silhouette perfectly.

'You can't scare me any more than I already am,' she responded. 'What if this goes wrong? First I got Beatriz mixed up in this mess, which cost poor Encarni her life. And now I've got you involved too.'

For the first time since it had all begun, Ana felt an uncontrollable urge to cry. It wasn't just the fear; it was the guilt and her self-recrimination for allowing herself to get drawn in by her ambitions.

'I'm sorry, I'm so sorry,' she said between her tears.

Pablo got up and hugged her. Ana rested her head on his shoulder.

'You're going to get cold,' Pablo said into her ear. 'You should lie down again.'

'I don't want to go back to bed. I'm afraid to fall asleep, afraid of the nightmares.'

'Then come.'

He led her, with his arm around her shoulder, to the sofa where he slept, lifted up the sheets and gestured for her to lie down.

'And you?'

'I'll stay in the armchair. Maybe tonight I'll start reading *Don Quixote*, and then I can impress my aunt tomorrow,' joked Pablo.

'You'd need to read a lot to impress her, she's a walking encyclopedia of literature,' she replied, unable to contain a yawn.

'Go on, lie down.'

Ana lay down. Pablo covered her with the sheet. Ana looked at him.

'If you want ...'

'No, I'd better not. You have a boyfriend, and ...'

'And he'll be sleeping, like we should be.'

'Fine, but I can assure you that you needn't worry.'

'About my honour? Spare me that nonsense, this isn't a comic operetta.'

Pablo lay down beside her, being so careful as not even to brush against her that he almost sent her onto the floor. They laughed under their breath.

At some point Ana came closer to him, appreciative of his warmth, curling up into a ball when he ran an arm over her and nestled against her back.

In those scant two hours of sleep she didn't have a single nightmare.

She woke up disoriented and confused. Pablo was sleeping, Beatriz wasn't any longer; she heard noises from the kitchen. Had she seen them? How could she not have? She had even been past the side table because the copy of *Don Quixote* was no longer there. She gently extracted herself from Pablo's embrace.

'Don't go yet,' he said sleepily.

She got up anyway and headed towards the kitchen. She was expecting to see a severe expression on Beatriz's face, but she found a melancholy smile.

'I'll make coffee while you get dressed,' said Beatriz. 'I grabbed several changes of clothes when I left my house, I can lend you one.'

Ana appreciated having something clean to wear. After washing and dressing, she went back to the kitchen. Pablo was already there. Going over the plan helped them overcome their initial embarrassment.

They worked out the right moment to head out to their appointment with Pepe the Spider. They didn't want to arrive too early and risk being seen.

At five minutes to twelve they were at the entrance to the Atracciones Apolo, mingling with families and excited, rowdy groups of young people. They went in and stayed close to the door to the Autogruta, a roller coaster that sent you into a huge, pointy-toothed mouth and through scenes of heaven and hell. From where they stood they could hear the screams of the people who thought they were about to slam into a giant rock, or had just seen a mummy.

They didn't see him arrive. All of a sudden, Pepe the Spider was simply there.

'You left word that you needed me, Señorita Ana.'

'I do, Pepe. I'm in a fix and I need your services.'

'Let's go somewhere we can talk.'

Ana and Pablo followed him to a small bench beside a stand that sold nuts and dried fruits. She and The Spider sat down. Pablo remained standing, keeping his eyes peeled.

'Pepe, I'm going to tell you what I want you to do, but I won't tell you why. If you don't think it's possible, let me know. I don't want you to take too big a risk.'

'Well, let me decide that. First tell me what you need.'

Ana showed him the bundle of papers and said, 'It would

mean leaving these papers in someone's house, so that they can be easily found, for example, on his desk.'

'And can you tell me who the person is, or is it better I don't know?'

'I have to tell you so that you can decide if you want to do it or not. I'd be asking you to plant these papers in the house of Joaquín Grau.'

'Who's that?'

'He's a public prosecutor.'

'He's never nicked me.'

'Good. He's a dangerous bloke.'

'The ones who nabbed me are too. Look.'

He showed her a gap in his teeth.

'From the last time?'

The Spider nodded his head.

'You need to give me the address so I can see whether it's a house I know how to get into or not.'

She gave it to him. The Spider screwed up his face and Ana realised that he was travelling through the city in his head. She waited in silence until The Spider looked at her again and said, 'Piece of cake, Señorita Ana. When do you want me to send the little message?'

'Could it be tonight?'

'Of course. Can I ask you something in return?' The Spider pulled an envelope out of his waistcoat pocket. 'I got a letter from my girlfriend.'

Ana took the letter and began to read it very slowly. They brought their heads together so that only he could hear what it said.

Dear José,
I hope this finds you in good health . . .

70

The room was suddenly bathed in red. Rage escalated within him so powerfully that it plugged up his ears and he had to shout because he was afraid he would explode.

'That son of a bitch!'

He scanned the letter again.

That swine had dared to break into his house to leave this carrion on his desk. This stinking letter that reeked of arrogance and, above all, of betrayal. How dare he threaten him? Him!

Joaquín Grau went through his study, sullied by the presence of that letter filled with veiled warnings. Before his eyes everything he had done for Fernando passed like the pages in a family photo album. Every step, every conversation, every recommendation, until he had him in Barcelona, preparing to fly even higher. It was like having taught a son to walk only for him to stamp all over his father.

'*Bastard!*'

And that mocking envelope impudently rested beneath a lit lamp, as if it were a love letter.

It was all so degrading.

He had to do something. Right away.

He dialled the home number. 'Hello, Dolores. I want to speak to Fernando.'

'He isn't back yet. I think he had a meeting with some businessmen. He'll be back for dinner.'

So he was still at the office.

'Is it something urgent, Joaquín?'

'No, don't worry about it. It can wait until tomorrow.'

He said goodbye to her. Then he called one of his men.

'Juanito, get the car out. Bring it to Ernesto so that he can drive; I need you in the back seat.'

Juanito had worked for him for fifteen years. He was large, strong and obedient.

They left soon after and parked the car near the Civil Government building.

They waited in silence. Neither of his two men dared open their mouths without permission, and he wasn't in the mood for talking.

During the long wait, the possibility of pardoning him, if he handed over the papers, ran through his head, but he ruled it out. He had had them in his hands, he had seen them, he was contaminated.

Only one thing could save him: if he knew nothing of the matter, if the letter was a fake. But that was a preposterous idea. Who would do something like that, and why?

'Start the engine, Ernesto.'

The car began to move. Soon they had caught up with him.

Grau lowered the window and called out to him. Fernando's face twisted when he saw him.

'What's going on, Joaquín?'

'I need to speak to you.'

'They're expecting me at home.'

'It's important. It won't take long.'

Fernando had already stopped. Grau saw him glance at the street, as if looking for someone to ask for help. Meanwhile, Juanito had already got out of the front passenger seat and opened the rear door, inviting Fernando to climb in. Grau moved across. Fernando got into the car.

'Come closer, Fernando. That way Juanito can fit in too.'

'But wasn't he in the front?'

Fernando tried to get out of the car, but hulking Juanito blocked his path while pushing him towards Grau. Juanito sat down and closed the door.

'Let's go, Ernesto.'

Grau noticed that Fernando's breathing was panicky. He turned towards him.

'What? Now that you have me face to face, you have nothing to say?'

'What am I supposed to say?'

'Don't play the innocent with me. I know you better than your own mother.'

'I don't understand.'

'It's strange how suddenly you have such trouble understanding. Your letter, on the other hand, was very easy to grasp.'

'What letter are you talking about?'

'A letter in which you refer to certain papers.'

It was only a second, a flickering glance down towards his jacket pocket. It was so brief that perhaps not even he himself was aware he'd done it, but Grau saw it.

'Juanito,' he said. 'See what he has in that pocket.'

Fernando, with terror in his eyes, made an instinctive gesture to protect it. A grave mistake. He struggled with Juanito, whose physical superiority won out. Juanito pulled out some papers that were crumpled from the skirmish.

Grau glanced at them. Then he looked at Fernando.

'I wasn't going to do anything with them, Joaquín. If you want I'll give them to you. It's not what it looks like.'

'Of course; nothing is what it seems.'

Joaquín Grau stepped out of the car.

'I'll walk home. Air the car well before leaving it in the garage.'

He could still hear Fernando's pleading voice, but he couldn't make out the words. Then he heard a dull blow. Perhaps it was the door slamming. He didn't know; he didn't turn around.

EPILOGUE

There was nothing in the papers about Fernando Sánchez-Herranz's body showing up in the Somorrostro dressed in women's clothing. Such a deplorable and shameful fact couldn't be seen amid the pomp and pageantry of the Eucharistic Congress that filled the newspaper pages, newsreels and radio hours.

The public prosecutor's office, 'out of respect for the family's honour', ordered that the investigation be conducted with the utmost discretion, which Castro clearly took as an order to do nothing at all.

Grau, who had given the order, didn't know that the First Class Inspector had also grasped that he'd used the same method on Sánchez-Herranz that he'd utilised to avoid the investigation of Mendoza's death.

Two days after the ill-fated encounter between Grau and Sánchez-Herranz, a call from Isidro Castro informed them that they were 'out of danger'. They didn't feel happy, merely relieved. Sánchez-Herranz, the instigator of the murders, was dead, his body battered. They had brought on his death, by pitting one giant against the other. Although it was in self-defence, as Pablo had argued. But that didn't absolve them. The result had been that one giant had killed the other. Had they really not considered that possibility when they came up with their plan? They wondered if, deep down, they had even wished for it.

'What about the material killers of Mariona, Mendoza and Encarni?' Ana asked the policeman.

'They're retiring Burguillos. He was left deaf in one ear and unfit for service. Since his injury occurred in the line of duty, they're going to give him the concession for a tobacconist's in Albacete, I think. They sent the other one, Costa, to Melilla.'

Far away. Very far away from Barcelona. Just as they heard his name for the first time, they knew they would never see him again.

Relief; that was what they felt.

They were able to attend Encarni's funeral. Beatriz gave her a place in the family mausoleum; Encarni's mother had accepted because that way she would be close to the slum where the family lived.

After saying goodbye to her relatives, they separated at the cemetery gates.

'I have to get on with sorting through my things,' said Beatriz.

And making noise in the house, which was too silent without Encarni. She wanted to get back to her work and try to fill the void with the chatter of her books.

Pablo had to go back to the firm. He still didn't know what to do with what he'd found out. Use it or keep it quiet. Beatriz knew him well enough to be able to read the dilemma in his eyes.

'If I had wanted an honourable profession, I wouldn't have become a lawyer, Tieta,' he had told her at one point during their enforced confinement, when they scarcely dared to make plans for the future.

Ana told him that Sanvisens hadn't wanted to cause a commotion and so he'd got rid of the bitter journalist, Belda, by promoting him to Madrid correspondent, near the Ministries, at the centre of power. He'd offered Ana a staff position at the newspaper, 'Belda's desk'.

'I'd prefer my own, if you don't mind.'

Beatriz watched Ana and Pablo walk down the slope of

Montjuïc. Maybe her eyes were playing tricks on her, but she thought she saw them holding hands.

She knew that, while everything went on as normal, nothing would ever be the same again.

ACKNOWLEDGEMENTS

The research for this novel was not only nourished by reading, but also by the stories many people generously shared with me. I won't attempt an exhaustive list; the task would be doomed to failure. So instead I want to thank Juan Ribas and Montserrat Moliné, whose vivid memories impregnate the entire text; Professor Isabel de Riquer, a wonderful narrator who allowed me to relive the period; and Marga Losantos from the National Library of Catalonia, who introduced me to the ins and outs of one of this novel's most important settings.

The manuscript had the privilege of being read by Társila Reyes, Pilar Montero and Karin Hopfe, whom I thank for their comments, criticisms and enthusiasm.

I am indebted to Klaus Reichenberger for the most generous form of critique I know.

Finally, I would like to end by remembering Celia Jaén Rodrigo, who was by my side from the initial idea for this novel until its final full stop. Celia accompanied me by reading, commenting, critiquing, encouraging and correcting. My appreciation is infinite, so I will close by repeating the dedication of the novel here: to you, Celia, forever in my memory.